Crown of Confessions

Mafia Matriarch Series Book 2

E.J.TANDA

Copyright © 2023 by E.J. Tanda

All rights reserved.

Thank you for buying an authorized edition of this book and for complying with copyright laws that protect the author's intellectual property by not scanning, photocopying, transmitting, or distributing any portion of this edition by electronic, mechanical means, photocopying or recording or otherwise without permission from the publisher.

Requests for permission should be emailed to
Sweet Violette Publishing at: info@SweetViolettePublishing.com
San Ramon, California

Tanda, E.J.
Crown of Confessions/by E.J. Tanda
ISBN: 979-8-9857497-2-4 (eBook)
ISBN: 979-8-9857497-3-1 (paperback)

Visit my website: www.ejtanda.com

This book is a work of fiction. Names, characters, places, storylines, and encounters come from the author's imagination. Any resemblance to actual persons, live or deceased, events, organizations, or locales is entirely coincidental. The book contains mature content which may be disturbing to some readers. Suitable for 18+

All product and company names and logos used herein are trademarks™ or registered® trademarks of their respective holders. Use of them does not imply any affiliation with or endorsement by them.

Edited by Laura Mitchell
Proofread by Sabine Sloley
Book Design by Tatiana Vila
Formatted by Stacey Blake

To my boys: Michael, Patrick, and Justin, my "silly rabbits,"
remember to always follow your hearts
and never give up on your dreams.

And to all the escape artists like me who fall in love with
imaginary friends, this story is for you.

In memory of Julia Marie Langone Tanda,
March 8, 1921–July 26, 2022.
Nani, may our little story serve as a beacon of hope and possibility for all those in need of reminding.
I miss you every day and love you always.
Your Pumpkin #1

Crown of Confessions

Part One

Una Nuova Recluta

Chapter 1
Mafia Man

San Jose, California
May 2003
Barbara

P oor Ms. G.
Red rosary beads wove through her fingers. Her eyes were closed.

My heart ached. It seemed like only yesterday I'd said goodbye to my former patient, Mrs. Passarelli. Here I was again.

Chants echoed through the mortuary. "Pray for us sinners, now, and at the hour of our death..."

For the past few months, Ms. G. divulged secrets to me about her forbidden love affair with her beloved, Gaetano, and her arranged marriage to one of the most famous gangsters in the country. I'd learned of the damage the Mafia did to her soul and of her eventual comeback. I thought of the picture I'd found in her hope chest of her and Gaetano after the war. Her face lit up when she saw her grape grower in the old photo. I couldn't wait to hear the rest of the story.

Then everything changed.

I looked at the coffin before me. To my right, Ms. G.'s great-niece, Sofia, blew her nose into her handkerchief. Her tears caused a pang of sadness to ripple through my gut. I put my hand on her back to steady her as her body shook with grief. I patted my eyes with a tissue.

A familiar hum echoed through the room, followed by a loud whistle. The sound blared through the mortuary.

"God damn this thing," Ms. G. roared. "I can't hear shit with this stupid hearing aid."

The ceremony stopped. Everyone looked at us.

"Here," I whispered, embarrassed we'd interrupted the entire ceremony. I pulled another hearing aid from my purse and handed it to her. "This is the third one this month. You'd better not throw this one away."

"They don't work. And then I don't have to hear you going on all day. Gives me peace and quiet for once," Ms. G. snapped back, then rolled her eyes as she shoved the tiny object into her ear.

"Yeah, all right. Until you want to watch *Judge Judy*. Then whatcha gonna do, huh?"

"Okay, smart ass."

"*Shhh*," hissed a voice from the back.

"You *shhh*," Ms. G. fired back and scanned the room. "This is my brother's funeral. I'll be as loud as I God damn want!"

The room erupted with laughter. Sofia gave a look to signal me to quiet Ms. G.

My cheeks warmed. "Everyone's staring at us, even the priest. We have to be quiet," I whispered. I put my hand on her arm.

"Yeah, yeah. *Minchia*. How much longer is this guy gonna talk anyway?" She tapped her wristwatch.

I gave Sofia an apologetic grin. She smiled back through tears and swollen eyes. Eyes that, months ago, seemed to look right through me when she handed me the non-disclosure agreement and offered a threat-filled job offer to care for her rambunctious great-aunt. I felt guilt when I looked at the young woman.

Days ago, Ms. G. was about to tell me how she and Gaetano got back together in Rome when the phone rang. Selfishly, I told Ms. G. to continue with her story and let the machine pick it up. Sofia's voice sobbed on the recording as she broke the news that her grandfather had suffered a heart attack. Ms. G. trembled in my arms. Listening to her cry hurt my heart. Sofia had arranged for his body to be brought to San Jose and buried here with his family.

The next few weeks would be difficult. With advanced Alzheimer's, Ms. G. would forget what happened to her brother. She'd forget we were at his funeral today. I didn't want to think about her expression every time she'd ask why Vinny didn't call. Part of me wanted to lie, say he was busy, and hope she'd let it go. But since we'd exposed our pasts and our shared bond of domestic abuse, she knew me better than anyone. I couldn't lie to her. The truth meant I'd have to break the news to her repeatedly.

I hated her disease.

Ms. G. was my dearest friend now—a second mother to me. I smiled down at her little head of grey hair and placed my hand on top of hers. I'd help her through it. I wasn't just her caretaker anymore. We were family.

"I'm fine. I'm fine," she snarled and brushed my hand away.

Hmmph. Still a pain in the ass, but I loved her. She saved my life. In some ways, I'd saved hers.

I glanced around the room. Men in tailored three-piece suits with matching pocket squares and trench coats sat in the back. Typical mourners to most. After everything Ms. G. told me, I knew better.

They were Mafia.

One of the men gave me a nod.

My spine stiffened.

A few of them smiled, but one old man had my attention. A

single red rose clung to his lapel. Two guards flanked his sides. He had to be someone important. Mafia important.

We exchanged stares. He scowled at me.

The man to his right unbuttoned his suit coat and revealed a gun holster at his waistline. He caught me inspecting him, squared his shoulders, then shot me a death glare. I swallowed against a bone-dry throat and forced a faint smile to break the tension. The man adjusted his jacket and bent over to whisper something into the ear of the man with the red rose. They probably wondered who I was and why I was there. I was the only non-Italian in the place.

I definitely stuck out in this crowd.

I wanted the service to be over. I needed to get away from the grief-stricken faces. Away from men who could kill me without a thought. I gripped the wooden pew in front of me while the priest finished the service.

"Let's pay our respects and then get some fresh air." I reached for our belongings and handed Ms. G. her cane. "How's the ankle feeling? It looks better today, but you should still use the cane. No more sneaking out in the garden without my help, okay?"

"I don't need it except maybe to hit someone with it. I told ya, Barbara, I'm fine." She stood, then winced.

"Fine, huh?" I shook my head.

"All right, all right." She yanked the cane from my hands.

I followed her to the front of the mortuary. She approached the casket and bent her head over her brother's body. "I'm gonna miss you, Vin." She brushed away a loose tear. "Tell Mama and Pop I love 'em. Peace be with you, brother. I love you, kid."

She grabbed my hand.

As we walked out, I focused on the entrance doors. I wanted to avoid more dirty looks. Something in my peripheral vision shifted my attention to the right.

A man with teal blue eyes fixated on me. The same eyes I'd met the first time I took Ms. G. to Angelo's Deli: Angelo's son, Alessandro.

Ms. G. and I were about to pass his row when our eyes locked. My forehead felt feverish.

Alessandro looked handsome in a black suit and tie. His shiny black hair crested over his brow. A slight smile escaped his lips.

I smiled back, then lowered my head and ushered Ms. G. toward the door.

My attraction to Alessandro was inescapable. From the first day I'd moved into the ranch, he'd poke his head around every corner. Some days, he'd say he was there to bring his aunt her favorite sausage and peppers. Other days, he did odd jobs around the ranch, from installing security cameras to constructing a ten-foot-tall iron gate with a keypad. After the night my ex-boyfriend, Marcus, forced his way in and tried to kill us, Ms. G. "made the call."

Overnight, the once-open ranch turned into a top-secret fortress. But I suspected there was more to why Alessandro came around. He looked at me like my forehead scar didn't exist. His jeweled eyes had some strange sort of power. They were hypnotic and dangerous and pulled me toward him when I should have run the other way. He was Mafia, and that scared me.

I didn't need more problems. Nope. My days with bad men were over.

With Ms. G. by my side, I stepped through the doors of the mortuary, eager for a change of scenery.

"Let's find a place to sit. I know just the spot." I aimed us toward the wooden bench where I'd met Sofia months earlier. "I'm sure your family and friends will want to pay their respects."

"Family and friends, huh? What kind of family leaves you here to die? Friends? Yeah, I saw them in the back. There are only a few wise guys left that I care about anymore."

Men in trench coats with guns at their sides ambushed my memory.

Hit men.

Killers.

Thieves.

Mafia henchmen.

And so was *he*. Alessandro. In this family, he had to be.

We sat under the shade of a weeping willow as mourners trickled from the building. They gathered, hugged, and lit cigarettes. I was about to pull my pocket mirror from my purse when the man with the red rose walked over to us with guards at his sides.

Hairs on the back of my neck tingled.

"Hello, Violetta. How you been?" the man asked with a wolfish grin.

Ms. G. gave him a careful glance. "Hello, Anthony." She shook his hand. "It's been a long time."

"Yes, it has. How are things with you? You still at the ranch?" he asked.

"Where else would I be? Back in New York under *your protection*? No way. My brother died an early death because of you," Ms. G. said with an icy tone. "He was your slave."

"Feisty as ever. I see there are still hard feelings here."

"Hard feelings? You got to be kiddin' me." Ms. G. reached for her cane.

I grabbed her arm.

"Who are you?" the man asked.

"Her caretaker. And you are . . . ?" I asked protectively.

"He's Anthony Molanano," Ms. G. blurted out in a glacial tone.

Holy shit. Is this the boss of the Molanano family standing right in front of me? My legs shook.

"Caretaker, huh? Good to know that someone is caring for this sweet lady." Mr. Molanano patted Ms. G. on the cheek.

She swatted his hand from her face. "Get your God damn hands off me."

"Let's not be disrespectful. It's your brother's funeral, for Christ's sake," the man admonished.

Ms. G. stood and lurched forward with her hand poised to strike. One of his bodyguards charged us.

I pulled her back. "Easy, Ms. G. Calm down."

"I tried to make peace, Violetta," he said. "It's obvious we'll never break bread."

"Peace, my ass," Ms. G. scoffed, then slumped back onto the bench.

"Take care." He smirked, then placed his hat on his head and walked away, mumbling, "Rat bitch."

Ms. G. jumped up and hit him in the back of the neck with her cane.

Mr. Molanano yelped and crouched down. A guard pulled the crime boss close to him.

I pulled her back and seized the cane. The other guard got in my face, his hand on his gun.

"Please, no. She has Alzheimer's. She doesn't know what she's doing," I begged.

"I know what I'm doing all right," she said through clenched teeth.

Mr. Molanano locked eyes with Ms. G. "Frank shoulda killed ya when he had the chance."

She spit at the ground near his feet.

"Stop it. Sit." I pointed to the bench.

Ms. G. plopped herself onto the bench but not before she gave him the finger.

"Come on, fellas. Let's leave this bitter old bat to mourn." The men laughed. Mr. Molanano turned on his heels. Bodyguards followed.

"Are you crazy?" My voice was pitched high enough to squeak. "What's gotten into you? Is he who I think he is?"

"Yes, his nephew. The new Don," she said, winded from her attack. She reached for her ankle. "He took over the business a few years ago. I knew him when he was a teenager. He's still the same cocky brat he was before, only more powerful now."

"See, you've inflamed it." I placed my hand on her ankle. "That's what you get for being a tough ass. You'll get us killed!"

"Let 'em try. He won't do anything unless he wants a war."

"I just want to get out of here alive. Can we do that, please?" I handed her back the cane. This is for walking *only*," I admonished.

I grabbed our things to make our way to the car. Angelo and Alessandro approached.

What now? One minute I'm getting a gun pulled on me, and now him? This day can't get any worse.

Angelo hugged Ms. G. "I always liked Vinny. He was a good man."

"To me, he'll always be my pesky little brother who hid cigars and nude pics under his bed. I'll miss him dearly." Ms. G. brushed a straggling tear from her cheek.

"Hey, *Zia* Vi." Alessandro leaned over to kiss his aunt on the cheek. "I'm sorry. You gonna be all right?"

"I'll be fine." She patted his cheek.

While Angelo spoke to Ms. G., Alessandro stood next to me. With his body close, my breathing accelerated. I reached for my hat and pulled it down over my new scar, compliments of Marcus on that dreadful night. The gash above my right brow made me look like a monster. There was no way I'd let Alessandro see that.

"Hello, Barbara." A grin played across his lips.

"Hello." I tried to avoid his hypnotic stare.

"I came to the ranch the other day to bring some food, but you weren't there. Your daughter told me you were at a doctor's appointment."

"Leticia said you came by. She helps when I have errands and such. She's training to be a doctor. Ms. G. was in good hands."

"Of course. The family has full confidence in you." He nodded. "So, Dad and I are hosting a reception at the deli. A celebration of life for my *Zio* Vin. You and *Zia* are coming, right?"

"I'm not sure it's a good idea. She'll be exhausted after the burial service. We're headed there next. She wants to see her brother laid to rest." After just having a gun pulled on me, I wanted to get the hell out of there. More than anything, I needed to get away from *him*. Alessandro.

His face dropped. Light in his eyes dimmed. "Really? That's too bad," he said softly. "Dad went all out. We made every Italian dish you can think of."

"Hell yeah, we're coming," Ms. G. interrupted. "I'm starving." She grabbed her cane, stood, and pushed past me. "The food will be better than anything this one cooks."

Damn it. Of all the times I wanted her to hear me—this wasn't one of them. I should have never given her the new hearing aid.

I sighed. "Sounds like we're coming."

"Good." Hope returned to his face. "I look forward to seeing you later," he said with a teasing twinkle in his eyes.

Waves of heat burned onto my cheeks.

What's gotten into me? You're at a funeral, for God's sake. He can read right through you. Mafia man, remember? Why am I such a magnet for trouble? Look away from his eyes.

"See you there," I said, trying to sound impassive.

"Time to go, Pop. We gotta get ready for the guests." The two turned and made their way to the parking area.

"Come on, Ms. G. Let's go." I grabbed her purse.

We passed a long black limo in the parking lot. Don Molanano stood with his guards. Alessandro kissed the back of his hand. The two men discussed something. An earshot away, Don Molanano said, "Did you take care of that little thing I told you to do?"

"All taken care of, boss," Alessandro replied.

Pure validation. Eyes or no eyes, Alessandro was Mafia. I'd been a magnet for bad boys in the past, and it almost killed me. I'd fight back every urge I had for him, or I might not be so lucky next time.

We rushed to the car. Once I'd secured Ms. G.'s seat belt, I shut her door and ran to the driver's side. I hopped in and slammed the door shut.

"Follow that hearse," Ms. G. belted out.

I turned the key in the ignition and pressed the gas. We flew past the long black limo.

Bye-bye, Mafia man.

In the rearview mirror, Alessandro stared at the back of my car as we plowed through the parking lot.

"Hey, easy," Ms. G. yelled. "*Minchia*. You trying to kill me? I wanna go, but not today, kid."

I made my way onto Willow Street and blew through the yellow light at the intersection. I couldn't get away fast enough. My pulse surged through my fingers as I gripped the steering wheel. How could I be so dumb? This wasn't goodbye. In a few short hours I'd see Alessandro again.

Chapter 2
Things Said at Funerals

Ms. G. swung open the door to the deli and shuffled her little feet across the room. I walked cautiously behind her as smells of fresh bread and spices circulated in the air.

Where metal racks of aged meats and cheeses once stood, round tables dressed in white linens filled the deli. Large flower wreaths stood at the front of the room. On the main wall, Italian food filled a giant table. From what I'd witnessed, Italians used every opportunity to have a party—even funerals. To avoid awkward conversations, I'd get food and hide in the back—especially from *him*.

Ms. G. went straight to Angelo and mingled. People kissed her cheeks and told stories about Vinny. While everyone looked occupied, I grabbed a plate. Someone tapped my shoulder.

I turned. Alessandro shot me his signature smile. He could pass for a model.

My spine turned to jelly.

"You sure left in a hurry," he said.

"Ms. G. wanted to get to the cemetery when the hearse arrived ... and you know how she is about being on time."

"I should call you Mario Andretti."

I scowled at him. "I don't drive fast."

"I'm kiddin." His eyes were softer now, apologetic and soulful. In a gentler voice, he said, "Hey, can we start over? Have I done something to you that I'm unaware of?"

His pupils were wide and pulled me back into his private abyss. *You mean like you being in the Mafia? Or the fact that you're super-hot and your hypnotic eyes have some kind of power over me, forcing me to ignore all logic?*

"You haven't done anything at all," I lied.

"Sometimes I get the feeling you don't like me very much."

"What gave you that impression?" My voice was thick with sarcasm.

"I don't know. Since I've been coming around the ranch, there are days I get you to smile, and then there are days when it feels like you want to run away from me."

Maybe that's because you kill people for a living? "The times you've seen me, I was busy tending to your aunt."

"My mistake, then." He nodded his head. "Are you hungry?"

"Yes. I was about to make a plate for Ms. G. and me."

"Here, let me do it." He took the plate from my hands. "Someone needs to take care of you for a change. Do you like gnocchi?"

"Yes."

"I made it myself." Alessandro ladled a heap of pasta and handed me the plate. "Let me pour you a glass of wine. We got a few new ones in this week." His strong hands held the bottle; hands that could crush a man's throat in seconds. I swallowed and studied his firm grip around the glass. The name *SANNA* was wrapped around the top of the label. The letter *S* came up from the horizon, just like Ms. G. had described.

I gasped.

His brows pulled together. "You have a thing against red wine?"

"Um, no. It's just that . . . the name of the wine is familiar to me.

I must have heard about it before, somewhere." I didn't know how much he knew about his aunt's secret love life.

"It's a popular wine. Made right here in California, up in the Napa Valley."

"I think I'll have some water instead." I grabbed a water bottle from the table. People did crazy things on that wine. I didn't want to be tipsy around him. I didn't trust myself around those eyes. Mafia man or not, he was gorgeous. Besides, I was on the clock.

"Why don't you find a place to sit, and I'll make *Zia* a plate. No wine. I promise." His smile sparkled. Muscles along his cheekbones pressed against his perfect jawline.

"Thank you." I scanned the room for Ms. G. She sat next to Angelo like a queen on a throne as everyone gathered around her to talk about old times. Alessandro brought her food, and her face lit up. Knowing she was safe and in her glory, I dashed to a private table at the back of the room. It was far enough away to have privacy but close enough to keep an eye on Ms. G.

I chugged on my water to moisten my dry lips.

Alessandro came toward me. "Mind if I join you?"

My heart accelerated. "Of course. It's your place." *Of all the tables in here, he has to sit next to me?*

"*Zia's* happy. I gave her two servings of manicotti."

"Thanks for doing that."

"My pleasure. You do a lot for her. I'm happy to give you a break. We appreciate all you've done."

"I love your aunt very much. She's like a mother to me."

"*Zia's* great," he said, then undid the button on his jacket and sat. With his suit open, I looked for a gun on him. To my surprise, there was none. While adjusting his silverware, his pinky grazed the side of my hand.

I flinched.

"Pardon me." A seductive smile webbed its way across his face. "So, Barbara, why don't you tell me a little about yourself?" He poured himself a glass of Sanna wine. His inquisitive eyes were there again, holding me hostage.

I took a deep breath of air to lower my blood pressure. "Not much to tell." I fumbled with my water bottle. "I grew up in South Carolina, then moved with my mother and sister to California after my parents divorced."

"South Carolina?" He stabbed some pasta with his fork. My eyes watched as his tongue wrapped around the metal utensil while taking the food into his mouth. Even the way he ate was sexy.

He caught me staring. My eyes darted down to my plate.

"I've never been to the South. Do you miss it?"

"Sometimes."

"Aren't you gonna eat? I made all this food, and I want you to enjoy it. Life is about enjoyment, and food is only *one* part of it." He cocked his head to the side and teased a suggestive grin.

I scooped up some pasta and put it in my mouth. The flavor was amazing, and the thought that his strong hands made the food that was in my mouth made it taste so much better. I wiped my lips after each bite for fear I had sauce on my chin. I didn't want to give him another reason to study my face.

"It's delicious. I can taste the fennel in the sausage and the basil makes the sauce sweet."

"I'm glad you like it." He beamed. "I'd like to get to know you better. With the noise in here, I don't think this is the best place. When can I take you on a date?"

I tugged my hat brim lower, past my scar. "I'm not ready." *Not with a Mafia guy. I want a Gaetano, not a Frank. But was he a Frank?* I wasn't sure yet.

"I heard about your troubles. I'm sorry you had to go through that. It's a good thing I wasn't there, or *maronn* . . . things would've gotten ugly." He grabbed his wine glass.

"I don't like violence. Period."

"Men who hit women are scum. Women are to be worshipped

and loved." He took another sip of his wine. "Let me take you out. I think we'd have a good time. I'm a nice guy. You'll see."

"All men are nice in the beginning." I sipped my water. "And from what I've heard . . ." I stopped mid-sentence. *Shut up. Oh no. I've said too much.*

He licked his lips and used his napkin to wipe the corners of his mouth. His brows inched together. "*Hmm*," he mumbled as he swallowed a bite of food. "I don't know what my aunt has told you, but . . ."

"Oh, nothing," I mumbled, trying to think of a quick lie to escape interrogation.

"You're not a good liar. I'm not as bad as you think I am." He moved his finger along the stem of his wine glass. "If things go the way I hope, maybe one day we can trust each other enough to have those conversations."

I looked up from my plate. His eyes peered right through me, cradling my vulnerability. He licked his lips and followed up with a warm, contagious smile.

I smiled back.

From the stories Ms. G. told me about Frank, Mafia men were hard on their women. I wouldn't get involved with someone who'd hurt me again. But there was something in his eyes, a softer light that came through when he spoke, that made me think he might not be like the rest.

"With everything that happened, it's been difficult for me to trust men. I don't want any trouble. I have to think of my kids. They've seen enough bad things to last them a lifetime." Guilt reared its ugly head.

"I can tell you've been hurt. We all have pasts. There was a time in my life I experienced my own share of grief." He grimaced. "I'm not perfect, but I know how to treat a lady. Let me spoil you, Barbara."

My heart ignited while he searched my face. I drew in a quick breath and pulled down my hat.

"You don't need that. You're beautiful with or without it." He gently placed his hand on top of mine and guided my hand to my side.

"Me? Beautiful?" I chuckled. "I bet you say that to all the women."

He rested his elbows on the table and folded his hands. His face grew serious. "The only woman I'm interested in is you."

"Me? I'm nobody. I'm just the person who takes care of your aunt."

"You are *not* a nobody. From what I've seen, you're the most caring, loyal, and beautiful woman I've ever met."

"I'm sure you've met *lots* of women." *Of course he has. Look at him. He's an Italian god. Women must throw themselves at him.*

"That came out wrong. What I mean is that when you work retail, you meet lots of different people."

Did he just say retail? Laughter escaped my mouth. "Yeah, I'm sure you meet many people here at *the deli*." I shook my head.

"I met you here, didn't I? The day you brought *Zia*."

"I remember." The memory caught me off guard and choked me up. He was nice to me when Marcus was so horrible. For a brief second, he'd made me feel wanted at a time when things looked so bleak. "That was a nice day. You and Angelo have been incredibly supportive of Ms. G. through all this. Thank you for that."

"We should be thanking you. You're loving and patient with my aunt. Then I watch you with your kids. You're a great mother, Barbara. I'm a pretty good judge of character and you're a very kind person."

I straightened in my chair. "Thank you." My voice shook. "Please don't take this the wrong way, but I've been foolish with men in the past. I can't afford to do it again." I tried to sound convincing—even to myself.

"I understand the need to protect yourself after what happened, but I'm not the bad guy here. If anything, I want to protect you, and I *can* protect you, Barbara," he said confidently. His hands balled into fists, and he turned his head to the side. "Shoulda left him dead in a ditch," he said under his breath, almost inaudibly, but I'd heard him. Muscles in his jaw tightened.

"What did you say?"

"Oh, nothing." A coy grin weaved its way across his face. "I said it sounds like your ex was a real son of a bitch." He recovered smoothly.

Was he the one Ms. G. called? The one who beat Marcus up that night? Marcus said it was an Angelo's Deli truck that came for him. A strange feeling came over me. As the seconds ticked on, my heart and mind wrestled with each other. Could the one force I tried so hard to get away from be the same force that tried to save me that night? Deep down, I knew the truth.

A red rose in a small vase on the table caught my eye. The man with the rose on his lapel crept from my memory. Don Molanano: head of the Molanano family, Mafia leader and one of the heads of the five families, with his armed bodyguards. Alessandro had talked to him and even called him boss.

Nope. Not gonna happen.

"Thank you, but I can take care of myself." I placed my napkin on the table.

"I'm sure you can, but from my experience, some of the strongest people in the world need a safe person to rely on. I'd like to be that person for you. My offer stands."

I bit my lip, unable to think of what to say next.

"It's only dinner. Think about it. Besides, if I ever did something to hurt you, my *Zia* would make it so that my body was never found again. She knows a guy or two." He laughed as if to confirm that I was right about him.

"Alessandro," a man's voice called from the other side of the room.

Alessandro looked to the right. He locked eyes with his father. Angelo shook his head in disapproval and signaled him to come over.

"*Hmmph*," Alessandro grunted. His nostrils flared.

"Everything okay?" Angelo's reaction confused me.

"Everything's fine," Alessandro said in a low voice. "You're not the only one taking a chance here. I have as much to lose as you." He paused. "Maybe more. But I'm willing to give it a shot—when you're ready, of course . . ." His eyes lingered on my face for a long moment, then he got up from the table and pushed his chair in. "I think my Pop needs me. Can I take your plate?"

"Yes, thank you," I answered, dizzied by his gaze.

As he leaned in, his cologne—a bold and delicious mix of amber and sandalwood—wafted from his neck and filled the air around me. He smelled delicious.

I looked up to find him staring at me again.

"Barbara, it's been a pleasure." He winked, then smiled.

As he walked away, I wondered how long I'd have the strength to resist him.

After a few tearful speeches, it was time to go home. Ms. G. was repeating herself, a sign that she was tired. Alessandro walked the room. Occasionally he'd search for me in the crowd. I grabbed my things and walked over to Ms. G. She held onto Angelo's arm.

"This beautiful lady's getting tired," Angelo said with warmer eyes on me.

"I'm not tired, damn it. We just got here." She tried to free herself from Angelo's grip.

"Well, I'm tired, and I have an early morning appointment tomorrow," I said.

"I'll help her out," Angelo offered.

"I don't need any help," Ms. G. snapped.

"Maybe I want to hold onto you a little longer." He winked at her.

"Don't get fresh, Ang." She elbowed him in the ribs.

"One thing's for sure, you haven't lost that Giordano temper." Angelo chuckled. "But I wouldn't have you any other way." He smiled at her fondly.

We walked to the car. Angelo helped Ms. G. in as I opened the driver's door.

Alessandro yelled from behind. "Hey, wait! *Zia* forgot this."

I turned and he handed me her purse.

"Thanks, I should've checked."

"No problem. Happy to help." He leaned past me and stuck his head into the car. "Hey *Zia*, how's about I bring you some manicotti tomorrow? There's still some left over from the party."

"Sure, kid, I'd love some. I could use it." She pulled the waistline of her skirt. "Look at how much weight I've lost with how this one cooks." She glared at me.

I rolled my eyes at her. "We can take them now and save you the trip." I needed time away from him to get my head on straight.

He stood tall and faced me. "Gives me an excuse to visit with my aunt."

"Of course." I cleared my throat. "You should spend time with your aunt. I mean, because you're busy with your work at the *deli* and all." I let out a nervous giggle, then let my eyes rake over his body. With his jacket off, muscles on his chest and arms filled out the shirt in all the right ways.

The man definitely worked out.

"I like visiting with my aunt and spending time at the ranch. I have lots of good memories there, and . . . seeing you of course. I hope that's okay. See you tomorrow, Barbara." He flashed the sweetest of smiles, then leaned in close and whispered in my ear, "I hope one day you say yes. You'll be safe with me—always."

I swallowed deeply. My pulse surged through my veins.

"Hey, love birds. Whatcha doin' over there?" Ms. G. barked. "Let's get goin'. I wanna get home."

"Sleep well. Sweet dreams," he said, then stepped away from the car.

I shut the door and started the engine. This time, I edged my way out of the parking lot. In my side mirror reflection, Alessandro waved goodbye.

I'd need to double up on my anxiety meds, gets lots of sleep, and maybe even visit a shrink, a priest, or both. Staying away from Alessandro Sunseri would be harder than I thought.

Chapter 3
Battle Wounds

"Y*OU'LL BE SAFE WITH ME—ALWAYS.*"
Alessandro's velvety voice played in my ears. He bent down and kissed my lips. I grabbed onto his muscular frame and let his mouth explore. Desire pooled between my thighs . . .

The sound of the door snapped me into focus. Panting, I drew in a breath. For a split second, I didn't know where I was until I looked at the wall in front of me. A large poster displayed the before and after pictures of various nose jobs. I was at the plastic surgeon's office, getting my pre-surgery evaluation.

"Whew." I shook my head. *Damn this man! What is he doing to me?*

"Hello, Ms. Jackson. May I come in?" Dr. Padua's voice rang behind the door.

"Yes, of course. I'm sorry. Come in," I replied, embarrassed that I'd drifted off in thoughts of Alessandro. I wiped the sweat from my forehead.

Doctor Padua entered holding a clipboard and shook my hand.

"You feeling all right, Ms. Jackson?" She stared at me. "You look a little flushed."

"I'm fine. Just nervous." Which wasn't a lie. I *was* anxious to be talking about my future surgery, but it was Alessandro who'd brought on the beads of perspiration.

"Today's evaluation won't hurt. No need to be nervous." She adjusted her glasses and examined my scar. "This looks better than I expected. I estimate one or two minor procedures. Luckily, the scar is located on a natural frown line that transitions nicely into your eyebrow. With the laser treatments it should become less visible over time."

"Really?" I touched the skin above my right eyebrow. The scar was a good two inches long, slightly raised, and fibrous. Most days, I covered it with a thick headband low across my forehead. Other days, I wore a hat. On days I felt brave, I set long curls in front to conceal it. No matter what I did, evidence of that night was always there.

"Certain foundations and makeup also help," she reassured. "But I'm fairly confident I'll be able to achieve the results you want."

"That's reassuring."

She glanced down at my chart and back at me. A mist of concern spread across her face. "Have you seen a therapist about what happened that night? Domestic violence can lead to post-traumatic stress disorder. It might be a good idea to talk to someone."

"Social services offered therapy after the incident, but I was so busy moving into my new place that I didn't think about it."

"It's time to think about your health, physical *and* mental. I have the number of a psychologist in the area. Gwen Bevier is a good friend, and she's highly respected."

A therapist? With the family I worked for, I couldn't talk to a therapist.

"Okay," I said reluctantly, "but I'll be fine."

"You'd be surprised how PTSD presents. The most common symptoms are anxiety, restless sleep accompanied by nightmares, and flashbacks. Eye movement desensitization and reprocessing therapy, also known as EMDR, helps people get through past traumas. Domestic violence affects the whole family. If not for you, then maybe think about going with your kids. You could all benefit."

"I'll think about it."

"Good." She smiled and looked back at my chart. "When would you like to set up the appointment for the first procedure?"

"As soon as possible." I was ready to get my life back.

"I'll need you to fill out some paperwork for consent and a few standard forms." She wrote something in my file and handed me a stack of papers.

I scanned them briefly and put them into my purse.

"And here's Gwen's number." She handed me a small paper, then walked out of the room. Without a second thought, I dropped it in my purse. It was better than putting it in the garbage and taking the chance of her seeing me throw it away. She'd been so nice. I didn't want to be disrespectful.

I stood in front of the mirror and tugged my bangs low over my forehead. With shaky hands, I put on my sunglasses. Time to buy more makeup.

I cruised up the one-lane road that led to the ranch and passed a half-dozen farmhouses. Neighbors who had ignored me when I first came, now waved. The ranch finally felt like home.

With Marcus in jail and my new rent-free living arrangement—thanks to Ms. G.—I'd bought myself a brand-new blue Cadillac Seville. It was fully loaded and gorgeous. Because of Marcus's gambling debts, it had been a long time since I had something new. It felt good.

Since I'd moved into the big house out back, I'd offered to pay rent to Ms. G. several times, but she cursed in Italian and threw the money back in my face. I tried to write a check to Sofia, but it was returned with a note that said, "*You have done so much. We will never take your money. Think of this as a favor for a favor.*"

With the extra money, I got on top of my bills. No more late notices. I was free of financial burden thanks to my new boss—the real boss of the Giordano family, Ms. G.

As I came around the last bend of Alum Rock Avenue, I spotted a familiar scene: a white Angelo's Deli van parked in front of the ranch.

Oh, great. He's here again. Leftovers, remember?

Nerves shot up my back and forced me to adjust my seatbelt. I looked in the rearview mirror and pulled down my long, curly bangs.

At the gate, I pressed the entry code. The giant metal fence slid to the right, allowing me to pass. I parked and searched for Alessandro, but it was Darnell who spotted me first. He ran up to my driver's side door.

My heart jumped. "What happened? What did she do this time?"

"Ms. G.'s fine, Mom. I'm just glad you're back. She's extra feisty today. She got mad that I beat her at poker, so I made her some lunch. She asked for you, but I told her I was in charge until you got back from the doctor. That's when she got angry. She started saying stuff in Italian and waving her arms around."

I harnessed my laughter. "She does that from time to time."

"She's happier now. She's watching *Judge Judy*. Oh, and you got a flower delivery today. I put them on the kitchen table. There's a card attached. I wonder who'd send you flowers?" Darnell pressed.

"No idea." *No. They couldn't be from Alessandro, could they?* "You better get in that room and study for those finals, son."

"I know." Darnell swung open the screen door. As Darnell trudged to his new room, I stepped into my newly furnished three-bedroom home. The house, which once hosted many

Italian parties and Mafia meetings in the basement, was now my new sanctuary. If the walls in this place could talk.

I set my purse on the table near a huge arrangement of a dozen long-stemmed red roses. The picture on the front of the card was a beautiful sunset. Inside, it read:

I'd like to see many sunsets with you. I hope these flowers put a smile on your face the way you put a smile on mine.
Thinking of you,
Alex

The man was persistent.

I sat down at the table and inhaled their scent when Leticia came into the kitchen.

"Who sent you flowers?" Leticia asked while pouring herself some juice.

"A friend."

"A *friend*, huh? I bet they're from Alex. I see the way he looks at you, Mom. He's interested." Leticia smiled.

"Doesn't matter. I'm not ready to date. And not someone like him," I said, reaffirming my plan to abstain from Mafia men. I blinked away images of how he looked in a suit.

"What do you mean, someone like him? Isn't he Ms. G.'s godson?"

"Yes, but . . ." I bit my tongue to keep from going any further into the conversation.

"He's handsome, and every time he's been here, he's been nice. He's always helping Ms. G., bringing food, and doing odd jobs around here. From the looks of it, he's gonna start on the barn."

"The barn? What's he doing to the barn?"

"He came right after you left with some paint cans and rollers."

"Oh?" I peered out the window to find a shirtless Alessandro standing on a ladder, sanding the barn's exterior. Thick muscles on his back and chest stretched and contracted along his torso. They gleamed in the sun as a layer of sweat covered his body. I looked away. *Ugh . . . This man will find any excuse to be here and mess with my head!* I threw back the sheers.

"He even offered Darnell a job at the deli."

"Oh, he did, did he?" *Now he's trying to get to me through my kids?*

"Darnell needs a job, Mom. Have you seen the guys he's hanging around with lately? Trouble. With Dad as a role model, who knows?"

My heart sank to the soles of my feet. I didn't want my son to turn out like Marcus. "I don't like them, either. Last time they were here, one of them said he had to meet with his probation officer."

"He should take the job. It will keep him outta trouble."

"He can find another job somewhere else."

"What are you not telling me, Mom? What is it? Is Alex, like, in the Mafia or something?"

"What do you know about the Mafia?" My voice jumped an octave. I rubbed at the sudden tightness in my chest.

"When I told people at work where we moved to, I mentioned Ms. G.'s name. Someone said her family was known in San Jose for being in the Mafia."

"Keep our business, our business," I snapped.

"Geez, what's got you on edge?"

"Nothing. I'm sorting through some things in my mind."

"I know that you and Dad fell out of love long before anything happened. I want you to be happy, but I also want you to be safe. That's most important to me. Maybe give Alex a chance? Just be careful, Mom."

I peered at the roses on the table. *Perfect. Now I'll have to thank him for something else. First Marcus, then the flowers, and now the job. Was this another favor-for-a-favor Mafia thing?* I shook my head.

"There's always Dr. Lawrence. He asks about you. He's a nice guy. Wouldn't hurt a fly."

"Doesn't matter. I'm still not ready."

Just as Ms. G. and I finished our leftover manicotti, Alessandro came to the back door. He was shirtless and covered in dust and paint.

"Hi, *Zia*." He peered around me to catch a glimpse of his aunt. "You look beautiful today."

"Thanks, kid, but don't bullshit an old lady," Ms. G. yelled from her recliner. "And don't drip paint on my floors, either."

"I won't come in. Promise. But I'll be back soon to tackle the other side."

"Thanks for your help out there today, but you don't need an excuse to be here to talk to Barbara. Just talk to her. She's right here." Ms. G. flashed me a smile.

"You're impossible. Do you know that?" I glared at her.

"Barbara, can I speak to you outside for a minute?" Alessandro asked.

"Go out and talk to him, for Christ's sake," Ms. G. shouted.

I walked out to the patio and shut the glass slider behind me, trying to hold onto any shred of willpower I had left. "Thank you for the flowers and the card."

"You're welcome. Just a little something to let you know I was thinking about you." His face went shy. "I meant what I said in the card. I hope we can see many sunsets together."

"I heard you offered my son a job?"

"I should've spoken to you first, but once we got talking, it just came up. He's a great kid. It doesn't pay much, but it's honest work. A solid first job. Builds character."

"I'll talk to him about it when I get home."

"Let me know what you decide. The job's his if he wants it."

"Thank you. I will."

"Look, I know it's only been a day, but have you thought any more about what we talked about?"

"Yes."

"And?"

"I'm not sure it's a good idea. I have responsibilities here. Your aunt. My kids . . ."

"I understand." His chin dropped to his chest.

"I can't get involved. It's too dangerous."

"What's dangerous about dinner?" He dangled a smile. "No wine. I promise."

I exhaled sharply. "This isn't about the wine, and you know it," I said firmly. "Please don't make me say it out loud. I signed contracts and everything. Trust me, your secret is safe with me. My life depends on it. I won't tell a soul. But that doesn't mean I want to get involved. You seem like a nice person, but . . ."

His brows shot up. "But what?"

"Although I'll never understand what you see in me, it's too risky." I worried about his reaction to my words.

"I don't know how much you know about the family, but from what I've heard, you're someone we can trust. If you weren't, my cousin Sofia wouldn't have hired you."

"I'm . . . afraid," I stammered and looked away quickly.

Alessandro stepped closer. His warm breath fell softly onto my cheek. I turned back to look at him. Our noses touched. "I'm not your ex," he whispered. "You don't need to be afraid of me. I'll never hurt you."

He grabbed my hand. With a featherlike touch, his thumb grazed over my knuckles. He peered into my eyes. The teal blue effect radiated throughout my body and devoured any resistance I had left.

"Please . . ." I licked my lips. "Don't do that." I pulled my hand back.

"I'm sorry." He winced. "I don't know what came over me. I need to be careful with you." He put his hands at his side.

I fought for breath. "Don't make this harder," I said, ignoring the ache between my legs. His shirtless body so close to mine sent ripples of heat through my insides.

"Can you honestly tell me you aren't the least bit interested in spending time alone together? Because your body language tells me differently." His breath came rougher, and his face grew serious. "If you dislike me that much, tell me now, and I'll never bother you again." His eyes blazed a bewitching blue.

For fear of falling, I locked my knees and took a deep breath. My eyes scanned his bare chest and glorious six-pack abs. Peeks of hair came up from the top of his jeans past the waistband.

"I . . . I can't just leave and go on a date with you. Who will watch your aunt?" I choked out with ragged breath, thoroughly aroused.

"So, you don't want me to go away, then?" The ghost of a smile tugged at the edges of his mouth. "Take a chance with me." His voice was satin. He grabbed for my hand again. The pad of his thumb softly kneaded my clenched fist. Within seconds my fingers relaxed.

"Please understand, I have a job to do. Ms. G. needs me." I struggled to breathe.

"I have an idea."

"I told you I can't leave."

"You won't have to leave."

"What do you mean?"

"You'll see."

I pulled my hand away and placed it on my hip. "See what?"

He grabbed his toolbelt off the porch and walked through the gate.

I rubbed the sweat from my face. I'd never believed in witchcraft before. But there was no denying it—I was under some kind of magical power, and only he knew the spell.

After Alessandro left, hours passed like days.

What did he mean, I won't have to leave?

Questions loomed and left me anxious. To fight the nagging feeling in my gut, I tried to stay busy for the rest of the night. I cleaned Ms. G.'s kitchen, gave her a long bath, then tucked her into bed and walked back to the big house.

 I flicked on the kitchen light and reached into my purse to find the number to the therapist. The slightest knot formed in my stomach as I rubbed the edges of the paper. What would I say if I had the courage to call? My kids had seen so much violence. There was no way they hadn't been affected after what they saw that night when Marcus came to the ranch to shoot Ms. G.

 We were trying to adjust to our new lives at the ranch. The kids did their best to get back to their normal routines. Leticia was almost finished with her term, and Darnell was weeks away from graduating high school. Our new home gave us a fresh start, but there was still unresolved grief. I saw it on their faces when they threw Marcus's letters from jail into the trash, and I felt it every time my mind told me I was a bad parent.

 Avoiding the weight of my past, I shoved the vase of roses from view the same way I wanted to push away guilt.

 Darnell had been visibly troubled since the night he witnessed his father attack me. In the last few weeks, he'd shown a range of emotions—sometimes distant and avoiding eye contact, and other times displaying signs of rage like his father. A week ago, he got in my face when I reminded him to do his chores. Maybe it was these new friends of his, but I swear he looked high the other night. Something was off.

 Although Leticia appeared unphased, she was a lot like me—a stuffer. I worried about how she handled her emotions. I'd have to sit them both down and discuss the benefits of long-term healing—something I didn't know that much about yet.

 I placed Dr. Bevier's number on the table. There was no way around it—we all needed some kind of therapy. But how? It was impossible. Well, maybe not for the kids, but for me . . . I was a different story. If anyone found out that I'd talked to a shrink, I could be killed. I'd have to keep things to myself. It would be a breach of contract, and I'd be a sitting duck. I'd never told anyone about Ms. G.'s past with the Mafia, and I wasn't about to start now.

Alessandro complicated matters. I'd never been pursued by a white man before and definitely not by someone in the mob. At some point, I'd have to talk to Ms. G. about him. She'd be the only one I could speak to about this. Just like I'd admitted my past with Marcus, I could tell her things, private things, that only she and I understood. When the time came, I would tell her about my feelings for Alessandro. I suspected she already knew.

I changed into my nightgown. Sleep would help clear my mind. I nestled into bed and closed my eyes. Flashbacks of hooks slicing my face caused tears to fall. I held my pillow tightly. There was no denying it. My near-death experience with Marcus haunted me. Dr. Padua was right. I had the beginnings of PTSD.

Ms. G. would know what to say and do. She'd suffered far worse than me and lived to talk about it. She'd help me to be strong. We needed each other like that. Tomorrow, I'd ask her what happened when she and Gaetano had reunited after the war. Maybe the rest of the story would give me hope and a way to overcome my fears. I'd live vicariously through her. Her stories of the past were always a welcome escape from reality. Thankfully, those memories were still intact. Like most Alzheimer's patients she couldn't remember what happened yesterday, but could tell me in great detail what happened in her younger years. All I had to do was pray that her disease hadn't progressed enough to devour those memories for good.

I slammed my hand against the alarm button and rubbed the sleep from my eyes. "It can't be morning yet." I yawned.

My lids felt heavy. I'd tossed and turned all night. Old memories of Marcus beating me mixed with dreams of Alessandro, shirtless, left me feeling like a limp noodle. Today would be a long day, but one that I hoped would give me all my answers. I dressed and shut the door, medical bag in hand.

I was determined to ask Ms. G. about the picture I'd found of her and Gaetano in Rome. The more I thought about it, the faster I walked to the main house. With every step forward, my heart swelled. I was happy and excited. I hadn't felt this good in a long time.

I took a few more steps when I heard Ms. G. singing and laughing. My joyous mood halted, and my blood pressure rose. *Damn it, I told her not to go outside without me! Oh, that woman never listens.*

"What did I tell you about coming into the garden without me? You could get hurt," I yelled.

Ms. G. stood in her nightgown, throwing pieces of bread at the cement.

I ran to her side.

"You see 'em? You see my pretty fish?" she asked, tossing breadcrumbs everywhere.

Years ago, there had been a pond with small fish and ducks here, until her father cemented it over. With wide eyes and a childlike grin, she grabbed handfuls of bread and threw them at her feet. Ms. G. was in some kind of trance. Tangled in visions of the past, she looked down at the cement as if the pond was still there. Watching her, I felt helpless. She was in the grasp of her disease—faltering and succumbing to it. A lump formed in my throat.

I grabbed her hand. "Hey honey, I think you've given those fish enough food for now. They're gonna get fat. Let's go inside." We strolled to the living room. I sat her on her brown recliner. She appeared confused. She studied her hands, still holding pieces of bread, and then looked up at me.

"Time for your pill." I grabbed the bread from her hands.

Her eyes held no emotion. She offered no words and no movement, only gentle breaths. I went to the kitchen and threw away the mashed-up bread, then poured a glass of water and grabbed her pill box.

I handed her the medication. "Here you go, sweetheart."

She placed the tablet on her tongue. Her hands shook as she held the glass to her mouth. Droplets dribbled onto her lap. I placed my hands over hers. Together, we gently tilted the glass upward. She gulped slowly.

"I'm gonna get some breakfast started." I turned on the TV, hoping the noise would bring her around.

When I returned with food, she stood in front of the pictures on the wall. One by one, she touched them.

"Here's some toast with your favorite jam." I placed it on the TV tray by her recliner.

"I'm not hungry," she mumbled, expressionless.

"Honey, you have to eat. Have a bite or two."

When she turned around, I met her with a slice of toast. She gummed a bite and turned back to the shrine of pictures. She grabbed one off the wall and stared at it.

"Is that Carmela?" I hoped that talking about her family would put the light back into her eyes.

"Yes." She grinned at the picture. "My big sister, Carm."

"Whatever happened to her?"

"She moved to Los Angeles. She died a few years ago. I have a few nieces and nephews down there. They were at the deli. I should've introduced you." Her brows pulled together. "Wait, why were we at Angelo's?" Her eyes searched mine for answers.

I didn't respond. I waited for her to make the connection. I didn't want to upset her after what I'd seen in the yard. She wrung her hands together. A single tear fell.

"Oh yes, I remember." She looked away from me. "It's just me and Paulie now. But Paulie will never see the light of day again. He's gonna die in prison."

"That's so sad. When was the last time you saw him? Would you like me to arrange a visit? I could take you."

"No," she said, then handed me back the toast. "I don't talk to my brother anymore." Her hands balled into fists.

"But I thought you said he writes you?"

"I read his letters, but I never write back. Too painful after what happened . . ." Her voice trailed off. "You know that crap they say about blood being thicker than water? That's bullshit when it comes to the mob. You're loyal to them and only them."

"What about Tony? You seemed close to him."

She reached for the St. Anthony's charm that hung around her neck. "I always loved my big brother. He saved my life. Ended the madness," she said with a dazed look on her face.

"Ms. G., tell me what happened when you reunited with Gaetano after the war. You told me that I needed to hear the rest of the story. I still can't believe you found each other. That's the kind of stuff that movies are made of."

"Movies? Ha! In this life, there are no fairy-tale endings," she scoffed. "You know where I put my crochet needle? I used to have a big metal one. I must have misplaced it somewhere. Have you seen it?" She turned to me for an answer.

A shiver swept its way across my body. I'd stabbed Marcus with it.

She rummaged through her craft box.

"The police have it." My shoulders slumped.

"The police?" she shouted. "What in the hell were they doing here?"

"They were here the night Marcus showed up. The night you shot him and the night I got this." I pointed to my forehead.

She eyed me cautiously. With one eyebrow raised, she pressed her lips together. "Oh yeah, I remember. They don't make 'em like they used to. Winchester." She beamed proudly. "The old woman that used to make 'em lived right here in San Jose. Did you know that?"

"Yes, I did."

"I remember readin' that she thought the ghosts of the people who were killed with her guns would come back to haunt her. That's a scary thought. I wouldn't want anyone to come back and haunt me. Not after what happened . . ."

"I feel like I'll go crazy if you don't tell me what happened between you and Gaetano. *Your* love story gave me hope that good guys still exist."

"My nephew, Alex, is a good guy. He sure seems to like you, or he wouldn't be here every *God damn day*." She grabbed for a different crochet needle and her yarn. "I've seen the way you two look at each other. Whether you want to admit it or not, you're interested."

"I don't know what you're talking about."

"You can fool others, but you can't fool me. No matter what you think about him, my nephew's a good boy, but like the rest of us, he was left with no choices. With Angelo in the business, it was only a matter of time before Alex became a *made man*. When they come, you do what they want, or you suffer the consequences."

"That's why I can't get involved with someone like him. After what you told me about Frank and the Mafia, I can't expose my kids to that." I touched my scar.

"Quit touching it," she admonished. "It's not *that* bad. I have plenty of scars. Did I ever tell you about the time I bit Frank in the face? That left a nasty scar." A small, devilish grin crept over her face.

"You did."

"Frank was pissed about that. Son of a bitch deserved it. He tried to kill me, after all. I was free after that day. Well . . . not really." Her words turned into whispers, and her gaze fell.

"What happened? Did you ever see Frank again? And how did you and Gaetano reunite?"

She dug her crochet needle into the yarn and took a deep breath, a sure sign she was ready. "Okay, kid. If you've got time, I'll tell you what happened when Gaetano Sanna came back into my life. No living soul knows everything that happened all those years ago. You'll be the first."

My heart flooded with excitement. "You were his sun, and he

was your wind," I swooned. "I love that." I needed the escape of their love story.

Her expression looked miles away. "Funny thing about the sun and wind. You put them together long enough, and they make fire. Come to think of it, it was a God damn inferno. I had to make tough choices and sacrifice parts of myself to end the destruction that this life creates." She looped the yarn around her finger. "See, kid, the Mafia is like an infectious, generational disease. As lethal as any cancer. It preys on the need for power and protection. That's how it claims its victims. And it comes at a high cost. Some pay for it with their lives. There were times I would've happily taken a bullet. That would've been easier." Her voice turned to a whisper. "I paid the ultimate sacrifice . . . one worse than death, and one that no woman should ever have to make. I couldn't allow them to harm anyone else."

Muscles in my back stiffened like thick rubber bands ready to snap.

"It all started the night after Carmela's wedding. I enlisted in the war effort to be a combat nurse."

"Combat nurse? You never told me that."

"I've told you plenty. Hell, if anyone was to find out what's in that little head of yours, they'd whack me for sure, then you."

My mouth went dry. "Go on."

"When I returned home from Brooklyn, I felt lost and needed a purpose. I'd read that the government had programs to train women with some medical experience like me. After working at my father's clinic, I wanted to do something with what I'd learned. Next thing I knew, I was shipped off to England."

"It must have been difficult to leave the ranch and your family behind."

"I don't like to think about the war. I saw things no one should see. I was up to my armpits in blood and pus. Hundreds of men died in front of me, and there was nothing I could do about it."

The same was true in my profession. I'd seen so many patients die during my time with them. Thinking about losing Ms. G. made my heart crumple into a tight ball. I placed my hand on her shoulder.

"After my tour of duty, I traveled to different parts of Europe. Italy was as lovely as I'd imagined. It was the perfect place for a loving reunion with *my Guy*," she sighed. "I was in one of the holiest places in the world when God placed Gaetano back into my life. That's where I made peace with myself after everything that happened in Brooklyn—losing my daughter, the drugs, my involvement with the Mafia—all of it. For a moment, I felt absolved of my sins." She paused in thought. "But that didn't last long. My circumstances quickly changed."

Tears welled at the sides of her eyes.

"If this is too difficult, you don't have to tell me." I patted her hand.

"No," she snapped. "It's time you knew everything." She reached for her necklace, kissed St. Anthony, then laid the medal back on her chest. Her eyes peered up at me. "The story I'm about to tell you can never be repeated. If someone were to find out, they'd come for us."

This wasn't the first time she'd cautioned me about her life as a Mafia queen and the illicit things she'd seen and done. Only a few short months ago, she'd told me a story I'd never forget. As scared as I was to learn the truth, I couldn't wait any longer. I had to know the whole story, no matter the cost. I swallowed hard, then finally spoke. "I won't say a word. Go on. I'm ready to go back . . ."

Chapter 4

An Answer to a Prayer

Rome, Italy
Early June 1947
Violetta

I WIPED MY EYES WITH A HANDKERCHIEF. IN THE GRAND room of St. Peter's Basilica, I stared into the eyes of the Virgin Mary. Her dead son lay across her lap. When I looked closer, it was as if I was staring into a mirror. Her eyes told her story. She was shattered, empty, and broken. It was the same way I'd felt the day I held my daughter, Adelina, in my arms. My precious angel. Gone too soon.

Shame-filled drops streamed down my face. How could I still have tears? After watching countless men die, and spending endless nights sleeping in a lonely bed, I never cried. But when it came to my daughter and Gaetano, the regret-filled drops were there to remind me of my past. My soul stored sadness like an abandoned warehouse. Grief thrived there, in the vacant place of my mind that exists after such a tragedy. Prayer was my only salvation.

Dear God, please forgive me.

I know it's been a while since I've been to church and to confession. It was that damn war, and . . . the war within me. I promise I'll make more time to be in your heavenly presence, Father. I ask for your forgiveness for all that I've seen and done. The drugs, the robberies, the sleeping around, the fight . . .

I blinked back images of Rose's red-stained lips and the blood that poured from her head when I beat her unconscious after I found her in bed with Frank. I choked at the feeling of not being able to breathe when Frank kicked me in the gut and broke my ribs. I rubbed my chest. I took a deep breath and made the sign of the cross.

I can't keep thinking about the past and living in fear, Father. I've done some bad things, but I'm not a bad person. I have to move on, or I may never return to my true self. Please guide me with your ultimate wisdom and protect me and my loved ones in the days ahead. Help me find love and happiness again. With you by my side, I know I'll never really be alone, but I'm human, God. As much as I've tried to move on, I miss him.

"Gaetano." Saying his name out loud made him real again.

Lord, please heal my heart.

"Adelina, if you're listening," I whispered, "not a day goes by that I don't think of you. Please forgive me. I love you always, *piccolina mia*."

The lump in my throat grew so thick that I struggled to swallow. I turned to walk away—to leave my past behind me and lock it away in that holy space forever. I hurried through the entrance, down the giant steps, through the piazza and out onto the Roman streets.

Italy was alive with tourists again and buzzed with chatter. Men and women held hands and took pictures while children laughed and played. Seeing this beautiful country thrive again made me happy.

Something sparkly caught my eye in one of the windows of a small shop. I took a second look, then went in. Religious symbols, from crosses to statues of the Virgin Mary and all the saints, sat on tables. I perused, then made my way to the front, where various strands of rosary beads were strung on hooks behind a glass cabinet. The beading was breathtaking. Some were made of silver and multi-colored glass, others of pearl and semi-precious stones. A few were even made of gold.

On a piece of black velvet lay a brilliant St. Anthony's medal. It was solid gold with tiny diamonds, attached to a matching gold necklace. I stared at it until the clerk spoke up.

"*Signora*, do you want to see something?" the shopkeeper asked in Italian.

"*Si. Lei parla inglese?*"

"Yes."

"I'd like to see the gold Saint Anthony's charm. The one on the right with diamonds. Yes, that one." I pointed.

The man picked up the necklace and placed it in my hands.

"It's beautiful."

"Did you a lose someting?" the man asked in broken English.

"Yes and no."

The man cleared his throat. "*Sant'Antonio* itsa da saint to pray for lost tings. But soma people say itsa better to pray to him dan to *San Valentino* if you looking for *amore*. Uh," he mumbled, trying to find the words in English. "Love. I tink you finda love in *Roma*." The man's brows moved up and down.

"Better than Saint Valentine, huh?" I asked skeptically. He looked at me curiously, then a smile edged past his bushy mustache. "Not sure about the love part, but yes, I've lost some things in my life. Maybe Saint Anthony can help me." A glimmer of hope blossomed in my heart. "May I try it on?"

"*Si*," said the man as he watched me clasp it behind my neck.

"How much is it?" I asked curiously.

The man cocked his head to the side.

"Um . . . *Quanto costa?* The price? Money?"

"Oh, itsa honna dolla US."

I gasped. "A hundred dollars? I had no idea it was that much. I can't afford that." I undid the clasp and handed it back.

The man placed it back on the velvet. My life was different now. Without Mafia money, a hundred dollars was significant. I'd have to do without. "I'll take the rosary beads." I pointed to a strand of red glass beads.

"Dis only two dolla US."

I handed him the money. With a heavy heart from the day's emotions, I grabbed the beads and put them in my purse.

"I like the other one better on you," a familiar voice said from behind.

I felt like I'd swallowed my tongue. Prickles of panic tugged at the hairs on the back of my neck, causing the tips of my ears to burn. When I tried to focus, the room spun around me.

I knew that voice like no other. With wobbly legs, I turned around. There he was—the man of my dreams. Gaetano stood before me in a dark suit and tie with his dreamy eyes, smiling my favorite crooked smile.

"Hello, Violetta," he said with his cashmere voice.

I tried to respond, but words wouldn't come. Everything around me moved in slow motion. Seconds felt like hours. Gravity shifted, forcing my body to sway, but I couldn't stop it. My vision blurred, and my legs gave way.

Then, without my permission, the beautiful, familiar face faded into darkness.

Chapter 5

Miracle

"Violetta, wake up." A hand brushed my face.

I blinked my eyes open. My vision rolled in on a fog. Gaetano loomed over me.

I reached for him and cupped his chin in my hand.

"Gaetano. It *is* you. I must be dreaming. Please, don't wake me," I mumbled, then pulled his face to my lips. Instinct took over, and I kissed the man in my dream. As my fingers laced through his hair, I felt the softness and fullness of his mouth and a feeling of warmth enveloped me.

Two hands pressed at my cheeks.

My lips chilled as he pulled away.

"You're not dreaming. I'm here. It's me, Gaetano," he said softly.

I went to kiss him again but he moved his face to the side, dodging my advance. Gaetano had never denied my affection before. My heart stopped, and my eyelids fluttered when reality set in.

This was no dream. This was real.

"What happened?" I choked out while looking at the pair of honey-brown eyes staring down at me.

"You fainted."

"Fainted?" Blood rushed to my head and cheeks. "I'm sorry. I . . . I shouldn't have kissed you."

"You don't have to be sorry. It's okay. I'm here." He pressed a cup of water to my dry lips. A pained expression took hold. "Please drink. You'll feel better."

I sipped the cool water.

A smile streamed across his face, making my heart flutter. I tried to get up. "Whoa. I'm dizzy."

"Stay still," he said, his hand on my arm.

Strangers stared.

"She'll be fine. *È svenuta*. She fainted." Gaetano spoke to the people gathering around us. "Give her room, please." His soft eyes peered at my face.

I looked at my surroundings. I was on the shop floor with something soft under my neck.

"I was afraid you'd hurt your head on the ground, so I put my jacket under your head." He crouched protectively over my body.

"Thank you."

"You're welcome. Please, take another sip. Then I'll try to sit you up."

"You okay, *Signora*?" the shopkeeper asked.

"She'll be fine," Gaetano assured.

With double vision, I grabbed the cup and let the water cascade down my throat.

He picked me up in his arms. "There's a bench outside. Let's get you out in the fresh air. That should help."

Afraid I would pass out again, I closed my eyes and gripped the cup. With each step, his muscular arms cradled me. He stared down at my face, then looked away quickly and placed me on the bench. He grabbed the cup from my hands and sat next to me.

"My purse. Do you have my purse?" I asked, panicked.

"Yes." He placed my purse next to me. "The man in the store

gave us this cup of water. We should thank him later. I asked for holy water for you, but they wouldn't give me any," he joked.

We both laughed, and my body relaxed. Even our laughter felt familiar.

"You're the same. You still know how to make me laugh."

"It's wonderful to see you smile again, Violetta."

"Thank you. It's wonderful to *see* you at all. What are you doing here?"

"I was going to ask you the same thing."

"Well . . ." I stammered as a pang of nausea crept up from the adrenaline.

"Are you all right? Do you need more water? You don't look so good. Have you eaten?"

"Not since this morning."

"Let's get you something small to eat. I know a good *trattoria* around the corner. Can you walk?"

"I can try." I attempted to stand. My body swayed.

Two arms grabbed at my hips to steady me.

"It's a good thing it's close, but if I need to, I'll carry you."

"Thank you. Stand close, just in case."

"Here," he said, then reached for my hand. "Is that better?"

"Yes, thanks."

Dream or no dream, this was nothing short of a miracle. My heart felt whole again. My sadness ebbed, and as I was about to embrace the moment, I glanced down at the hand that firmly held mine.

No wedding ring.

He wasn't married? What happened?

He might not have been married, but I still was—*technically*—to one of the biggest Mafia bosses in the country.

After a short walk along cobblestone streets, questions filled my mind. Answers would ultimately provide hope or add more confusion. Either way, we needed to air out our truths.

Gaetano squeezed my hand and guided us to a charming little *trattoria* on the corner. Tables and chairs sat on a patio with a pergola overhead, providing much-needed shade. Bougainvillea and wisteria grew through wooden slats and gave the air a welcome scent. A waiter sat us at a table that faced the street.

"*Grazie*," Gaetano said to the man.

The waiter handed us menus.

"What are you hungry for?" Gaetano's dreamy eyes peered down at the menu then back at me.

"Right now, I'll eat anything."

As soon as the waiter came by to pour water into our glasses and place bread on our table, Gaetano ordered for us in Italian.

I was captivated by the way he blended both languages almost perfectly now. His lips moved while his tongue massaged the words. It was intoxicating. The more he spoke, the more I was reminded of the days at Antonelli's dinner table when he'd stumbled to read Shakespeare.

"You speak English very well now."

"Yes. It's good for business."

"You've come a long way." I smiled.

"We both have."

"So, what are you doing here?"

"I'm here on business, looking for property. I plan to expand." He spread his napkin over his lap. "And you? What are you doing here?"

"After serving as a nurse in the army, I decided to stay and tour Europe. Until about a month ago, I stayed with family in Calabria."

His eyebrows shot up. "But wait, how? You were pregnant the last time I saw you."

My daughter's face burned a hole in my heart again. I sipped some water to dislodge the giant lump forming in my throat. "My daughter died. I miscarried after six months. And, well, Frank and I . . . he's in jail. I left him," I explained, holding back that I still wasn't divorced. I rubbed at my temples.

"I had no idea. I'm so sorry." He placed his hand on mine.

My pulse surged from his touch. "When I returned from Brooklyn, I needed to do something to help people. The army had nursing programs, so I enlisted and, well, here I am." I took a bite of bread.

"And here you are." He smiled.

"After the war, I had no reason to go home. I always wanted to visit Italy, and I'm so glad I did."

He grinned. "It's a beautiful country, isn't it?"

"Yes, it is."

"I also fought in the war."

"Really?"

"I was drafted and deployed here in forty-four. I didn't want to leave because my father had grown weak after his stroke, and I didn't know how the winery would survive with only my mother and sisters running it. José and a few other workers stepped up to help out."

I'd forgotten how unbelievably handsome he was. The same face and dreamy eyes stared back at me. He'd grown into his body. Firm shoulders and a perfect build filled out his suit. He was no longer the boy I remembered. He was a man. His hair was cut short and most of his curls were gone, but the same long brown lashes flickered against his irises in the sun. I focused my attention back on his mouth and held onto his every word.

He placed his hand on my arm. "Are you still dizzy? You look like you weren't here for a minute."

"I still can't believe you're here. I'm sorry, go ahead."

He flashed my favorite crooked smile and continued. "Where was I? Oh yes, so when the war started, the wine business took a hit. People needed food, not wine. To keep my family afloat and the workers fed, José and I planted fruit to stay profitable. Now, the winery also produces apples, apricots, and peaches. We sell to local markets across California."

"How's your family?"

"They're managing. It's been tough on my mother with my father so weak."

I thought about how much his mother despised me for my family's allegiance to the Mafia. Time wouldn't have changed that. "That must be hard. And your sisters? They must be so big now."

"They're doing well in American schools. They've made friends with the other children who live at the winery."

"Oh yes, I remember. Who was that one girl? José's daughter? The one who had a crush on you. E-something," I teased.

"Espi, short for Esperanza. She's terrific." He smiled brightly. "She's been a huge help to me over these few years. She knows the business from growing up in the winery. She helps my mother with everything from reconciling the books to handling large events. You name it, she does it. The girls are close to her and treat her like an older sister. After everything that's happened, it makes me feel good to know that my mother has her by her side when I'm away."

He spoke of her with reverence and admiration. I knew that look. That was the way he used to talk to me. A part of me was envious and also angry at myself for leaving him that day. But if I hadn't, Frank would've killed him. I'd do it all over again to save his life. I loved him too much to let him suffer that fate. I tried not to be jealous of his past but hopeful of our reunion.

"She sounds lovely," I said with a half-smile. "The war hit our family too. My father had to work with the US government and agricultural department to keep my brothers on the ranch. Ranchers and farmers took a huge hit since most men were out here, fighting."

The waiter brought us a bottle of wine with our salads.

"*Grazie,*" Gaetano thanked him. "Wine?"

"No, thank you. I'll have water today." I hadn't had any alcohol since I'd almost overdosed after Adelina's death. "Please, continue."

"When I returned, I told my father I wanted to expand our business in Italy. A few winemakers out here are doing well for themselves, so I came back to view property."

"Sounds like business is good."

"We've managed." He took another sip of wine, closed his eyes, then swirled it in his mouth. He swallowed down deep, then licked his lips. "*Hmm* . . . Now that's good wine." He relaxed into a smile. "I've been visiting the many wine festivals in Italy and sampling our wine out here. I might try and open a winery right here in Rome. One day I'd like to have a vacation home here. I miss Italy." A flash of sadness crushed his face. "It feels different now after all that's happened, but some things are the same."

The waiter came with a tray of antipasti.

"Here. Eat. *Mangiate.*"

I grabbed a piece of cheese and took a bite. I ate slowly. "How did you serve in the war?"

"I started as a foot soldier. Over time, they used me more as an interpreter. My knowledge of the English language has served me—and America—well." He took a sip of his drink.

"An interpreter?" I smiled proudly. "Do you remember when *Signora* Antonelli used to watch us like a hawk?"

"What about your mother with her gun?" He laughed.

I cringed, and my lips pressed together. "God rest her soul."

"I'm sorry."

"She isn't suffering anymore, and that's what matters. She's looking after my daughter in heaven. Does your family keep in contact with ole man Antonelli? I haven't seen them in years. Pop still works with them from time to time."

"My mother is very close with *Signora* Antonelli. They talk often. She feels indebted to them for taking us in after everything that happened."

"To think I used to hate picking prunes, but then I met you." He smiled.

"I'm sorry. You were saying that you were an interpreter."

"It was difficult at first. I felt disloyal. I grew up here, but America has given my family so much. I knew that what I relayed got people killed, and that part was hard." His eyes went suddenly empty, followed by a brief strained silence. After a few seconds, he dragged his eyes back up to my face. "Cheers, Violetta. It's amazing to see you again." He forced a smile, then raised his glass to toast.

With his hand around his glass, I looked at the finger that was absent a wedding band. I clinked my glass against his, then set it down on the tablecloth. "Last time I saw you was at my mother's funeral. You introduced me to someone. Are you married?"

He grimaced at the question. "That relationship is over," he clipped, then looked down at the table.

"I'm sorry," I lied.

"Long-distance relationships don't seem to work. Time away from someone changes things." His gaze fell. "Angelina worked for her father's winery and had responsibilities to her family, as I have to mine. Besides," he said, then gulped, "she wasn't the one."

My heart stopped and started again.

With renewed hope, I chose my words wisely. "I understand. Sometimes you meet someone, and you know there'll never be anyone else like them—ever." I stared into his eyes.

He broke focus and sipped on his drink. "Yes, well," his voice stammered. "Right after we ended things, I was sent off to boot camp, so I haven't had the time to pursue the company of a female." He flashed a half-smile. "What about you?"

"There's no one. Actually, there was someone . . . you."

He shook his head. "Violetta . . ." His voice was pained.

"Gaetano, I need to apologize to you for what happened. I know I hurt you. I was only trying to . . ."

He put his hand up. "I don't want to talk about that. It was a long time ago," he said as the waiter arrived with our last course. "*Grazie*, good," he exhaled as if the interruption was welcome. "Let's eat."

He avoided my eyes. He spun his pasta around his dish and then looked up at me. "Violetta, all I want to know is if you're happier now that you left him. Everything else is in the past."

"Yes, I'm happier. Happier because if I hadn't, I wouldn't be here having lunch with you," I said, hopeful.

"*Salute.* To friendships like ours." He held his glass to mine.

I felt like I'd been kicked in the gut.

Friendships like ours? Really? Is that what we are now? Just friends? Was I misreading something?

We were alone in one of the most romantic places in the world together, and he only wanted to be *friends*? With our history, how could he appear so aloof? I lifted my glass to hide my disappointment. "To *friends.*" I let my glass touch his and put my head back, gulping what I wished was some finely aged Scotch. Water caught in my throat, and I coughed with force.

His brows shot up. "Are you all right?" He patted my back.

"Yes. Wrong pipe." I cleared my throat. "I'm fine. Really. About today, I'm sorry I kissed you. I don't know what came over me."

He laughed. "You don't need to apologize. I've had dreams like that too, but then I wake up." His face grimaced, then a slow, forgiving smile warmed his cheeks. "No need to feel embarrassed. We have a history, you and me. It's natural to return to old habits."

"Yeah, I guess it is," I said, trying to hide the sadness from my face. I needed to escape before I made a fool of myself and cried. I had to maintain some kind of dignity. I put down my fork. "I don't think I should eat anymore. I don't want to be sick." I reached into my purse for money. "Here, this should cover my lunch. As for what you did for me today, I'm not sure I'll ever be able to repay you." My voice quivered, and my cheeks flamed.

He pushed my money back to me. "When a man takes a woman to lunch, he pays. It's on me."

"I don't want you to feel obligated. I can pay for my lunch. We're just *friends*, remember?" My voice caught in my throat as I said the word *friends* out loud to the man I'd loved forever.

"I never do anything I don't want to do. I'm not like *some* people." Contempt coated his voice.

"*Some* people?" I suspected he meant me.

He reached for his wallet.

I rose from the table and grabbed my handbag. "I know you'll never understand, but I left to protect you because I loved you. I didn't have a choice. And after everything I've seen and done for those bastards, I know I did the right thing. I couldn't let you die. I'm sorry, and I hope one day you'll forgive me." I blinked back tears.

Unable to meet my eyes, he spoke. "Violetta," he sighed and reached for my hand. It was obvious that indifference was his weapon of choice to deal with the past.

If I was the only one to still have these feelings, I wouldn't let him pity me. Tears filled my eyes. I adjusted my skirt and pushed in my chair. "Thank you for a lovely lunch. I should be getting back now. I need to lie down. This has been an emotional day. Goodbye, Gaetano," I whispered, and pressed a kiss to his cheek. I pulled away fast and moved quickly around the other tables, passing the entrance and onto the street.

"Wait," Gaetano yelled.

I glanced over my shoulder. Gaetano threw money on the table and chased after me. "You shouldn't be alone after what happened. Please let me walk you to your hotel."

"You don't need to do that. I'll be fine," I said proudly.

"Please. I'll feel better knowing you got to your hotel safe."

"I'm a big girl now. I can take care of myself." I flicked my hair behind my shoulder and continued walking briskly.

"If that were true, you'd still be on the ground in front of the Basilica."

I slowed and turned to him. Muscles in my arms and legs tensed, and my hands turned into balls. "How dare you! I'm sorry I hurt you, but you don't have to punish me this way. You aren't the only one who got hurt in all this. I'll have you know that I never loved..."

"Stop," he interjected. "Please stop."

"I'm sorry I ruined your day and that you felt you had to help me. Good day, Mr. Sanna," I clipped, and turned on my heels.

"It's me who should be sorry. I shouldn't have said that," he said, trying to catch up. He grabbed my hand and turned me around to look at him. "Please, Violetta. I know you're capable of taking care of yourself."

"It's fine." I rolled my eyes. It felt so strange. I'd never rolled my eyes at Gaetano—ever. Who had we become? Past hurt lingered around us.

He took a breath as softer eyes returned. "It was careless of me to speak so rudely to you. Please, let me walk you to your hotel." His voice sounded defeated.

"If you must." I let out a sharp breath. "I'm up the street." We walked side by side in awkward silence for a few blocks. "This is it." I pointed to the old building. We stopped in front. "It's not fancy, but my father knows the owner. It was the only place I could rent for weeks at a time, and they promised a hot breakfast. The room is small, but it's clean, and I have my own bathroom and tub," I explained, then counted the seconds to get back to my room and cry my eyes out.

He put his hands in his pockets and stared at the ground. He kicked a pebble on the street.

"I should go." I turned toward the entrance.

His hand grabbed my arm. "Wait," he pleaded. His eyes were pensive and demanding. "How long will you be in *Roma*?"

"A few more weeks."

"If you don't have other plans, would you like to see *Roma* with me? Not the tourist traps but other places—special places that will take your breath away. I love this country." He waved his hand at our surroundings. "And I want to share it with you." He smiled my favorite crooked smile. "I can pick you up in the morning. Would you like that?"

As much as I wanted to fight it after what he'd said, I was helpless against him. His dreamy eyes looked right through me as they always had—holding me in place, making him the center of my universe. I surrendered to his request. "Yes. That would be nice."

"I'll be here at nine a.m. Get some rest and be ready to do some walking."

"I will."

He bent his head toward mine and studied my face. "I'll see you tomorrow," he whispered. A smile played at the end of his lips.

"Tomorrow," I said, admiring the light in his eyes.

He turned and walked away. I skipped into the entryway of my building. I'd be spending tomorrow with the love of my life. This was the second chance I had prayed for. I ran up the stairs.

A voice called out to me. "*Signora* Di Natale," the owner of the building yelled.

My stomach churned. I felt sick again. I hated that name. I cringed and walked down the steps slowly. "Yes, *Signor* Corbisiero?"

"*Scusi, Signora.*" The man handed me an envelope. "A letter coma for you, from America," he said in broken English.

My arm shook as I grabbed the note. "*Grazie.*"

It was from the ranch, in Carm's handwriting. I hadn't received a letter from home in weeks. I looked over my shoulder and ran up the stairs to my room to read in privacy. Once in, I bolted the door and threw my purse on the bed. A shiver snaked its way up my back.

In Carm's previous letter, she'd written of rumors that Frank had been spotted around town. From what I knew, he still had a few more years in prison. Did he escape? Under Don Molanano's orders, Pop had hidden him before, so it was a possibility. Frank's words still rang in my ears. He'd called me a rat and threatened to come after me.

Before I left Brooklyn, Frank's father told Don Molanano that I had put his son in jail. He called me a whore and started a rumor that the baby I'd lost wasn't Frank's. When I got home, I told my father everything, which soured the relations between

Pop and Frank's father. The only reason I wasn't turned over to Don Molanano before I left Brooklyn was because of Pop's and Don Molanano's business relationship. There was no way the Don would muddy the waters with Pop.

Pop told the Don about the trouble I'd had with Frank and that I'd stay under his supervision. He knew I'd never say anything. I think that's why, when I came to him about my intentions of enlisting in the army, he didn't object. He wanted me far away from Frank, his father, and the whole outfit.

I wished Frank would find some whore and leave me alone. He could have all the *goomahs* he wanted. Even Rose, if she ever got out of that insane asylum. I didn't care. They'd kill each other, and that would solve everything. But to a Sicilian in the Mafia, I was his property—his problem to handle until the day he died.

My fingers trailed over the envelope's seal. When I got home, I'd talk to Pop about a divorce. That wouldn't go over well. I was Catholic, and I was married to a mobster. My marriage bridged the gap between families. But the biggest reason I couldn't divorce Frank was that if I did, I could testify against him in court. To the Mafia, that would make me a traitor, and that would surely get me killed. If that happened, I'd have started one of the biggest West Coast-East Coast wars in history.

More death on my hands.

More people I loved, hurt.

As much as I'd thought about my options, it seemed there was no way out, but I'd have to do something. I couldn't stay connected to that monster any longer. I needed to free myself of him once and for all. My only hope was that maybe he'd get whacked.

If only I was so lucky.

I shook my head. *Stop it. He won't do anything. They're rumors.* My chest tightened.

With shaky hands I ripped open the seal. There were two letters. I opened the one with Carm's handwriting first. The date was postmarked four weeks prior.

May 2nd, 1947

Vi,

 I hope this letter finds you well and gets to you in time. I think the rumors are true. I didn't believe it until I received this in the mail. There was no return address. I asked Pop and Tony, but they don't tell me much. Pop had a meeting in the big house. A few of the bigwigs were here. I tried to sneak and listen, but Paulie caught me snooping and made me leave. Paulie's been a real stronzo lately. He thinks he can run things over here because he's a soldier now. You should see him. He's in deep. I asked Louie, but he doesn't want me to get involved. After you told me about what happened, I thought you should know. There was no signature and no return address. Maybe you should stay in Italy—just in case. If you need money, I'll wire you some.

 Love,
 Carm

I opened the second note:

You owe me, Violetta,
I'm coming for you.
I have eyes everywhere.
Rats die~

My heart skipped a beat.

I studied the penmanship. The words were scribbles, written in a dark black pen. Ink was everywhere. There were faint splotches of red on the paper. Blood, maybe? I couldn't place the hand. Come to think of it, I'd never watched Frank write anything except for signing his name on our marriage certificate. I was the one who paid the bills.

Or was it Rose's handwriting? The mob wife who took me under her wing only to stab me in the back. Rose never pressed formal charges against me for the bodily damage she suffered when I split her head open with the lamp. I'd heard rumors before I left Brooklyn that she hated being locked up with the other crazy people. Knowing her, she must have felt like a caged animal. She'd want her revenge too.

My mind raced, thinking of all the possibilities.

Even behind bars, as a boss for one of the most powerful families in the country, Frank still had the resources and power to find me if he wanted. There was nowhere on Earth to hide from him. The mob had spies everywhere. He'd probably order a guy to put a hit on me and finish the job that he couldn't.

My intestines pulled together into a tight knot.

I couldn't tell Gaetano about the letter. He thought Frank was in jail. I didn't want to tell him I was still married to Frank. Not yet. He wouldn't understand. He'd never want this kind of trouble again. The first time had been too much already. I'd been given another chance to get close to the man I loved, and now this.

"You fucking bastard, Frank," I screamed. "Why can't you leave me alone?" I threw the letters on the desk.

Panic gripped me. I ran to the window, drew the curtains, then grabbed my army knife from my purse and placed it under my pillow. I crawled into bed with my shoes on, ready to run at a moment's notice.

I couldn't let Frank win. I'd suffered enough. And Rose—I'd be ready for her, and I'd finish the job this time. This time I'd kill anyone who threatened my happiness. I wasn't the same naïve girl anymore. I was a Mafia queen. I'd learned how to shoot a gun and fight back with my fists. I'd even sawed off soldiers' limbs and watched them bleed out. I wasn't afraid of blood or death. I was a survivor. Tomorrow would be for Gaetano and me. I wouldn't squander that.

"Stop being paranoid," I huffed. "He's not here. You don't even know if it's him. He's thousands of miles away. Locked in a jail cell."

I leaned over and pulled out the rosary beads from my purse. With one hand I prayed the rosary. With the other, I held onto the knife under my pillow. Gaetano told me to get some rest, but there would be no sleep for me now.

Not tonight.

Chapter 6

A Picture Says a Thousand Words

I ROLLED OVER IN BED AND PEERED AT THE LETTERS ON THE desk. I didn't sleep a wink except for maybe an hour or two. Every noise, from the creaky stairs in the *pensione* to cab drivers' horns on the street below, caused my eyes to spring open. Carm's letter was written weeks ago. Who knew when the other letter was written? I took solace in the fact that if it were Frank, he'd have done something already. His Sicilian temper would have gotten the best of him by now.

A cleansing breath escaped my lips. "You're fine," I said. "Don't waste another minute on that bum."

I looked at the clock. It was only seven a.m. I had two hours to get presentable before Gaetano arrived. I walked to the bathroom and peered at myself in the mirror. I looked like hell. A scalp full of knots and a pair of swollen eyes stared back at me. "Oh, God. Not today." I dragged the comb through the mats and started the tub. I lowered myself into the warm, relaxing water.

Once dressed, I placed my camera in my bag and marched down the stairs to grab a pastry and some coffee from the kitchen.

I didn't want to be woozy again with Gaetano. I ate quickly and was out the door by nine. After everything that happened yesterday, a small part of me was worried he wouldn't show. Butterflies swarmed my belly.

While I was waiting on the street, a man approached me. He wore a silk suit with a matching pocket square. He was dark-skinned and had a thick mustache.

He looked Mafia.

My body froze as he got closer. I slipped my hand in my purse and felt around for my knife.

"*Buongiorno Signora.*" The stranger tipped his hat in my direction. He smiled and walked past me.

I pulled my hand from my purse and wrung the nerves from my fingers.

God damn it! Frank's not here. Enough. Gaetano should be here any minute.

"Whew." I exhaled and patted my beating heart. I turned, and a man whose face lit up my world strolled up to me.

In brown slacks and a white button-down shirt, Gaetano took my breath away. His sleeves were rolled up, exposing his muscled forearms. His thick dark hair was brushed back. His eyes searched my face.

"*Buongiorno.*" His mouth curled up on one side. "Hey. You okay? You look like you saw a ghost." His brows furrowed, and his hands rested on my shoulders to steady me.

"I thought I saw someone I knew." I licked my dry lips.

"Oh really? You have friends in *Roma*?"

"No. There's only you." I smiled. No truer words could be spoken.

"Were you able to sleep?"

"A little. The wind kept me up," I lied. "But I eventually drifted off."

"I heard the wind too, but today is full of sunshine." He looked up at the sky. "In late spring, you can never tell."

"Do you remember what we used to tell each other about the sun and the wind?"

"Of course, how could I forget that?" He flashed his crooked smile at me, leaving my knees weak. "Are you ready to see *Roma* with me?"

I nodded. "I even brought my camera. My father bought it for me as a going-away present."

"I meant to ask you about your father yesterday, but our day got cut short." His tone tinged on apologetic.

"He's fine. Lonely without my mother."

"I understand that. It's crushing when you lose someone you love." He grimaced. "New camera, huh? May I see it?"

I handed him the camera.

He fumbled with the buttons. "Smile," he said, then snapped a quick shot.

"Hey! No fair. I wasn't ready."

"You look wonderful." He beamed. "Let's find a taxi. This way." He reached for my hand.

"Where are we going?"

"It's a surprise. But it's beautiful. Some of the most beautiful things show up in the most unexpected places." A smile streamed across his face "You'll have to trust me." Gaetano winked with his long eyelashes. "Taxi," he said as he hailed a cab.

I peered over my shoulder to see if anyone was watching, then put my hand in his, ready for anything. "I trust you."

We ran toward the taxi.

I stared out the cab's window while the driver sped through the streets, occasionally looking away from the scenery and back to Gaetano. His eyes were deep and pensive. I wanted to read his mind. What was he thinking? Was he feeling what I was feeling? I couldn't be sure. My mind vacillated between excitement and nervousness as images of the letter hung over my head.

"Villa Borghese," the driver said. He stopped the car, forcing us to look away from each other.

"*Grazie.*" Gaetano handed him some lire. "We're here. Prepare to be astounded," he teased.

Like a gentleman, Gaetano exited and reached for my hand to help me out. I'd forgotten how it felt to be treated respectfully. Frank never did that. He used me like a punching bag. I swallowed past the giant lump in my throat, then placed my hand in his. Our eyes met as he lifted me toward him.

"Thank you."

He grinned. "It's one of the few places that didn't get destroyed from the war. I remember how much you liked parks when we were younger."

I recalled our time together at Alum Rock Park.

"It's pretty here." Excitement filled me.

"I've missed your radiant smile, Violetta."

"Thank you." I squeezed his hand. "And I've missed yours." I drew strength from his touch while his words forced my heart to beat faster. To see him happy and smiling again was a dream come true.

"Come."

His hand with mine felt familiar and safe. I'd craved his touch for so long. But could I be misreading him? He'd said he only wanted to be friends. I couldn't be sure. My heart fluttered about the possibilities. If we were to ever have a chance, I'd need to declare my feelings. I'd have to tell him I was still married. A divorce from Frank meant possibly signing our death warrants. My vision darted around for any suspicious characters.

There were none.

Gaetano accompanied me past tall trees that lined the walkways. We wandered deeper into the maze of historic statues along the luscious green gardens. Large, tiered fountains poured water into the pools beneath. Fragrant orange blossoms filled the air while the sound of rippling water nearby reminded me of our first kiss by the babbling brook.

An old building stood in the distance. It had tall, solid, white pillars and was located at the edge of a lake. "What's that?"

"An ancient temple." A smile spilled across his face. "Want to get a better look?"

"Yes."

"*Andiamo, sole mio.*" He cleared his throat as if to correct himself. He hadn't called me his sun since the days I'd spent with him in the guest house of the winery so long ago. His words warmed me. I let my thumb graze the top of his hand to let him know I'd made the connection.

"Everything's so beautiful. It's too pretty for words. Thank you for bringing me here."

"I'm glad you like it."

"Here, let me take a picture of you."

"Where should I stand?"

"Right here, with the temple in the background." Gaetano stood there like a god. Sunshine picked up the honey in his irises, and his smile came into view.

My eyes glided down his body, from the top of his shoulders, down his broad chest, then past his hips to his long legs. Tremors coursed through my pelvis.

"Are you all right? You look flushed. Did you eat this morning?"

"Yes," I replied casually, but food wasn't what I was hungry for. I craved something else entirely.

"Don't move." I hit the button. I drew in a sharp breath and then moved the camera away.

A man approached—the same man I'd seen on the street in front of my *pensione*. Protectively, I ran to Gaetano.

"Hello," the man said.

My body stiffened. "Who are you?" I demanded.

"I'm sorry. I didn't mean to startle you," he said politely. "I thought you'd like to have a picture together. I can take it for you."

"Oh," I exhaled. "Yes, of course. Sorry. It's just . . . I saw you earlier. I thought you might be following us."

"No. I'm just an American touring Rome, like you. It seems we like the same places. Sorry to have caused any concern."

"No apology necessary. You can never be too cautious in a foreign city, right? With pickpockets and all," I said, trying to cover up my extreme reaction.

"I understand," the man said.

"Please excuse my friend," Gaetano interrupted.

There was that word I hated again.

"She's been a little jumpy lately," Gaetano explained.

I handed the man my camera with a smile. "We'd love a picture together." I wiped sweat from my brow and straightened my blouse. With the temple behind us, Gaetano placed his hand at the small of my back. I held onto his arm tightly as the man snapped the picture.

We thanked him. The man handed me the camera. "Enjoy your day," he said, then walked off.

Gaetano turned to me. His brows were creased. "Violetta, tell me the truth. What's making you so frightened?"

"I don't know what came over me. I've heard of men following tourists around the city and holding them up at gunpoint for their money. I thought he might be one of them."

He looked skeptical but put his arm around my shoulder. "When you're with me, I won't let anyone hurt you."

"I know." *How could I be so stupid? He's going to think I'm crazy, and run.*

"Maybe we should go back?"

"No, I'll be fine," I said. Anger flowed through my veins. *I won't let you take him from me this time, Frank Di Natale, you son of a bitch. I won't be your victim again.*

I was only promised today with Gaetano, and I'd guard it with my life.

We filled the morning with sightseeing, which was exactly what I needed to keep my mind busy and off the mysterious note. At the Galleria, we marveled at the sculptures and precious pieces of classical art that hung on the walls. He explained the history to me, and this time I was *his* student. As he spoke, I witnessed his love and admiration for this country. He mesmerized me with his knowledge and passionate spirit. Throughout the day, we exchanged smiles. Each comforting grin rid me of any worry.

We strolled along the Tiber river that flowed between the city streets. The more we talked, the more we became familiar with each other again. We reminisced of the past when we were young and free. Conversation felt healing. He made me miss my innocence.

Before the beatings and the drugs.

Before Brooklyn.

Before Frank.

I didn't mention my time with Frank. He didn't mention Angelina. I didn't want to upset him. I wanted these moments to be solely about us. But time felt strange. As much as I wanted to savor every second with him, I feared that telling him my feelings might cut our time short, so I stayed quiet and present in the moment. I needed to explain how I still felt about him. But how? And when?

From what I'd witnessed yesterday, Gaetano tried to appear unaffected in matters of the heart, but I knew he'd been protecting his feelings from me. I think he was afraid to be vulnerable like I was. And after what he'd said yesterday, there were no guarantees.

Before we made our way back to the inn, we came upon an old church with a tall steeple and a large crucifix. The old building drew me closer. "That church. There's something so enchanting about it. I want to see it." Like magnets, my feet steered me in its direction.

"Okay, but I must warn you. It might be condemned. Many buildings around here were affected by the war." Gaetano followed me.

Our pace slowed as we climbed the steps of the ancient structure. The church had been severely damaged by the war. Boards covered openings, and the walls had crumbled in places. Broken depictions of saints and other religious symbols covered its rocky exterior. I took a picture, then followed Gaetano to the side of the building, where we came upon a small door-like opening framed by stones. It, too, was boarded up.

He placed his hand on the little shrine. "It sickens me to see what men can do. They've desecrated it." His eyes were void of any sparkle.

My heart felt for him. "What is it?"

"It's called *ruota degli esposti*. The foundling wheel."

I looked closer. "What's it for?"

"Women placed their children here when they couldn't care for them."

"What do you mean, *couldn't* care for them?"

"For women who have children out of wedlock or for young girls who didn't have a choice and were forced to give up a child without their permission."

I swallowed back awful memories of my wedding night and so many other nights when Frank raped me.

"Either for fear of public scrutiny or family obligation, they'd come here," he explained in measured tones. "Sadly, some women can't afford to have a child. Big families mean more mouths to feed, and with the war, things have been hard. For most women in poverty, this decision is a matter of life and death, for them and the child."

"I hadn't thought of it that way, and I know how it is to make life-and-death decisions to protect the people you love, even if that means your child." I clutched at my heart. "I can see how it could be right for some women." I stared at the tiny shrine and thought about how Rose had given up her daughter to be part of the mob, for a life of turning tricks and selling drugs. Her need to be a player in the game didn't allow her to be a mother. She didn't want her daughter to suffer the same consequences, so she walked away to give her a better life. It was one of Rose's few redeeming qualities, and I respected her for that.

My throat grew thick, remembering that I'd had those feelings when I was pregnant. A part of me didn't want to bring another innocent life into this world. The irony that I'd been the one to hurt my child because of my choices and my addiction choked me up.

His fingertips gently tilted my chin up toward him. "What's wrong?"

"Losing my daughter almost killed me. It's hard for me to think about giving up a child since mine was ripped out of me because of my . . ." I stopped my words as my stomach knotted deep inside. "Addiction."

Gaetano's brows drew together, and a pained gaze spread across his face. He placed his hand on my shoulder.

"You don't have to tell me. I can see it hurts you. I never wanted this day to cause you pain. Let's get back." He reached for my hand.

"I'd do anything to hold my daughter again, and I feel guilty about her death every day. But she's in heaven now, away from all of the danger and death. I know women in the life who've given up children. Certain circumstances warrant those decisions." I thought about Frank, the pills, and my life as a Mafia queen. I put my hand to my barren stomach. "Sadly, I've given up the thought of being a mother. After what happened, I have scar tissue. My father said it would be almost impossible for me to conceive."

Gaetano's jaw tightened, and a shadow of fury crossed his face. "I'm so sorry. I had no idea." He gently tucked a few stray hairs behind my ear. "Your daughter is an angel now, and you're safe. That's all that matters."

"Thank you." I flashed a reassuring smile. "Enough of that. I can't change the past. I can only be present. And right now, I'm happy to be here with you."

"I'm happy to be here with you too. You were an unexpected surprise." The shine in his eyes reaffirmed my faith in us.

I refocused my attention. "What happened to the children?"

"At night, a mother placed her baby next to this door and rang a bell to alert the nuns. The babies were taken in and raised in the church. As the children aged, they were sent to orphanages. The foundling wheel was a safe place for mothers who had no other choice. It was discreet, and in truth, it saved many lives—including my grandmother's." A reverent smile spread over his face. "My *nonna* was a foundling wheel baby. Without this," he touched the stones around the tiny door, "I may never have existed, and I might never have met you. I'm so glad I did." He stared into my eyes with a deep, penetrating gaze.

His words caused my cheeks to burn.

"Then I'm so grateful for this." I placed my hand on the rocks close to his. "What an amazing story."

"All children deserve good families and homes."

I nodded. "They're innocent to the ugliness of this world and the environments we expose them to. Look at my family. I love them, but I didn't get to choose my parents or the circumstances behind my father's allegiance." I sighed.

His eyebrows knit together, then became soft again. "Things are different now. You're free from all of that." Hope threaded through his face.

Sadly, I wasn't free.

"You might be tired, but would you like to have dinner with me tonight?"

My heart leapt in my chest. My opportunity had presented itself. I would tell him my feelings tonight. A mix of excitement and nervousness filled my body. "That sounds wonderful. I'd like that."

"Well then, we'd better grab a cab."

On the ride back, silence left me to my thoughts. Tonight, I'd tell Gaetano that I never stopped loving him. I'd expose my vulnerability and ask for a second chance. I'd be truthful and tell him I was still married. I didn't know how he would react to that sort of news.

Our love and commitment to one another would have to be strong enough. Was he willing to fight to the death for what we had, or was our love story a memory now?

Fear of rejection loomed, making my stomach tangle in knots.

Chapter 7
Revelations in the Rain

I WASHED IN WARM BATH WATER AND REHEARSED THE LINES IN my head. "Gaetano, I love you. I'm sorry I left. Please forgive me. I promise I'll never leave you again," I said, while lathering bubbles on my arms. "Oh, who am I kidding? He won't forgive me—not after I left him to be with another man! How could he?"

Could he?

"Not to mention you're still married to that man! Damn it, Vi, who you kiddin'? He won't believe you. He'll think it's a way to lure him to bed."

Bed. "*Hmm.*" I sighed at the thought. I missed being intimate with him. How many times had I imagined his face on Frank's so that I could endure sex with that monster? Wine bottles came to mind. My cheeks stung hot as the memory of my attempt at ménage à trois crept up, making my nipples tingle against the bubbles.

I rubbed my washcloth over my breasts, imagining Gaetano's strong hands touching me. My actions reaffirmed my sexual desires. I wanted him inside me again. I wanted Gaetano, body and soul. This was more than want—this was need.

I closed my eyes and submerged my head under the water. I wanted the warmth to drown out the what-ifs and the maybes. What I'd say to Gaetano tonight would change our lives. If he said no, there'd be no more fantasizing about him. No more dreams to satiate me.

The idea of him kept me going on some of the hardest nights of my life. If he didn't want to try again, I'd have to move on and say goodbye forever. But after losing Adelina, I didn't like goodbyes, and I didn't have the strength to do it again. They didn't have a drug strong enough for that. With the constant grief, my sobriety hung by a thread, and my choices would be limited. I tried to use church-like AA meetings, but they didn't feel the same.

My lungs burned from being underwater, and pressure mounted in my ears. When I couldn't hold my breath any longer, I came up for air. It was a conscious choice to breathe again—my way of taking another chance at life and another stab at love instead of drowning in my fears. For so long, I'd turned to pills to help me in times like these—times of uncertainty. I didn't want pills, but they were on my mind.

I decided on a purple dress I'd bought in Brooklyn. It was a tight fit with a plunging neckline. I wanted to watch Gaetano's gaze glide over my body in this dress. I took one more look in the mirror, fixed a few unruly strands of hair, and added a layer of red lipstick to my lips. With my hair back, I fantasized about Gaetano peppering kisses from my ears to my breasts. My pulse quickened.

I grabbed my black satin handbag off the desk. Carm's letters fell to the ground. I picked them up and rubbed at the paper. My eyes zeroed in on the words "*Rats die.*" I wondered when I'd be confronted by my past. Until I was back at the safety of the ranch, I'd need to stay vigilant.

I crumpled up the letters and threw them in the wastebasket.

That's where you belong, Frank Di Natale. You no-good excuse for a man. I grabbed my knife and shoved it into my handbag. After a deep breath, I locked the door behind me.

I stepped from the building and gasped. Gaetano greeted me with a smile, wearing a navy-blue pinstriped suit with a hat and tie. He looked amazing. The suit made his shoulders stand out, broad and strong.

His eyes widened as I got closer. "*Sei bellissima.*" He raked his gaze down my front. "Stunning."

I smiled at his reaction. "Thank you."

"Shall we?" He extended his arm for me to grab.

I glanced over my shoulder to see if anyone was watching us. We were alone. I clutched at my purse to feel for the knife, then looped my hand under his arm. "Yes, Mr. Sanna, we shall."

The restaurant was only a few blocks away. It was secluded enough not to draw attention to us and quiet enough to have the kind of conversation I hoped to have with him.

With his palm on the small of my back, Gaetano pulled out my chair, and I sat while the waiter handed us menus.

"*Grazie.*" I turned to the waiter. "At least this time, I can order for myself." I laughed.

Gaetano smiled in response.

To calm my nerves, I unfastened my handbag and pulled out a cigarette and lighter. I pressed it to my lips. My hands shook as I flicked the ignitor.

"Here, let me help you." Gaetano took the lighter from my hand. "When did you start smoking?"

"A few years ago. Everyone in Brooklyn smokes."

"*Hmm,*" he mumbled, then shot me a quizzical stare.

I lit up, inhaled, then blew smoke out the side of my mouth.

"I've never seen you with lipstick before."

"Also, Brooklyn. A lot of the women wore it this way."

"It's a nice touch, but in my opinion, you're beautiful without it."

I blushed. "Thank you."

The waiter took our order, grabbed our menus, and walked away, leaving us in our quiet thoughts.

"It was a lovely day today," I said to break the silence. "Thank you for taking me. I'll never forget it."

"You're welcome. I'm glad you enjoyed it," he said, almost avoiding my stare. "Violetta, I must ask you a question. I should've asked you before, and you can tell me if it's none of my business, but I must know." He paused. "Are you divorced? You mentioned that you left Frank some years ago, but you never actually said that you were no longer his wife."

I chewed on the side of my mouth, "Um... well." My pulse rang in my ears. *Here we go.* "Not exactly. When Frank was sent to prison, I left Brooklyn and returned to the ranch. I planned to divorce as soon as I returned home, but things happened so quickly—my sister's wedding, then me enlisting in the war."

"*Hmm.* Well, thanks for being honest," he said in a steely tone. His lips pressed together in a firm line.

"Please understand, my family is Catholic, like yours. Divorce isn't something that is looked upon highly in the church. But more than anything, a divorce would mean that I could testify against Frank and the Molanano family. That could mean war, and that was the last thing I wanted before I left for an even bigger war."

Muscles in his jaw tightened. His face went blank before he diverted his gaze.

"Look at me." I reached for his hand across the table.

He recoiled, breaking the connection we'd had all day.

Waves of disappointment crashed over his face. "I'm sorry to hear that." His eyes turned cold.

"I don't love him. I never loved him. I'm always having to please everyone around me; my father, the mob—everyone but me. But you have to understand that me leaving Frank, divorce or not, was an act of betrayal. Frank thinks I'm the one who turned him in, for Christ's sake," I snapped. "For all I know, there might be a price on my head when I return home. I'm lucky Don Molanano trusts my father, or I'd already be dead."

Gaetano's shoulders stiffened. "I'm sorry I asked. Let's enjoy our dinner and call it a night. I've heard all I needed to hear on the matter." He took a sip of his wine.

We sat in silence. He avoided eye contact. Divorce was only a piece of paper and time in a courtroom. After all that had happened in Brooklyn, I didn't want to be surrounded by cops and lawyers. I hated cops. I didn't trust them. I didn't want to be near a courtroom for fear they might turn me in for something. But for Gaetano, I'd do it. For him—I'd do anything.

"Gaetano, please, I love . . ." I said as the waiter placed our plates in front of us.

"*Grazie. Mangiate.*" Gaetano grabbed his fork and stabbed his pasta. Bite after quick bite, Gaetano ate fast. He gulped huge mouthfuls and washed them down with red wine. He looked uncomfortable and continued to dodge my eyes.

With a shaky hand, I dug my fork into my food and chewed quickly, thinking about what to say to break the layers of ice between us. I wanted him to feel safe with me again and trust me with his heart as he'd done so many years ago.

About halfway through the meal, I placed my napkin on the table. I couldn't eat another bite. Sweat trickled down my back as I planned my next words carefully.

"Gaetano. I've been meaning to say this to you all day, and I need to get this out. Forgive me. I never wanted to hurt you. As you said today, sometimes people must make life and death decisions. Marrying Frank was a life and death decision."

"*Basta,*" he clipped. "Life and death, huh? I would've given my life to save you, Violetta."

"That's exactly why I did it."

"By offering yourself to *him,* you were doing something noble. Is that it?" His nostrils flared, then he took a deep breath to calm himself. "Look, what happened between us was a long time ago. We were kids, and we've both moved on. If forgiveness is what you seek, then you're forgiven. All right, Violetta? We can be friends. Does that make you feel better?" His jaw tightened.

There was that word again—*friends.* I hated that word. I didn't want to be his friend. I wanted to be his lover, his lifelong companion, and eventually, his wife.

"Are you done?" he asked, motioning the waiter over for the check. "I'm tired. I'm sure you are too. We should get back. It's been a long day." His face looked withdrawn and empty.

I bit my lip. *Think of something. Fast.* Different scenery might change the mood. "Before we return, I'd like to see something with you. I've never seen it in the dark, because I've been too afraid to go there at night, but I heard it's beautiful. It's not far. Will you come with me? Please?" My voice shook.

A light huff escaped his lips. "All right, but just for a little while. I need to get back." He rose from the table and pushed in his chair.

I reached out my hand to grab him, but he placed his hands in his pockets.

After handing the waiter money, Gaetano marched to the front of the restaurant and hailed another taxi. He opened the cab door stiffly.

I moved past his unreadable eyes and sat in the backseat.

Gaetano followed, then slammed the door. His body language screamed hurt and anger at my admission.

"*Ponte Sant'Angelo, per favore,*" I said to the driver.

Gaetano avoided my eyes and looked out the window as the cab raced through the dimly lit streets. Small raindrops hit the windshield.

"A late spring storm, I suppose," I said nervously. *Damn it, just my luck.* With the rain, he'll want to cut the night even shorter.

"We shouldn't be out long in this. You'll get sick." He handed me his jacket.

I wrapped it around my shoulders and breathed in his scent. My insides quivered. The driver pulled up to the bridge. It was bathed in the soft glow of yellow light from the lamps above. A light, wet sheen covered the ground. Gaetano handed the man some money, and I opened my door. Drops of light rain fell from the dark sky and hit my cheek.

I turned toward him. "It's exactly how I've seen it in pictures."

We walked to the middle of the bridge. Sparkles of light flickered over the water, then dimmed as more clouds moved in front of the moon. Gaetano looked over the side of the bridge. His soft lashes flickered as tiny droplets kissed his face.

"It's getting wetter by the minute. We'd better go soon, or you'll be soaked by the time I get you home. You don't want to ruin your dress."

"I don't care about this dress. I only care about you." I grabbed his hand and stepped closer. "I'm not leaving here until I tell you what I set out to say earlier. I love you, Gaetano Sanna."

He pulled his hand away.

"Please, listen." I grabbed his hand again. "I've loved you from the first day I met you, and I never stopped loving you. I've thought about you every day since I left the winery."

His brows drew together.

"You've taken over my dreams. You've saved me in ways you'll never know. I didn't want to leave you. I did it to protect you because I protect the people I love—those who matter most. I'd never let you suffer at their hands, so I started a life of hell. I was beaten, raped, and abused. To cope, I abused pills and accidentally killed my unborn daughter because I was too afraid to leave Frank. And when I knew I'd lost you and that you'd found someone else, I almost took my own life."

His eyes grew wide from my admission. "Why would you try to kill yourself?"

"I'd lost my mother, then you, then my daughter, all in a matter of months. I felt worthless and alone. I didn't want to go on." I blinked away tears. "But when I saw you, after all these years, I had hope again. What I'm trying to say is I want another chance, Gaetano."

Gaetano took a deep breath and cast his gaze back onto the water. "Another chance?" Lines formed between his brows. "You're still married," he snapped.

"I'll divorce Frank," I said into the cold night air. My breath formed clouds around us. "I'll get a lawyer and draw up the papers. I'll move with you to the winery."

He shook his head. "It's too late now."

"It's never too late." Tears filled my eyes.

He grimaced, then turned away from my stare.

"Gaetano." My voice was almost a whisper.

He faced me. "I'm sorry that happened to you, and I wish I could've protected you, but that's the life you chose." His hands curled into fists.

"I never had a choice. My father chose for me. I didn't want to see my father killed, or you, or anyone I loved. That's what the mob does when they don't get what they want."

"You don't think I know that? My mother was almost raped in front of me because of those *bastardi*," he spat. "I know *Cosa Nostra*. I know what they're capable of, and I was ready to protect you from that and sacrifice everything for you. But you left. You never fought for our love." His voice cracked, then went silent.

"Sacrifice? You think you're the only one who sacrificed? I gave up the life I wanted and almost died while trying to protect you," I scolded.

His eyes were withdrawn as he shook his head at me. "I would have taken us away, but instead, I woke up to a note. A God damn note," he fumed. "How do you think I felt after everything we'd shared? Do you know how often I got in my car to drive to the ranch and get you away from him? Do you know how often José had to pry a gun from my hands so I wouldn't drive down and kill him? About a hundred times," he yelled. "I would've gladly killed him and watched him die in the street so he could see how it feels when your soul rots and leaves your body. That's how I felt after you left. Putrid and empty," he seethed, then turned away.

"Look at me." I turned his face back to mine. "There were so many days that I felt the same. But it doesn't have to be that way anymore. Be with me. I'll never leave you again. I need you in my life. You're my wind, and I'm your sun. Remember?" I moved closer.

He put his hands on my shoulders to stop me from taking another step. "This is crazy talk. I can't listen anymore. I don't want you. I don't want this. I can't." His voice was thick with pain. "We had our chance. You left. It took me years to get over you. Years."

His voice stung my ears.

"Don't you understand? I can never put myself in that situation again. I hate *Cosa Nostra,* and you're still married to one of them!"

"Then why did you take me with you today?"

"I don't know. I thought that since we were both here alone, I wanted to see . . ."

"See what? See if you still loved me? We still love each other. I know it in my heart." I gently pressed my palm to his cheek. "I read the newspaper article where you told the interviewer about your plans for the winery. You were talking about me."

Gaetano's eyes widened.

"Don't you see?" I tugged his body toward mine. "I know it when you look at me. I see it in your smile. I felt it today by the church when you gripped my hand as I told you about my daughter. I felt it when you looked at me tonight in this dress." I twirled around. "I know you love me, and I love you. Don't be afraid anymore. I'm right here, baring my soul to you. That's got to mean something."

"We should go," he said, then looked toward the street.

"Right before I saw you, I prayed for God to reunite us. And then you were there—the real you. God answered my prayers." I wept. "Don't you think that us being here at the same time is more than a mere coincidence? It's divine intervention, for Christ's sake. We were brought together for a reason. We can't waste the chance," I pleaded through tears. I reached for him.

"Stop this," he shouted and took a few steps back. "You broke my heart in a million pieces." His eyes blazed. "I'm sorry if I've given you the wrong impression, but I don't want you anymore, Violetta. You and me, we had our chance. It's over. My family will never give their blessing, and your allegiance will always be to *la famiglia* Molanano before me." His voice tinged with disgust. "I'm not even sure I believe in love anymore. I've changed. I'm not the same man you used to know."

"Yes, you are. You're just scared. I'm scared too, but I want to try again. I'll fight by your side, whether they come or not. I'd rather die than leave you again." I approached him with caution, afraid of more angry words and rejection.

"Maybe I haven't been clear enough," he said in a glacial tone. His eyes turned dark as the night sky—cold and barren. He took a deep breath. "I could never be with a drug-addicted Mafia puppet."

His words cut like daggers to my heart, but my mind refused to process them. Breathless, I blinked a few times. The impact punched me in the gut—a feeling I knew all too well. Tangled in the paralyzing hurt, I couldn't speak another word.

I reached my hand back, palm open, and slapped him across the face.

Whack.

The sound echoed off the water down below. My hand stung as my blood boiled. "You bastard. Don't you *ever* call me that. You have no idea what I've been through. You're no better than Frank," I said, shocked at his verbal assault on me.

He winced.

"You aren't the only one who can hurt with words. How does it feel? Are we even now? I hope you're happy with yourself. I'll never allow another man to mistreat me again, including you. Never talk to me again," I hissed, ripped off his coat, and threw it into a puddle by my feet. I kicked off my heels, scooped them up in my hands, and ran through the streets. Cars and taxis honked their horns around me. With the rain on my face, I couldn't see where I was going. I didn't care, just as long as it was away from him.

"Violetta, stop," Gaetano roared. "You'll be killed. Stop running. I'm sorry."

"Stay away from me," I yelled back as I ran into a dark alley.

I bolted through side streets where he wouldn't see me and arrived at the *pensione* soaked. My feet bled from running barefoot through the war-damaged streets. I hurried up the stairs, unlocked my door, and stripped off my soaked clothes. When the room settled into a noiseless void, I picked up one of my heels and threw it across the room.

The shoe caught the bathroom mirror's edge. It shattered.

I thought of only one thing—to find a way to numb the pain. I didn't know anyone in Rome who could get their hands on pills, but there were a few bars. They'd have what I needed. I wanted to get drunk—so drunk that I'd never wake up and think about him again.

I wiped tears from my eyes and searched for dry clothes.

Chapter 8

Surrender

"God damn you, Gaetano Sanna! How could I be so dumb? That's what I get for pouring my heart out to someone I thought loved me."

I stared at myself in the one piece of broken mirror that hadn't fallen yet. Makeup dripped down my face from the rain, and traces of lipstick smeared down my chin. I rubbed away at the streaks of red and pushed my wet hair back from my eyes.

"After a few drinks, it won't matter what I look like. A few drinks . . . more like a few bottles." I snatched my purse from the nightstand and rushed to the door. Memories of whiskey flushed my mouth.

Without a care, I ran down the stairs of the *pensione* and onto the street. It was dark. The rain was heavy. I was determined to completely erase Gaetano from my brain.

Through tears, I looked down at my feet on the slick pavement to keep from falling. Trudging through puddles, one of my heels got caught. My body fell forward until a pair of hands held me upright.

"Violetta, is that you? Oh, thank God you're safe," Gaetano

exhaled and held me tight against his chest. "The roads are so dark at night, and with all this rain . . . Are you crazy? You could've been killed by a car."

"Let me go," I yelled and fought his hold. "Get away from me."

"Wait." He pulled me close and looked into my eyes. "I ran after you, but you slipped down an alleyway, and I lost sight of you. For the last hour, I've been combing the streets. I had to know you were safe. I couldn't bear the thought that something I'd said might have put you in danger. I was so worried."

"Worried? About me? Why? I'm just a drug-addicted Mafia puppet, remember? Leave me alone." I yanked my arm from his grip.

"Please, Violetta, don't." He reached for me again. "I was wrong to say what I said. I behaved badly. I was hurt, and I said it out of anger. I didn't mean it."

"You've changed. The Gaetano Sanna I knew would've never said those things to me. I don't want to know you anymore."

His face grimaced as my words pelted him like acid. "Please don't say that. I know you're angry, and you have every right to be. I was cruel and heartless. The minute the words were out, I knew I was wrong for saying them. I tried to apologize right then, but you ran away."

"What did you expect me to do? Stand there and look like a fool?"

"No. I never want you to feel that way."

"It doesn't matter. You'll never trust me again, so I'm giving you what you want." I tried to push past him, but he held my arm, then drew me close.

"That's not what I want. I want you. And if you can find it in your heart to forgive me, I plan to spend the rest of my life making up for it."

"And when are you going to forgive me, huh? Or will you make me feel bad for the rest of *my* life? I won't live like that."

"Look at me." He tilted my chin up so I could meet his eyes. "I forgive you. I mean it. You know me better than anyone. I'm still the same man you remember. Just more afraid... afraid of what losing you again might do to my heart. But I realize my love for you is bigger than any fear I'll ever have. You were right all along. I love you. I've always loved you."

My heart stopped, then started again.

He still loves me.

His words left me weak in the knees.

"I need you in my life." He cupped my face in his hands. "You are my life. The best part of my life. I lost you for years. Let's not waste another minute," he whispered against my mouth.

I stilled from his advance. Tears filled my eyes and spilled over my cheeks as I searched for courage. "Your words hurt me," I stuttered.

"I know. I'm sorry." With his thumbs, he wiped my cheeks.

"I forgive you, but never speak to me like that again."

"Never," he promised. His eyes searched my face. He leaned in and pressed a kiss on my wet lips.

I melted into his embrace and kissed him long and deep. My insides warmed as he held me. Rain dripped down our mouths. I pulled away slightly. His warm breath was still on my lips. "I'm sorry too." I pressed my hand over the cheek I'd slapped.

"I'll be all right." He took my hand from his face and kissed it. "I'm better than all right with you in my arms."

"We've both done things we regret out of anger. I was afraid to tell you how I felt, but I couldn't wait any longer."

"When you know what you want and have always wanted, you have to take the chance. You're my sun. You give me life." He yanked off his tie, then undid the top buttons of his wet shirt, grabbed my hand, and placed it on his heart. "Do you feel that?"

I nodded and rubbed the water from my eyes.

"That's yours. Please take care of it. Please never leave me again. I don't think I'd survive if you do."

"I'll never leave you again."

Our heads moved in toward each other. His tongue entered my

mouth with vigorous intent. His grip on me was tight. I wrapped my arms around his shoulders and let our mouths continue to explore.

He grabbed the back of my neck and stared into my eyes. "You're the only woman I've ever loved. I came back because I wanted to show you what it means to fight for us." He pressed his hands on my hips and kissed my cheek.

My eyes darted around. I glanced over his shoulder to make sure we weren't being followed, then studied his face.

He tracked my gaze. "What is it?"

"You know what this kind of commitment means. There will be consequences."

"We'll face them together. I'll do everything I can to protect us and everyone we love." He pressed another kiss to my lips.

"I want you," I panted as more drizzle fell onto our faces. "Take me to my bed," I whispered against his mouth.

Without another word, he scooped me into his arms and carried me to the front door of the *pensione*. He set me down, and I searched my purse for the key. From behind, he moved my hair to the side and sent a trail of kisses down my neck. His erection pressed hard into my backside as light moans escaped his mouth. With his warm breath in my hair, I worked to insert the key into the lock.

"*Shhh*," I whispered, trying to steady myself enough to turn the handle. "Someone might see us. We have to be quiet. I don't want to wake *Signor* Corbisiero."

Gaetano pulled back, then placed a soft kiss behind my ear and carried me up the stairs to my room.

I tapped the door shut with my foot. "Lock it."

His eyes held onto me as he placed me down on the bed. He turned to bolt the door, and I switched on the bedside lamp. Light flickered from the bulb against the walls. The storm tested the electricity—but my sexual energy burned bright and steady for Gaetano. In the glow, I needed to see his body again. I wanted to reacquaint myself with his muscles, his hands, his touch, and his mouth. I wanted to allow his eyes to possess me as they'd done so many times before.

When he returned, he leaned over and claimed my mouth with his. His kiss was intense and full of need. The slightest taste of wine from dinner was still present on his tongue. Hints of spice and fruit washed over my taste buds like an erotic elixir, sending signals to my private parts.

He raked his gaze up and down my body, making me tremble. As much as I'd thought and prayed about this moment, was I ready? It had been so long. Would he think differently of me because I'd been with Frank? My body had changed since we'd last been together. Would he still crave me the way he did all those years ago? My gut twisted in knots for answers.

"Violetta," he panted while he kissed behind my ear.

"Yes?" The sound of my name against my skin made me quiver in his hold.

"On the way here, I discovered that you were right."

"About what?"

"About God bringing us together again." He peppered kisses down my neck. "I didn't want to believe it. In fact, I refuted it, but it's true. Being with you right now, right here, is a blessing, and I plan on honoring our miracle by reveling in this moment with you." His once dreamy eyes now flamed with hunger for me. He leaned in for another kiss.

His words were like honey. They smoothed out any wrinkles of trepidation I had left in me. "I want you, Gaetano. Forever. I've never wanted anything more," I muttered as rain pelted against the window.

Slowly, he reached under my skirt and undid the clasps of my stockings. The graze of his knuckles against my thigh sent chills down my spine. One by one, he tugged them over my knees and dropped them to the floor. He undid my skirt and pulled it down my wet legs along with my garter and panties.

I lifted my blouse over my head while he watched. I lay there in nothing more than my satin slip. He stared at me as rainwater dripped off my hair and onto the pillow.

He touched the lace between my breasts and let his fingertips trail the pattern down to the tops of my thighs.

He kicked off his shoes, then sat up to unbutton his shirt. I stared at him anxiously as he pried it off his drenched body. Drops fell from his forehead and dripped down his chest, making his muscles glisten in the room's soft light. His body was familiar except for some hair that now sprouted from his chest. His arms were my safe place. I rubbed my hands along the grooves on his back, neck, and chest while he peered down at me through his soft lashes.

With apologies behind us and an understanding of our commitment to one another, our future was in our grasp. God had given us this gift to share. I'd thought about this moment for so long.

I'd wanted this.

I'd prayed for this.

I'd fantasized and even dreamed about this.

I loved this man with every bone in my body. I was his, and his alone, for the taking. I always had been his from the day I met him all those years ago.

He kissed me again, hard and deep, as thunder shook the window.

Startled by the noise, I pulled away with ragged breath, sat up, and stared out the window.

"It's okay. It's just a little thunder from the rain. It'll pass," he panted against my neck as his erection pressed into my leg.

Another flash of lightning illuminated the room. The bright gleam energized every sexual nerve in my body. I needed to see him. Every inch of him. "Here, let me help you out of those," I whispered against his neck as I undid his belt, then unzipped his pants. I yanked them down his hips and let them fall to the floor. I reached into his boxer shorts, grabbed him, and glided my tongue behind his ear.

He lifted my slip over my head, tossed it to the side, and pressed another kiss to my mouth. My nipples hardened against his skin. He released my lips, and I fought for breath.

"I want to look at you." His eyes raked over my naked body. "You're so beautiful." He let his fingertips graze over the ends of my hair, then down to my breasts.

Goose pimples bloomed across my skin from his touch.

He kissed my neck, then brushed the tip of his tongue from my chest down to my hardened nipples. He grabbed my breast and rolled my nipple between his fingers. He took the other breast into his mouth and sucked and nibbled around my areola.

I yelped out in pleasure, then wove my fingers through his wavy hair while he continued to suckle on my nipples. He detoured from my breasts and kissed my mouth softly.

"I want to taste you. All of you." He moved down my stomach. My body trembled as the tip of his tongue flicked against my skin. Featherlike, he let his lips graze my hips. Once he reached my pelvis, he paused and drew in a breath.

I looked down.

He stared at the skin on my stomach.

"What's wrong?" I panted.

"Nothing. You're perfect," he smiled, then pressed soft kisses around my belly button. His knuckles grazed against my skin, then he descended past my hips and between my legs.

He nudged my thighs and spread me apart. He stroked the hair between my legs.

It tickled. I moaned in response as pressure built under my navel.

He let his lips drag around my inner thighs. He stroked my spot with his fingertips, then inserted a finger.

I yelped out in pleasure.

He slid his fingers inside of me, then back out, and in again. His movements made a wet, popping noise. "You feel so good."

Moisture dribbled out of me and onto the bed as I trembled under his touch. I closed my eyes and concentrated on breathing while he licked his fingers of my taste. "Please, don't stop," I begged. "I can't wait any longer. I'm going to burst."

"You taste sweet, like a fine wine. I'm going to fill my cup with you and swallow every last drop," he said in a thick voice, then took the flesh into his mouth and sucked. With his plump lips, he let his tongue lap over my soft nub in circles, then up and down.

"Gaetano," I yelled out as I writhed under him and dug my nails into his back. I reached for his head to pull his face in deeper.

His tongue flicked faster and faster against my flesh until I felt my whole body tighten.

"I love you," I cried out as my body shook in ecstasy.

He continued to suck on my spot relentlessly. We rode the waves of my orgasm together, then our bodies stilled. He released my flesh, took a deep breath, and then moved up my body to my face. As thunderous booms bounced off the walls and flashes of light lit up the air around us, he stared deep into my eyes. A myriad of emotions crossed his face.

I touched his cheek and let my thumb graze over his right brow and down his jawline.

Gaetano bent down and kissed me tenderly on the lips, then on my cheekbones and neck.

"I love you too," he said softly against my skin. "Do you know how beautiful you look right now?" he asked, then placed another kiss behind my ear. "To see you like this, in this light. Your face." He kissed my mouth again. "Your body," he murmured and sprinkled kisses over my breasts.

His lips on my nipples made me giggle in pleasured bliss.

He locked his fingers around mine. "And one day," he said as he drew my left hand up to his mouth, "I want to place a ring on this finger." He kissed my knuckle.

"That's all I've ever wanted."

"There was a time I thought I'd never see you like this again." He tucked damp strands of hair behind my ear.

We shared a smile.

He held my face between his palms and kissed my cheeks. His face was soft. He stared at me with a look so intense and a love so deep it couldn't be measured. His expression made me feel like I was his whole universe.

"Don't look at me like that, or I'll cry again," I whimpered.

"*Shhh.* It's all right." He swept a few straggling tears away with his thumb. "You don't need to cry. I'm here with you, and I'm not going anywhere. I want to worship you. I want to show you not only with my body but with my heart how much you mean to me." He moved onto his side and pulled my body close.

"There aren't strong enough words for how I feel about you. I love you so much."

He wrapped me in his arms and pulled the blankets over our bodies.

"I know of another way to get warm." I tossed the blankets aside and rolled him over onto his back. I tugged his boxers down his legs.

"My turn," I said.

His eyes were wide from my advance, and his arousal sprang forward.

I stared at his body, kissed his chest, and licked down his torso and past his hips. I held him in my hand and stroked his foreskin. He closed his eyes as I massaged him.

"Climb on top of me. I love it when you're on top. I like to watch you," he encouraged me.

"I want to do something else first." I licked my lips. Time and other experiences gave me the confidence to explore him in new ways. I moved down between his legs and took him into my mouth. I brushed my tongue up and down his shaft. He was warm and thick.

He put his hands through my hair as I worked. Muscles in his thighs grew tight, and light moans escaped his lips.

"I want to be inside you now," he whispered with measured breaths, then patted the pillow beside him.

I lay next to him.

"I know what you said at the church, but is it safe? Did you count your days?" He rolled over me and kissed behind my ear as his erection pressed against my inner thigh.

"We'll be fine," I whispered against his lips, then looked up at his face. "I don't think I can get pregnant anymore." A pang of guilt flooded me. "But now that you mention it, maybe you should think about that before we . . ." I recoiled slightly.

"Think about what? I don't want to think about anything but you."

"Maybe this is wrong." I withdrew from his grip. "I wasn't thinking." I covered my face with my hands. "I'll never be able to give you a child," I whimpered.

"I love you, no matter what. Even if we can't have a child, I want only you." He tried to free my hands. "Please look at me. If we can't have our own baby, we can always adopt. Look what happened to my grandmother. You're the one who said God listened to your prayers, and look, here I am. Here *we* are." He kissed my knuckles. "So, whatever happens, we'll leave it up to God." He placed a kiss on my forehead.

I nodded, then he rubbed away my tears.

He took me into his arms and kissed me deeply.

I climbed on top, straddled his hips, and reached between his legs. He stiffened from my touch. Slowly, I inserted him inside me. I moaned as the folds of my skin wrapped around him. I rocked my hips, pulling him in and out of me. I loved to feel him inside me. I let my body's rhythmic movements set the pace. I wanted to give him pleasure and watch his face as we rediscovered our lovers' paradise together. He clutched my hips as I moved. Trickles of sweat dripped down my back and between my legs.

While still inside me, he sat up. I wrapped my arms and legs around his body. He took my breast into his mouth while the muscles around my thighs and pelvis contracted with every thrust.

With one breast in his mouth, he grabbed my ass with both hands. I moved my hips back and forth as I pushed against him, again and again. We were a perfect storm. Our bodies crashed into each other like roaring thunder against the bright lightning outside. Sparks of our own light filled our bodies as we moved toward the finish. Years of wanting to be together had been bottled up and boiled down into this one moment. With every pump of our hips, we pushed past feelings of anger, resentment, fear, and regret, followed by forgiveness and an unyielding love and respect for one another that couldn't be harnessed or forgotten. The sound of the storm edged closer with every second, encouraging me to move faster. Then, without warning, he stilled and came inside me.

"I love you, Violetta. Be mine forever." He held me tight as he finished.

"I love you too." I kissed him softly as he regained his breath. Trembling, we held each other tightly and cradled our vulnerability. Our hearts beat hard against our chest bones as if speaking to one another again. I held him in my arms and wrapped him in all my love and admiration.

"You feel so wonderful. Just to be with you like this . . ." He nuzzled into my hair. "I feel whole again," he whispered against my neck, then hugged me tightly.

"I missed you so much. Your touch, your love, your kisses," I said and kissed him again. "Tonight was even better than I'd imagined."

He smiled. "It was for me too," he said, then dappled kisses along my neck.

Minutes passed, along with the storm, and silence filled the room. Our lovemaking was more than just an act of passion—it was a hurricane of emotions. We'd come through our storm, and with our bodies intertwined, we'd made it to the other side.

He slowly pulled away from my grasp and looked out the window. "Looks like the storm's passed us now. Late spring storms tend to do that. They come in quick, then go away just as fast. Tomorrow should be clear and beautiful." He turned back to me, cupped my cheeks, and stared into my eyes. "Speaking of beautiful, you're like the sun coming out after a long storm. Without your light, I've been living in darkness."

I studied his face as he spoke.

"Thank you for your forgiveness and for giving me the chance to make this right. And for choosing me to share your life with."

"That's all I ever wanted—to be close to you again, like when we were kids—when things made sense. Before . . ." I put my head down as remorse flooded me.

Gaetano tilted my chin up. "I'm here now, and I'm not going anywhere. When I look over my life, I will think about this night and know it's the night I reconnected with my soulmate. These precious moments are not lost on me. You are my soulmate, Violetta. You always have been and always will be." He played with the ends of my hair, then looked back up at me. "I tried so hard to fight my feelings for you. I've gotten good at stuffing the pain. I'm just glad I followed my heart tonight because it led me right back here to you. Now, we have a chance at a future. I will love you until my last breath."

Tears welled in my eyes. "Your words overwhelm me." I reached up to touch his face. "To know that you love me that much, after all this time, fills my heart with so much hope and happiness. I'm so grateful for you."

He held my face in his hands. "*Il tuo corpo è la mia casa, sei il mio santuario. Sei il sole che mi dà la vita. Il tuo sorriso da solo potrebbe illuminare l'universo. Ti amo, Violetta, per sempre.*"

I pulled away slightly and stared into his soulful, honey-brown eyes. "Still the poet, are we?"

"Only for you," he smiled, then kissed my chin and neck.

"My turn."

"Let's hear it," he said, then lay back down.

"With every bone in my body, I'm yours. I love you, Gaetano Sanna. You are my wind. You have the strength to make trees dance and kites fly. You have the power to make dark clouds disappear. Without you, every day has felt like a thunderstorm; frightful and gloomy. Thank you for blowing away my past and my fears."

"Not bad." He smiled. "I promise to protect you from any storm. I love you." He kissed my forehead.

"You aren't the only one who can be a poet. Remember, I'm the one who introduced you to *Signor* Shakespeare."

We both giggled.

"There's my beautiful girl," he beamed. "I love to see you happy and laughing."

"You still know how to make me laugh. Please, never stop."

"Deal. I want to spend the rest of my life watching you smile." He kissed my mouth.

"When I'm with you, how can I not?" I cupped his face.

He rolled me onto my back, then placed his face between my breasts and fondled my nipples.

"And I thought you said you were tired?" I reached up and threaded my fingers into the waves of his hair.

"Who, me? No, I'm just getting started."

Chapter 9
Voices in the Night

GAETANO STOOD AMONGST THE VINEYARDS. HE SMILED AT ME and then back, toward the tiny voice.

"I'm gonna get you," Gaetano said.

A little voice giggled and ran. A small head of brown curls bobbed up and down through the miniature trees of the Sanna vineyard. Gaetano ran and scooped up the tiny blessing in his hands. "Gotcha."

His voice echoed through the field. I ran to my future ahead of me. With every step forward, they got further and further away. I yelled for them, but they didn't turn around. I tried to move my body through the countless vines.

"Stop, wait for me," I bellowed.

Their bodies disappeared from view. My heart fell into my stomach. Where had they gone?

Lost in a maze of green, not knowing which way to turn, I called out again, hoping I'd hear their sweet voices. "Gaetano, where are you guys?" My heart clenched under my rib cage. I tried to run again, but this time I sank into a deep pit of mud. I slogged around the wet dirt and crawled from its grip.

With all my strength, I dragged my body closer to their voices until I came upon reddened, muddy earth. I followed the trail of red, slithering my body from side to side, searching. The pool of red got bigger and bigger as I came upon something solid.

Gaetano's body, face down in the dirt.

I screamed his name and rolled him over to see his face.

Nearby, laughter filled the field.

It was Frank, and he held our child in his hands, with a knife to my angel's throat.

"No, Frank, don't do it. Please. Take me instead," I cried while my child squirmed in his clutch. Frank pulled the knife back, stabbed my angel in his chest, and then lunged at me.

"No," I shrieked.

Gaetano shook me awake. "Violetta, wake up. Please, *sole mio*."

I reached for his face. "You're alive? Where's Frank? Please, we must do something," I bellowed through the tiny, dark room. The rain had stopped.

"You had a nightmare. He's not here. You're here with me. You're safe." Gaetano held me tight while I shook.

"It was so real. He was right there," I panted.

"It's over now. He can't hurt you anymore. I won't let him." He pushed my hair from my watery eyes.

I took deep breaths to regain my sense of location and well-being.

"I'm okay." *Oh God, when is that man gonna stop haunting me?*

"How long have you had these nightmares?"

I put my head down. "Now and again. It was worse during the war. The long hours made them creep up more."

Gaetano's lips pressed into a tight line. "I don't think you realize how much it angers me that he did those things to you. It makes me feel like I could . . ."

"Please don't let Frank ruin our night. Too many great things have happened. It was only a dream." I climbed into Gaetano's loving arms.

He brushed his thumb along my arm and the hairs stood from his touch. "You're very courageous." He placed his finger under my chin and tilted my head up to look at him. "Do you know that?"

"I did what any woman would do, trying to protect the people she loves." I ran my fingers through his chest hair.

"I want to protect you from him. It kills me to watch you in this much pain. He has certainly left his mark. Sadly, he resides in your mind." His eyes blazed red in the dim light of the room. "He's the devil."

"The devil?"

"Yes, he's pure evil, and I hope he burns in hell for what he did to you. All of them—devils and thieves who rob and kill. They're only here to do harm. Every last one of them."

"Frank's not as powerful as the devil." I laughed. "He's a coward of a man who didn't even say goodbye to his daughter at her funeral. He's an embarrassment and a loose end for the Molanano family, and I bet Don Molanano knows that. The only reason he isn't dead yet is because of his father."

Gaetano gathered my hair in his hands and smoothed it over my shoulders while he listened.

"The last time he hit me, I fought back. We almost killed each other."

One brow rose on his forehead. "You should've killed him."

"I gave him a nasty scar. I bit the bastard's face." I tried to bury the memory of how his flesh tasted and the sound of his skin popping in my mouth when I bit down on his cheek.

"You bit him?"

"Yes, and hard."

Gaetano laughed.

"It was the night I left him. We got into a huge fight, and I fought back. I wanted the madness to stop."

"Did it?" He looked skeptical.

"Not completely. But with you in my life now, I know it'll get better. Besides, we don't need to worry about Frank. He'll be in prison for a long time." I turned to kiss him.

"Is there something else you need to tell me about him?" His eyes grew serious. "Anything I should know?"

"No. Not really. It was just a dream."

He sighed, then put his face close to mine. "You can tell me anything. I'll never let anyone hurt you, Violetta—even me." His eyes scanned my face as if he was searching for something.

"I know," I whispered. I needed to tell him about the letter. He needed to know what would come for us. But I couldn't take the risk he'd leave me over it—not after what just happened between us.

"It's been a long night," he whispered, then put his arms around me.

I let my head fall into the crook of his neck. "Let's get some sleep. We can talk more in the morning." He hugged me tightly.

Chapter 10

Secrets and Sparkles

I MOVED MY LEGS AROUND THE SHEETS. I WAS STICKY. LAST night's rain mixed with the morning's heat made the air sultry. But I was also sticky in other parts of my body—evidence of Guy's need for me. I turned over to find Gaetano dressing. His pants were unzipped, and his bare chest was exposed.

"*Buongiorno.*" He grinned, buttoned his shirt, and zipped up his slacks.

"Good morning." I kept my eyes on his body.

"I need to head back to my hotel for a shower and a fresh change of clothes, but then I'd like to take you to the land I'm thinking of buying for my expansion. If you're to be my wife someday, I'd like you to see it."

Wife. The word jolted me. I couldn't be his wife until I was divorced. My stomach clenched. "Okay," I mumbled with swollen lips. I struggled to sit up in bed.

"What's wrong?"

"Oh, nothing, I slept wrong, is all." I didn't want to admit where I was sore. Every muscle in my body ached from our long night of lovemaking. It had been such a long time for me. Even the sheets burned against my tender nipples. Images of Gaetano's mouth sucking my flesh while he moved in and out of me consumed me. A titillating ache returned, dulling the pain and making me moist again.

Gaetano was different in the bedroom. We both were. We were older now and more experienced. We weren't afraid to try new things. He took my body to new places that I'd never experienced before. He ignited a fire in me again, and it burned red hot. With him inside me, we were one, sharing the same heart and breathing the same breath. Time and space didn't matter. Our lovemaking was medicine. With every kiss, we healed each other's pain.

He came to the side of the bed. "See you soon." He bent down and kissed my forehead. "By the way, I cleaned up the glass in the bathroom. I didn't want you to cut your feet." He grazed his knuckles over my cheek.

I put my head down. "I forgot I broke the mirror. I was angry..."

"It was my fault for upsetting you." His eyes carried his shame. He kissed me goodbye. "I'll be back soon."

I thought about how close I'd come to breaking my sobriety. Self-loathing enveloped me.

Gaetano picked me up in a black Fiat—courtesy of his realtor. The drive was beautiful. Long patches of undeveloped land butted up against lush hillsides. As we got closer, glimpses of vineyards lined the horizon. We stopped at a little town outside of Rome, surrounded by fertile meadows. It was a winemaker's paradise.

He grabbed a bag and blanket from the backseat.

"What's all that?" I asked.

"I remember how much you loved to have picnics, so I figured some wine, a little food, some interesting conversation, and maybe a few more kisses would be nice."

"That sounds wonderful." I smiled and opened my door.

He came over to my side of the car and pressed a kiss to my lips, then stared deep into my eyes. "I can't wait to show you." He beamed, then turned and pointed.

"Do you see that small building to the right, there? That's where we're going."

I looped one arm around his, and we walked up a tiny dirt road to a small farmhouse. The land was fenced in on one side but wild and untamed on the other.

Gaetano turned to me and smiled. "Are you ready?" His eyes were wide and eager. "Come."

I grabbed for his hand, our fingers intertwined, and I felt safe again. We wandered the fields, and Gaetano pointed to various landscape features for his future expansion.

"This is a good spot for a picnic." He pointed to a shaded area under a tree. He opened the bag and laid out the blanket.

From the sack, I pulled out a giant loaf of bread and a bottle of Sanna wine.

"Oh, good. You found the wine. I forgot glasses, but I remembered the corkscrew. I guess we'll take sips from the bottle."

I squeezed the bottle between my fingers. The last time I held a bottle of Sanna wine was with Frank. The time that I willingly succumbed to him with the help of alcohol.

"I shouldn't have any." I handed him a hunk of bread and cheese.

"Why?" he asked and took a bite.

"After what happened with the pills, I need to abstain."

A small laugh escaped his lips as he chewed. "How is the future wife of a winemaker not going to sample the wine?" he joked.

"You're all the alcohol I'll ever need," I said suggestively and went in for a kiss. His mouth smiled against my lips.

When we pulled away, I looked down at the blanket. Life was so different when we had our first picnic. We were young and innocent. The full weight of my family's involvement in the Mafia had not yet made itself known to us.

"So, what do you think?"

"It's beautiful here."

Gaetano kicked off his shoes and lay against the blanket. "Lie next to me. We need to talk."

I took a piece of bread and lay down next to him.

"Look, Violetta." He pointed to the horizon. "This can all be ours."

My eyes followed his finger.

"Over there is where I'd like to build the main house. I want it to have plenty of room for extra bedrooms. And over there I'd like to put a hotel. Not as large as the one in Napa. More of a bed and breakfast—a place where people can enjoy the grounds and sip on the wine." A pair of hopeful eyes stared back at me. He turned his body to mine and placed his hand on my hip.

I tried to imagine walking hand in hand through the fields when flickers of my nightmare came into view. I shook the memory from my mind. "It sounds wonderful."

"Is there something *you* want? Maybe a large master bedroom for us? A built-in tub? What makes you happy?"

"Just being here with you makes me happy. Would we live here year-round?" I asked, frightened that I'd no longer see my family.

"No. We couldn't stay here all the time. I have too many responsibilities back in California. Maybe we'd spend half the year here." He touched the ends of my hair. "Just look out there." He moved onto his back and peered at the land before us. "It's a winemaker's dream come true. And up until yesterday, I planned on buying it."

"Wait, what? Why aren't you going to buy it? It's what you said you wanted." I gazed over the rolling hills around us.

"I did want it. I wanted it with you. After our commitment yesterday, I wanted this to be a second home for us. A place we could get away and let our children run through the fields. Can you see them out there?" He pointed to the vast stretch of green in front of us. "They'd be so happy here. We'd all be happy here. I had a vision for this place, but something has come to my attention that makes me think otherwise."

"What do you mean?"

He exhaled and his focus sharpened. "When were you going to tell me about the note?"

I sat up quickly. My voice felt caught in my throat. "What?" I choked out. "Did you snoop through my things while I slept?"

"Not exactly. I got up to use the bathroom, and when I returned, I wanted to write you a love letter telling you how sorry I was for the things I'd said and how happy I was to have you back in my life. The only paper I found was in the trash."

Heat rushed up my neck. "I was going to tell you last night, but I was afraid you'd leave. I couldn't let Frank come between us and take the chance of losing you again."

"When I surrendered to the idea of *us*, I accepted the complications of your family's allegiance. I know the chance I'm taking and that I'll have to take a stand against them. Because you're worth it." He pulled my hand to his mouth and kissed the back of my knuckles. "I need you to feel safe enough to tell me anything. How can I protect you if I don't know everything?"

"I know. I'm sorry. I don't even know if it's him. I don't understand how he could have gotten out so soon. I thought he had a few more years to go. It may only be rumors. Carm isn't sure. Pop doesn't tell her much, but he would've told me this. He knows what a son of a bitch Frank was to me."

"Are you sure about that? He's the one who married you off to that bastard in the first place." His voice was glacial.

I couldn't defend my father. Gaetano was right. Pop had a hand in my marriage, but once he found out Frank had been beating me, he had a different opinion of him. "I know you're angry at my father. So was I."

"Not sure I trust any of them. That's why it's so important that I can trust you. There may come a time when you must choose between your father and me."

His words stung like a hornet's nest. I didn't want to have to pick. We both knew that in this world, everyone has a price to pay, even Pop. I hoped he loved me enough that, after everything I went through, he'd protect me this time. I blinked back tears. "I hope I don't have to choose."

"Neither do I. But it's a real possibility. We may even have to move away. I'll do everything in my power to fight them, but they own the winery, and that will present its share of problems. Are you willing to leave everyone you know and never talk to them again?"

I thought about my family. My mouth turned to dust. "It might not even be Frank who wrote the note. It might be Rose, another mob wife I met in Brooklyn. She has good reason to come after me. She was the one screwing around with Frank when I caught him cheating. One thing led to another, and we got into a fight. When the cops came, they took her away. Last I'd heard, she was in a mental hospital. But who knows? Maybe Frank's trying to scare me. The letters were written weeks ago, and nothing has happened. It's probably a farce." I rubbed at the goose pimples that grew on my arms.

Gaetano pulled me into his tight embrace. "He can't hurt you anymore. I won't let him. I'm right here," he whispered into my ear. He pulled his face back slowly and locked his arms around my waist. "Listen to me. When the time comes, we'll be ready. José has some friends in Mexico that can help us. They're mercenaries but could act as bodyguards until things settle down. It will come at a price, but that's a price I'm willing to pay to be with you. You know as well as I do that there may come a day when we must make other arrangements, and I want you to be ready for that."

Gaetano was no longer a half-cocked, angry kid ready to fight. He'd thought about this, and he had a plan this time.

"I just want him to leave me alone." Emotion flushed my eyes. "I'm a liability to the family. And to Frank, I'm property."

Gaetano's nostrils flared. "Not for long. I'll call my lawyers and have them start the paperwork when we return. If they can pay off lawyers and judges, so can I."

"This will start a war."

"A war started the day they almost raped my mother in front of me."

I thought about my wedding night to Frank, the first time I'd been raped. Another shiver jerked its way through my body.

His eyes observed me. "It hurts to see you like this. What can I do to make you feel safe again?"

"Hold me."

"My God. What did that monster do to you?" His eyes welled.

"He did what monsters do." My bottom lip trembled as I blinked back tears. Gaetano held me close to his chest, where I listened to one of the most soothing sounds I'd ever heard—the beat of his comforting heart.

After a few loving embraces, encouraging words, and some wine, Gaetano fell asleep in my arms. We'd made love on what was to be *our* land. The sun was about to fall behind the horizon. I lay with Guy's arm around me, feeling whole and protected. I put my ear to his chest and listened to his heartbeat. Two big hands tangled themselves in my hair.

"That felt great. I haven't had a nap like that in years." He removed his hands from my hair and stretched out his long, muscular body. "What time is it?" He peered down at his wristwatch. "Wow. It's late. We should go. It'll be dark soon."

He yanked his white undershirt over his head, then buttoned up his shirt. He grabbed his jacket and patted the pockets.

"With all the *activities* this afternoon, I almost forgot to give this to you." He smiled my favorite crooked smile and took something small from the side pocket. "Close your eyes. No peeking."

I squeezed my lashes together.

"This is for you." He placed something small in my hand. "May we never lose each other again. Go ahead. Open them."

I looked down at my hand. A small black box lay in my palm.

"You shouldn't have. Really. You've given me enough already. Having you back in my life is a gift." Momentary warmth filled my body, followed by anxious silence. This couldn't be a wedding ring, could it? I hadn't even talked to my father yet.

"Don't worry. It's not what you think—at least, not yet. For that, I want you to pick whatever you like." He gauged my reaction. "Open it." His eyes were wide.

I opened the box. A shiny necklace adorned with tiny diamonds sparkled in the sun.

"Saint Anthony." The same one I'd tried on in the tiny shop. "Oh, Gaetano, you shouldn't have. It was so expensive."

"The man at the store said that this is the saint you pray to when you've lost something. I'd lost you, but now I've found you." A warm smile spread across his face. He took the necklace out and opened the clasp in front of me. "Pick up your hair so I can put it on."

"It's too much."

He reached behind my head and fumbled with the clasp. "I'm now a firm believer in praying to Saint Anthony." He brought his hands in front of my chest, lifted the dazzling charm to his mouth and kissed it. "It looks beautiful on you. May we never lose each other again."

I peered down at the charm.

"Wear it as a symbol of our love. For now, use it in place of a wedding ring to show that you're mine. Only this time, I won't be asking your father for his blessing. This decision rests on you."

I nodded and swallowed against a bone-dry throat.

He rubbed the golden medal. "We've waited so long. I don't want to wait any longer. I want to be with you every day. I want to marry you and begin our life together. When we get back to the hotel, I will send word. Maybe they can mail the papers overseas?"

"It won't be long, my love. I don't want to wait any longer, either, but I want to speak to my father first, face to face. I don't want to blindside him with this kind of news. Besides, I haven't seen my family since I left for the war. I want to be with them one last time." My throat swelled. "Before I may have to leave them forever."

He tilted my head up to his. His lips parted, and he placed a soft kiss on my mouth. "I understand." His thumbs stroked over my cheekbones. "Let's not think the worst." He touched the shiny pendant that swung between my breasts. "We need to have faith."

"Yes," I whispered. "I'll pray that God watches over us now."

He nodded. "We should get back now, and I was thinking . . ." he said with a devilish grin.

"Thinking what?" I eyed him curiously.

"Tonight, I'd like us to stay at my hotel. I have a bigger bed and . . . we'd have more room." He winked at me.

"Gaetano Sanna, you have a one-track mind." I tapped his arm.

"I've waited so long to touch you again. I'm making up for lost time," he teased.

"You're impossible. You know that?"

We giggled.

As we packed up our things, I looked around the countryside. Would I ever be here again with him? Safe and free from the Mafia's hold? Or would this place serve as a memory of what could have been? Time would tell. My chest tightened when I thought about what I'd say to my father, and the inevitable fallout from what I was about to do.

Chapter 11

Telegrams

Sun poured through the windows of Gaetano's opulent hotel room. I tried to move, but his legs were intertwined with mine as he slept. I studied my necklace. The pendant was worth more to me than any ring. It was a symbol of his commitment to us. A commitment that would be met with fury and blood. Nerves twisted in my stomach.

"*Buongiorno, sole mio,*" he croaked with a rough morning voice, then leaned over to kiss my cheek.

"Good morning."

"How did you sleep?"

"Good, once I *finally* went to sleep. You had me up late last night." I giggled into the crook of his neck.

"I'll never get tired of making love with you." He kissed my forehead.

"So, what are we going to do today?"

"Stay in this bed. All day." He hugged me tightly.

"You want to sleep all day?"

"I never said *sleep*," he joked. He skimmed his fingers over my hip and squeezed my ass.

A knock sounded on the door.

"Who could that be?" Alarmed at the intrusion, I pulled the blankets over my naked body.

"*Un attimo. Sto arrivando!*" Gaetano threw on some pants and opened the door. A bell captain stood there with a small note in his hand. The two men went back and forth in Italian, then Gaetano shut the door.

"What is it?"

"A telegram from home."

A slight pang of anxiety rushed through my abdomen as Gaetano read the telegram. His eyes looked frantic.

"What's wrong?"

"I must go home immediately," he said with stiff lips. He handed me the note.

```
Gaetano,
Your father's had another stroke.
He's in the hospital.
Your mother requests your prompt return.
My father and I will look after things until
you get home.
Thinking of you, Espi.
```

The salutation was concerning, but this wasn't the time to question. I placed my hand over his. He looked at me, and I smiled softly to comfort him.

"Come with me." He cupped my face. His words held desperation. "I can try to get you on my flight."

"With everything that's happened, it's not a good idea for you to bring me around your mother just yet. I know how she feels about me. We don't know what we're walking into. I'd make things worse for you and everyone right now. And I need to speak to my father, alone."

Gaetano squeezed his eyes shut, then opened them again. "I can't leave you here. Not after everything we've shared. Not after the letter. I'm afraid that—"

"Don't be. I'm not going anywhere this time. This time it's forever." I pulled him close. His tight body slumped into my arms.

"What if something happens? I can't protect you when I'm gone. You must come back with me at once."

"I'll be fine. I've been in Italy this whole time, and nothing's happened. Come get me at the ranch when things settle. I'll be ready. By then, I'll have talked with my family and packed my things to move with you to the winery. We both need to take care of our affairs. You need to be there for your family right now. I'd be in the way." I felt as if I'd swallowed something sharp. I'd been so close to him these last few days that being away from him would hurt.

He nodded in agreement. "As soon as I can, I'll come for you." He grabbed my hands in his and kissed my forehead. We held each other tight.

I gathered my things and dressed quickly. With a few unsure glances, a strange, foreign distance crept between us. Uncertain of our future, I reached the door when he stopped me.

He grabbed my hips and turned me around fiercely. "I won't let anything come between us again. I love you, Violetta. You're mine," he said, his voice full of trepidation.

"I'm yours, always." I smiled up at his beautiful, dreamy eyes. Then with an energy and tension I'd never felt before, he pulled my face toward his and pressed a deep kiss on my lips. A low moan escaped as he pried open my mouth with his urgent, warm tongue. While our lips locked into place, he pulled me into his frame. His movements were so intense that it felt like he wanted to climb inside me. I held onto his body with everything I had left to give.

The kiss was a declaration of our love for one another. It was possessing and pleading—a signal of our future intentions. No more words were needed. I loved him, and he loved me. When we needed air, he released my lips, leaving us both panting. His hooded eyes blazed into mine as he let his thumb glide against my bottom lip. To avoid saying another painful goodbye, I turned away quickly and opened the door. I slipped through the frame, too afraid to look back.

Tears streamed down my face as I wandered along the cobblestone streets. Like the wind, he'd come back into my life as a powerful gust, only to vanish like a soft breeze. I'd never get used to saying goodbye to Gaetano—the last time almost killed me.

What would happen when I returned home? If history had shown me anything, it was that life always had a way of pulling us apart. My heart squeezed into a tight ball. I reached for my St. Anthony's medal and pressed it to my lips. I prayed this time would be different, but the consequences would surely be dire.

Chapter 12
Coming Home

For the next few days, I dragged my hollowed body down the streets of Rome. The city wasn't as alive as it had once been. Without Gaetano by my side, life felt dull again. I missed his crooked smile gleaming back at me when he'd made me laugh, and the way his eyes studied my face while we made love. No amount of gelato satiated my hunger for my grape grower. My room was filled with memories of our time together. Even my bedsheets still smelled of him. All that was left was a shiny pendant that dangled from my neck—a remembrance of our time together—to indicate it was more than a dream. I held it between my fingers.

Why was I still here? I was paid up until the end of the month, but I didn't want to be in Rome anymore. I wanted to run to my new life with him. I needed to go home and talk with my father.

It would have to be a surprise. News of my arrival might tip off the wrong people, and I couldn't afford that. Without further thought, I packed my things and made my way down the stairs en route to the airport. I was halfway down when I heard *Signor* Corbisiero speaking to a man. He sounded upset.

"Don't fucking lie to us," a voice yelled. "Look at the damn picture, old man."

"Ahh," *Signor* Corbisiero yelped out. "Please, stop."

"We got word she's stayin' here. What room is she in?" a different man's voice snarled at the *pensione* owner. "Tell me now, or I'll blow your fuckin' brains out on this nice desk you got here."

They were in *Signor* Corbisiero's office next to the main entrance.

"She no here," *Signor* Corbisiero explained with a shaky voice.

"If we find out you're lyin', we'll kill you. *Capeesh*?"

"*Si. Si.*"

Then I heard what sounded like skin-to-skin contact.

Signor Corbisiero let out a loud groan. Something hard fell to the ground.

My legs shook. *Oh, God.* They must have knocked him out.

"Let's check the rooms," the man said.

I reached into my purse for my scarf. I wrapped it around my hair and face and then threw on some sunglasses to hide my identity in case they came to search. I pulled out my knife and held it in my hand, ready to stab anyone who came close.

Come and get me, Frank. This time, I'll cut your fucking eyes out!

I surveyed exit routes from the building. There were none except the front door. If I tried to climb out of my window I would surely break a leg, and then they'd nab me. Every muscle in my body stiffened.

"She leave. She no stay here no more," *Signor* Corbisiero whimpered.

"Oh, so you were lying, old man?" the voice said. "I should kill ya for lyin' and wastin' our time."

"Easy, Carlo. Easy." Another man said. It wasn't Frank's voice. "He's better off alive than dead to us. The boss might want to question him."

"She say she go to *Milano*."

Signor Corbisiero lied for me. Thank God he was loyal to my father.

"Milan, huh?" one of the men said.

"*Si.*" Then I heard more fighting and glass crashing to the floor. *Signor* Corbisiero groaned. I hated hearing them beat him on my account.

"Let's go, Johnny. Time to call the boss and let him know."

Footfalls rushed from the building, followed by a loud slam of the door.

I waited a few seconds, then ran down to *Signor* Corbisiero's office. He lay bleeding on the floor. I dropped my knife and knelt next to him. Glass from his desk lamp surrounded him. He looked disoriented.

"*Signora*, you need to leave. Now. Or dey gonna kill you," he warned as blood dripped down his chin.

"*Grazie.* Thank you for not telling them where I was." I held his head in my hands. "My family will be forever indebted to you. I'll tell my father of your service to us."

"Go and be safe."

I picked up my things, placed my knife back into my purse, and rushed out the door in search of a taxi.

San Jose felt just as I'd left it. With every turn through the foothills, my stomach tightened. I hadn't seen my home in years. It was strange to be away from something for so long and fear that it might look and feel different. The ranch was the one place that knew my secrets and loved me anyway. I didn't want to admit it, but after I spoke with my father, this might be the last time I called this place home.

The cab pulled up to the mailbox. I handed the driver cash and opened the door. Suitcase in tow, I approached the front door. Memories of Mama on her rocking chair on the porch crept up. I blinked back tears. The rocking chair was still there, but no Mama. My heart withered in my chest. I knocked on the door.

Tony appeared on the other side. His face lit up. "Violetta." He picked me up and spun me in his arms. "How the hell you doin', kid?"

"Put me down," I fussed and shoved at his shoulders.

"Hey everyone, Vi's home," he yelled from the foyer.

"Shut up, *stunad*. You're yelling in my ear," I snapped as he set me down.

"I can't believe you're here. Why didn't you tell anyone you were comin' home?"

"I didn't want anyone to know." I shot him a careful glance.

His brows pulled together. "What happened?" His face looked pained.

"I'll tell you later."

With stiff lips, he nodded. Carm pushed him out of the way to hug me.

"Vi, welcome home!" Carmela flung her arms around my shoulders and then pushed me out in front of her. "Let me look at you." Her eyes scanned my face and body. "You look different, somehow."

"What do you mean?"

"I don't know. You look happy. Happier than I've seen you in years. Peaceful even. Your face is glowing." She raised an eyebrow.

"I don't know about that. But I'm happier, that's for sure."

"I can tell." She held out my arms.

I pulled her in close for another hug and whispered in her ear. "I need to talk to you in private. I got your letters. You were right."

She pulled away fast and eyed me cautiously.

"I'll tell you later," I whispered, then smiled at Tony. "I have much to tell you all."

Carm wrung her hands. She looked like she wanted to cry.

To avoid her stares, I turned to Tony. "I missed you guys."

Tony grabbed my luggage and placed it on the sofa. "We missed you too. Pop tells everyone about his 'daughter who went to help in the war.' We're all real proud of you." Tony grinned.

"Where's Pop? I need to speak with him."

"He's in the barn, talkin' to Sal Sunseri," Tony said.

"Sal Sunseri? The name sounds familiar."

"He's an old timer from the old country. He's been around. Pop's workin' a deal with him for our livestock."

"Our livestock?"

"Sal started a butcher shop and a deli in Goosetown. He's doin' great over there. Says he can hardly keep up with all the new business. He even put up a huge sign—World Famous Sausage and Peppas." He sized up an invisible marquee with his hands.

"How many pigs we have this season?" I asked.

"We had some big litters. It's a good thing too. Things got tight for a while with the war. It slowed business. Even Molanano business," Tony explained.

I rolled my eyes.

"But with Sal having the new butcher shop and deli, he and Pop worked out an arrangement, and Pop makes a generous profit," Tony went on.

"Good for him and Pop," I placed my purse on the sofa next to my luggage. "The more money we can make legitimately, the better."

"Yeah, it's a cute little place with good food. I think he'll do well there," Carm said. "Pop even had Louie give Sal one of his trucks so that he can come up here for the pickups. Wait till you see his son, Angelo," she said in a bubbly voice. "He's such a looker and so polite too. He's Paulie's age. The two of them got along real good the last time he was here. I heard that Angelo asked Paulie if he wanted a job at the deli, but you know Paulie. He makes more money in the streets. Paulie's not about to get his hands dirty slaughtering pigs and chickens." She looked over her shoulder. "He'd rather get his hands dirty doing other things," Carm whispered, then shook her head.

"Where is Paulie?" I asked. "I want to see him."

"He came in late. Again," Carm said in a disapproving tone. "He's passed out in bed. He won't be up until later tonight."

That had been my life with Frank. He was up all night conducting business and slept all day. Paulie was surely gone.

"Man, when Pop sees you, he's gonna want to invite the whole town over. It'll be a welcome-home party in your honor," Tony said.

"I'm not up for a party, Tony," I said in an earnest tone. I didn't want to attract unwanted attention to my arrival. "I'm too tired."

"Well, you better wake up, because you know Pop."

"*Maronn*. Only family, then. I don't want outsiders."

"What are you worried about?" Tony probed. "What's goin' on, Vi?"

"Nothing. That's just how I want it. It's been a long day, and I don't feel like entertaining."

"Well, I got gravy on the stove, and I don't want it to burn. It's good to see you home safe, sister." Carm kissed my cheek. "We'll talk later."

Tony and I walked past Carm to the back door. Carm stood over the stove, and a giant hole pierced through my heart. Mama's absence was everywhere. I imagined her standing there with her Winchester by her side, making food for us. The reality of her death weighed on me. To stop myself from sobbing, I turned back to Tony. "With all the excitement, I forgot to ask. How's it going with you?"

"Fine. Just busy. Pop has me doin' lots of work out here. We're headin' to the track this weekend. Pop's been training another horse. He's a real winner this time, Vi," Tony said as we walked through the back door and onto the porch.

"Pop and his ponies." I smiled. "How's things with Christina? When you gonna marry that girl? I like her, Tone. Don't lose this one."

"She's fine. I like her too. A lot." He beamed.

My feet slowed as we moved through the garden into the field. I looked up at the foothills. They'd turned from green to yellow, and the smell of chicken feed was heavy in the air as we strode past the chicken coops. My stomach clenched, thinking about the last time I stood there with blood running down my legs when I lost my daughter. To abandon the pain, I changed the subject. "And Vin? How is he?"

"He's doin' real good in school. Wants to go to college and be an accountant or somethin'. Maybe he'll go into bookmakin' like you used to do for Pop."

"I hope not. I hope he gets a legitimate job after college."

"We all got to make a livin' somehow."

"There are other ways to make a living that don't require killing people."

A puff of air escaped Tony's lips as he shook his head. "*Maronn*, you only been here a few minutes, and listen to you already."

"Yeah, yeah." I nudged him with my hip.

Tony stumbled. "Cut it out, or I'll put you over my shoulder and throw you into the manure patch."

My eyes shot up. "You wouldn't."

"Oh, I would." A mischievous grin pulled at the sides of his mouth.

"Don't even think about it." I moved a few feet away from him. We both laughed. "And Paulie? Tell the truth. How deep is he in?" I asked, afraid of the answer.

Tony's eyes shifted to his feet. "He's doin' all right. He got into a little trouble, but Pop got him out of it."

Disappointment crashed against my heart. "I knew he was wrapped up in it. Maybe you should talk to him, Tone. You're his big brother. I tried a few years ago, and it didn't do anything."

"Paulie's a soldier now. There's nothin' I can say that will change his mind. Even if I did, Pop might not like that. It's always good to have someone on the inside who'll look out for the family's interests," he said as we passed the big house.

"If Paulie stays in it, he'll go to prison for life. Or worse. He could die, Tone."

"No one wants that, God forbid."

"You can't say you haven't seen Pop's face when Paulie's around. He's sad. I know it."

"After all this time, what's Pop gonna say? He'd look like a damn hypocrite. He's been tryin' to go legit for a while, but you know how hard it is to break away."

"I don't know, but we have to do something. When I was pregnant, one of the scariest things to think about was what might happen to my kid in this life." A knot formed in my belly. "Pop doesn't know if one day he'll read the paper to find out that one of his kids got whacked. Reporters like to use Mafia families as examples of what not to do—to shame us. I'm afraid something bad will happen if we don't do something soon."

"I'll talk to him, but no promises. He won't take me seriously because I still help Pop occasionally. He knows that good and well."

We walked toward the barn when I caught the scent of Mama's roses. No matter where I stepped, the place was filled with memories. Some good. Some bad. Memories, all the same. Nostalgia took over, leaving me quiet in my thoughts.

"Pop, Vin, get out here," Tony yelled. "Look who came home."

Pop walked from the barn and grabbed his glasses from the pocket in his overalls. Vinny followed behind him.

"Violetta!" Pop cried and put his arms out for me.

I ran to him. "Papa. Oh, how I've missed you." Warmth filled me. I kissed him on the cheek while he hugged me tightly.

"Welcome home. I missa you too," he stammered with tears in his eyes.

"Hey, Vi. How you doin'?" Vinny asked. "Pop's been moping around without you helping out in the clinic."

"I'm sure you did a good job in my absence." I wrapped my arms around my baby brother. He towered over me. "How've you been, Vin?"

"Good. I'm going to college to be an accountant."

"I'm real proud of you, kid. Look at you—all grown up. You must've grown a foot since the last time I saw you. So, you gonna be a college boy now, huh? I'm happy you found a good life for yourself." I leaned into his ear. "I bet Pop's happy. No more of this life for you, kid. You made the right decision. It's not worth it. Believe me."

I looked up when two men approached.

"Violetta, you remember Salvatore?" Pop asked.

"Yes, I think I remember meeting you at my sister's wedding."

"Yes," he said, and we shook hands. "Dis isa my son, Angelo," the burly man said.

"Hi, I'm Violetta." I reached out to shake the young man's hand.

"Hello." He gripped my hand firmly, followed by a slow smile.

"I hear you make the best sausage in town," I said.

Angelo eyed me. "Yeah, we like to think so, anyways." He grinned. He was tall, with a slight black mustache beginning on his upper lip.

"I can't wait to try it." I smiled back.

"For you, it's on the house," he said confidently, almost flirting.

"We gonna get going," Sal said, gripping his son's shoulder to exit. "See you in a few weeks, *paesano*," Sal said to my father, then shook his hand. "We gonna load da truck now."

"Vincenzo, you go and helpa dem," Pop ordered.

"Sure, Pop," Vinny said and followed them out.

While the three men walked away, a strange feeling came over me. Something deep inside me knew that I'd know Angelo forever.

"We gonna hava pati for you. Da whole family comin' ova," Pop said proudly.

"Pop, I'm tired. I don't want a lot of people here—only people we can trust. Something's happened, and I need to speak to you. It's important."

Tony and Pop exchanged glances. "Okay, we'll talk later, but right now, we get ready."

"This can't wait. I need your help. I think Frank's after me."

I told Pop everything—except for wanting to divorce Frank to marry Gaetano. I needed to rest up for that conversation. Pop listened and said he would talk to Don Molanano privately when he saw him at the track this weekend. Tensions would be high, but I had to know who was after me.

When I returned to the house after spilling my guts, I wanted to talk to Carm about the letters, but she'd already left, so I checked on Paulie. I opened his bedroom door and peeked in.

The room reeked of liquor and tobacco. He was snoring like a chain saw, face down on his bed.

"*Stunad*," I whispered under my breath and pulled the sheets over him.

A gun peeked out from under his pillow.

I gasped, causing him to stir.

I backed away quickly and shut the door. He was my brother, and I loved him, but Carm was right. Paulie was in deep.

Pop ignored my warnings and invited the family over. To him, I was a war hero. I didn't want to deprive him of his moment, but I also didn't want to draw too much attention. I didn't know who the players in the game were yet. I trusted the family, but the people who worked for the family were a different story. Their loyalty was based on the size of their pockets.

While my uncles drank whiskey and smoked cigars, I told stories about my time in the war. The men listened to every word with genuine curiosity and asked lots of questions, but the minute I started talking about the horrible things I'd seen, my aunts retreated inside.

One by one, the family kissed me on the cheek, shook my father's hand, then left while rubbing their stuffed bellies. When everyone was gone, I sat on the porch to watch the sunset. I held my pendant in my hand. "I miss you already, Gaetano."

"Gaetano. Did I hear you right?" Carmela spoke over my shoulder.

"You did. Gaetano bought me this necklace in Rome."

"You saw Gaetano in Rome?" Her voice was light with excitement.

"Yes, and we plan to marry."

Carmela's eyes widened like she'd seen a ghost. "Wait a minute. I thought he was seeing someone."

"That's over," I said, beaming at the new St. Anthony medal in my hand.

"How? You're still married. Have you talked to Pop about this?" Carmela cautioned.

"Not yet. I thought it best to wait till we were alone."

"*Maronn*. I don't know, Vi. I can't stand Frank for what he did to you, but divorce? I don't know how Pop's gonna react to that. And the church . . ." Carm shook her head. "The Molanano family will think you're a rat. Have you thought about what this will do?"

"I don't care what anyone thinks anymore. I can't keep living my life for others. I've done that for too long, and it almost killed me." Feelings of anger assailed me.

Carm sat down and put her arm around me.

"I love him, Carm. He's the only man I've ever loved. He said he'd pay for my lawyer and everything."

"Whachoo needa lawyer for?" Pop interrupted, with my three brothers in tow.

"Has everybody gone home now?" I looked at Tony.

"I think so. Maybe just Sal and Angelo but he's loyal to us. He won't say nothin'," Tony explained.

I looked at the familiar faces around me. "I wanted to tell you all, but I didn't want to do it until we were alone. I figured if you were going to hear about this, it's better you hear it from me." I stared at my father, square in the eyes. "While I was in Italy, I ran into someone from my past."

"Oh yeah, who?" Paulie asked while he brushed dirt off his new leather shoes.

"Gaetano Sanna."

"Never heard of him," Paulie said.

"Gaetano Sanna? You mean the guy who stayed with the Antonelli's a while back?" Vinny asked. "The one you took to the park?"

"Yes, him." I looked directly at my father. "We plan to be married."

"Ay *minchia*," Pop shouted. "Oh no, not again, Violetta. *Aspetta!* You stilla marry. How you gonna getta marry?"

"I'll be filing paperwork with the court for a divorce from Frank."

"*Che cazzo*," Pop shouted.

"He's the only man I've ever loved, and after what happened with Frank, I think I've paid enough dues to *la famiglia* Molanano."

"*Maronn,*" Tony said under his breath. "All hell's gonna break loose now." He shook his head at me.

Paulie laughed. "You can never leave *the family,* and you know it, Vi."

I rose from my chair to look my brother right in the eyes. "I can do whatever the hell I want," I fired back.

"Pop, you can't let her do this. It'll screw up my plans. I'm finally running things ova here. I got my own rent collectors now and everything," Paulie said.

"Rent collectors? Is that what you call it now? I didn't know you'd bought property, little brother. You think you're some big boss then, huh? Rumor has it that without Pop, you'd still be in jail. *Stronzo,*" I barked.

"I'm a boss whether you like it or not. They're gonna send me to Vegas soon. Then I'll really be runnin' things."

My father's brows shot up with Paulie's admission.

"The casino business, huh?" I said through clenched teeth. "The fact that you're tooting your own horn is why you'll be a weak boss, like Frank—that lousy piece of shit."

Paulie took a step toward me when Tony pushed him away from me.

"Take it easy," Tony barked.

"Look, I don't want to fight with you. I don't want to fight with anyone here, but I will do what I must," I said.

"Oh yeah?" Paulie said. His eyes pressed into thin lines. "Well then, so will I. I can't be the brother to a traitor, and that's what they'll think, and you know it. You know what this means. They won't trust me anymore, and if they don't, how am I supposed to get close?" Paulie planted his feet and pushed his shoulders back.

"Do what you have to do, but I won't be their puppet any longer."

Paulie spit on the floor next to me. "You're dead to me now, Vi. *Viva la famiglia* Molanano," he shouted and walked away furiously.

Carm ran after him. "Paulie, wait. You don't mean that."

"Do you realize what position you'll put Pop in if you do this?" Tony warned. "Paulie's right. They won't trust us anymore. Pop could get whacked, for Christ's sake."

"I have no control over that. I won't be their property anymore."

"I neva like Franco. You know dis, but to divorce? What about da church? Dis willa disgrace da family. If you wit dis udder man, you looka lika *puttana*," Pop said, his breath heavy with whiskey. Tension in my father's body was palpable.

"No, I won't," I fumed. "And there's nothing you can do about it this time. I'm a grown woman."

"Even if you were to date this guy, they'd find out," Tony said. "Once word got out, Frank would make sure the situation was dealt with. He's a son of a bitch, Vi. You know he is."

"I'm not afraid of Frank."

"When they come, it won't just be Frank, and you know it," Tony warned.

"Pop, you told me you wanted me to be happy. Gaetano can give me a good life. Isn't that what you want for me? Or do you want me to wander around the ranch miserable and alone for the rest of my life?"

"No. I no wan dat," Pop said with empty eyes.

"Then I'm moving to the Sanna Winery as soon as Gaetano

can make arrangements for me. His father suffered a stroke, so he's busy tending to his family. Lie all you want about my whereabouts. Tell them I'm still in Italy. I'll fake my death if I have to. Whatever you want. I don't care. But I've made my decision."

Pop shook his head at me and trudged back to the house in defeat.

"What are you looking at, squirt?" I smiled at Vinny.

"Nothing," he said, then shot me a half-smile. "I'm scared for you, Vi. I wouldn't want anything to happen to ya."

"Nothing's gonna happen."

"You don't know that," Tony spat.

"Look, I'm sorry my decision will cause some waves, but . . ."

"Some waves?" Tony raised his voice.

"I love you guys with all my heart, but I'm in love with someone else. I have to do this, or I might as well . . ."

"Don't even think it." Tony licked his lips. "Look." He placed both hands on my shoulders. "Me and Pop are headin' down south for the races. When we get back, let's talk about this. I'll come up with a plan that won't cause a war. Maybe we can even arrange a meetin' with Frank's dad and Pop to try and work things out."

"If that plan doesn't include me moving to the winery, then I don't want to hear it." I pressed my lips together tightly.

"Give me a week or two. If you get any heat from the Molanano family after that, we'll deal with it." Tony's nostrils flared. "I'll never forget how that son of a bitch Frank was when he held a knife to my throat, actin' real tough that night. No respect," he spewed with his hands in fists.

"It was the night before my wedding. How could I forget?"

"Keep things quiet for now, and when we get back, we'll work something out. I promise. Pop and Don Molanano have been friends since the old country. Maybe he'll be okay with the arrangement. Who knows? Maybe it's time for another sit-down." Tony pulled me into his arms and kissed the top of my head. "Somehow, it'll be all right. Trust me. I love you."

"I love you too." I pulled him in for a hug, then turned to Vinny. "I love you too, you little pest." I scuffed up his hair.

"I better go inside and talk to Paulie," Tony said.

My hand shook holding the receiver while I waited to hear Gaetano's voice.

"Sanna Winery."

"May I speak to Gaetano Sanna, please?" I asked.

"One moment."

"Hello?" he answered. His voice sounded exhausted.

"It's me. I came home early."

"Violetta? How long have you been home?" he asked, surprised.

"A few days. I stayed back in Italy for another week, but I missed you too much. How's your father?"

"Not so good. He's back home, and me and Mama have been trying to nurse him back to health, but this last stroke was brutal on him. He can't speak or walk. I have to help him to the bathroom."

"I'm so sorry. Is there anything I can do?"

"No. It's been hard. Lots of work to tend to around here, and with the way my father is, I have to help my mother."

"I miss you. Even though it's only been a few weeks, it feels like forever."

"I miss you too. Are you safe? Has anything happened? I can arrange to come down today."

"Nothing's happened. I'm safe here. Don't worry. Be there for your father right now. Besides, I promised to stay around the ranch to help out while Pop and Tony are away. They're headed to the track with one of our horses. They should be back by next Monday. Come then. I'll be ready. I told them of our plans and my feelings for you. There isn't much for me here anyway. You're my home now." My heart warmed in my chest.

"I'll pick you up Monday. I love you."

"I love you too. Can't wait to see you. Then it's forever."

"Forever." I heard the smile in his voice. "I'll ask Espi to watch my sisters so I can make arrangements."

There was that name again. Who was she to him? I'd have to find out.

"Do you want me to speak to your father?" he asked.

"No. He'll never understand. Just come Monday. I'll sign whatever papers you want. Oh, and Gaetano?"

"Yes?"

"Might be a good time to hire some of those mercenaries you talked about."

With Don Molanano's new winning horse secure in the trailer, the truck engine roared. Carm and I waved goodbye as Pop blew us a kiss and Tony reached over to press the horn. Vinny sat in the back of the truck with his head down. He hated going to the racetrack with Pop. He knew Pop would embarrass him by introducing him to the Don, telling him all about his brilliant son and that he'd be good with the numbers, all to find him a place in the business.

"Hopefully, Pazzo will win again, then Pop will be happy," Carm said.

Heartsick, I watched the trailer go off in the distance. The horse was another one of Don Molanano's possessions, like I was for Frank. He just wanted to be free. "I'm sure Don Molanano will be happy, considering he's been laundering through that track for years. Everyone will make loads of money. Pop will be in everyone's good graces again, and all will be well, right? What a joke. I feel sad for that horse."

"Sad for him?" Carm shook her head. "That horse is a winner. He's gonna do great. You know, sometimes you act real high and mighty, Vi. Like you're better than us or somethin'. Everything you've had growing up, every meal you've eaten at Pop's table, and even the clothes on your back come from that money. Ever since you been back from Brooklyn, you act different."

"I am different. I've seen and done things you can't imagine."

"Oh yeah, like what?"

Bags of drugs shoved in the seat cushions of cars, the smell of the Cuban's breath on my face as he threatened to rape me, the look of my dirty fingers as I dug holes in the backyard to hide drugs and money, the thrill I got when I pulled the trigger in that dark field, the look on Officer Tewey's face when I used his body to avoid incarceration, and the cold emptiness of my daughter's nursery, a consequence of my drug habit, when I didn't bring her home.

"Vi. You there?" Carm waved her hand around my face. "You look like you've seen a ghost."

"I did. The ghost of myself." I drew in a cleansing breath. I'd never told Carm the whole truth about what happened in Brooklyn. I didn't want her to think badly of me. "When I was with Frank, I did things I'm ashamed of."

"Like what?"

"Lot of things." I looked down at my feet. "People gave me the clothes off their backs, and the last bits of cash from their bill folds, and I took all of it." I wanted to tell her about the drugs, but I couldn't bear the look on her face. "I had everything. Money. Power. But it wasn't enough. I wasn't like the rest of the mob queens—like Rose."

"Who's Rose?"

"A mob wife who taught me a lot. She taught me about the streets, how to shoot a gun, and how to play the game, but then she betrayed me. Her betrayal became my freedom."

"Listen to you, collectin' and shootin' guns. Next, you'll tell me that you whacked a guy." Carm laughed.

"Laugh all you want, but it's true. I've changed."

"Just don't get too big for your britches, little sister. All hail the queen." Carm bowed in front of me.

"Get up." I pulled her upright. We both laughed, and Carm put her arm around me. No matter how much Carm and I fought, she loved me, and I loved her.

"I'm gonna start callin' you *la regina*."

"Cut it out." I pinched her arm.

"Ouch," Carm shrieked.

"I'm guessing Paulie was too busy with his new job to go with Pop?" I changed the subject to get her to stop teasing me.

"Paulie's never been a rancher. You know that. According to him, he has *more important work* to tend to. I don't care how important his work is. He's gonna clean out the pig pens like the rest of us," Carm said.

We both giggled and walked toward the back.

"We haven't had a chance to talk, but you were right about everything. I need to tell you what happened in Italy. Someone's after me and they came to the *pensione* where I was staying. I'm afraid, Carm."

"You're shakin'." My sister held me tight. "No one's gonna hurt you. We're family. We'll protect you. Was it Frank?"

"I don't know."

I told Carm I'd help around the ranch so she could spend some time away with Louie. She and Louie never had a real honeymoon because she worked two jobs. When she wasn't at the cannery, she helped out in the clinic and cooked for my father and brothers, all while trying to be a new wife.

She accepted my offer and handed over Pop's black book. I looked through the mess she'd left me. As I read through her chicken scratch, I found deposits that weren't accounted for, unrecovered cash, and loads of receipts. I had no idea what belonged where. The books were a disaster.

During the day, I fed the chickens and hogs. I walked the mules and weeded the garden. After I fed myself a small meal at night, I sat on the porch of the big house and sorted Pop's books. I wasn't sure if it was from all the hard work, but I was tired and sleep was welcome.

I was alone for the rest of the week except for the occasional run-in with Paulie. Pop had told him to watch over me until he got back in case someone wanted to try something, except he was usually out doing Molanano business. We hadn't spoken since the day I told my family I wanted to divorce Frank and be with Gaetano. Paulie was angry with me, but I hoped he'd forgive me in time.

Nights were the hardest. That's when I'd think about Gaetano the most. I decided to crochet him a blanket. I sat in my old living room, grabbed some yarn, and pressed it to my cheeks. The material was soft, and I wondered how it would feel against our naked bodies as we made love. Visions of Gaetano's muscular body on top of mine excited me. It'd been a little over two weeks since I'd seen Gaetano, and my body craved him. I took a deep breath and wiped beads of sweat from my neck.

The sound of someone hitting the front door startled me.

"Paulie, is that you? Why you poundin' so damn hard? It's late. I was about to go to bed," I yelled and raced down the hall.

I opened the door.

A face I hoped I'd never see again stared back at me.

I froze in place as doom wrapped its dark hands around my throat. I fought to breathe.

Oh, God, no. It can't be.

Chapter 13

Some Stories Should Be Locked Away Forever

East San Jose Foothills
May 2003
Barbara

Ms. G. sat in her recliner. She looked like she'd seen a ghost. I reached for her hand.

"Are you okay? What is it? Who was at the door?" I squeezed her hand.

Then all at once, her body tensed and shook violently. A stream of urine ran down her legs. Puddles formed around her feet. The stench of feces wafted around us.

She'd lost her bowels.

I jumped up from my chair.

A low, deep sound came from deep within her sternum, crawled its way up her chest, and snaked its way to her throat. She paused only for a second to breathe, then stood.

And screamed.

The outburst was so loud it stung my ears.

It was the biggest roaring scream I'd ever heard—feral and fierce. The sound sucked the air from my lungs, causing me to swallow my voice.

Blood vessels in her eyes popped. Muscles twitched in her face. She let out another blood-curdling scream. "NOOOOOOOO, STOP, GET OUT," she shrieked, then put her hands over her face.

I knew that position all too well. Instinct took over, and I sprang into action.

"Ms. G." I placed my hands on her shoulders. "It's me. Barbara. Come back to me. You're here with me—safe in your house. It's okay, honey. I'm right here."

She turned to face me and stared as if I was an intruder. "STAY AWAY FROM ME! GET OUT OF MY HOUSE!"

"It's me. It's Barbara. Look," I said, then released her and snatched a picture from the wall of the two of us in the garden. "See this? This is us." I shoved the frame in front of her face. "Leticia took this picture of us. You see? I'm Barbara. Please, God, help her remember." I looked up at the ceiling.

"Barbara?" she said with softer eyes. She looked at me, then back at the photo, then back at me. She fell back into the recliner with the picture in her hands. I bent down next to her and held her in my arms as she trembled. "Barbara?" she asked.

"Yes, it's me. Do you remember now?" I brushed away her tears.

"Yes. I think so."

"I'm your nurse." I trembled next to her.

She searched my face and rubbed tears from her eyes. "I remember. What happened?" She placed her hands on her pants. "Why am I all wet? What's that smell?"

I didn't have the heart to tell her. I looked at her careworn face and said, "You were telling me about the story with Gaetano, but something scared you."

"Gaetano? Why would I be scared of Gaetano? I loved him." She worked to catch her breath.

"You weren't scared of Gaetano. It was something else. When you came back to the ranch, something happened."

My heart withered in my chest as silence hovered around us.

She looked up at me and then back to the pictures on the wall. She felt around her body. She rubbed her fingertips together and then put them to her nose.

"Oh no. I didn't. Oh God, no." She began to sob.

I held her in my arms. "It's gonna be okay, sweetheart." If I had known the story would cause her this much pain, I wouldn't have pushed. "Here, honey, let's go clean you up."

I held onto the phone as adrenaline ebbed from my body, leaving me weak and nauseated. "Yes, she's fine now. She had a hallucination this morning. She thought she saw fish in your great-grandfather's pond," I explained to Sofia on the phone, concealing some of the context of what had been shared to protect my patient.

"The pond? They cemented that years ago."

"Well, she thought she saw them."

"Poor *Zia*." Her voice cracked. "I'll be on the next flight out," Sofia said frantically.

"You don't need to do that. These things can happen as her disease progresses. I gave her a bath and a light sedative. She'll probably sleep for the rest of the day. When you hired me, you asked me to tell you if I thought her Alzheimer's had progressed. Until today, I would have said her condition was the same. But after what happened today, there's no doubt in my mind." I couldn't tell Sofia everything Ms. G. told me during our time together. I knew too much about Ms. G.'s past with the Mafia.

"Is there anything else we can do to help her? Any other treatments, maybe? I feel so powerless."

"She needs to be seen by her doctor as soon as possible to

increase her medication. I'll take her. From there, other decisions will have to be made."

"What other decisions?"

"As the disease advances, she'll need more help. At some point, hospitalization may be required. I'll be with her every step of the way. I've seen patients who forget the basics—even how to eat. When that happens, she may require other interventions. I'm not saying we're there yet, but it could happen. I want to make you aware of the worst-case scenario. If the disease takes over, the patient can lose all physical and cognitive ability."

"Oh, my God."

"I'll do everything I can to provide her the best care," I said, trying to convince myself that I was strong enough to watch her until the end. This was Ms. G., and we were way beyond the patient-nurse relationship. "I'll call her doctor and make her an appointment."

"Let me know what we need to do, and I'll make sure it happens."

"I will."

"Thank you for taking such good care of her, Barbara. My aunt loves you. She even went so far as to say she considers you like a daughter. Like it or not, you're part of the family now."

The family.

"I've come to love her like a mother. As much as I've helped her, she's helped me. Your aunt is a special lady."

"Yes, she is. Take care. We'll be in touch."

I hung up the phone and peeked into Ms. G.'s room. She was asleep. Peering down at her, I thought about all she'd told me. I was at an impasse. On the one hand, I'd become so invested in her stories that I had to know what happened next, but on the other hand, our story time seemed to be causing her harm. I wanted to see her happy, and she seemed happiest when she spoke about Gaetano.

Selfishly, I needed her stories to help me escape. I needed to know who was at the door. But would she ever be ready to tell me the *whole* story? Only one person on this earth could get that kind of reaction from Ms. G. Was he the one who wrote the letter?

I took mental notes. Then I remembered the search I did when I began work for the family. Frank Di Natale went missing. It was one of San Jose's biggest unsolved mysteries. With this family's history, I had no idea what to think at this point.

Quietly, I opened her window so she'd hear the windchimes—a reminder of the one person who still put a smile on her face—Gaetano.

"Sweet dreams, sweet girl." I put my hand over hers. My heart ached. "I love you." I walked out and shut the door behind me. Pangs of guilt struck my heart.

I did this.

It's my fault.

"And to whoever it was behind that door, it's your fault too." Protective anger stirred within me. "May God have mercy on your soul."

Chapter 14

Prank Calls

Ms. G. slept until dinnertime. She was quiet while we ate. I thought about all she'd said about her affair with Gaetano, but I still had many questions. I didn't know if she remembered what she'd told me, but I didn't push. Seeing her upset hurt me. She'd been through so much. After what felt like the longest day, I tucked Ms. G. back into bed and trudged home for a long shower.

The house was quiet. Leticia had taken another night shift at the hospital, and Darnell said he'd be at the movies with a friend. Happy to decompress, I threw my purse and keys on the kitchen table.

Exhausted, I exhaled.

I pulled out the business card Alessandro had given me the first time I met him at the deli. I walked toward the phone. It rang before I reached it. It was probably Darnell, asking if he could extend his curfew.

"Let me guess. You want to stay out later, right?"

Someone breathed on the other end of the line. A deep voice said, "Tell your son he owes me money. If I don't get paid soon, Imma kill him."

I drew in a sharp breath. "What money? Who the hell is this?" I fired back.

"He knows who this is." The man's voice blazed. "I know where you live. You better get me my money, bitch!"

"Don't ever call this house again, and stay away from my son," I shouted. There was no answer, only a dial tone.

My stomach jumped into my mouth. Oh, God. What trouble had Darnell gotten himself into? Receiver in hand, I fell to the floor and pulled my knees to my chest. *This can't be happening.* I trembled in the fetal position while the dial tone echoed through my not-so-safe house. Darnell and I would have a serious conversation the minute he walked through the door.

I woke to the sound of the door slamming shut. My alarm clock displayed three a.m. I grabbed my robe and charged out of bed. As I approached the kitchen, Darnell stood there, his body swayed left to right. His eyes were red, and his breath reeked of liquor and pot.

My heart sank to the pit of my stomach.

"What in the hell is going on, Darnell? Where have you been?"

"Out. At a movie," he slurred.

"I don't like your new friends. It's three in the morning. You weren't at any movie. Don't lie to me," I clipped and tried to steady him. "Someone called today saying you owe him money and threatened both of us. What kind of trouble are you in?"

He laughed, then burped. "I'm not in trouble. I don't know what you're talking about."

"Tell me the truth. What's gotten into you?"

"Nothing. Just having some fun."

"There are other ways to have fun. Getting high isn't one of them."

"Well, tonight I tried all of 'em," he stuttered, then laughed.

"I might be able to help you if you tell me. The man on the phone said he will kill us if you don't pay."

"Someone's messin' around. Stay out of my business."

"Who would mess around like that?"

"Who knows." Darnell grabbed his stomach.

"Are you okay?"

"No." He bent over and moaned. He ran to the bathroom and threw up.

I helped Darnell to bed. A sheen of sweat coated his skin. His eyes closed as his body passed out. I pulled out the bleach and cleaned the vomit off the toilet. The memory of the man's voice made the hairs on my neck stand up. How much did he owe?

I mapped out my son's gene pool in my mind. Would Darnell turn out like his father? I couldn't allow that to happen. I'd talk to Darnell before I left for Ms. G.'s house.

I'd have to set some ground rules. Maybe Leticia was right—it was time that he got a job. That way, he wouldn't have so much time on his hands to hang out with his new loser friends. I'd do everything in my power to keep my children away from any more harm.

I pulled the blankets over Darnell's clammy body and shut off the light. With watery eyes, I plopped myself back into bed. Tomorrow would be another long day.

Wait. Tomorrow is today.

To make matters worse, Alessandro would be here again, tormenting me with his dangerous blues and his Mafia magic.

I sat up quickly. With all the commotion, I'd forgotten to call him. What was he planning? I couldn't handle any more stress. With a pounding heart, I laid my head on my pillow. Perfect, just perfect. Another near-sleepless night.

I peeked into Darnell's room before I left for Ms. G.'s. He was still passed out, and his room reeked of a night's worth of bad decisions.

Knowing there was no chance we'd have a meaningful conversation in his state, I locked the house and checked in on my other patient. I opened the door quietly and found an angry Ms. G. tapping on her watch.

"Where you been?" Ms. G. snapped. "You're late."

"I have a good reason. I hardly slept."

She huffed and sat in her recliner.

"Look at you, back to your old snarky self again." I smiled, then walked over and kissed the top of her head. That was one of the perks of her disease. Her mind erased things.

As I took her vitals, my hands wouldn't stop shaking. I kept looking over my shoulder every time I heard a noise, unsure if it was Alessandro or the voice on the other end of the phone.

"What's with you today? You're acting like the feds are following you. And I should know."

I placed my stethoscope around my neck. "Oh, it's nothing, really. I have a lot on my mind."

"Oh yeah? Like what?"

I avoided her stare.

"Spill it, kid. Maybe you'll feel better if you tell me."

"For starters, Darnell came in drunk at three a.m."

A small laugh escaped her lips. "Not my sweet boy, Darnell. He's a good kid. I hope you weren't too hard on him. But if he keeps acting up, I have a nice strap somewhere. My father used it on us from time to time."

"I don't need a strap. I'm worried he's getting involved with the wrong people. Some guy called the house and made threats."

"What kinda threats?" Ms. G.'s hands balled into fists.

"He said that Darnell owes him money and that if he doesn't pay, he'll kill us both."

"Why don't you take matters into your own hands? I got a spare twenty-two around here somewhere." She looked around the room. "It's a pretty good shot, and it can fit in your purse. You know how to shoot a gun, honey? I can teach you if you want."

"No. No guns. But I do have to protect my son." Tears welled in my eyes.

"No one messes with my family. Maybe it's time I make a call." Ms. G. grabbed the phone next to her.

I placed my hand over hers before she could pick it up. "Don't even think about it. I don't want any more problems. This might get dangerous."

Ms. G. giggled. "Dangerous. Ha! That's a laugh. You handle your problems your way, and I'll handle them mine. This is why you need a gun."

"No, I don't. I can take care of this myself. No calls."

"All right, all right, no calls." Her voice trailed off slightly. "But you never said I couldn't *tell* anyone who visits, right?"

I shook my head.

"*Maronn*, okay, okay," she yelled and put her hands in the air. "And what about these friends you talk about? Do they drive a hot rod kinda car?"

"I don't know, why?"

"I heard a car pull up last night and some kids laughing and talking loudly. When I went to the front window, I saw a red car. By the time I grabbed my gun and went outside, they were already gone."

"The next time you think you wanna grab your gun, call me first. My number is written right next to the phone. I put it there when I moved into the big house, remember?"

With a blank stare, she looked down at the phone.

"See? It says 'Barbara, dial 1.'" I pointed to the telephone.

"Why do I need to call you if I get my gun? If some son of a bitch wants to wake me up, then they're gonna be greeted by my Winchester."

"What if you had accidentally shot Darnell?"

"Then tell those damn kids not to drive like maniacs around here. I like it quiet," she scoffed, then grabbed the TV remote.

"Will do," I said in a frosty tone. "You know, if you keep acting this way, wanting to shoot everyone, I'm going to have to hide your guns."

"The hell you will," she fired back. "No one touches my gun. Only me and Mama. You got that?"

"I'll do whatever's necessary to keep you and my family healthy and safe. That's my job. Always has been. That's what I was hired to do."

She looked back at the phone again.

"Go ahead. Call Sofia. I'll tell her how you're going around here with your gun, threatening to shoot people. I don't think she'll like that, do you?" I pulled my shoulders back.

Ms. G. glowered at me. "You know, you can be a real pain in the ass."

"I learned from the best," I said with a smile.

Ms. G. threw her hands in the air and started cussing in Italian. Then she grabbed the remote and turned on *Judge Judy*.

I sat next to her. "Can we watch something else?"

"No."

I took a deep breath and crossed my arms over my chest.

"You got hormones or somethin'?" she asked. "Why you being so sassy today?"

"I'm fine. Actually, no, I'm not fine. I have a son who's getting involved with the wrong people. I'm praying that he's not going to turn out like his father, and, well . . ." I touched the edge of my scar. "I think your godson, Alessandro, is coming over here later. He wants to take me out, but I can't leave you right now with everything that's going on."

"Sure you can. I'm fine."

"No, you're not," I said. Guilt flooded me.

"Yes, I am, damn it."

"After what happened yesterday? No, you're not," I said firmly.

"What happened yesterday?"

I made sure not to bring it up again. I didn't want her to relive it. "Nothing, it was a long day. You were exhausted."

Ms. G. got quiet and ignored my words. "Look honey, Darnell's gonna be fine. You can't blame him. He's seen a lot. You guys might need to go to one of those head shrinkers or somethin'. As for that scar you keep touching, I have scars too." She placed her fingers under the hair behind her ear, revealing a thick mass about three inches long from the top of her ear to the back of her skull.

I'd seen it when I'd bathed her, but never asked about it. I didn't know if it was Frank's handiwork.

"See, kid, things happen. We both have scars to remind us of our pasts. But that is exactly it—the past. We can't change who we were, but we can change who we become."

"How did it happen?"

"Frank did it during one of his drunken tirades. He hit me and banged my head on the bathroom vanity. A few stitches later, and this is all that remains. When Frank took me to the hospital, he threatened he'd do worse if I told the doctor what happened. So, I lied, as most survivors do. I told the nurse that I'd slipped on the bathroom floor. They bought it. I had a massive headache for days, and Frank was in the clear—*again*. That *stronzo* piece of shit."

When she said his name, I wondered if it jarred some kind of memory from yesterday, possibly jolting her back into a whirlwind of feelings. With little sleep, I had no energy to probe. But there was no flicker of remembrance. She continued to watch TV.

"So, you say my godson is coming over? When?" she asked with wide eyes.

"I don't even know if he is coming. If I'm honest, I'm not sure I want him to. I didn't get much sleep," I huffed, then looked out the window. "Hey, instead of watching *Judge Judy*, let's go outside for some fresh air. It would be good for you."

"Sounds good, kid. I want to check on Mama's roses," she said, and I helped her outside. I glanced at the gate for any signs of an intruder or the sight of a man who took my breath away in an instant. Both weighed heavily on my mind.

After a day of gardening, Ms. G. was tired. To get out of the sun, we retreated inside. I sat her down and gave her something cold to drink when I heard a knock at the door.

My chest tightened.

"If it's a solicitor, tell them to go away."

My blood pressure rose. "I don't think it's a solicitor." I walked slowly to the front door and peered out the peephole. It was Leticia. Surprised, I opened the door.

"Hey baby, you all right? You need something?"

"I'm fine. I'm here to relieve you."

"What do you mean, relieve me? Where am I going?"

"Out."

"Huh?"

Within seconds, a sleek black Mercedes sedan with tinted windows pulled up. Leticia walked past me with a smile on her face.

"Hello, Violetta," Leticia yelled down the hallway. "Tonight, you're gonna teach me how to play five-card stud."

"Get over here, cutie, and give me a hug," I heard Ms. G. say. "I feel like I haven't seen you in ages. You need to eat. You look like a rail, and it's no surprise with your mother's cooking. I'll make us some ravioli."

"Don't even think about it, Ms. G," I hollered from the front door, still staring at the mysterious Mercedes.

The car door swung open, and Alessandro got out in a dark gray suit. He shut the door and hit a button on his keys. Holding two bouquets in his hand, he walked toward the front door. His mirrored sunglasses obstructed my view of his eyes, but it was him—all of him.

"Hello, gorgeous." He pulled off his sunglasses and placed them in the inside pocket of his suit. His eyes welcomed me with their magic and were accompanied by a brilliant smile.

"Um, hello." I pulled my bangs down over my forehead.

"These are for you." He handed me one of the prettiest bouquets of pink flowers I'd ever seen. "They're peonies. For you and *Zia* Vi, only the best."

"Thank you. My kitchen table looks like a florist shop." I smiled at his gift.

"May I come in?"

"Yes." I smelled the fragrant flowers. "Nice car."

"Yeah, I suppose it's a big change from the catering van. I don't always wear a sauce-stained apron," he teased.

"Clearly." I admired his well-tailored suit.

"Sofia called me and told me about *Zia*. How she doin' today?" His brows drew together as he crossed the threshold.

"Better, I think," I stammered, mesmerized by his look. His hair was lightly gelled with a slight flick in the front. Light stubble covered his face. His scent filled the air around me. "She doesn't remember any of it."

"That's good."

"So now you know why I can't go out with you. She needs medical supervision."

"We'll see about that."

"What do you mean?"

"We have reinforcements."

"Reinforcements?"

As if to ignore my question, he said, "I hope she hasn't eaten yet because I have the guys coming over to bring a full-course meal from the deli."

"She hasn't eaten dinner yet."

"Good. So, if you decide you don't want to go out, I told you I'd bring the date to you." He walked past me down the hall.

"What do you mean, *date*?" I closed the door and followed him to the living room where Ms. G. hugged her godson.

"You're looking good, kid." She patted his face with her liver-spotted hands.

"So are you, *Zia*."

"Ah, bullshit. I'm an old lady."

"These are for you." Alessandro handed her the other bouquet.

"I'll get a vase." Leticia walked to the kitchen.

"Well, thank you." Ms. G. smelled the flowers. "See, Barbara? He knows how to treat a lady." Ms. G. smiled fondly at Alessandro.

"Wait. I'm not sure what's happening here, but I can't go on any kind of date with you. I can't leave her. Not after what happened yesterday." I looked at Alessandro.

"What happened yesterday?" Leticia interrupted while arranging Ms. G.'s flowers.

"I'll tell you later," I said to Leticia.

"Yeah, what happened?" Ms. G. asked.

"Nothing." I shook my head at Leticia and Alessandro.

"So, you gonna take my Barbara somewhere good tonight? You'd better," she scolded. "She deserves a fun night out."

"I'll take her wherever she wants to go," he replied to his aunt. "Or we can stay here and play a game of poker." He looked at the deck of cards on the table. "I've heard I have a pretty good poker face." He flashed a flirtatious smile.

"In this family, I'm sure you do," I replied, not caring if he caught on to my accusation.

"No way. You need to take her out," Ms. G. chimed in.

"Yes, Mama. It'll be fine. Show me where her pills are before you go."

"Wait a minute, how did you know he was coming here?" I asked Leticia as she shuffled the cards.

"I think I should answer that," Alessandro interrupted.

This ought to be good.

A coy smile edged at the corners of his mouth. "I wanted to get permission from your children before I whisk you away. So, I found out where Leticia works and went to the hospital. We had a good conversation, didn't we, Leticia?" Alessandro said, then turned back to me.

"Yes, we did, and you *so* have my approval," Leticia said behind Alessandro's back with two thumbs up, then dealt the cards.

Mafia men—master manipulators. He was good. Very good. "So, how'd you find out where she works?" I asked.

"I have my ways."

I remembered hearing those words from Sofia's mouth the day she offered me the job. "Your ways, huh? I've heard that before."

"If it makes you feel better, I'll have the guys stick around for a while to help keep an eye on her. Just in case. I want you to feel safe. But if you'd rather stay here, I'm fine with that too. Even with your daughter's and *Zia's* supervision if you want. I'm at your disposal. Whatever you want, the sky's the limit," he said as the light in his eyes shined straight through my heart.

I licked my lips and took a breath. "I don't know."

"What's one date, Mama? Violetta's in good hands. I'm gonna be a doctor, remember? Stop worrying."

"*Maronn*, what else do we have to say to get you movin'? Go get dressed already," Ms. G. prodded, staring at the cards in her hands.

I clutched the flowers. "I guess. If you have the guys stick around, that would be good," I said, thinking about the prank caller. I was pretty sure anyone who worked for Alessandro would kill anyone who tried to get in here. That's what Mafia guys did. I looked down at my clothes. "I'll need to shower."

"Take all the time you need. I'll be over here playing cards. If you're up for it, I'd like to take you to the city for dinner. I know a great spot."

"Daylight's wasting," Ms. G. yelled from her recliner.

"Go get ready, and I'll be by in an hour," Alessandro said.

I nodded and looked at Ms. G. and Leticia. "Are you sure?"

"Yes, damn it. She's sure. Now go." Ms. G. slammed down her cards. "Full house. Read 'em and weep."

Chapter 15
First Dates

WHILE ALESSANDRO PLAYED CARDS WITH HIS AUNT, I PULLED Leticia aside and explained what had happened to Ms. G. the previous night and where her pills were. I told her to try and keep her calm and, most importantly, not to let Darnell leave under any circumstances. I informed her of the prank call and to hang up if she didn't recognize the voice.

With a bottle of aspirin on his bedside table, Darnell continued to sleep it off. Thankfully, Alessandro's crew would be here to keep watch while we were gone. And with the newly installed security fence and cameras, Darnell was safer here than anywhere else. I shut his door and turned on the shower.

After five dress changes, I settled on a teal dress that was hidden in the back of the closet. Luckily it still fit. I liked it because it wrapped around my shoulders, but mostly because the color reminded me of his eyes.

I'd found the dress in one of those fancy shops in the mall when I'd gone to buy more makeup to cover up my bruised cheeks. It stuck out in memory because it was one of the few dresses I'd bought myself when I was with Marcus. I felt strange in a dress. For years, my only attire was medical scrubs and sweatsuits that I'd found at a second-hand store by my old house. Money was always tight with Marcus, and the kids had to eat, so I usually went without nice things.

I stared at myself in the mirror. For the first time in a long time, I felt sexy. A small smile crept its way across my face until I saw my scar. I fell back onto the bed with my hands over my face. *What am I even doing?* Maybe I should tell him to wait a few weeks, until after the first surgery. Then maybe I wouldn't be so self-conscious.

Stop it. If he's interested in me, he'll like me—scars and all.

I grabbed for my compact and continued to apply generous amounts of makeup to my face, then scrunched my curls so they dangled over my forehead. For the final touches, I sprayed on some perfume and added a layer of lip gloss. I slid on my heels, then heard a knock at the door.

Showtime.

I smacked my lips together and gave myself one last look. *Forget about the scar and all the makeup. How about the fact that you're going on a date with a Mafia boss?* The minute I walked out of this house, I'd be taking my first real step into this life. There would be no turning back. Butterflies swarmed my stomach.

"Coming," I yelled. I walked down the hall to the living room.

"Mom," Darnell yelled. "Mr. Sunseri's here for you."

I walked in and listened to the two of them talk.

"Sorry I haven't answered you about the job. I still haven't talked to Mom about it. I'm kind of in trouble," Darnell said with a froggy voice.

"Trouble, huh?" Alessandro said.

"I thought you were sleeping." I bent over and kissed Darnell's head. "Yeah, he's in big trouble."

"You look amazing." Alessandro teased a tantalizing grin.

My cheeks warmed.

"We're going out for a bit. Your sister is next door sitting with Ms. G. I'll be home later. There's food in the fridge. Don't even think about leaving this house after last night. You're grounded until further notice. Alessandro's going to have some of his crew deliver food here tonight. They may stick around a bit, so I'll know if you try and sneak out. And your sister's watching the cameras just in case you thought you were slick. At some point, we'll need to talk about what happened. I'll need the keys to your car."

Alessandro gave me a strange look.

"I'm not going anywhere. I still feel like crap." Darnell rubbed his stomach.

"That's what happens when you drink too much, son."

"Before we go, I'd like to talk to Darnell, if you don't mind," Alessandro asked.

"Why?" Darnell's brows drew together.

"Don't worry, you're not in trouble with me," Alessandro joked. "I wanted to make sure you were okay with me taking your mom out tonight. Since you're the man of this house, I want you to know that my intentions are honorable. I like your mom, and I want to get to know her better. If you're not okay with it, then I'd like to talk about it."

"I don't have a problem with you. I only have a problem with my mom grounding me. I'm too old to get grounded, don't you think?" Darnell asked, then glared at me.

"I can't get involved. She's your mom, and she makes the rules. I'd do what she says. But I'll talk to her," Alessandro said. "I can be pretty persuasive when I want to be." He shot me a gorgeous grin.

He wasn't lying. Here I was, about to go on a date with him. "I forgot my purse. I'll be right back, and then we can leave."

"Sure," Alessandro said.

When I returned, I grabbed Darnell's keys from the kitchen and put them in my purse. Darnell and Alessandro laughed and talked about sports. It felt nice to see my son smile again. In the short time I'd known him, Alessandro had that same effect on me.

"Ready," I said.

"Darnell, it was nice talking to you. Maybe one day soon we can catch a game sometime. I have season tickets for the Niners."

"That'd be cool," Darnell answered with a smile.

"Sounds good. We'll plan it. But I can't take you if you're grounded, so you gotta keep your nose clean."

"Yeah, I know. I only had a few beers." Darnell looked back at me.

"A few beers? You reeked of pot and threw up half the night," I said in a reprimanding tone.

"He's a good kid. He knows better now. Don't you, Darnell? Remember what I told you. Two aspirin every two hours. Believe it or not, a greasy cheeseburger has been known to cure many hangovers. I bet you're hungry since you don't have anything in your stomach."

"Greasy cheeseburger?" Darnell wrinkled his nose.

"I'll have the boys bring one over when they come. The bread soaks up all the booze. You'll be all right, kid. And don't worry about the job. It'll be there if you decide you want it."

Darnell nodded.

"Be good, son." I pressed a kiss to his forehead and grabbed my sweater. "If anything happens, call 911 immediately. You hear me?"

"Yes, Mom, nothing's gonna happen. It was someone messin' around."

"We'll talk about it tomorrow," I said and walked to the front door.

With his hand on my lower back, Alessandro escorted me from the house. "Everything okay?" Alessandro turned to ask.

"Someone called the house saying things . . . I don't know. For all I know, it might have been a prank call, but there was something about the man's voice that I can't shake."

"What did he say?" Alessandro asked as we walked through the yard.

"He said Darnell owed him money and that if he didn't pay, he'd . . ."

"He'd what?" Alessandro grabbed my arm so that I'd face him.

"Kill us."

His jaw tightened. He took a deep breath and said, "I'll never let that happen," then ushered me through the gate.

We walked to his car and he opened the passenger door. "Here you go."

"Thank you." I sat on the black leather seat. I waited for him to get in the car, but he stood at the driver's side window, his cell phone to his ear. I couldn't hear what he said, but he looked mad and shook his head a lot. He caught me staring at him and flipped his phone shut. He opened the car door. "Sorry, I didn't mean to keep you waiting." He unbuttoned his jacket and placed it on the back seat. "I had to make a quick business call."

"No problem. Everything okay?"

"Everything's fine. The boys are on their way. I ordered a few of *Zia's* favorites and a cheeseburger for Darnell."

"That was nice of you. I'm sure they'll be happy."

He turned to me. "Are you ready for a good time?"

"I'm here, aren't I?"

"I plan on spoiling you and pampering you all night."

The sting on my cheeks spread, and I looked down at my hands.

With his fingertips, he tilted my chin toward his face. "Do you know how gorgeous you look tonight? This dress . . ." His eyes raked over my body. "It's stunning on you."

We exchanged a heated glance.

"Thank you. I like the color." I moved my hands over the fabric on my thighs. "It reminds me of the ocean and . . . your eyes."

A warm smile laced over his lips. He brushed a strand of hair from my face and tucked it behind my ear. "Buckle up. We have a little drive ahead of us." He reached back into his suit pocket and put on his mirrored sunglasses.

I put on my seatbelt. Oddly, I felt safe with him next to me, which scared me even more. The Mercedes engine turned on, and we were off for a night I was pretty sure I'd never forget.

Chapter 16

Alessandro Salvatore Sunseri
Defender and Protector

THE SUN LOWERED AS WE DROVE ALONG THE 280-FREEWAY, AND the sky turned a brilliant shade of orange.

"What kind of music do you like?" he asked.

"I like lots of music."

He reached into the armrest compartment. "I have one that I think you might like." He inserted a CD. The singer's voice was soothing, and the emotion behind the words was infectious. I listened intently. Alessandro was bashful at first, only humming a few ballads. But as he got more comfortable, he sang along. His voice was beautiful: smooth, silky, and deep.

As he continued to sing, his tough Mafia exterior ebbed away. What remained was a man with a smile and a song. I closed my eyes and let the music distract me from my worries.

"I don't know what he's saying, but it sounds romantic in any language. Maybe one day you can translate it for me? You have a wonderful voice."

He turned the volume down. "My mother made me sing in Catholic school."

"Wow, a nice Catholic boy, huh?"

"Once upon a time. Thankfully, there's always confession, and I've confessed a few sins in my life." He half-smiled.

I chewed on his words, then spoke. "Sounds like we've both done some things we're ashamed of." *My sin was not leaving Marcus sooner and that our kids suffered from what they witnessed.* Guilt squeezed my stomach tight.

"Yeah, I guess we have."

We were more alike than I once thought. We'd both done things to survive that we weren't proud of—him by order of the Mafia and me by order of Marcus.

I began to see him in a new light. Sometimes, he'd take his eyes off the road to look at me. Between songs, he'd say something sweet and leave me breathless. Maybe I'd heard too many Mafia tales and was desensitized to it all, but when he looked at me with those eyes, I was pretty sure I'd forgive him for whatever he'd done—or would do in the future. And for a moment, I felt something I hadn't felt in a long time.

Uninhibited.

We drove up the steep hills of San Francisco. The city came to life around us. Alessandro smiled at me and opened our windows.

"Smell that? That's the ocean air. I love that smell," he said as a gust of wind whooshed around my face.

The breeze kicked up my hair. Reflexively I reached for my forehead and turned my face away from him. He grabbed my hand. My heart pounded in my chest.

He stopped at a red light. "It's okay. Look at me."

I turned my face toward him.

"How can I make you understand how beautiful you are?"

"I don't know, I..."

"When I see what he did to you." He lightly touched my forehead. "What he's done to your self-esteem. It makes me angry. When I look at you, I don't see your scar. All I see is you. I see your smile. I want to see your mind and heart next. Will you show me?" His knuckles grazed my cheek.

"Be patient with me."

"I will. I promise." His thumb grazed the back of my hand.

When the light changed, we continued toward North Beach. Alessandro pulled up to a building where a huge neon sign displayed the words *O' Sole Mio*.

"I've heard of this restaurant, but I've never eaten here. Is the food any good?" I peered up at the colorful sign over the entryway.

"I think so." Alessandro parked and got out of the car. I pulled down the visor and inspected my forehead one last time before he opened my door and extended his hand.

"Thank you." I straightened my dress.

"No, thank *you*." His breath whispered on my cheek as he pulled me close.

"For what?"

"For agreeing to go out with me tonight. I know you were nervous. I am too."

"You, nervous? How's that possible? You're the epitome of confidence. Look at you."

He caught me staring at his frame. He smiled and went silent. After a few seconds, he said, "I'm nervous because I don't want to screw this up."

His eyes became full of secrets. "There are things about me that I'm not proud of. I'm afraid that once you find out what they are, you might have reservations. I need you to know that my job and personal life are two separate things."

A gangster with a conscience? Isn't that some kind of occupational hazard? My eyes fixed on his face. "I guess you'll just have to prove it."

He stared at me with unwavering focus. "Oh, I intend to."

He opened the glove box. There it was—his gun. He quickly put it at his waistline, then grabbed his jacket and put it on.

My pulse quickened, and I licked my lips. Of course he had a gun. He was in the Mafia. A reality I'd have to accept.

He scanned my reaction, grabbed my hands, then pulled them to his chest. "It's for protection. You don't need to be scared. You're safe with me, remember?"

With his warm hands around mine, I felt his heartbeat against his chest. "Yes," I mumbled.

"There can be some rough people out here in the city. Better to be safe than sorry."

"Do you always carry a gun? I mean, because you're in the . . . well, you know. I don't want to say it out loud." I looked around the parking lot.

"Not always. But I won't take chances with you. Not after you told me someone threatened you."

I looked down.

He tilted my chin to his face. "If it makes you feel better, I can leave it in the car, but I think you should trust me on this. Do you trust me, Barbara?" His voice was intense and shielding.

His protectiveness excited me in ways I didn't know existed. No one had ever shown me this level of concern. My breathing hitched. I tried to focus and collect myself. "You haven't given me a reason not to. So, yes, I trust you."

"Good." He grinned.

"But the night is young," I teased with a smile.

"That it is, and I plan to use every minute of it to dazzle you." He offered his arm. "Shall we?"

"Yes." I smiled back.

He escorted me to the entrance and opened the door. Everyone greeted him and shook his hand like he was a king.

"You must come here often. Seems like you know everyone."

"I have a lot of friends."

"I bet you do. Ms. G. says that a lot too."

"It helps to have a big family."

"That's what I've heard."

One brow shot up on his forehead. "I have a feeling you've heard many things about my family and me." He looked amused.

"Your table is ready, *Signor* Sunseri," said a host in a black tuxedo. "This way, please."

"*Grazie*, Paolo."

People stared at us, mainly Alessandro, as we walked past the dining area into a private room that had a partial view of the city. The other walls were lined with wood paneling, giving it an old-fashioned feel. A table for two sat in the middle of the room.

"*Signora*." Paolo pulled out my chair and handed me a menu.

Once I was seated, Alessandro sat across from me.

I looked down at the beautiful presentation. Crystal stemware was arranged on a fancy linen tablecloth and twinkled in candlelight, giving the room a warm glow.

"*Paolo, per favore portaci una bottiglia di Dom Perignon. Grazie.*"

"*Sì, certo, signore.*" Paolo nodded at Alessandro and left the room.

"Champagne?" Alessandro asked.

"That's a pretty fancy bottle of champagne. What's the occasion?"

He let out a light laugh. "You. Only the best when you're with me. It's time that you're cared for in the right way. And I mean in *all* ways," he said suggestively. A wolfish grin spread over his face. His blue eyes burned into me.

I looked away to avoid his penetrating gaze.

Within moments, the waiter returned with a metal tub filled with ice and a bottle of Dom Perignon.

"Perfect timing." Alessandro said.

Paolo opened the champagne. The loud pop echoed through the room.

"I'll take it from here, Paolo."

"I'll be back to take your order."

"*Grazie.*"

"Enjoy, *Signore.*" Paolo left the room and shut the door.

Isolated. This must be the place where Alessandro hosted sit-downs.

"This is nice."

"I like this restaurant a lot." He poured the bubbly into our glasses, then lifted his. "Cheers, *cent'anni.*"

"Cheers." I clinked our glasses together. I took a sip. Tiny bubbles popped on my tongue and rolled down my throat. "What does *cent'anni* mean?" I asked in my best accent.

"It means a hundred years."

"One hundred years?"

"Yes, and I don't know if that will be enough time."

"Enough time for what?"

"To count the variations of your smile." He reached over the table and gently rubbed his thumb over my bottom lip.

I recoiled slightly when his fingers touched my lip.

"I hope you don't mind. There's a tiny drop of champagne."

I pulled my hand up to his with my napkin.

"It's gone now. I got it." He smiled and rubbed the moisture of champagne and lip gloss between his fingers. "You don't need to be afraid of my touch," he said in a husky voice. He rubbed a finger over the back of my hand and gauged my response. When I didn't move, a seductive grin tugged at the sides of his mouth.

I took a deep breath. "So, Alessandro. Your turn to tell me about you."

"What do you want to know?" His eyes peered through dark lashes while he scanned my face.

"For starters, your name. Alessandro. It sounds exotic. I've never heard it before. Is it a traditional name?"

"My full name is Alessandro Salvatore Sunseri. Alessandro is Italian for Alexander. My father wanted me to be his namesake. But my mother said the moment she saw me, she wanted to name me after Alexander the Great." He laughed and waved it off. "Salvatore is Salvador, which was also my grandfather's name. It means the protector of all men and the defender, or something like that." Another laugh escaped his lips. "My mother was weird like that." His bottom lip trembled slightly. "She died a few years ago—cancer."

"I'm sorry to hear that," I said, witnessing his pain.

"I don't like to talk about it much, but she was one of a kind. Mom was *Zia's* cousin. That's how we're related."

"She must have been very special."

"She was." His lips relaxed into a warm smile. "Well anyway, she thought our names represented who we'd become."

Oh man, was she right. He sure looked *great* to me. *Great* and a *protector*? "Oh really, that's interesting." Of course, that would be his name. One more reason to find him attractive and irresistible. A protector. I looked down at my St. Christopher's medal that was given to me after my past client died. *Mrs. Passarelli, are you sending me a sign?* "Protector, huh?"

"Yes, I protect what's mine."

"I know you said I could call you Alex when I first met you, but I prefer Alessandro. I like the way it falls off my tongue. *Alessandro.*" I paused on the *S*. "I have to concentrate when I pronounce it. It's sexy."

"Sexy, huh?" He reached over the table and held my hand. His gaze lingered on my eyes. "I know what it means to have to concentrate on something. I concentrate a lot when I'm with you. Sometimes I can hardly contain my thoughts."

"Oh really? What are you thinking about?"

"Lots of things . . ." His thumb glided over the back of my hand as he studied it. "Like how I can't keep my eyes off of you, among other things . . ." He looked down at the table. "Things that might not be appropriate for a first date."

"Is this just sex for you?" I asked, curious about his answer.

"You are straightforward, aren't you?"

"At this point in my life, I can't afford not to be. I thought that's what you liked about me."

"I do." He smiled approvingly. "In my line of work, you don't know how refreshing that is. Now, let me be honest with you." His face became suddenly serious. "Sex is the easy part of a relationship, but falling in love with someone's soul? That's entirely different. It's delicate and requires time. And I want to get to know your soul, Barbara. So no, sex is not all I want. I'd be lying to you if I said I hadn't thought about it with you. I mean, look at you. You're sensational."

"Thank you," I said, still unsure how to handle compliments like that. "I appreciate you being patient with me. I'm not used to this. I haven't been on a date in a long time, and after what happened . . ."

"You don't have to explain. When I decided to get involved with you, I knew what that would mean for both of us. You'll never be a one-night stand to me—ever. You're different. I want you to feel comfortable, and I want you to trust me. I know that takes time, and I have all the time in the world for you."

"Thank you." I blushed again.

"Tell me about yourself, and not just the generic stuff. I want to know about your hopes and dreams. Places you want to see, your passions, and what gets you up every morning. I want to hear everything," he said. "It's a five-course meal, so we have plenty of time. Have you decided what you want to eat yet?" His eyes were wide with interest.

Alessandro, how can you be so wonderful yet such a bad boy at the same time?

"So, what will it be?" he asked, interrupting my thoughts.

"I think I'll go with the ravioli."

"Good choice. It's fantastic, but I'm probably biased."

"Why's that?"

He hesitated. "I own the place."

My jaw dropped. "This is *your* restaurant?"

"Yes. I have a few others like this around the Bay Area, but this one was my first. I wanted to take you here for sentimental reasons."

"I had no idea." I looked around the room with different eyes. "I'm impressed."

"I learned a lot from my father about the restaurant and catering business, but I wanted to do something bigger, so I invested some of my money, and here I am. Having a business degree also helps."

"Where did you go to school?"

"Santa Clara. I almost didn't graduate, though. I was so busy tending to the deli and other family business . . . that my grades suffered."

"Oh." I sighed, then took another sip of champagne. The kind of business he spoke about had nothing to do with restaurants.

"Yeah, I'll never forget. My father threatened to kill me if I didn't finish. Said he'd spent his whole life working hard to provide me an education, and there I was, blowing it off."

"Kill you?" I croaked.

Alessandro laughed, "My dad was a legend back in the days, but he didn't mean it. Someone else maybe, but not his son, unless . . ." His words trailed off.

"Unless what?"

"You ever see *The Godfather*?"

"Yes.

"Remember what happened to Fredo?"

"Are you serious?"

"I'm kidding. You should've seen the look on your face." He laughed. "Jokes aside, I got involved with things my father had always tried to keep from me. He didn't want me caught up like he was, but the life always finds you."

I looked at the door to make sure no one was coming before I spoke. "How long have you been working for the *family business*?"

His eyes narrowed, and his face got serious. "It's a little early for this conversation, but I knew it would come up eventually. I'm bound by life not to say anything, and I'd deny everything if questioned, but if I want you to trust me, I guess I will have to trust you for this to work." He eyed me cautiously.

"You don't have to tell me anything. I don't want to cause you problems."

"You aren't causing problems. But it's silly to dance around the subject any longer. I want to be as honest as I can with you, and I say *can* because there are lots of things I *cannot* and *will not* share."

I listened intently.

"If you're to get involved with me, that will have to be enough for you. But I know that if we're going to see more of each other, there might be things that come up in conversation that might make you feel uncomfortable. I think you know what would happen if you were to tell the wrong people. Do we understand each other?"

"I understand." I cleared my throat.

"I'm also fairly certain that my godmother, even with her wonderful heart, has said things to you—private things that shouldn't be discussed outside the family. With her condition, how can you blame her? I can't even call her a rat. It's her disease that makes her say the things she says."

I put my head down in response.

Alessandro grabbed my hand firmly in his. "Don't do that. Look at me, please."

I met his eyes.

"See, this is what I was worried about—that look. I don't want you to be afraid of me. That's the last thing I want after everything you've been through. You don't appear to be the kind of woman who can be lied to easily—not after living with an abusive alcoholic. Lying doesn't get you to trust me, does it?"

"No. It wouldn't. I don't like being lied to."

His candor was refreshing. These Mafia guys didn't mince words.

"Ask yourself if this is something you can accept. I'm not really *in* the life much anymore, but no one is *ever* truly free from it. The decision is, and always will be, yours."

"Since we're being honest, are you the one who beat up Marcus that night? He said a white deli van pulled up on him at the gas station. It was you, right?"

"What do you think? Trust your gut. You already know the answer." A devilish smile ribboned its way across his face. "Two parties at the same gas station at the same time. Maybe my guys needed gas? There's nothin' there. Or maybe he was in a blackout and doesn't remember what happened. He has a history of drug and alcohol abuse, does he not?"

"Yes."

"That's the answer my lawyer would give if we were ever to go to court. Sofia's my lawyer."

I took a deep breath. He'd never tell me the whole truth, but he'd told me enough.

"*The family* doesn't lose. We have resources at our disposal—even gas station security footage. Everything has a price."

I grabbed my glass of champagne and chugged it down. Every. Last. Drop.

We ate by candlelight. When I wasn't ruminating about what he'd said about Marcus and it being my decision to get involved with him, Alessandro made a joke to lighten the mood. Despite his comments about *the family*, he remained a gentleman, always asking questions about who I was and what I stood for. I told him about my life as a nurse and caretaker, my southern roots, places I'd love to travel, and my kids. He mentioned he had a son, but the topic seemed to hurt him, and he quickly changed the subject. When I spoke, he listened genuinely, then asked questions that sparked more engaging conversation.

Everything about Alessandro intrigued me. He told me of his love for fishing, his fascination with motorcycles, and the time he won the state boxing championship. He was smarter and more compassionate than I'd thought he'd be about social issues. He was a powerful businessman with an intense love for his family, and well versed in his beliefs. I was powerless against my growing feelings for him, and I wanted to know more.

While nibbling on dessert, the light from the candle flickered in his eyes. I studied Alessandro up close. Thick hair matched up with intense eyebrows against good skin, with a perfect nose and chin. And his fleshy lips—I'd never seen lips like his. They were in the shape of a heart. Soft and plump, they acted like curtains opening and closing against his perfect smile. I wanted to brush my fingertips over them.

When it was time to leave, he asked if we could take a quick detour before returning to the ranch. He wanted to show me something beautiful. To make me feel safe, he gave me his cell phone. We called to check in on Ms. G.

Leticia said she was fine and getting ready for bed. Before I hung up, Alessandro told Leticia that if she saw a few guys in catering vans in front of the house, not to be alarmed. He was always two steps ahead, doing everything possible to ease my anxieties. This must have been what he meant when he said, *'It's time that you're cared for in the right way.'* So far, he'd lived up to his name.

Alessandro escorted me through the main dining area and passed the bar. A man approached us. Alessandro pulled me toward him. Appearing unimpressed, the man looked me up and down. His top lip curled up in disgust as he looked back at Alessandro.

"Hey Alex, how you doin'? I tried to get a meetin' with you, but you haven't returned any of my calls." The man stepped toward me. The smell of alcohol was heavy on his breath.

"Back up, Mikey. You're drunk, old man." Alessandro pushed him back from us.

"And who do you have with you tonight?" The man slurred his words. "I didn't know they served chocolate pie here." His eyes scanned my body then he laughed as the vodka spilled from his glass.

Alessandro lunged forward, grabbed the lapels of his jacket, and stood him upright. Alessandro was in his face. "Hey! You watch your mouth. You're outta line. Don't ever talk about her like that again. You got that?" Alessandro seethed. Veins in his neck pulsed.

I stepped back, afraid the two men would come to blows.

"Hey, take it easy. I'm sorry," the man begged.

Alessandro lowered him to his feet and slowly let go of his jacket. "I never wanna see you in here again. Paolo, get him outta here," Alessandro demanded. Paolo came over and escorted the man to the front door. A few of the women around us started gossiping, shot me dirty looks, and whispered to themselves. Alessandro looked at them. "What are you looking at, huh? Mind your business. Come on, Barbara, let's go."

We drove over the Golden Gate Bridge in silence. Hues of silver moonlight cast over the bay. Cables of the famous bridge zoomed by as Alessandro drove with purpose. His fingers gripped the steering wheel, and his face was still red from the confrontation.

"You didn't have to do that."

"Yes, I did, and I'll do it every time. No one disrespects you. I won't have it." His eyes narrowed. "Mikey's a drunk old fool, and that mouth of his is gonna get him into trouble."

"Maybe we should go home," I said, disheartened.

"Go home? No way, we're almost there." He reached for my hand over the middle console.

"I was afraid of this. This is why my parents got divorced."

He tilted his head to the side.

"My father's white and my mother's black."

"I didn't know that. But it doesn't matter."

"Maybe we should stop now. People will talk. Society doesn't take well to interracial couples."

"I don't care what society likes. All that matters to me is what *we* want. Everyone else can go to hell."

"I'm trying to save us from future problems. Falling for a guy in the Mafia is problematic enough, don't you think?" I'd finally said the *M* word out loud. "And you—will you fight everyone who says something derogatory about us? Because there will be more. Trust me."

"I told you before. I protect the people I care about. I'll fight every last one of them if I have to. I will defend your honor no matter what."

"You shouldn't have to do that."

"Don't give up on this."

To avoid his reaction, I looked out onto the water again.

With his right hand, he gently reached under my chin and turned my face toward his. "Don't let others ruin this before we've even given it a chance," he pleaded. His voice dripped with concern.

After some hesitation, I nodded.

While we continued to drive, I fought a silent battle between my mind and heart. I wasn't sure which would win, but I hoped it was my heart.

"We're almost there," he said. "I'm glad you brought a sweater. It can be cold by the water."

We pulled into the town of Sausalito. I'd forgotten how cute and quaint the downtown area was. Big houses were nestled on cliffs overlooking the San Francisco Bay. On the other side were many waterfront restaurants and shops.

Except for the few people sitting in front of the restaurant windows, the town appeared quiet at night. With most of the shops closed, we parked along the main road. The San Francisco city skyline came alive. Lights from the Transamerica Pyramid and various other buildings stood out in the distance.

"I'm thinking of putting another restaurant here. It's a pretty great location. Less traffic, a few shops, and easier to park."

I looked at the line of restaurants that hovered over the ocean. "That's a great idea."

"It's a spectacular view of the city, isn't it?"

"It's breathtaking." I put on my sweater.

Alessandro opened my door and grabbed my hand to help me out.

Holding hands, we walked the cement path along the water's edge. There was a supreme lookout point past the shops. Cool sea air felt good on my flushed cheeks. I took deep breaths, remembering where I was and who I was with. I looked up at the night sky, comforted that the darkness shielded my scar from view.

Alessandro stopped and pointed to various points of interest in the distance. We looked out at the bay and sailboats docked to our left. Overhead was the brightest moon I'd ever seen. Ripples of silver washed up against the giant rocks in front of us, causing spray to mist our faces.

"I've never been here at night."

"We're lucky. There's no fog tonight."

"It's perfect."

Alessandro grabbed my hands and pulled my body close to his. "You're perfect. I wanna kiss you, Barbara. Are you okay with me kissing you?" he asked gently. "I want this with you. Let down your walls and let me in." He cupped my face with both hands.

His warm breath tickled my face, and our noses touched. I closed my eyes and met his lips with mine. They were as I'd imagined—soft and plump, like biting into a ripened peach. Tiny hairs of his stubble grazed over my chin. He grabbed the back of my neck to pull me closer, then claimed my mouth with his. His tongue was warm and thick like his body. My heart moved like crashing waves in my chest, and my legs felt like they'd come out from under me. But his arms held me in place.

For some reason that I couldn't explain, I felt safe in a man's arms for the first time in my life. I wanted him to hold me like this forever—to protect and shield me from my past hurts.

He provoked every one of my senses to spring to life simultaneously. It made me want his kisses that much more. Sweet and wet, we moved our mouths together until a gust of mist sprayed us.

We pulled our mouths apart in surprise.

"Are you all right? I hope that didn't mess up your dress." His eyes raked over my body.

I peered down at the tiny water spots that peppered my skirt, then back up at him. "Right now, I don't care about my dress." I grabbed him by his tie and pulled his muscular body back toward me, where I waited with parted lips.

Chapter 17

Under the Influence

My surgery date had come faster than I expected. I sat in my bedroom and stared at myself in the mirror while my head throbbed from the procedure. It was one thing to have a nasty scar but another for my forehead to be covered in gauze. I looked like a mummy. I grabbed my pain medication and swallowed two pills with a glass of water.

Thankfully, Dr. Padua said I wouldn't need a second surgery, and I'd be happy with the results. I hoped that Alessandro wouldn't come over. I didn't want him to see me like this, but something told me he'd drop by. He'd been by every day since our magical night in Sausalito.

The ranch became our shared place. It acted as a safe haven for us to explore our minds and hearts and offered a private escape from our pasts. It was the perfect place for us to connect on a deeper level, each of us dismantling our walls one brick at a time.

Some days, he'd sneak a kiss after working on the barn. Other days he'd make dinner, and we'd watch the sunset from the big house porch. Every time he came through the gate, a nervous excitement rang through me. He was becoming someone I counted on. My heart had grown for Alessandro.

He'd offered to take me to my appointment, but knowing my insecurities, he seemed to understand why I asked Leticia instead. But now that I was home, I was sure he'd arrive at any minute to check on me. I tried to ignore the slight ache in my head when the doorbell rang.

Yep. Right on time. Damn it. I don't want him to see me like this.

"I'll get it," Darnell yelled.

I jumped in bed, covered myself with a blanket, and pulled it around my face to hide my bandages.

"Hey, Darnell, how you doin'?" I heard Alessandro say from the kitchen.

"Fine. Mom's in her room."

"I thought I'd check in on her, if that's okay."

"That's fine. She's pretty out of it. The doctor gave her some pain pills," I heard Darnell say.

"I brought over some chicken soup. I'll put it in the fridge for her."

I heard his heavy feet walk down the hall. His gorgeous face appeared in my doorway.

"Can I come in?"

"I suppose. I'm resting." I pulled the blanket over my face.

"Hello, beautiful. How do you feel?"

"I have a headache, and my forehead throbs," I muffled under the blanket.

"Do you want some aspirin?"

"No, I took some pain meds. I should warn you I'm a lightweight. I'll probably be sleeping in an hour. But I hope this pain wears off by this afternoon. I have to relieve Leticia. She's been helping me out with Ms. G. today."

"I have a better idea. You stay in bed, and I'll watch *Zia*."

I peeked my face out slightly. "Don't you have work?"

"Don't worry about that. I have enough people on the payroll that it won't be a problem. Get some rest, and let me take care of you." He bent down to my face. "I can't see you with all these blankets. I'm trying to find those luscious lips of yours." He stood at the edge of the bed and pulled away the covers.

I caught his hand as he tugged.

"I don't want you to see me like this," I croaked out as tears welled.

"Oh, baby, stop that. You know how I feel about you. This bandage doesn't change anything."

I let go of his hand.

He removed the blanket and looked at me. A smile played at the edges of his mouth.

"I look horrible." I turned over, avoiding his stare.

"You don't look horrible. This is temporary. Don't cry. If me coming over makes you cry, then I'll go."

I turned to look at him. "You're so . . ."

"So what?"

"So sweet and so damn irresistible. I mean, look at you. You're freaking gorgeous. Have you looked at yourself in the mirror lately? You can get a thousand girls. Why do you want me?" I tried to focus my drugged-up eyes on his face.

"Yeah, but they don't have this." He leaned over me and placed his hand over my heart. "I see what you do every day. You care for others before yourself. Only people with big hearts do that."

"See, it's that kind of stuff. Where did you learn how to talk like that? Did they have charm class when you were in school? Like some book on how to get a girl in ten minutes or something?"

I sat up and placed my hands on his forearms to steady me while the room spun around us. "You're so smooth and gorgeous." I rubbed my palms over his arms. "You have such amazing eyes and soft lips." I grabbed his lips between my fingers. "And your butt," I said, reaching around to grab him. "I mean . . . this is a nice ass. It's a frickin' piece of artwork," I slurred my words.

He laughed, grabbed my hand off his butt, and pulled it to his chest. "How many pills did you take?"

"Two . . . maybe three. I can't remember," I stammered. Three of him stood before me.

"Get some sleep." He kissed my cheek and pulled the blankets back over me.

My eyes sprang open. It was dark in my room. Panicked, I looked down at the clock on my nightstand. It was eight p.m.

"Oh, Jesus." I sifted through bits and pieces of my conversation with Alessandro. My stomach flipped. *Did I grab his butt? Oh God, please tell me that was a dream. And what about Ms. G.?*

I jumped out of bed. Lightheadedness took over, and the whole room swayed. I grabbed for the nightstand to steady myself. Once the room stilled, I slid my feet into my slippers and made my way over to check in on my patient.

The house was quiet. Loads of photo albums and playing cards littered the living room table. I listened for voices and movement. Water ran from the bathroom faucet. I followed the noise to find Ms. G. in her nightgown, brushing her teeth.

"Oh, thank God. Whew," I huffed. "Are you here all by yourself?"

She looked at me with her toothbrush in her mouth then spit in the sink. "No. Alex is fixin' my bed. Where you been all day?"

I pointed to my forehead.

"What happened to you? Why you got that gauze hanging off you?"

"I had surgery today. That's why Leticia was here this morning. Then Alessandro said he'd come over and watch you."

"Watch me? Why the hell does anyone have to watch me? I'm not a baby," she fired back.

"Okay *Zia*, you ready for bed?" Alessandro's voice came from behind us.

I turned around to see those wonderful eyes staring back at me. "I'm sorry. I just woke up. How's she been?" I asked.

"Ya, you were pretty drugged up," Alessandro said. "I checked in on you, but you were snoring and drooling. I figured I'd let you sleep."

"I don't snore," I refuted.

"You do, but they were cute snores," he joked.

"Drool?" I asked, while feeling the side of my cheek, still caked with saliva. I wiped my face in front of him. "Those drugs did a number on me. Thanks for helping. I've got it from here."

"I can help her to bed. We had fun today, didn't we, *Zia*?" He walked Ms. G. to her room.

"Yes, it was good talking about old times again," Ms. G. said.

"Here, get in." He helped her into bed and covered her with blankets. "I love you. Sleep well. Next time I come, I'm gonna win my money back."

"In your dreams, kid," she laughed. "By the way, I forgot to tell you, the gnocchi was good, but make sure Ang keeps the sugar out of the sauce. Maybe next time you'll bring me some of his sausage and peppers. I miss that." Ms. G. nestled into her pillow.

"I will. Promise. Now it's time to go to bed." Alessandro kissed her on the cheek.

"Hey, wait, you forgot to open my window." She pointed at the small window of her room.

"She likes to have the window open to listen to the windchimes." I opened the window halfway. "Good night, Ms. G. I'll see you tomorrow." I followed Alessandro from the room. "Thanks for today." I closed the door.

"I don't have anywhere to be. I thought maybe we'd watch a movie or something. I brought you some soup from the deli. Have you eaten?"

"No, I haven't. As soon as I woke up, I rushed over here to make sure she was okay."

"We had a good time. She told me about the old days. Hey, now that I'm thinking about it, can I see what you've done with the basement? I remember it from when I was a kid, but it's kind of legendary."

"Sure. Let's walk over."

As I opened the door to the big house, Darnell was about to leave.

"Remember what I said, son. No drinking and be home by curfew."

"Yeah, I remember."

"I'm giving you a chance to prove I can trust you. Don't make me regret it."

"I know."

"Don't forget, you start work tomorrow. You wouldn't want to come in on your first day hungover in front of the boss, would you?" I reminded Darnell while looking at Alessandro.

"Thanks for the job, Mr. Sunseri." Darnell shook Alessandro's hand. "I'll be home by curfew, and I know . . . no drinking or smoking."

Darnell grabbed his keys and left.

"I can't thank you enough. After what happened to his father, Darnell's been displaying questionable behavior. He's been hanging around a new group of friends I'm not too keen on. We talked about therapy but haven't yet committed."

"Hard work builds character," Alessandro said. "Don't worry. I'll keep an eye on him."

There he was again, taking care of the people I loved. Comforted by his promise, I smiled. "He hasn't had a strong, positive male influence in his life."

"He'll be fine. I'll make sure of it."

"Thank you. Oh yeah, the basement. I almost forgot."

We walked down the steps into what was the notorious Giordano basement. I'd converted it into a workout room and office.

"Sorry for the clutter. I still haven't unpacked everything after the move." I pushed various boxes aside. Alessandro stood in awe and looked around.

"Wow, if I could've been a fly on the wall back in the old days. There are so many stories about this place." He brushed his hands against the walls. "I remember there used to be a table here where the men smoked cigars. You couldn't breathe from all the damn smoke. My uncles showed me how to load a gun right there." He pointed to the corner of the room. "To think of the things that were decided in this room. This is where the true Mafia existed. For you, I'm sure it's just a room. To me, this place is a museum."

"We never talked about what you do for them now. I don't think I even want to know. I don't want anyone I love to get hurt. My children are everything to me."

Alessandro turned and cupped my face in his palms. "I won't let anyone hurt you or your kids, ever. Like I told you before, there are things I can't say and won't say, but I'll do everything in my power to keep you from harm. Always."

"I saw you talking to Don Molanano at the funeral."

Unable to meet my gaze, his chin dipped down, then back up again. "He asked me to take care of a few things."

"Have you ever killed anyone?" I put my hands over my mouth. Curiosity got the best of me. The words were out before I could stop them.

His brows creased, and he grabbed my hands in his.

"Sorry, I know there are things you can't tell me." My heart pounded in my throat.

"All I *can* tell you is that the Mafia operates differently now. I've been trying to legitimize my and my father's business for years, but it's not easy. I've paid my fair share of costs in this life, one of them being my son." His gaze fell.

"You don't talk about him much."

"It's too painful. My ex-wife didn't like some of the things I used to be involved in. So, one day she left and took my son. As much as I wanted to use everything in my power to get him back, the truth was I didn't want this life for him either. One day, I hope they release their grip on me so that my son comes back into my life."

"I'm sorry to hear that. I hope he does."

"You're blessed to have both of your kids here under your roof. You have a wonderful family." A warm grin spread across his face.

"Thank you." I smiled back. "Oh, and sorry about earlier. I feel like such a fool. The pills. I'm such a lightweight."

"Yeah, you said some pretty crazy stuff." A light laugh escaped his lips.

"I did?" I clutched at my stomach ready to run to my room and lock the door from embarrassment. "Like what?" I asked, afraid of his answer.

"You told me your deepest, darkest secrets and the things you wanted to do with my body when we were alone. There was something about nipple clamps . . . It was hot." A naughty grin played at the ends of his mouth.

"Oh, God. I didn't." I threw my hands up over my gauze-covered face.

"No, you didn't." He pulled my hands away and kissed me. "I was only teasing." He laughed. "You did say I had a nice butt. And you grabbed it."

"So, it wasn't a dream," I whispered, feeling the sting on my cheeks.

"No, but I liked it." He winked. "I like seeing that side of you. You can grab my ass anytime you want." He took my hands, placed them on his butt cheeks and held them there.

My insides flamed as my palms held onto the thick flesh of his ass.

"You don't need to feel embarrassed. It's okay to touch me. I want you to tell me what you want. Your needs are my needs." His voice was thick with heat. "You don't need to hide that part of you from me anymore." With his hands on mine, he pulled our bodies together even closer. "Look at me."

I squirmed in his hold. "I have this huge thing on my head." I reached for the bandage.

"I don't care about that. I'm glad it doesn't cover your mouth," he teased, then came in for a kiss.

My pulse throbbed in my pelvis, then in my head. I released him.

"I'm sorry. Did I hurt you?"

"No. It's not you. It's time for another pain pill."

"Let's get some food into your stomach first. Then I'll let you get some rest."

We marched back upstairs and into the kitchen.

"When you're feeling better, how about you come to my place? I want to make you dinner." He flashed his perfect smile.

"That would be nice. But I'll have to make arrangements for Ms. G. She's my first priority."

Alessandro pulled me close. "I'd never do anything to make you worry or to endanger my aunt. If I can't get a plan together, I'll cook dinner for you both here." He pulled my hands up to his mouth and pressed a soft kiss. "My job is to make your day easier and happier, not harder."

"Okay." I exhaled.

"I'd like to do something for her," he said with a glint of excitement in his eyes.

"Like what?"

"I was thinking of getting some old timers over here to visit her. Like my dad and some of my friends from the old days. All the pictures she showed me today gave me the idea."

His need to make his aunt happy was evident, making him that much more attractive. "She'd love that," I beamed, then pondered a thought. "But not anyone who knew Frank. She despises that man, and for good reason," I added in a frosty tone.

"So, she *did* tell you some stories, huh?"

I turned away from his stare. "Some," I whispered, running my sweaty palms together. "But I promise I won't say a word. Your aunt's been through a lot. It makes me afraid for us and what this sort of life can do to people."

"Frank Di Natale was a flip-floppin' piece of shit. I'm glad he got whacked."

"Whacked? I heard he'd gone to jail, then went missing."

Alessandro's lips pressed into a line. "I don't know what happened. Stories circulated, but who knows? I wasn't there, so I can't say anything," he explained. "It's getting late. Let me warm up your food, then straight to bed. You need your rest." He placed a kiss on my cheek, then looked back into my eyes.

I nodded, and we walked back to the kitchen.

"I'll let you know what family and old-timers I can round up. *Zia's* gonna love it. You watch." He grabbed the soup from the fridge and put it in the microwave while I sat at the table.

"Yes, she'll be happy." I watched him move around my kitchen. It felt strange to be waited on. He grabbed a bowl and spoon from the cabinet and placed them down in front of me. I'm usually the one taking care of everyone else. Now, someone was taking care of me.

The microwave sounded. He poured the warm soup into my bowl. "Here you go."

"Thank you."

"You eat, and I'm gonna head out now. Sleep well, baby." He pressed a kiss to my cheek.

The phone rang.

"Want me to get it so you can eat?"

"No, it's fine, I'll get it," I said, worried it might be my mother. She'd be shocked to hear another man answer my phone. I hadn't told her about Alessandro yet. I walked over to the phone. "It's probably Ms. G. I programmed my number into her phone, and sometimes she likes to press buttons. I swear she tries to mess with me." I laughed.

"If she needs something, I'll go back over there so you can rest."

I picked up the receiver. "You all right, Ms. G.? You need me to come over?"

Alessandro stared at me, waiting for direction.

"This ain't Ms. G., bitch," the deep voice said.

My heart pounded out of my chest while I waited to hear what he said next, but the caller was silent. The only faint noise that came through was some heavy breathing. Then out of nowhere came a sound I'd heard only once before—when Ms. G. found Marcus on the ranch.

A gunshot.

"You hear that? Your boy's dead if he doesn't get me what he owes. He tried to get away from me the other night by hiding out in that deli, but his time's run out. You better talk to your son and get me my fucking money, or you'll be next!"

I gasped. Jumbling the phone in my hand, I cried out, "Who is this, God damn it? Leave us alone." The phone slipped from my hand. The long cord dangled from the mount on the wall.

"Who is it?" Alessandro rushed to my side.

Tears formed in my eyes. "It's him. The same voice as before. I heard a gunshot. He knows where I live and where Darnell works," I choked out.

Alessandro picked up the phone. "Who is this?" he asked and waited for a response, but there was none. His nostrils flared as he roared into the receiver. "Look, you fucking piece of shit. I don't know who you are, but if you even think of stepping foot here, you'll deal with me, you got that?"

His voice was tinged with rage—a rage I'd seen once before when we left the restaurant but had seen in Marcus many times.

"The son of a bitch hung up." Alessandro slammed the phone down. The sound of plastic hitting plastic echoed through the kitchen.

I stood stiff as a board, afraid of his reaction. His words said one thing, but what I witnessed was a different Alessandro. This was the Alessandro in the restaurant, ready to pounce, but there he'd had witnesses. Here, we were alone. Old habits made themselves known. I took a few steps back from him and stood paralyzed in my kitchen, afraid of what might happen next.

"Come here," he said. "You're shaking." He reached out his arms and held me tight as I trembled into his frame.

"You're scary when you're angry. This whole thing scares me."

He held my face in his hands. "On the lives of my family, I'll never hurt you. I'm here to protect you. You must believe that. I'm not perfect, and I have a temper when someone I care about is threatened. You aren't alone in this."

I took a deep breath. "I can't believe this is happening again. Living with Marcus and his gambling addictions, I used to get threats from banks and even loan sharks. I thought I was done with all this. Now Darnell . . ."

"Hey, you don't even know if it's some asshole messin' around. So, Darnell got a little drunk a few weeks ago. What high school senior hasn't? That doesn't mean he's into anything deep. Maybe it's just some asshole bully kid at school, talking shit."

"He shot a gun," I snapped.

"You sure it was a gun?"

"I'm sure. I've heard a gun go off up close," I explained with a lump in my throat.

"I'm sorry. Of course, you have." He pulled me close and whispered into my hair. "No one will harm you as long as I'm alive," he pledged with a voice so honest I couldn't ignore it. He placed a light kiss on my lips. "If you get any more calls, I want to know immediately," Alessandro insisted. "Maybe it's time we changed your number. Let's call the phone company in the morning."

"Okay."

"I'm gonna have a few of the guys drive by the ranch at night and on days I can't be here. Just in case."

"No, please. I don't want any more trouble for anyone," I begged and grabbed at his shirt.

"There won't be any more trouble. I promise," he whispered

into my ear. "You said Darnell had some new friends. Have you met them? Have they been in this house?"

"Yes, once. One of them said they had to meet with their probation officer. And Ms. G. said that a couple days ago, some red sports car sped off in the middle of the night."

"Did she get any plates?"

"No. She ran out with her gun, ready to shoot them, though."

"*Maronn. Zia's* got a temper."

"Tell me about it."

"I'll talk to her more tomorrow and see what she remembers—if anything."

"I don't think she'll remember, but you can ask."

"I'll check the security footage from the side gates. Do you think Darnell gave them the passcode?"

"I don't know. I can tell him not to."

"It may be too late. Do you think it's one of his friends?"

"I can't be sure. The voice on the phone was older, not a teenager."

"What about your ex? Has he been in contact? Any calls from jail? Are he and Darnell close?"

"There's been a few letters, but I usually find them in the garbage, unopened. From what I know, they haven't said much to each other since the incident. But Marcus *is* his father. No calls that I know of, but I'm at Ms. G.'s for most of the day."

Alessandro picked up his cell phone and dialed. "Hey Joey, I have a job for you. I need you to get some guys over here to watch my aunt's house. Call me back as soon as you get this." Alessandro ended the call and then put his phone back in his jeans pocket.

"What are you planning to do? Maybe we should call the cops?"

"No cops. I don't want them nosin' around here. They won't do anything anyway. They have nothin' to go on but some crank calls. And if Darnell's into something big, they'll investigate, and he could be arrested. You don't want that. You'll have to trust me on this. Let me handle things my way." He hugged me tight. "The last time I checked, the name Molanano still means something around here. I feel sorry for anyone who wants to test that theory."

The famous mob family I had feared for so long was here, ready to help me not once but twice. "Please be careful."

"The only one who needs to be careful is the person on the other end of that phone."

I nodded.

"As far as Darnell is concerned, I'll do some digging. Me and the boys will watch over him at work. I'll even have one of the guys follow him home. He'll be fine. Nothing's gonna happen to him on my watch." He placed a gentle kiss on my lips. "I'd like to give you a better kiss, but I don't want to hurt you."

"You've made it clear that you'd never hurt me." I pressed my lips to his for a proper kiss. His arms wrapped me like a warm blanket, cradling me with comfort. I wanted to stay like that forever.

He pulled away slowly. "You gonna be all right? I can stay longer if you want. I can sleep on the couch, and if anyone calls, I'll deal with it."

I was too proud to ask him to stay. "No, I'll be fine. Thank you for everything today. For letting me get some rest and watching Ms. G., for the food, and for looking out for us."

"No, thank *you*," he said, cupping my face in his hands. His sapphire eyes dimmed right in front of me. Seconds ago, they were fierce and full of wrath. Now they were tender and pleading. "You're changing me from the inside out, you know that? You're giving me a purpose again." He lightly kissed my cheek. "Don't worry about anything."

I laid my head on his shoulder but felt the instant pain from my surgery. "Ouch," I yelped. "In your arms I almost forgot." I put my hand up to my forehead.

He released me gently and searched my face, then tucked some hair behind my ear. "I'll stay with you until you fall asleep."

"Thank you," I whispered as the sound of the gunshot still rang through my ears.

Chapter 18
Surprise Guest

After much anticipation, Dr. Padua removed my bandage. The scar was much less noticeable, but like my time with Marcus and our turbulent life together, the memory was still there. Dr. Padua said it was up to me if I wanted another procedure done, but she couldn't guarantee I'd get a much better result. She gave me a follow-up appointment for three months to discuss further options.

When I returned home, Dr. Mancuso made a house call to check in on Ms. G. He was an old family friend and had been her doctor for years. Besides her father and now me, he was the only medical person she ever trusted.

We discussed her latest episode, and he agreed that her disease had progressed. Her medication was altered, and he and I set up a medical plan if she'd need more advanced therapies and further care.

Ms. G. complained of faint dizzy spells—something she'd never mentioned to me before, but if her stories told me anything, she was good at hiding things—a symptom of being a Mafia queen. It explained why she fell in the garden a few months ago. I'd made her use a cane to help with her ankle, but that could've masked her symptoms.

The doctor thought it might've been a case of vertigo from a possible inner ear infection, so he ordered some antibiotics and various tests to rule things out. He made a few recommendations about her diet and left. With this news, I'd have to watch her more carefully and look for signs of a possible stroke or heart problems. My experience as a caretaker told me that the next few months would be a challenge.

The next morning, I was up early to check on Ms. G. I helped her get dressed and served her breakfast. "You never told me you were dizzy."

"Big deal," she clipped.

"It *is* a big deal. I'm here to care for you, and I need to know when something is bothering you." I placed the blood pressure cuff around her arm for our daily checkup.

"Don't you know enough?" Ms. G. barked. "You watch me eat. You watch me take a crap. Hell, you know everything. I got no privacy. All I do is sit around here getting ready to die."

Sadly, I'd seen this many times with my clients. They felt vulnerable and dependent. For someone like Ms. G., the feeling of isolation made her feel like a caged animal. I'd have to do something to perk her up.

"You want to go out for lunch? Maybe take a drive to Goosetown? But we need to watch your salt intake. Too much sausage and peppers. Maybe a salad today."

"A salad?" She raised her voice. "Greens are for the goats. I'm not hungry, and I don't want to go anywhere. I'm tired." She reached for her crochet needle and yarn.

"How about a walk in the garden for some exercise?" I looked down at the blood pressure cuff. The reading was slightly elevated.

A nice walk would help bring it down. "After you eat your breakfast, I'll grab your cane and we'll go outside. Okay?"

She rolled her eyes.

I got up to put the cuff back in my bag. The doorbell rang.

"I'll get it."

"Who in the hell is it now? Tell them to go away," she snarled from the living room.

"Boy, did you wake up on the wrong side of the bed today," I said under my breath. I opened the door to a familiar face.

Sofia stood in her six-inch heels with two Louis Vuitton bags at her side. She waved away a black limousine and came toward me with open arms. "Surprise! I thought if I told you I was coming, you might tell my aunt."

"I'm pretty sure I've proven that I can keep a secret." I hugged her back.

A slight giggle escaped her lips as she lifted her black sunglasses on top of her head.

"Hey, isn't that Joey Flora in that van?" Sofia squinted into the distance, then waved. "Hey Joey, you coming in?" she yelled at the van. Sofia turned back to me.

"I think he's here because of me," I said as the man waved his hand at Sofia.

"Why, what happened?"

"Oh, it's nothing. Someone's been calling the house. Like prank calls. The last time they called, Alessandro was here. He thought it was best to have some guys watch the house for a while."

"My cousin can be protective."

"Very."

"After your call, I thought it was time I spent some time with my godmother, and I need her to sign some papers in the will. The estate now passes into her name."

"She'll be thrilled to see you. I should warn you now, she's been a little cranky today. The doctor adjusted her meds. She says she's been experiencing some dizzy spells."

"She's dizzy?"

"Apparently. She hadn't said a word until today. I haven't noticed any balance issues, but she uses her cane from time to time because of the fall. It may be an ear infection. The doctor ordered some antibiotics. But now that I know, I'll keep a closer eye on her. A salt-free diet should help reduce the risk of any blood pressure fluctuations."

"Okay. Well, you know best. Where is she?" Sofia looked down the hall.

"She's in the living room."

"*Zia*, I'm here," Sofia yelled and whisked past me with luggage in tow.

Sofia's energy changed things in the Giordano home. For the next few days, people I didn't know filled the house. Cousins, friends, and many older Mafia men who still wore three-piece suits with hats, ate, drank, and smoked cigars outside. When they weren't drinking and smoking, they'd sit around the table and tell old stories. The minute I entered the room to check on Ms. G., they'd change the subject.

Angelo and Alessandro stopped by and brought food from the deli. I'd asked them to make Ms. G. some healthier options, but she turned her nose up at the flavor and told Angelo he should close up shop because his food "stinks" now.

There were even a few intense poker games. Sofia promised she wouldn't let the guys stay too late, and it made Ms. G. happy, so I sat back and let her relish it. She was surrounded by *her* people telling stories in *her* home. The past few days made her look youthful, and I was extremely grateful for her visitors, mafiosos or not.

Alessandro made sure to introduce me to some of the biggest Mafia men that ruled San Jose, and when they talked about Ms. G.'s father, Giuseppe, it was like I knew him. They told me about the parties they'd had over the years, and I felt like I'd lived it through Ms. G.'s stories.

I met not only the older generation but their families as well. Some were realtors, teachers, and well-known businessmen. One guy was the chief of the fire department, and another was a famous singer who serenaded Ms. G. with Italian songs all night. I even met an author who wanted to write a story about the family. I wasn't sure how that would go, considering the pledge of secrecy required in this life, but if I ever saw it on a bookshelf, I'd probably buy it to see how true it was to the stories I'd been told.

On the surface, they looked like regular, law-abiding citizens, but with this family's history, if anyone knew the whole truth, it would be cause for alarm. They were friendly and welcoming to me, and that was all that mattered. Many of them thanked me for taking care of Ms. G. Sometimes, she even introduced me as her daughter.

As strange as it was, I felt part of something much bigger than myself—part of a family with rich history and a need for one another. I was naturally drawn to them. But I knew enough about them to know that although they were loving people, they were also fierce—a clan of sorts, bonded by blood, where family and loyalty meant everything. If I crossed them, I'd pay the consequences, no matter how many years had passed. I wouldn't let their age and wrinkles fool me. As I'd seen with Ms. G.'s power wielded on Marcus, it only took one phone call.

I opened the sliding door to find Ms. G. sitting in her recliner with Sofia fixing her hair. She had on a dress she'd never worn before, but for some reason it seemed familiar.

"You look beautiful. Where are you two going?"

"I'm taking *Zia* to Bakersfield to see her nieces and nephews. My *Zia* Carmela's grandchildren."

My pulse picked up. "Sofia, may I speak to you in private?"

"Sure," she said. "Hold this brush, *Zia*. I'll be right back."

"Are you sure this is a good idea?" I whispered. "She hasn't been anywhere except a few occasional trips to Goosetown in a long time. It might cause her some confusion, not to mention the dizziness."

"I don't want to do anything to upset her. I promise I'll give her the meds and watch what she eats." Sofia pleaded her case.

"I understand. It's just that . . ."

"I thought it would be good for her to see some family."

"No matter what she tells you, I'm goin'," Ms. G. yelled from the living room. "You should be happy. I put in my God damn hearing aid today." Her voice bellowed through the house.

I rolled my eyes.

"I rented a car. If it gets too much, I'll bring her right back. My cousins will understand."

"Okay," I said, skeptical. "I suppose *one* night would be okay, but if something happens, call me right away."

"I will. You have my word," she said in a bubbly voice. "By the way, my cousin told me he wanted to have you over for dinner, and now you have a night off."

"We talked about it. He said he wanted to make me dinner. Since you'll be gone now, I guess that works."

"Seems like you two are hitting it off. *Zia* says he's here every day and that you guys can't keep your hands off each other." She laughed.

My cheeks flamed. *I wonder where Ms. G. came up with that? We've never kissed in front of her or the kids.* "Your aunt's funny." I looked out the window to see if she could view the inside of my house from her recliner.

"Come on, you can tell me," Sofia teased.

"*Hmm*, yeah, well . . ." I avoided her teasing look. "So far, things are good. He's been a big help around here, and he's sweet to me."

"Sweet, huh?"

Out of habit, I reached for my scar.

"I meant to tell you, that doc did a good job. It looks much better."

"Thanks." I put my hand down.

Sofia placed her hand on my arm. "He'll love you for you, Barbara. Unconditionally. And if he doesn't, he doesn't deserve you. Now go get ready. Put on something sexy. Do you have a strapless dress? Maybe put your hair up? Men always like the bare shoulders look."

I reached for my bangs and pulled them forward. "Dress... dress... Oh, that reminds me," I said, walking back to Ms. G. "Where did you get this dress, Ms. G.? I swear I've seen it somewhere." I touched the soft lace overlay.

"I'm surprised the damn thing still fits. I bought it years ago from Zavlaris's shop. I only wore it once for a picnic in Alum Rock Park." Ms. G. winked at me.

I winked back, and a feeling of warmth filled me up. It was the dress she'd worn for Gaetano the first time they kissed. The day by the brook.

"It's gorgeous, *Zia*. I found it at the back of your closet. It smelled like mothballs, of course, but it's still beautiful. The prettiest shades of yellow, and the lace..." Sofia ran her hand over the fabric. "It's breathtaking."

I placed my hand on her shoulder and let my fingers graze over the webbing. The dress had so much history behind it. It was a vintage relic with a story of its own. She sat in the tattered brown recliner with her salt-and-pepper hair in curls.

"You look beautiful," I said.

"You do, *Zia*."

"I love this on you for so many reasons. I can't even begin," I said.

"Can you believe she even let me paint her nails for the occasion?" Sofia said.

"Wow, she never lets me paint her nails. She says she'll be in the garden all day getting them dirty and doesn't see the point."

"Well, it's true, damn it," Ms. G. piped in.

I turned to Sofia. "Okay, have a good time, you two. Her pills are in the medicine cabinet. Directions are on the bottle. I'll see you tomorrow night. Call me if you need me for anything. If I'm not here, I'll be at Alessandro's house. You have his number, right?"

"Yes, I do. Don't worry. I got this covered. I work for one of the biggest firms in New York City. How hard can it be to care for my aunt for one night?"

"You'd be surprised," I smirked.

"Very funny," Ms. G. said. "Now, will you go already?"

"All right, I'm going, I'm going. Good luck, Sofia. You'll need it."

Something hard hit the back of my head. When I looked down, it was a hairbrush tangled in grey hair, followed by a ton of Italian expletives. I didn't know whether I wanted to yell or laugh.

"What am I gonna do with you?" I said under my breath when I heard Ms. G. say, "Where are we going? Why am I all dressed up?"

I walked over to Sofia. We exchanged a concerned look. "We're going to see *Zia* Carm's grandchildren. Remember?"

Ms. G. looked confused and covered her face with her hands.

"You okay, sweet girl?" I placed my hand on her shoulder.

She moved her hands from her face and put them on her lap. "Will Carm be there? I haven't seen her in ages." She searched our faces for answers.

A look of panic and sadness passed between Sofia and me.

Sofia bent down in front of her and spoke. "*Zia* Carm passed away a few years ago."

"What? How? Why didn't anyone tell me?" Tears welled at the side of her eyes.

"We did," Sofia said. She pressed her lips together to keep them from quivering further.

"You did?" Ms. G. asked, still in shock.

"Yes," Sofia confirmed.

Ms. G.'s face went white. Her eyes darted around the room.

"You're going to see Carm's grandchildren—your nieces and

nephews. What better way to be close to your sister again? They're your family," I explained.

"Yeah, and they miss you a lot. They're so excited to see you," Sofia added.

"You've been missing your family and friends for so long, and now you get to see them."

She wiped her cheeks, then her brows came together. "What if I don't remember them?"

"They'll remember you, and I bet you'll see Carm's face in their eyes."

She nodded. "Okay."

"I can come with you if you need me," I said to Sofia.

"I'm going to talk to Barbara for a minute, okay, *Zia*?" We walked to the back door far enough that she wouldn't hear us.

"You told me, but now I've seen it myself." Her gaze fell. "Should I cancel?"

"I'd normally say yes, but she seems to do well around the family. She likes talking about old times. The past few days with everyone here, she was in her glory. It would be a good idea to bring a few photo albums so she can tell stories about Carmela. They might want to hear how their grandmother grew up. And . . ." I took a deep breath. "It may be the last time they see her." The words cut like razors as they came out.

Sofia swallowed and thought for a minute, then looked back at me. "It's important that they see her, then. We're going. I'll be back tomorrow," she said, resolved.

"If you need me to go, I can. You don't have to go alone."

"No. We'll be fine. I want some time alone with her. The car ride will be good for both of us."

"I'll be at Alessandro's. Call if anything should happen."

Blinking back tears, she nodded. I let myself out and carried my heavy heart with me.

Chapter 19

Liquid Courage

There it is, the one on the corner. Of course, Alessandro would have the biggest house on the block. And closest to the lake. His home was massive, like something out of Architectural Digest magazine.

"No way." Then I remembered the Mercedes, the restaurants, and the fancy champagne. "Yep. This is it, all right."

I pulled into the driveway and parked in front of his three-car garage. To the left were brilliant views of Lake Vasona. The home was beautifully landscaped. A small deck jutted out from the top of the house as a lookout point to the water. Peering at the lake, memories of riding bikes with my kids on the Los Gatos Creek Trail warmed my heart. How many times had I passed by this house, not knowing that someone like Alessandro lived here? Dozens.

I took a deep breath and looked into the rearview mirror. I grabbed the compact from my purse, added some thick concealer to act as a last-minute shield, and pushed my bangs down. I looked at my watch. It was four thirty. I was early. Partly because I wanted to avoid Santana Row shopping traffic on a Saturday, and also because I was nervous. His house meant his territory.

"Here goes nothing." I got out and locked the car.

Since he said it was only dinner, I'd opted out of wearing a dress with heels. I decided on black jeans and a pink blouse. Sexy, yet comfortable.

At the double doors, I pressed the doorbell. A beautiful chime rang.

A woman answered. "Hello," she said, "I'm Lucy. You must be Barbara." She reached out her hand to shake mine.

Alarmed, I put out my hand to meet hers. "Um, yes." *Was I missing something?* I shook the mystery woman's hand.

"I'm Alex's house cleaner. He wanted me to give the house a fresh touch before you arrived. Come in."

"I'm sorry. I'm a little early. I didn't know if there might be traffic. Sometimes two-eighty can be a little crazy."

"With the new tech companies around here now, the freeways get packed. Good for business, bad for traffic. Alessandro should be done soon. He's finishing his workout. I'll take you to him."

"Thank you." I followed Lucy down a hall to a pair of French doors where some heavy metal music blared.

"Sorry for the loud music," Lucy apologized on Alessandro's behalf. "Mr. Sunseri plays it loud when he works out."

She cracked the door to his workout studio and peered in. I looked over the top of her head. Alessandro stood before a punching bag. Sweat dripped from his body and onto the black mat at his feet. Muscles in his arms and back contracted with every punch. When he stepped forward, he let out a grunting noise. It was guttural and manly. It made me think about the noises he'd make when we were alone. I'd never seen his body with so few clothes on.

I crossed my legs to dull the ache between my legs.

"Mr. Sunseri," Lucy yelled over the music.

No response. Alessandro was in the zone. He was laser-focused on his target. He bobbed and weaved from side to side, landing punch after punch.

I needed to see more. I put my hand on her shoulder. "Let's not disturb him."

She turned back to me. Her brows pulled together. "Mr. Sunseri would want to know you're here. He mentioned that you are important. He wouldn't want to leave you waiting."

"I'm the one who's early. It's not his fault. I don't want him to cut his session short on my account," I said, hoping for the show to continue. "I'll tell him I told you not to disturb him."

"Are you sure?"

"Yes," I said anxiously.

"You're welcome to sit in the living room if you want." She clutched her apron.

"Thanks."

"He shouldn't be much longer. He knew you'd be coming soon. Please tell him I put the sauce on low."

"Will do," I said, tapping my foot.

"It was nice meeting you."

"Nice meeting you too."

She turned and went down the long hall.

I stayed quiet and put my head through the cracked door. I didn't want him to catch me watching him. When he wasn't punching, he kicked the bag. Again and again. Right, left, then right again. Blows continued as his thick calves held him in place. His actions were aggressive and alluring. I should've been afraid.

I wasn't.

The song changed. He held the bag with one hand while he wiped the sweat from his face with the other. He turned around and caught me staring. His hair was soaked, and his hands were covered in boxing gloves and tape. He smiled.

"Sorry. I left early. I didn't know how much traffic there'd be," I explained. "Lucy let me in, but I told her not to disturb you. I know how much you love boxing."

He bit down and ripped the tape off his gloves. Once loosened, he unfastened the glove laces and placed them next to the CD player. Alessandro turned off the music.

"I was just finishing up."

"You're good."

"In my profession, it's good to keep up my skills. Making sandwiches doesn't have the same effect. Boxing also helps to relieve tension." He grabbed his water bottle and took a sip. His lips wrapped around the bottle as his Adam's apple pulled more water down his throat.

He came toward me. "I'd kiss you, but I'm all sweaty."

He could kiss me all he wanted right now. He was sexy—sweat and all.

"Let me pour you a drink, and then I'll take a shower." He wiped his face with a towel.

"Okay." I followed him to his oversized kitchen. He flicked on the light and washed his hands in the sink. There was a pot on the stove. A familiar smell filled the air—garlic and olive oil, a staple of Italian kitchens.

"Oh yeah, Lucy said she turned down the sauce."

"I had her keep an eye on it while I worked out. I didn't want it to burn. She's a great help. I haven't been home much lately, so I thought the house needed a once-over. I wanted everything to be perfect for you." He shot me a brilliant smile.

He reached into the refrigerator and looked around. "What sounds good? I have beer. I have some good Scotch in the liquor cabinet. You a Scotch drinker?" He looked over his shoulder at me. "I have a bottle of sparkling water around here somewhere. I know you hate wine." He moved things around in the fridge.

"I don't hate wine. Red wine makes me flushed."

"So, you're okay with white then?"

"White is good." I looked around his chef-inspired kitchen.

He pulled out a bottle of white wine, and two glasses from a cupboard.

"I have a bottle opener here somewhere. Lucy's great, but sometimes she puts things in places I'll never find." He laughed, then opened a drawer close to his hips. "Here it is." He began uncorking the bottle. "Same brand but this time, white." He showed me the Sanna label.

My heart thumped in my chest. Holy crap. I was about to sample the infamous Sanna wine.

He winked at me and poured. "Sip it slow and enjoy."

I swirled the Chardonnay around the glass. I smelled it and took a sip. It was lush and fruity.

"Well?" he asked with a glint in his eyes.

"It's delicious." I thought of Gaetano. If it gave me half the effects it gave Ms. G., then I was in for an interesting night. I studied the liquid in my glass while Alessandro stirred the pot on the stove.

"What are you making?"

"You mean, what are *we* making?"

"Huh?" I asked curiously.

"We're going to make gnocchi, and you're going to help me. I started the sauce early this morning." He grabbed a loaf of bread from the countertop. He tore off a piece and dipped it into the sauce. "Come here, try it."

I put my glass down and went toward him.

He put the sauce-covered bread close to his mouth and blew on it. "Open your mouth," he commanded in a husky voice.

I parted my lips, and he gently fed me the sauce-soaked bread. A mixture of spices touched my tongue. It was robust from the garlic but sweet from the basil.

"I'm going to shower. I'll be back in a few minutes. Make yourself comfortable. Put on the TV if you like, or I have some CDs if you want to listen to music. But I'm not singing this time."

He lifted his shirt over his head, exposing his chest. I couldn't help but study him. He didn't look his age of forty-five. He hardly had one grey hair on his head, and his pecs were that of a twenty-year-old—firm and defined. As he moved, his washboard abs compressed, and the perfect V shape formed around his obliques. I dragged my focus up over his hips, past his stomach, to his neck. A gold necklace hung from his neck with a charm that dangled in his chest hair.

"What's that?" I pointed to his charm.

"It's the *Corno*."

"Corn?"

"Not corn. *Corno*." He grabbed it between his fingers. "It's an Italian symbol for good luck. It's supposed to protect against the evil eye."

"The evil eye? You aren't superstitious, are you?" I joked.

"Most Italians are. I need all the protection I can get. Look at you. You wear a Saint Christopher." He touched the charm.

"It was a gift."

"And has it protected you?" His eyes blazed at me with sexual heat.

"It has."

"See?" He gleamed back at me. "If you don't want to eat at ten o'clock tonight, I'd better shower. See you soon, gorgeous." He turned and walked away.

An Italian flag with the word Sunseri was tattooed between his shoulder blades, along with a huge scar that stretched from the middle of his back to the top of his right hip. I put my hands to my mouth to muffle my gasp. Maybe we had more in common than I thought. Every scar had a story, but with his history and his past with the Mafia, I was afraid what he might tell me.

I took another sip of wine. As it traveled down my throat, warmth started in my cheeks, past my nipples to my groin. I imagined what he looked like when he showered.

Glass in hand, I browsed around. To the right of the kitchen was a formal dining room with a long table. A matching china cabinet sat on the back wall. To the left was a step-down family room with one of the biggest televisions I'd ever seen. I stepped closer and picked up the remote, but it had several buttons on it and seemed too complicated. I put the remote down and peered at the various pictures along the mantel.

The first photo was of Alessandro with his dad on a fishing trip. They both stood proud next to a marlin. Next to that was a picture of Alessandro and a little boy with sapphire-blue eyes like his. It had to be his son. I studied the young boy's face. I mainly saw Alessandro in him, but the boy's hair and chin were a little different, reminding me he had a past. I wondered who his ex-wife was and what she looked like. My imagination took hold as I perused the other pictures until I heard a door close.

To not appear nosey, I turned quickly and sat on his leather couch. When I looked up, Alessandro walked barefoot down the stairs. He wore faded blue jeans and a black V-neck T-shirt that hugged his muscular build. Even his feet were cute.

"I tried to put on the TV," I said nervously, "but it's way too complicated."

"How about some music, then?" He grabbed a CD from an oak cabinet next to the fireplace and turned on the stereo. Soft notes drifted from surround speakers.

I stood and walked toward him. "Are you going to serenade me again?"

"Maybe later if you want me to." He grabbed at my hips and pulled me close. "Can I have that kiss now? I'm clean." He bent down.

I took a whiff. "You smell good. What kind of cologne is that?"

"I got it in Italy the last time I was there."

"You always smell amazing."

Noses touching, he cupped my cheeks and pressed his soft lips against mine. Our mouths parted, and our tongues rubbed against each other, making the pulse in my groin thrum.

I shut my eyes and let my fingers tangle in his wet, tousled hair.

He gently pulled away. "Your kisses are my weakness."

I looked down to see the bulge in his jeans.

"See what you do to me?"

I laughed.

"Time to stir the sauce." He grabbed my hand and escorted me to the kitchen. Barefoot, he stood in front of the pot and stirred. "It's ready. I can turn it off now. I don't want it to burn. I might get distracted," he teased, then pulled my body in for another kiss.

Once he released me, he grabbed a large pot on the granite countertop. He lifted the lid. "Perfect, it rose." He reached for a pastry board and sprinkled it with flour. "Get your hands dusted," he said.

I put down my wine glass, dipped my hand in the white bag, and let the softness fall through my fingers.

Standing behind me, he intertwined his fingers with mine as we massaged the white powder. "Now, put some here." He lifted one of my hands from the bag and onto the pastry board. He pulled out the dough and placed it in front of me. "Have you ever done this?" he asked while his eyes consumed me.

"Yes, actually. I made ravioli with Ms. G. once." I waited patiently for his next direction.

With my hands laced in his, we rolled the dough into a long rope. "Now we do this." He took a knife and cut the rope into cubes. Then he rolled the piece of dough over the tines of the fork. "See, you want it to leave this mark. Now you try." He handed me the fork.

I placed one of the powdery squares in front of me.

He pressed his head into the nape of my neck and grabbed my flour-caked hands.

While he guided the fork over the dough, his breath teased my hair.

"You smell good too." His words felt moist against my neck.

I thought I'd catch on fire. I shifted my weight from hip to hip to search for control, but my insides blazed as his body pressed against mine. "Stop it, or we'll never eat."

"Are you hungry?" he whispered into my ear. His tone was thick and suggestive. He turned me around and kissed me deeply and passionately. Our mouths connected, and our smiles turned into moans.

Once we pulled away, he looked at me with a devious grin. He put his hand in the bag of flour, then pulled it back out.

"Don't even think about it."

"Or what?" he teased, then flicked a handful of white fluff in my face and laughed.

I yelped.

He laughed at my flour-covered face.

I wiped my nose. "No fair. I wasn't ready." I pinched some powder from the bag and smeared it over his face. "Two can play that game," I yelped, then bellied over in laughter.

"You got me. I should've waited to shower." He laughed, then wiped the white from his face. He grabbed the bag to douse me again, but knowing what he was about to do, I ducked. He caught me in his arms and kissed me again. This time, sexual energy radiated through his body. His lips pressed harder against mine as he pushed my hips against the counter. He lifted me onto the countertop, running his tongue over my lips, then down my neck. My breathing accelerated from his advance.

Desire took over. I hitched my legs around his torso and pulled his body toward me. I wrapped my arms around his neck while he sprinkled kisses down my chest. He reached under my blouse and squeezed my breast. My nipples burned against the lace of my bra.

His erection pressed against my inner thigh.

He paused and yanked his hand out from my blouse. "We should stop. I only have so much willpower with you," he panted.

I looked over his shoulder. "Is your housekeeper still here?"

"No, I checked. Her car is gone."

I wanted him now, here, on the countertop. I dragged my gaze over his glorious body and stared into his deep blue eyes to signal my intentions.

"I want you, Barbara," he said against my neck as his hands clutched at my ass on the counter.

I tightened my legs around his body and pulled him closer.

My God, what is it about this damn Sanna wine anyway? His warm breath caressed my ear.

He pulled himself from my grip and took a deep breath. "I want you to know, I didn't invite you here expecting this to happen." He cupped my cheeks in his palms and looked at me with tender eyes. "Are you sure you want to do this? I'll understand if you aren't ready. I'll have to take another shower. This time, a cold one."

Maybe it was the wine or that it had been so long that I'd been with a man, but I ached for him. I wasn't scared anymore. He'd been the perfect gentleman all these weeks.

So sweet and caring.

I stared at his heart-shaped lips. "The next shower you take will be with me." I opened my mouth and thrust my tongue into his. With my legs around him, he picked me up with his hands securely around my ass and carried me upstairs to his bedroom.

Chapter 20
The Gangster with a Heart

HE PUSHED OPEN HIS BEDROOM DOOR AND PINNED ME AGAINST the wall. I devoured his kisses. Pictures fell from the walls as our bodies moved. Without conscious thought, I clawed at his shirt and yanked it over his head. I kissed his chest and let my fingers slide down his firm abs.

He groaned, then pulled away slowly. "Wait. I want to take my time with you. If you want rose petals and candles, say the word." He set me down on the edge of his bed and brushed flour from my face and hair. "Let me get a towel to clean us up. I'll be right back." He grinned and walked into an enormous bathroom with a double shower and tub.

Surrounded by black satin sheets, I rubbed my hands against the soft fabric. My eyes darted around his room. Surely, there'd be things here that told me more about him. I sat up on my elbows to get a better look.

A peek into his large walk-in closet revealed shiny leather shoes set on neat, spacious racks, different-colored suits and ties that hung from wooden hangers, and a tall safe mounted in the wall between his belts and various cologne bottles. One of those scents lingered on the sheets around me. I inhaled deeply, letting his essence fill me.

Expensive paintings of Italy covered the room's walls. Alessandro liked nice things. Dark curtains partially covered a sliding glass door that opened to a private deck overlooking the lake. I stared out at the water. I was in his bedroom, about to do things I'd dreamed about for weeks. My stomach knotted. It felt unreal. My pulse ticked back up and pounded in my throat.

He returned with a wet towel, in nothing more than his low-cut jeans, and rubbed the warm towel over my fingers and face.

"That's better. Now I'm ready," he said in an urgent and wanting tone. "Let me do this right." He pulled off my sandals one by one and massaged my feet.

I moaned as the last grips of my anxiety faded away while his hands worked.

"You like that?" His voice was seductive.

"Yes, it feels amazing." His touch was firm but gentle—just like him.

He massaged the balls of my feet then kissed my instep, sending currents of pleasure to my pelvis. To ground myself to the moment, I swallowed deeply and looked down at his face. He peered up at me with his blazing blues.

His warm touch smoldered inside me.

He untucked my blouse from my jeans and unzipped my pants, then moved his face to my neck and kissed behind my ear. While his mouth pressed velvet soft kisses against my skin, he cupped my breasts, lightly, then harder, making my nipples burn with desire.

"Sit up," he commanded. With one quick move, he lifted my blouse over my head. He kissed the bulging flesh that bubbled from my push-up bra, and reached around to undo the clasp. The last clip came undone. He helped me out of it.

I lay back against the pillow.

"My God, look at you. You have beautiful breasts." He cupped them with his hands. "They're so soft and plump." He grazed his face and nose over my skin. In one swift action, he took the flesh into his mouth and sucked, making me heat up again as his tongue lapped over my nipples. I looked down at my half-naked body, and my throat became as dry as the desert. "I'm nervous." My voice shook under his touch. "I haven't been with a man in a long time."

He released my nipple. "We'll take it slow. I'll only do what you're comfortable with." A slow smile spread across his wet lips. "I want to get to know every inch of your body." He spoke with unwavering intensity. His fingertips traced my breasts, sometimes grazing my nipples. Like a ribbon on a Christmas present, he was unraveling me with every stroke.

My palms grazed over his back as he kneaded my breasts. I felt his arousal swell onto my thigh. He dragged his eyes from my breasts down my torso, then pulled my jeans down over my hips and onto the floor. He trailed kisses from my breasts to below my navel.

"I like these." He felt the lace of my G-string panties. "Very sexy, but I think I like what's underneath more," he teased, then yanked them off my hips and down my legs.

"Can we please turn off the light?"

"I want to see you. All of you," he whispered. He glided his finger down my neck, past my belly button, and down my legs. "You have lines like an Italian sports car—sleek and sexy, and I love the feel of your skin. It's like silk." He let his fingers graze along my rib cage and back to my neck. He pressed butterfly kisses along my abdomen.

I'd never had a man worship my body like this. A man's hands used to scare me, but Alessandro's soothed.

"I want you to feel safe with me at this moment." His eyes searched my face. "With my hands." He rubbed the tension in my shoulders. "My touch." He swept his thumb against my burning cheek. He bent down and pressed feather-light kisses down my scar line. With every pass of his lips, he healed me, little by little.

His bare chest faced me. I stared at his meaty pectoral muscles and smoothed my fingertips over his warm skin.

"That's it. You can touch me, baby. I'm yours. There's no one else."

I moved my hands over his shoulders and down his back until I felt a hard, thick line. I flinched.

He grabbed my hand and placed it back over his scar. "We're the same. Just feel," he assured.

My fingertips traced over the thick line. It was bumpy where staples once fastened his skin. "Now you see." He pressed his hips into me. "You aren't the only one with scars." He leaned down to kiss me. "Our scars and pasts can't define us anymore."

"How'd this happen?" I let my fingers explore his back.

"I was in a fight. Son of a bitch stabbed me," he whispered against my breasts. "The knife pierced my kidney. I was in the hospital for a month. I almost died." He placed a soft kiss on my lips.

"Oh, my God."

"Don't worry. I didn't go down without a fight." He laughed and nibbled on my ear lobe.

"I'm afraid to ask what happened to the other guy."

"He wasn't so lucky. He died." His face became serious. "I'm not proud of it. It was self-defense."

My throat tightened. I recoiled from his grip.

He stopped his advance and watched my reaction. He blinked a few times, then his brows pulled together as he waited for my next words. When I offered nothing in return, he brushed the back of his knuckles along my cheek. "It was a long time ago, in a life I want to get away from." His gaze lowered. "I can't apologize for things I did when I didn't know you. But you're changing me—giving me a conscience. I want to do good in my life." He grazed the back of his hand against my cheek.

"Why didn't you kill Marcus when you had the chance?" I had to know.

He pressed his lips together and shook his head. "The truth?" He lowered his gaze to the bed and back up to me. "I didn't want your kids to mourn him. When I met you in the deli that day with

Zia, I was instantly attracted to you. So, when the order came in to take care of him, I didn't want to cause you pain. I didn't want to be the one responsible for hurting your children. You would've suffered to see them like that."

He cares about me. He's been protecting me since the day we met. My heart swelled. "I didn't know you get to decide who lives and who dies."

He paused. "Usually, we don't. But you were different. Even then you were changing me." He played with the ends of my hair. "My dad gave me hell for not finishing the job. He doesn't want me involved with you."

"Why?"

"It's nothing personal. He doesn't want anyone getting hurt—least of all me. Some stuff happened with my ex, and he worries."

"What happened?"

"During the divorce, we got into a big fight. She threatened to rat to the cops about things she'd witnessed. I talked her out of it because that would've gotten her killed."

I stared at him in shock.

"Look, I don't want to talk about her or any other woman while you're in my bed. This needs to remain our private space. A place for us, always. I'll tell you about it another time. I'm not ready to get into those details. I'm sorry." His face was pained.

"I understand. I never told anyone anything."

"It's not just that. Pop knows how *Zia* feels about you and what you've done for her. He would never go against her. He wouldn't want anything to happen to jeopardize your relationship with her."

"You mean like if we got involved and somehow you did something to get me upset, and I spilled the beans?"

"Yes. Or worse, you split on *Zia*. She needs you."

"I'd never do that."

"You say that now, but people say and do stupid things when they're angry."

"Tell me about it. Marcus never controlled his temper."

"And it cost him. Now you know why Pop's hesitant. *Zia* has made it clear that you are like a daughter to her. You may think *Zia's* an old woman with a deteriorating brain, but she still has a lot of say about what goes on around here. She's old Mafia. No one fucks with her. If they did, a war would start. But to the Molanano family, you're a civilian, so getting involved with me has made this a delicate situation, to say the least." He grabbed my hand and held it between his. "Bottom line, the family needs you to keep quiet and help my aunt, and sometimes you might need the help of the family." His eyes were serious.

I nodded.

"Now you understand the chance I'm taking. You're worth it." He cupped my cheek.

"That must be why Angelo looked at me strangely at the funeral."

"Yeah. In his own way, he was trying to protect us. He doesn't want any trouble. But he also knows I'm stubborn. I mean, how was I to know that after a beating like that, your stupid ex would go to the ranch and pull that kind of stunt? When Marcus went to jail, he became a loose string. The family doesn't like loose strings. Thankfully, we have people in the jails—inmates and paid guards who will carry out an order if needed. Your ex is being watched."

"I can't believe I'm even saying this, because there are days that I wanted him dead for what he did, but thank you—for my kids' sake."

"It's beyond me now. If he so much as whispers the wrong thing to the wrong person, he'll be dealt with. You'll need to prepare for that."

"Sometimes, when I'm with you, I forget who you are and what you do. What if one day you get caught and go to jail, and I'm left alone? What if someone kills you in jail? Then what? This must be what Ms. G. meant about the sacrifices you must make. I don't know if I want that. I'd miss you too much."

"That's not gonna happen." He pressed a kiss to my forehead. "Listen, I could've given the job to anyone. I took it on personally because I wanted to be the one to protect you that night. I'm not a strong arm anymore. Pop and I are getting older. We leave the hard jobs to the younger guys. The most I do now is take in the rents and check on things when the boss calls. The family's happy with me when I bring them money. If I launder things through my businesses and provide, I can stay under the radar. I've given the old man plenty of money, and he knows it."

I looked at him skeptically.

He watched my face. "I've seen that look before. It seems like no matter what I do, I can't get close to anyone because of my oath. I gave those fuckers everything. My body to fight with," he said as his hands curled into fists. He pointed at his temple. "And my mind to do their dirty work. And for what? I've lost my family, my son." He shifted his gaze away from me and sighed. "From the look on your face . . . now you too." He sat on the side of the bed and reached for his shirt on the ground.

"Wait." I touched his shoulder.

He turned back to me.

I searched his face.

His expression was intense. "What do you want, Barbara? Because if it's me, I can't keep feeling unworthy of you. Worried that if I'm honest, you'll get up and leave me forever. I spend my days finding ways to get out, to distance myself from it, and I know a few guys who got out. I'm not saying it won't be hard, but I want to do that for my son, for me, for us." He exhaled and pushed his hair back with his hand. "I'm not perfect. No one is. If you're looking for perfection, we should stop now. I'll never measure up to your standards."

My heart broke at his words. This rich, beautiful man looked lost in his enormous room. He had it all: money, women, and power, yet he was alone. They'd stripped him of the people he loved and left him a prisoner of their war, afraid and trying to escape a life he never wanted.

"I'm sorry, Alessandro. No one's perfect. Look at my situation.

No matter what you've done, I know you have a good heart and want to change for me. I appreciate you trying to find a way to live a legitimate life. I do." I reached for his hand.

"Then what is it?"

He'd been honest. It was my turn to expose my truth and the secrets I'd kept for so long. "A future with you seems daunting, but when I'm with you, you stir feelings in me that I didn't know existed. A life with you is also familiar. After all this time with Ms. G., your world has become my world too. I've never had a man care for me so intensely and intimately as you have these last few months. You've become a part of my everyday life now. You're someone I've come to count on. No matter what kind of day I've had, when I hear you come through that gate, I get that excited butterfly feeling in my stomach."

He smiled, sending a blush to warm my cheeks.

"I know this doesn't make sense, but I think I'd miss you even if we'd never met. And as much as I should run the other way after what you've told me, I want to get closer."

His brows shot up from my admission.

"My feelings for you scare me more than anything you've done in your past because I can't ignore them anymore. And I don't want to."

He cupped my face in his hands. "You're not the only one who's scared. It's only been a few months, but I'm getting feelings for you too, and it scares the shit out of me. Every woman I've loved, I've lost. I'm not asking if you feel the same, but you need to know. Sometimes we can't help who we love. We just love." He placed the softest kiss on my lips.

I dissected his words in my mind. He was right. With his countless efforts to make me feel safe and adored, he'd proven to be someone worthy of my heart. I'd give this a shot or regret it. I wanted this with him—I'd always wanted this with him.

We held each other tight as if to squeeze away our pasts. We both wanted a chance at love and a fresh start. I'd have to ignore the voice inside my head that said all men sought to control and dominate women.

The beaters.

The rapists.

The abusers.

Alessandro wasn't Marcus.

A lump formed in my throat. Then I looked into his eyes. "You've been forthcoming about your feelings with me tonight, even about things that are still difficult to talk about. Now it's my turn. Before I met you, I was in a loveless relationship and beaten almost daily."

Alessandro's jaw tightened.

"Marcus took our money and gambled it away. He made me feel weak, stupid, and ugly. I haven't been with any man since him." The sting of embarrassment burned my cheeks. "I thought I loved Marcus, but I don't know if I ever knew what love was. After being with you these last few months, I know what it looks like when a man sees you as the most beautiful woman on Earth. I know what it feels like when a man listens. You've taught me what it means to be revered. I'm forty-three years old, and I never knew what that felt like until I met you. I want to take this leap with you. You asked me to let down my guard so you can see the real me. Well, here I am. You told me to tell you what I want. I want you. Make love to me, Alessandro."

His face lit up from my admission. He cupped my cheeks in his hands and captured my lips with his. He kissed me tenderly as if he wanted to speak to my heart. I sank against the pillows. He reached to turn off the light.

"It's okay. Leave it on. Tonight, you can see all of me."

He pushed my bangs aside and studied my forehead then brushed feathery kisses up and down my scar. A warm smile crept over his mouth. He kissed me again, this time harder, claiming my lips. With each new kiss, our breathing became more irregular.

Struggling for breath, he fondled my breasts and ground his hips against mine.

I watched while he unbuttoned his pants. His erection stuck out of the top of his boxers while he unzipped his fly. Every erotic thought and dream I'd had about him since the day I'd met him was about to come true. His penis was fleshy, and the tip was wet from our foreplay. I had to touch it. I wrapped my palm around him. It was stiff from the blood flow. I let my thumb glide over the head.

He looked down between his legs at my fondling him and then back up at me. His pupils were wide with excitement. He kissed me again. With every tug on his penis, his eyelids squeezed shut, followed by more heavy breathing. After a few more jerks of my hand, he pulled his hips backward, breaking my grasp.

"Not yet." He smiled. "You're gonna make me cum. Let me take care of you first." He scootched his way down my body, gliding his tongue down my torso to my inner thighs until he buried his face between my legs.

I gasped as his thick tongue moved around and around, brushing up against my tender spot. My body stiffened as he took my clit into his mouth. I wrapped my legs around his back and held him firmly in place. My breathing became uneven, and the tiny nerve that connected to my sweet spot quivered deep inside my pelvis. With his powerful grip, he clutched at my hips as I moved from side to side, bracing for my orgasm.

He released my clit. "Don't fight it, baby. Let yourself go. I'm right here. Let me watch you cum," he whispered against my sensitive flesh. He pulled my lips apart and lapped his tongue against me again. To stop me from moving, he pinned my hips down with his hands. My butt tightened and my legs shook.

He pinched my nipples hard while sucking a life's worth of sexual tension from me. Every muscle contracted, and my body convulsed. My heart stopped, and I came all over his mouth. I felt the gush of my orgasm leak out of me. Unraveled, I came down from my peak and tried to regain my breath.

He crawled up my body, flushed from being between my legs, and raided my mouth, kissing me fervently.

I tasted myself on his lips.

"You taste sweet." His erection pressed against my legs as he kissed me.

I panted between kisses, still trying to recover from my release. "You okay?"

"Yes," I said, winded. "That was wonderful." I exhaled blissfully against his chest. "Thank you."

Alessandro yanked down his jeans and boxers and let them fall to the floor. From his side table he pulled out a condom, ripped open the gold foil package with his teeth, and rolled the condom in place.

Then he grabbed my legs and placed them over his shoulders. Kneeling, his rock-solid body towered over me. He reached down between his legs and inserted himself into me.

He was large, and I wasn't used to it. I winced.

"Am I hurting you?"

"I'm fine," I said, taking him inside me. He slowly pushed himself in further. Once he was in, I felt him hit my cervix. I liked the fullness of him in my belly. His size filled me up in ways I never imagined. He reached down with his thumb and stroked my clit.

Oh God, here we go again.

Sensitive after my first orgasm, I shut my eyes and concentrated on his warm thumb rubbing me. After a few strokes, my orgasm built again. I looked into his eyes and moaned.

A crease formed between his brows. "Do you want me to slow down?"

"No," I huffed out. "It feels good. Keep going. Faster." I reached behind him and squeezed his firm ass with my hands. He pushed himself into me, harder and faster. The sweat from our bodies made our skin slick.

"You close, baby?" he said, trying to catch his breath as the muscles on his forearms contracted.

"Yes." My clit felt hot from his touch. Tiny nerves under my pelvis tingled again as our bodies moved.

"We're gonna do this together, okay?"

"Okay. Don't stop," I yelled out in ecstasy. He thrust himself into me over and over, then bent his head toward mine to kiss me passionately. With his tongue in my mouth and his penis inside me, we were interlocked and woven together. I clutched my pillow tight. I'd never had this kind of penetration. It was lovemaking, and it was incredible.

"Here we go," he said as the same small crease formed between his eyebrows again. He shut his eyes as he squirmed inside me.

Muscles in my vagina clenched around him.

He plunged himself into me, pushing my head further back against the headboard.

I dug my nails into his back as my insides shook. "Alessandro," I yelled out.

He grunted and emptied himself into the condom. His body stiffened, then slouched over me.

We came together. It was beautiful and synchronized perfectly, just like he said.

He panted on top of me, then he pushed the hair back from my eyes and kissed me on the lips.

I wrapped my arms around him and lay there while we held each other in a powerful embrace. Kissing his neck, I inhaled a breath of his cologne. I licked my lips and tasted his salty skin.

He placed a stream of kisses on my face and neck. "I need you. All of you."

I held his face in my hands. "I need you too." I kissed his lips softly. "Your touch and your kisses heal me."

He beamed. "You don't know how good that feels to hear. And how good it feels to be inside you. I want to lie like this forever." He put his head between my breasts. "You're so warm and soft." He sucked on my nipple, then came back up and kissed behind my ear. My breathing quickened in response to his touch. "Tell me what you want."

He took my left nipple into his mouth and sucked hard. He let go of my nipple and looked up at my face. His eyes blazed an unbridled blue. "I want to do things with you tonight."

I felt his spell on me again. "What kind of things?" I asked lightly, panting, ready to beg him for more.

"Lots of things," he whispered, "but only if you're comfortable. You'd really have to trust me," he whispered, then kissed my lips. As our tongues met, he put a finger inside me, then massaged the skin by my anus with my finish.

"Do you like that?" He breathed his words into my neck.

"Yes," I exhaled, feeling the heat of my blush sting my cheeks.

"Relax," he commanded.

I took a deep breath and let my muscles fall.

"Good girl," he reassured.

"Alessandro?" I struggled to get the word out.

"What do you want, baby?" he coaxed. "Tell me. Don't be embarrassed about your needs in our bed. I want your body to crave me." He swallowed my nipple into his mouth.

I gulped down hard.

It had been so long. My body screamed for more. More of him. More of everything. He was a gangster with a conscience who'd stolen my heart. A man who'd do anything for a chance at a future with me, and that was enough for me to be brave. I wanted him to do things with me I'd only dreamed about. Now was my chance to be adventurous.

Tonight, I'd test my limits.

"Alessandro," I said, not fighting the words anymore.

He released my nipple from his mouth. "Yes?" he whispered, then licked my bottom lip with his soft, wet tongue.

"You don't have to be so gentle with me. I won't break."

A wolfish grin spread across his face, followed by a faint chuckle.

"Be careful what you wish for." He stared at me with hungry eyes that threatened to devour my body in one bite.

I drew in a trembling breath and bit my bottom lip.

Shiny black wisps of his hair fell against his thick eyebrows. "I promise you this . . . I'm going to give you what you want, and I won't stop until I see your toes curl and your eyes roll into the back of your head."

My breathing hitched against my bone-dry throat as I gulped down his words.

He paused in thought, then spoke. "I try to maintain a private life. I don't consort with the neighbors." He brushed his tongue against my lips. "But tonight, I'm gonna give you so much pleasure that everybody on this damn street will learn my name." A naughty grin pulled at the corners of his mouth.

"Turn over," he commanded.

Orange surrounded me. Sunrise had made its way into Alessandro's room. He lay on his stomach, tangled in black satin sheets. His muscular arms clutched his pillow tight while his ass cheeks pointed toward the ceiling. My eyes raked over his bottom. Alessandro was a fine specimen.

Except for the phone call I'd made to tell Darnell that I wouldn't be home because I'd had a few drinks, I slept most of the night in Alessandro's arms, only waking twice: once, to the sound of Alessandro's voice as he checked in with his crew to make sure both kids were safe and accounted for at the ranch, and twice, when we both woke up starving at two a.m. from our night's worth of lovemaking. Alessandro served us gnocchi in bed. For dessert, we dined on our bodies. There were still traces of his scent on my arms.

I covered myself with a throw blanket and got out of bed. I crept to the sliding glass door that opened to the private balcony. Quietly, I slid the door open and watched as the sun's light spilled onto the lake. On the horizon, dozens of geese swam in groups. Sun warmed my cheeks. I wanted to stay there for hours, but my bladder had a different idea.

I closed the door, went to his bathroom, and turned on the shower. While the water got warm, pictures of his body on top of me, under me, behind me, and on my side stamped my mind. I would never forget the way he looked at me when he came or how he held me throughout the night. I'd never felt more loved in my entire life.

He was right. I craved him now. He was a Mafia sex god, and I wanted more.

I shut the shower door behind me and let the water fall on my face and down my back. I put his soap to my nose. It smelled of him, like clean linen drying on the line. I washed gently, afraid to lather the swollen flesh between my legs. I rinsed my hair and shut my eyes as the water pelted my face when I felt Alessandro come behind me. He nestled his face in the crook of my neck, then reached around my torso to pull my ass up against him.

"Here, let me help you." He reached for the soap in my hands. He lathered my back, down to my butt, then turned me around and glided the bar down my neck to my pubic area.

"Last night was amazing," he said close to my ear.

"You're an incredible lover. I enjoyed every moment."

"Good. I'm glad. I had fun too." He pulled me close and peered down at me with a look of sheer intensity. "You're exceptional." His gaze fixed on me. "I especially liked the part where you were in control. I like you on top. I think you like it too." He smiled a devilish smile.

I blushed under the shower water.

"Don't be embarrassed." He grabbed my hips and pulled me close. "It was amazing to watch you. That's how I want you to feel every time we're together—empowered."

"Can I tell you something?"

"Yes, of course. You can tell me anything." He continued to lather me up.

"I'm always saying this to you, but thank you."

"For what? For the five orgasms? You're welcome."

We laughed.

"Those too. But no, thank you for making me feel safe enough to be brave. You gave me courage last night. I did things with you that I never thought I'd do. My body is new to this."

"I only did what you asked me to do." With a soft touch, he washed along my backside. "Are you okay there? I hope I didn't hurt you."

"I'm fine," I said, reveling in his touch.

He poured shampoo into his hands and rubbed it into my scalp, massaging my temples and the base of my skull.

I couldn't see him, but I felt him.

As the bubbles washed down the drain, he kissed me on the neck.

I opened my eyes to the color of the ocean. "Do you know how insanely beautiful your eyes are? I've never seen a color like yours." I brushed my fingertips over his brows. "They're a cross between sea glass and sapphires. They're breathtaking... So, when you look at me, if I can't respond right away, you know why." I took the soap and washed his chest and stomach. "Oh, sorry, I didn't mean..." I watched him rise against the shower water.

He clutched my ass and pressed our bodies together.

I wrapped my arms around his neck and hugged him tightly.

He pressed my back against the cool white tile and sent kisses along my neck. As water ran down our bodies, he turned to look me in the eyes. "I love you," he said.

Overcome, tears spilled over my cheeks. In his embrace, I was ready to say the words. "I love you too."

His eyes widened. He bent down and placed his lips on mine. His kiss was full of devotion, reverence, adoration, and a feeling of pure joy. I felt the smile on his mouth as he moved his tongue along with mine. Then he hitched my leg up, and I held on for the ride.

The smell of bacon wafted up the stairs as I wrapped my hair in a towel. I threw on a pair of Alessandro's shorts and a clean T-shirt that he'd laid on the bed for me. I opened the door to hear Alessandro yelling at someone on the phone. I crept down the stairs to the kitchen to listen to what he was saying.

"So what? So she stayed the night. Big deal." Then there was a long pause. "I love this girl, and I want her in my life," Alessandro said firmly.

More silence.

"She knows better. She's not Vicki. She gets it. Sofia had her sign an NDA."

Then another brief period of quiet.

I tiptoed toward him, then stopped in my tracks when I heard the slamming of a cupboard.

"She makes me happy. She's a good person."

More silence.

"Yeah, yeah. Whatever happens, I'll deal with it. She's my responsibility. It's time to get out now anyway."

A few seconds ticked on with no words before he spoke again.

"Even if things were to go south, and God help me, I hope they never do, she'll never let that come between her and *Zia*. She's a professional, and she loves her like a mother. You know that. She won't say anything." Alessandro huffed in frustration. "Pop, I know you're trying to help, and I love you, but you gotta get out of my business. This is *my* life."

I walked in.

He saw me. "I gotta go." He hung up.

"Everything all right?"

"How much did you hear?"

"Most of it."

"He'll come around."

"You sure about that?" I put my head down.

"Yes. He's my father. He loves me. If he wants a relationship with me, he's gonna have to love you too."

"I hate that I'm already causing problems."

"You're not causing problems." He scooped me up for a hug. "Enough about that. I made us breakfast, and I thought before you go home, we might take a walk around the lake." He poured me a cup of coffee.

"That sounds nice." I grabbed the cup and took a sip. "Can I use your phone? I need to check in on Darnell and Leticia."

"Darnell's fine. I called the deli. He just got there."

"Have you heard anything?"

"Not a peep. He's doing well. He hasn't been late yet, and the boys say he's catching on quickly. He did ask for an advance on his paycheck. He's pretty young to have bills, but maybe he wants to buy himself the latest pair of Jordans. Do you know why he'd be in such a hurry to get his check?"

"No, he doesn't have any bills other than gas money. I pay for his insurance and buy most of his clothes. I can't believe he lied to me."

"You don't know that yet. Don't worry. I'll get to the bottom of it." He pressed a kiss to my forehead as his phone rang again. "It's Sofia." He shot me a cautious look. "Hey, *cugina*. How'd it go? Everything okay?"

His brows pulled together tightly. "Okay, okay, calm down." His voice was frantic.

I heard Sofia crying on the line.

"She's with me," Alessandro explained.

I reached out for the phone. "What is it?" The walls of my throat caved in. "What happened?" My heart pounded against my rib cage.

"Where are you?" Alessandro demanded. "We're leaving now." He hung up the phone.

"Get dressed. We're going to the hospital. They're at O'Connor's. Leticia's with her. *Zia's* had a stroke. They don't know if she'll make it."

Chapter 21
The Place Where Life Meets Death

As often as I'd been here, I'd forgotten the smell of a hospital room. It was a mix of industrial cleaning solutions and bodily fluids. Babies were born on one floor. People died on another. Hospitals were strange like that.

I'd been here with other clients, holding their hands as their families and friends said goodbye. This felt different. This was Ms. G. lying in a hospital bed. I didn't like it one bit.

After two days on a hard pull-out chair, my back ached. When I wasn't asleep, I waited for her to sit up in bed and say something nasty to me or order me around, but she didn't.

She just lay there.

No cursing.

No yelling at me in Italian.

No stories.

No nothing.

The only sounds were of Sofia crying or praying between the buzzing, flashing, and beeping of the machines that kept Ms. G. alive. Her little body was covered with tubes and wires—tubes in her arms, tubes down her throat that allowed her to breathe, and wires attached to different parts of her body that took her vitals.

Sofia and I traded shifts.

"This is all my fault," Sofia whimpered.

"It's not your fault. We talked about this. There was nothing you could do. Even if I had gone, I couldn't have stopped this from happening. She tripped. It was a freak accident. Some things are out of our control."

"No. I knew she was dizzy, and I still took her. We should've stayed at the ranch."

"You did what you thought was best for her. She wanted to go. Seeing her family means everything to her." I patted Sofia's hand. "Have faith. If there's one thing I've learned from your aunt, it's that God answers prayers."

Sofia wiped her nose with a tissue. "I hope so," she said and reached for her aunt's hand again. "Before I forget, there's something I've been meaning to ask you. When I found her in the bathroom, she kept saying the name Gaetano. Do you know who she's talking about?"

"I'm not sure," I said.

Sofia looked back at her aunt. Her lips quivered. "I just lost my grandfather. I can't lose her too."

"Try and stay positive. We aren't going to lose her. No one could've suspected this would happen. She's seen a doctor. He adjusted her pills and diet. You didn't know that she would get out of the car. Ms. G. has a mind of her own sometimes. You have to stop beating yourself up."

I came around the bed and hugged her tight. "Thank God it was a small bleed, and that they didn't have to perform surgery. You got her here early. The medicine they gave her will help. You did the right thing. She has a fighting chance now."

Sofia blew her nose. "I'm frightened. Does it ever get easier? I bet you've been through this many times before."

"No, it doesn't get easier. Your aunt has taught me so much in such a short amount of time. I don't know what I would do without her. We have to pray that she pulls through. Go home and rest. I'll see you tomorrow morning."

"I can stay," Sofia objected.

"You're exhausted. You need sleep. I've got it. Your aunt wouldn't want you to be so upset."

Sofia yawned as sadness flushed her eyes. "You'll call if she wakes up, right?"

"Yes. Now go."

Someone put a blanket on me. A warm body slid next to mine.

I opened my eyes to see Alessandro curled up next to me. Two strong warm hands rubbed at my back.

"Man, your muscles are tight." He massaged my back.

"My body feels like a pile of knots. I want Leticia to tell them to get better chairs."

"That's it," Alessandro said firmly. "Tomorrow, you're going home. Pop and I will be here to give you two a break."

"I'll be all right, and I'm much better with you here to keep me warm." I nestled my face in the crook of his neck.

He wrapped his arms around me and raked his fingers over my back. "So how's she doin'? Any improvement? Has she woken up at all?"

"She goes in and out, but it's brief."

"Did Sofia tell you how it happened? You said she's been dizzy."

"Sofia said that when Ms. G. woke up that morning to leave, she was out of sorts. She thought it was just from her waking up in a strange hotel. It wasn't until she came out of the mini mart at a gas station in Gilroy when she noticed Ms. G. wasn't in the car—only her cane was left behind."

"Oh man. *Zia's* one hardheaded lady—literally. Always has been. A real *testa dura*."

"A testa what?"

He laughed. "It means someone who's stubborn."

"Oh."

"Sofia must have been so scared."

"She was. She searched the bathrooms and found Ms. G. talking to herself in the stall. So, she cleaned her up and got her back in the car safely, then continued for home. Sofia said she seemed fine and that she was talking up a storm about the old days. But she started rubbing her head and complaining of pain.

"Sofia pulled over and noticed the large lump on the side of her head. Ms. G. said she'd tripped and hit her head in the gas station bathroom. To rule out a concussion, Sofia drove straight for the hospital to get her checked out. When she pulled into the parking lot Ms. G.'s face started to droop and she began to slur her words. She passed out right when Sofia pulled up to the emergency entrance. She called you as soon as they'd admitted her."

"Thank God Sofia decided to come straight here. The doctors know what to do."

"I feel so bad for her. Sofia blames herself. But the truth is no one could see this coming. Sometimes you just never know." I looked over at my patient. "I keep waiting for her to call my name and yell at me for something. I need to hear her voice."

I sobbed into my lover's arms.

"Hey, hey." He patted my back. "It's gonna be okay. I'm right here. We'll get through this together, and if anyone can beat this, *Zia* can. She'll be talking in no time. You watch." He rubbed away my tears with his thumbs.

"I hope you're right," I muttered and closed my eyes against his chest.

Wrapped in Alessandro's arms, I stared at the clock in Ms. G.'s room. It was four a.m. I hadn't slept much—mostly from nerves, but also because nurses came in every hour to check on her. I pulled the tiny blanket back over us when I heard a strange sound.

Ack Ack Ack

Ms. G. was choking on the tube down her throat.

I jumped up and pressed the call button by her bed. Alessandro sprang to my side.

"Ms. G., you're okay," I said as two beady eyes stared back at me.

"What's wrong with her?"

"She's trying to fight the tube. She's waking up," I cried out. "Ms. G., they're going to come and take it out right now. Calm down. I'm right here." I squeezed her hand tightly.

She continued to squirm.

Alessandro opened the door to her room. "Hey, we need someone in here right away. She's awake," Alessandro yelled to the nurses' station.

The on-call doctor and two nurses came in and removed the tube from her throat. She wriggled and writhed as they probed her. Her eyes looked confused as she peered around the unfamiliar room. She tried to speak, but her voice was hoarse.

In an unrecognizable tone, she called for me. "Barrbaara." The right side of her mouth sagged.

I rushed to her side and held her hand. "I'm right here. Don't speak yet. Relax."

Another nurse questioned Ms. G. as she examined her. "Hello, ma'am. Do you know your name?"

Ms. G. looked spaced out. She turned toward me.

"Hello, sweet girl. You remember your name, don'tcha?" I smiled down at her.

She looked at me, wide-eyed.

I brushed my hand over her forehead.

Alessandro came to my side. "*Zia*, tell 'em."

"Al . . ." she mumbled and reached up to pat his face.

"Yeah, it's me." He put his hand over hers. He turned to me

with a shimmer in his eyes, then kissed her hand. "I told ya she'd remember. *Zia*, tell them your name."

A blank look covered her face.

"Let's give her some space," one of the nurses ordered.

Ms. G.'s eyes opened wide, and she spoke. "Myyyy nammme is Violetttttaa." She slurred her words.

"Ms. Giordano, my name is Dr. Hartman. I'll be assessing you today," the doctor said as he shined a light in her eyes. "You're in the hospital. You bumped your head and developed some bleeding in the brain that caused you to suffer a stroke. We gave you medicine to help with the bleeding, and put a tube down your throat to help you breathe. We've been monitoring you since you were admitted three days ago."

"Call Sofia and tell her to come immediately," I said to Alessandro.

"I'm on it." He reached into his pocket for his cell phone and left the room.

I pulled the chair closer to Ms. G.'s bedside and sat. The next few days were crucial. Her right hand was curled up, and her fingers were twisted like a hook. I quickly assessed that the stroke had affected her right side. She tried to move her hand but was unsuccessful. A mist of worry eclipsed her face.

"It's okay, honey. With some physical therapy, we'll get things working again. Relax. I'm here." I squeezed her tiny hand. "I'm so glad you're back. I've missed you."

The nurses moved around Ms. G., probing her and inspecting her IV. Ms. G. smacked away the hand of one nurse. "She's checking to make sure you're all right. Let her do her job." I smiled at Ms. G.

She gave us both a dirty look.

More tears fell onto my cheeks, along with a hearty belly laugh.

"Everything okay, ma'am?" the younger nurse asked.

"Everything's perfect," I said, knowing my pesky patient had finally come around.

After almost a week and a half in the hospital, multiple tests, and hours of rehab, Ms. G. was on the road to recovery. Except for Darnell's graduation, I hadn't left her side. The stroke impaired her speech. Her mouth hung down slightly on one side, and her right hand remained curled up. But when we left the hospital, she could move her fingers again.

On top of her new medications, she was required to attend physical rehabilitation three times a week in the stroke unit at the hospital. The doctor made it clear that the stroke had advanced her Alzheimer's. I didn't know if and when she'd return to her usual ornery self, but I would be with her for every step.

Sofia returned to New York. She promised she'd be back in a few weeks and would call every night. It was difficult for her to leave, and Ms. G. was sad to see her go, but the daily calls made it easier on both.

Ms. G. hated rehab—especially physical therapy—so much that she hit one of the therapists and called him a slew of expletives in Italian. To avoid her getting kicked out of the hospital, I spoke with her doctor to see if we could do her exercises at home. He agreed and ordered someone to come by the house three times a week to help with the exercises.

The days were long as she worked to get her mind and body functioning again. Alessandro decided to temporarily move into the big house with us. He cooked, cleaned, and got the ranch into shape while I tended to Ms. G. When I crawled into bed, he was there to help me relax in other ways.

For so many years, I'd done things on my own—the bills, the kids, and the household—but Alessandro wanted me to know that I'd never be alone again. With everything going on, I needed him there.

"Yes, Mom. I understand," I huffed, holding onto the receiver.

"No, I don't think you do."

"I love him, and he loves me. He's a good man. Why can't you let me be happy?"

"I want you to be happy, but you've only been dating him a few months. Truth is, you haven't had a good track record with men. Except for him giving me two amazing grandchildren, Marcus was a train wreck. I'm happy he's out of your life for good. You need to focus on yourself and the kids now and stop rebounding."

"I'm not rebounding. Marcus and I fell out of love years ago."

"How do you expect him to take care of you? Didn't you say he worked in a deli?"

"I make enough money that I don't need him to take care of me. And he owns and operates a few restaurants. He does quite well for himself." *And he's a Mafia boss. I left that little detail out.*

"Have you thought about the impact he'll have on your kids?"

"He loves the kids as if they were his own, and they love him. He even got Darnell a job."

"Say what you want, but I'd hate to see you throw your life away on some needless affair. You need to set a better example for your children. Don't do what I did with your father. You see how well that turned out. And to top it off, he's white," my mother shouted. "Haven't you learned? You saw what happened to your father and me."

"Mama, I gotta go. It's getting late. It's my life, my decision."

"Well, you better make a better decision than you did with that deadbeat Marcus, or your kids will suffer. You can't keep having men come in and out of your life. Go slow and think about this."

"Goodbye, Mama," I said and hung up the phone. *Oh Mama, I know you mean well, but sometimes you're too much.* I rubbed at my temples.

A loud motorcycle rumbled down the road. I walked out of the house to the front gate to see who it was.

Alessandro sat on a silver Harley motorcycle wearing a white

T-shirt, jeans, and black leather boots. I didn't think the man could look more handsome, but I was wrong. Dead wrong.

He cut the engine and pulled off his helmet.

"Hello, beautiful."

My heart ignited. "Hi." I approached him, and he wrapped me in a loving embrace.

"I want to take you somewhere. After everything that's happened with *Zia* lately, we could use a break."

"But who's . . ."

"Don't worry, Pop's coming over right now. I think you're gonna like it. Will you come with me?" he whispered against my neck, sending chills down my spine.

I backed away to refocus. "All right. As long as your dad's coming by, but on this thing? I don't know," I said hesitantly.

"Don't be scared." He reached his hand out to mine. "Please, it's important to me," he pleaded.

"Okay. Everything all right?" I searched his face while he handed me a helmet.

"Everything's great when I'm with you. Put this on and hold tight."

I fastened the straps under my chin and straddled the bike.

"Where are we going? Is it far?"

"Not too far. Just hold onto me. We'll be there in no time."

He strapped up his helmet, and roared the engine.

I put my arms around him.

As we made our way onto Highway Seventeen, the bike shook between my thighs. The ends of my hair blew in the wind as we cruised to the surprise destination. Alessandro had told me about his love for riding motorcycles, but I'd never seen him in action. His love for riding was evident. He drove with confidence and ease. He'd told me once that on his bike he felt free. Being on a motorcycle gave him a sense of control when his life had none. Like his love for boxing, riding blocked certain things from his past. He had to concentrate. Riding and boxing were forms of therapy for him.

We drove through the quiet town of Saratoga, south of San Jose, and up into the hills. Mature redwood trees lined the private roads until we came to a gated entrance. The sign read *Villa Encantada Est. 1913* in black and gold metal lettering.

As we edged closer, Alessandro slowed. A road sign blocked the entrance: *Closed tonight for a private event. Will reopen again tomorrow at 9 a.m.*

I tapped his shoulder.

He put out his foot to stop. We flipped up our visors.

"We came all this way. Next time, I guess," I yelled over the bike's loud engine.

"We'll be fine," he said.

"But it says it's closed."

"Not to us, it isn't. I know the manager. He owes me a favor."

"You know everyone."

"I have a lot of friends."

We laughed and continued down the narrow pass.

Alessandro parked in front of the estate. The building was massive. Grand steps led up to a private patio lined with white chairs. We got off the bike. A man in a tuxedo greeted us with a silver platter holding two champagne flutes and a single red rose.

"Hello. Welcome to Villa Encantada. This is for you." He handed me the rose. "Compliments of the staff."

"Thank you so much. It's beautiful here."

"Please enjoy the grounds. If there's anything you need, I'm here at your service."

"Thank you." I smelled the petals and remembered the red rose on Don Molanano's lapel at Vinny's service. I looked at Alessandro, and he smiled at me. We'd come so far since then. "Did you set this all up?"

"Maybe." He winked and handed me my glass.

I took a sip. The sweet taste lingered on my tongue. "What's the occasion? My birthday isn't for months."

"Us. We're the occasion. Come with me." He extended his hand.

We strolled along the property as the sun set. Birds flew in and out of their homes in the tall trees. Mermaid sculptures and other exotic symbols sat in flowing pools. Small waterfalls spilled water along river rock, giving off a melodious sound. I thought about Ms. G. and Gaetano when they visited Villa Borghese and witnessed the grand fountains.

"This is the closest thing to Italy I could find." Alessandro pulled me to his chest. "I'll take you to the real Italy for our honeymoon."

"Honeymoon?" My lips went stiff. My mother's words still echoed in my ears.

"Come. There's somewhere I want to show you."

"Okay," I said, intrigued.

"So, you've told me a little about your mom, but where's your father? I'd like to meet him." Alessandro held my hand along the private path.

"That might be hard. I don't talk to him much."

"Why? What happened?" He took another sip of his champagne.

"After my parents divorced, he took it hard. He was in and out of rehab. Their families warned them about getting into a biracial relationship for fear of the public scrutiny, but they didn't listen. Over time, things got harder for them. My dad's family said things about my mom that caused big fights. Eventually, they succumbed to the pressure."

He stopped and turned to look at me. "I'm sorry to hear that. I want you to know that my love for you will never change. I won't let anyone, or anything, come between us—even family." His love for me radiated from him.

"My father calls on holidays and sends the kids gifts on their birthdays, but we aren't close."

His face looked pained. "That's too bad. Maybe in time, you guys can reconnect."

"Maybe." I rested my head on his shoulder.

"Speaking of reconnecting, I spoke to my son, Dominic, today."

"You did?"

"It was his eighteenth birthday yesterday. Eighteen." He shook his head. "I still remember when he fit in my palm." Smiling, he spread out his fingers. His face went cold. "I've lost so much time with him." He let out a deep breath and then looked up at me. "When he was younger, Vicki didn't let me talk to him much. But now that he's an adult, I got his number and made the call. I needed to talk to him, man to man."

"What did he say?"

"At first, I didn't know it was him. His voice had changed. Made me think how much time had passed since I'd seen him. I told him I was sorry about what happened between me and his mom and that I knew things had been said that I wanted to clarify when he was ready. Then I asked for his forgiveness." Alessandro's eyes welled.

I squeezed his hand tight.

"Did he forgive you?"

"He did. A huge weight lifted off me. For so long, I felt ashamed because I looked like an absent father. I wanted to be in his life, go to his baseball games and see him at Christmas, but she'd told him things I'd done for the Molanano family. A part of me hated her for that and wanted her gone."

"Do you mean what I think you mean?"

"I was angry. She was the mother of my child. I loved her. I could never do that to her, but I was hurt." He looked away, ashamed of his admission.

"I sent her money every month—lots of money, hoping she'd let me see him. She never did. She even threatened to turn me in if I went over there. I didn't want trouble, so I stayed away. I stopped calling the house. I stopped writing letters, but I never stopped sending money. I needed to support him financially, but I didn't want to play her games."

"Why didn't you go to court to try and get visitation?"

"I was afraid she'd expose me. I'd done some time, and I didn't want to mess things up with my probation. I was too deep in the life to be a good father to him. As much as I was pissed at Vicki, he was safer with her. So, I walked away. It was one of the hardest things I've ever done." He brushed his thumb over my knuckles. "Dominic starts college next year."

"Like Darnell."

"Yes. He wants to be a software engineer. Can you believe my son, a computer guy?" Alessandro beamed with pride.

"That's great."

"He wants to visit me. I told him about you and the kids."

"I'd love to meet him," I said as we approached a tall black gate. A metal plaque read *The Italian Gardens*.

"There's more?"

"Lots more."

He pulled open the gate, and we walked through the entrance. Hundreds of candles flickered in lanterns along the walkway. Dozens of twinkle lights had been strewn across the junipers that grew overhead. It was magical—like something from a fairy tale.

"This is beautiful. You had them do all this?" I asked, breathless.

"Yes."

He smiled as the lights caught his eyes and gave them a warm glow. Their sparkle drew me closer—his magic at work again.

"I did it so I could put *this* smile on your face. *This* particular smile is my favorite." He touched my bottom lip.

I grinned even bigger under his touch.

"We're almost there. Follow the petals." He pointed to the left path.

Red rose petals covered the stone walkway. I followed the blooms to a sculpture of Adam and Eve. I touched the marble with my hands.

"It's so beautiful and romantic here. Thank you for making this day so special and for doing all this." I studied Eve's face.

Alessandro didn't respond.

I turned. He was on his knee with a black box open in his hand. Inside, a ring with a huge diamond glinted in the candlelight.

I gasped.

"From the first day I met you, I wanted you. That day when you walked into the deli, I remember thinking you were so beautiful. Then when I found out you were taking care of *Zia*, I wanted to get to know you. These past few months, you've made me believe I'm worthy of being loved. You're the one person who knows who I really am. You know my past and my family, yet you still love me. Every day I'm with you, you give me purpose. I want to marry you, Barbara. Be in my life forever. I want to see all my sunsets with you. I know it's only been a few months, but if I've learned anything from *Zia*, and from my son, time with the people you love is precious. I don't want to waste any more of it."

I swallowed hard and thought about my mother. I remembered her crying when my father left and how lonely I felt.

"With a long pause like that, I feel a *no* coming on."

"It's not that. I promise you. It just . . ."

"What is it then? I thought you loved me."

"I do love you. You know how much," I pleaded and held his hand tight, "but we've only been dating for a few months. I must be practical this time around. I don't want to be another mixed-race divorced couple. I told you before, it will be harder for us."

"And I told *you* before that I don't care about that."

"I haven't even processed all of what happened in my last relationship yet. In a few weeks, I start domestic violence survivor classes and, hopefully after that, family therapy." I paused. "I have to think about my kids. I'll need to speak to them. I need some time."

He closed the box, put it in his pocket, and stood back up. A thin veil of sadness covered his eyes. "I understand. You're not ready."

I pulled him close. "It's not a *no*. Just more time."

"See, that's the thing, I've learned that we don't always get as much time as we'd like." He brushed a few curls behind my ears. "I love you, and I want you to be my wife, but if you need more time, I can give you that." He kissed my forehead, smiled, and reached for my hand. "We can stay as long as you want, but it's gonna get dark soon."

Within seconds, his body language had changed. His eyes distanced themselves and avoided contact with me. His lips pressed into a thin line. I'd hurt him, and I hated myself for it.

"I guess we should go, then." I took the last sip of my champagne, and we walked back to his bike.

Chapter 22
When Memories Are All That's Left

AFTER OUR NIGHT AT THE VILLA, THINGS FELT AWKWARD. Alessandro spent much of his time working on the barn, and I kept busy with Ms. G. He came by every day to check in on us. Some nights, if he was exhausted, he stayed, but the intimacy slowed.

We were in a rough patch. To his credit, he never left without saying he loved me. We needed to find time to talk. I loved him, and I didn't want to lose him. A long engagement seemed possible.

With more alone time, I looked for things to do while Ms. G. slept. I uncovered a scrap box under her sewing table and read old newspaper clippings she kept in journals. Without her stories, I looked for clues into her past.

Photos of her father standing proudly in front of his clinic with his business sign overhead were mixed in with old pictures of Antonelli farms. Ole man Antonelli stood with his arm around his wife. I'd never seen her picture, but something about her face resonated with me. Her eyes looked sad, and she wasn't smiling. Ms. G. told me that their one and only son was shot by the Mafia when they arrived in the States, and *Signora* Antonelli was heartbroken over it for years.

As I continued to sift through journals, I found a picture of Giuseppe standing with another man who had to have been Alessandro's grandfather in front of a truck with a sign on the door that said *Sunseri's Butcher Shop and Meat Market*. Alessandro told me that, when Angelo took over, he'd renamed the shop Angelo's Deli. I looked out the window to see an Angelo's Deli van parked outside.

Some things were different, and some were much the same.

At the back of one of the journals was a small envelope with a picture from the *San Jose Gazette*, dated 1947. It was a photo of a truck being pulled from a body of water.

Why would she keep such a picture?

There must have been a story behind it. Maybe one day I'd ask her about it, but she was still too fragile.

"Hey, what are you looking at?" Alessandro said while carrying in groceries from the deli.

"Just some old pictures. What did you bring?"

"Sausage and peppers. And a veggie lasagna."

I shot him a look.

"Don't worry. I used turkey sausage and low-salt cheese."

"Thank you. You're so good to us. Can we talk later? I miss you."

"Sure. How's she doing today?" He kissed me on the top of the head and continued on into the kitchen.

"She hasn't woken up yet. Every day is different."

"Barbara," Ms. G. yelled from the bedroom.

I ran to her side. "Good morning, sweet girl. How'd you sleep?" I placed the clipping on the bedside table.

She turned to look at me. "Good, but I had lots of dreams. Some were nightmares." She rubbed the sleep from her eyes.

"That's probably from the medication. If it continues, I'll call the doctor to see if we can change the dosage."

Alessandro came in and stood next to me. "How you feelin', *Zia*? I brought you some food."

She grabbed the newspaper clipping from the side table and stared at it. "Where'd you get this?"

"I'm sorry. I was looking around, and I found it under some scrap books by your sewing machine. I like to see the old pictures. They remind me of the stories you've told me about your family. I'll put it back." I tried to take it from her.

She brushed my fingers away. "I haven't seen this picture in years. Brings back memories. This was when . . ."

"You don't have to tell me. Last time, the memories were too painful for you."

"You're like a daughter to me now. Besides our friendship and the big house, memories are all I have left to give you. And one day I'll lose those too."

"You don't owe me anything. I'm here because I want to be here. I love you, and I want you to get better."

"*Bella mia.*" She cupped my face. "You've helped me more than you'll ever know, and that's why I know I can trust you." She traced the edges of the newspaper clipping with her fingertips. "If I'm going to die, I can't be afraid anymore. I need you to find him."

"Find who? Gaetano? Is he still alive? I can drive you to the winery whenever you want to go."

"Who's Gaetano?" Alessandro asked, confused.

Ms. G.'s eyes darted around the room.

"Alessandro, please sit," I said.

He sat at the foot of her bed.

"I think you're about to hear some stories about your aunt's past that no one knows but me. Private things that can never be shared."

"Old Mafia tales? Sure, that's easy. I know most of them already," he answered proudly.

"Not just Mafia. I'm pretty sure you don't know *this* story. Are you comfortable telling Alessandro?"

"He can stay. I need his help too." Her voice became desperate.

"What do you need, *Zia*? I'll do anything for you."

She reached for both our hands and joined them together with hers. Alessandro looked at me as his fingers grazed against mine. I smiled. I missed his touch. With our hands clasped, she said, "If I'm going to die, I need to see him and know that he's alive. Bring him to me." Tears gathered at the sides of her eyes.

"Gaetano?" I asked.

"My son."

Alessandro and I exchanged a look. Then I shifted my focus back onto her.

"Your son?" I asked.

"What's she talking about? What son?" Alessandro pressed.

"I don't know," I said incredulously. "You don't have a son, honey. It must've been a dream."

"It's no dream. It's real," she fired back.

I looked at Alessandro. "Maybe it's the medication. It can have hallucinatory effects."

"I'm not crazy, damn it."

"We know that." I squeezed her hand to comfort her in her confusion.

"I'm ready to tell you what happened when I returned home from Italy—the day I opened my door to a monster. The day that changed everything..."

Part Two

Verità

Chapter 23

Informant

East San Jose Foothills
Late June 1947
Violetta

I OPENED THE DOOR TO FIND EVIL STARING ME IN THE FACE.
"Hello, Violetta."
Oh God, no. It can't be.

With eyes like the devil's, Frank Di Natale charged through the doorway.

I backed away. *It can't be. How?* Hairs on the back of my neck stood straight up.

He slammed the door behind him and stormed toward me.

"What'sa matta, you don't recognize me anymore?" The soulless voice spoke into my face. "Maybe it's because of this?" He pointed to the crescent-shaped scar I'd given him the night the cops took him to jail.

My legs shook as I walked backwards down the hall. Too afraid to speak, I swallowed my scream deep inside me. Air in my lungs felt like it had been sucked out. Who would help me? There was no one at the ranch but me. With no neighbors for miles, I was alone with a monster. The devil himself.

"How did you get out? What are you doing here?" I forced the words through my dry lips.

Like a hungry lion ready to pounce on its prey, Frank followed me into the living room and cornered me against the wall.

"They got this thing called parole, and let's just say I had an arrangement with the cops. I fed those pigs lotsa bullshit. They ate every fucking word for months. Then when they got comfortable, I gave them the slip." He grabbed my waist and pulled me close. "Me and Pop got other plans in motion."

"It was you all along . . ." A cold sweat made its way across my body. "The note. The guys in Rome . . ."

"I told you. I have eyes everywhere." He inched closer and yanked me toward him.

"Get your hands off me." I tried to push his arms off my hips. "You lousy piece of shit. You flipped, and now you're on the run? And all this time you thought *I* was a rat. How could you be so stupid? They'll come for us from both sides. When they find out, you're a dead man and you know it." I looked over his shoulder. My purse was a few feet away on the table. I needed to break free, get my knife and end him, once and for all.

"What are you looking at? No one's coming to save you this time." He shoved his face into mine. His filthy breath made me want to vomit. He placed his hands on the wall behind me to keep me from escaping. "After everything I did for you. I should kill you for turning me in."

"I didn't turn you in." I stopped myself from saying Jimmy's name—Rose's jealous ex-boyfriend. I'd never ratted, and I didn't want anyone else after me. I stayed silent and turned my face away from his reeking mouth and futile interrogation.

"If it wasn't you, then who?" His lips went stiff.

"I don't know. Get away from me. It's over." I tried to squeeze my body under his arm, but he threw me back against the wall. "Leave me alone."

He pressed his forehead against mine. "Is that anyway to treat your husband?"

"Treat my husband? You were fucking Rose in our bed after our daughter died," I roared. "But thank you. You gave me the freedom I needed to leave. I want a divorce."

Frank slammed my body against the wall. "Nice Catholic girl like you. You ain't getting one. I'll kill ya first before you try and divorce me." His vile threats landed on my face in the form of a frothy spizzle. He squeezed my breasts so hard it felt as if he would rip them off.

"Don't touch me, you pig!" I tried to push away from his hold, but he grabbed my wrists and held them above my head. "Get out of this house before you get us both killed. They're gonna come for you."

"No, honey, you got it wrong. I've come for *you*. My pop knows I'm here under your father's protection."

"My father's gone. He wouldn't have made any deal to protect you."

"You forgot how things run around here. My father doesn't make deals. He gives orders. Your pop would be smart to do what he's told. If something were to happen to me while I'm here, my father will seek justice. So, it'd be wise for all of yous to welcome your guest."

"No one wants you here, least of all my father. He can't stand you after what you did to me."

"He and I can have that conversation when he returns. I can't wait to hear what he says when I put my gun to his head. I'll let you watch when I blow his brains out."

"You bastard." I spit in his face.

He slapped me across the cheek.

My eyes watered. Being beaten again felt like riding a bike. I'd felt this pain many times before. Psychologically, I was numb to it.

"We're gonna have some fun, me and you. It'll be like old times." He ripped off my blouse. Buttons scattered across the floor, making a ticking sound as they landed. The corner of his mouth shot up in a heinous grin.

"If my brother comes home and sees you here, he'll kill you," I warned. I screamed Paulie's name.

Frank laughed. "You stupid bitch. How the fuck do you think I knew you were back home?" Like a snake tasting the air, his poisonous tongue slipped out and licked my neck.

My stomach heaved from his stench.

"Oh yeah, me and your brother, we got this arrangement now, see? He's gonna do good, your brother. He knows how his bread's buttered. He's not stupid like his *puttana* sister."

My heart squeezed into a tiny ball. "No, not Paulie. He'd never do that to me."

"You'd be surprised what people do. Loyalty ain't about blood. It's about who lines your pockets."

His words hit stronger than any fist. How could Paulie do this to me? He was my flesh and blood. "You're lying," I hissed. It couldn't be true, but something in my gut told me it was.

"Oh yeah. He told me about your new boyfriend. You think you can step out on me? On Frank Di Natale? I'm a boss in this family." His jaw clenched.

"You don't run anything out here. Go scuttle back to where you came from. No one around here wants to do business with you. You're a joke. Don Molanano knows it, and deep down you know it too."

"Oh yeah?" He squeezed my face between his fingers.

"Stop," I choked out. My teeth pressed together in his vise-like grip.

"Now that I've ditched those pigs, I'll be running things. Tahoe. Vegas. They'll be mine for the taking. I got deals with the big players out here. Your daddy will be beggin' me for jobs and money, and I'm gonna let yous all starve. Or maybe I'll kill every last one of yous for the trouble you've caused me."

"No," I stuttered.

"This is what you get for trying to make me look like a fool." He curled his hand into a fist and punched me in the gut.

I gasped for breath and looked him dead in the eye. "Go back to Brooklyn and marry one of those floosies you like so much."

"I have a secret for you." He grabbed the back of my hair and yanked my face toward his. His red eyes burned into me like hot coals. He reached between my legs, making my stomach churn. He thrust his body against mine. His erection pressed against my thigh. The whole exchange had aroused him.

Sick bastard.

"I haven't given you a gift in a long time. But, boy, do I have the best gift coming for you. I'm gonna wrap up your boyfriend's head with some wrapping paper and tie it up with a bow. An early anniversary present. Would you like that? Yeah, a fuckin' head on a spike, just for you." His spit pelted my ear like venom.

"Leave him out of this. Take your anger out on me. He's innocent."

"Innocent? He ain't innocent if he put his cock in ya. He's trying to take what's mine."

"No, don't. I beg you."

"Oh, I'm gonna pay this guy a visit, all right. He's gonna wish he never met Frank Di Natale. And when I'm done gutting him like a pig, I'm gonna bring you his head. Maybe I'll mount it to the God damn wall," Frank roared.

I had to get free to warn Gaetano. I needed to get my mother's gun. The knife would hurt Frank but a shot from that would surely kill him.

I yanked my leg back and kneed him in the balls.

Frank fell to the floor, grabbing himself between his legs. I jumped over his body. He grabbed my foot and tripped me.

I kicked and scratched his face and clawed at his eyes.

He yelled out in pain, then climbed on top of me and pinned my arms with his knees.

With his hand poised to strike, all the feelings of self-preservation returned at once. He punched me in my gut. I curled up in a ball.

"Pleeaasse . . ." I whimpered.

Frank pushed his full weight onto me. "It's been a long time, Violetta." He unzipped his pants. "You don't know how long I've been waiting for this. You're gonna give me a son if it's the last thing I do."

"No, don't. Oh God, no. Stop," I cried out while trying to fight off his grip. He pulled his hand up high above his head then closed his fist. His hand came down against my face.

Everything went dark.

Frank's loud snoring echoed off the walls. I tried to open my eyes, but my left eye was swollen shut. With only partial sight, the room swirled around me. From the little I saw, it was dark out. I was naked in the old bed we used to share. My head pounded, and every inch of my body ached.

Frank lay next to me, sweaty, with red scratch marks on his face and eyelids. The room smelled of liquor, cigarettes, blood, and bodily secretions. I tried to move my hand to my face to assess the damage, but Frank had tied my arms to the headboard. I rustled around trying to wriggle free but woke Frank instead.

"Don't even think about it. You ain't runnin' off nowhere. I ain't done with you yet." He pressed his lips together in a tight line.

"Let me go." I tried to tug free, but when I inhaled, a sharp pain ripped through my chest. Frank had broken my ribs again.

He advanced his body on top of mine and pressed his weight against my chest.

"Get off. I think you've broken my ribs. I can't breathe," I wheezed. I wanted to push his body off me, but with no hands I was powerless. I tried to twist my wrists to free one hand, but a jolt of searing agony shot down my arm. I looked up at my hands. Two fingers pointed in the wrong direction. They were dislocated and the pain was intense. It must have happened sometime during the night, but my memories were foggy.

My other hand was asleep from being overhead all night, leaving my grip useless. I was numb, both in body and spirit.

"What kind of monster are you?" I yelped out in pain. "Untie my hands."

"What do you need hands for? It's not like you ever worked. You just like to whore around." He tightened the ropes around my wrists.

The last bits of adrenaline sparked inside of me. I kicked my legs and kneed him in the groin again.

He gasped.

With every movement of my legs, his cum dribbled out of me. I kicked and kicked again until the back of his hand connected with my face. His knuckles felt like giant rocks across my chin.

The room spun again, and a loud buzzing entered my ears. I couldn't move. My brain wasn't connecting with my body. Nothing worked.

"Don't you move," he ordered.

The bed rocked back as he moved violently inside me. When he plunged himself deep, it ached and burned. I closed my one good eye and tried to go to a safe place. When my soul was cast into the dark again, I imagined vineyards and sunsets.

I woke again. This time it was daytime. Frank wasn't in the room. I was alone. I couldn't feel my arms, which helped with the pain. It was better to be numb than to feel the ache from my twisted fingers. I looked down at my naked body. Huge red blotches covered my inner thighs. My legs were tied to the bottom bed posts with sheets and more rope. I tried to move, but I didn't have the energy. My mouth was dry, and I felt sick. I needed water—anything to quench my thirst.

"Frank," I shrieked, trying to ignore my throbbing ribs.

Frank stumbled into the room.

"Please, I need some water. I can't even swallow. Please. Something. Anything."

Frank climbed on top of me.

"No. Stop it. Not again," I begged. The words came out like vapor and dust. I drew in a sharp breath. "You're gonna go to hell for this, you bastard."

"I'm sick and tired of hearing your mouth. For once in your life, shut the fuck up. All you do is complain." He grabbed his dirty sock off the floor and shoved it into my mouth. Dry, filthy fabric pressed to the back of my throat. My nose was swollen from the hits to the face, making breathing even harder.

"Good. That ought to shut you up," Frank said as he unzipped his pants.

I closed my eyes.

A knock came from the front door.

My swollen lids sprang open.

Frank put his hand over my mouth, pushing the sock even deeper down my throat. Afraid to choke on my vomit I fought the urge to gag while he lay on top of me, waiting to see if the knocking stopped.

It didn't.

Bang. Bang. Bang.

The noise grew louder and more persistent.

"God damn it. If this is that brother of yours, I swear I'm gonna give him a beatin'. I told him I wanted some privacy." Frank squeezed my face. "And if you think about screamin', I'll kill you both. You got that?" His eyes blazed. He zipped up his pants and headed for the door.

I tried to wriggle free, but it was no use. *Oh God, what if it's Carmela? Get out of here, sister! He'll hurt you.* For a split second, I hoped it was Tony and my father. Maybe they'd come home early to save me. But as I lay quietly, I listened to Frank talk to someone at the front door.

"She doesn't live here," Frank said.

"Is her father, Giuseppe, around? Or her brother Tony?" a voice asked.

"How do you know Giuseppe? You one of Mario's guys?" Frank asked.

"No. I'm not. My family has known them for years."

Then there was a long pause.

"You have a cat?"

"No. Why?" Frank said.

"Your face is scratched up. And that's a nasty scar you got there."

My heart pounded against my chest. From many feet away, I finally recognized the voice. It was Gaetano. He'd come for me just as he promised.

A burst of energy zinged through my body, giving me renewed life. The bed frame hammered against the floorboards as I thrashed around in the bed.

"Oh, that. No. It's nothin' Hey, uh, look, I gotta go. I'll tell the old man you were lookin' for him."

"I was told Violetta was here. I have to speak to her," Gaetano demanded.

"How do you know Violetta?" Frank asked.

"Where is she?" Gaetano's voice roared.

"Look out, boss. He has a gun," another voice yelled. Then something heavy hit the ground and a gunshot went off.

My body stiffened. *Oh God, no.*

"This is for everything you did to her, you son of a bitch," Gaetano yelled.

Frank and Gaetano shouted at each other. Then I heard a noise I'd become all too familiar with: the sound of skin hitting skin, followed by grunts and heavy breathing. They were fighting. Things crashed to the ground. Glass broke. The house shook like an earthquake.

This was it, my moment to get free.

My medical training kicked in. I moved my dry tongue back and forth against the putrid cloth that had been shoved down my throat. If I got it back far enough, my regurgitation reflex would take over and I'd retch up the sock. As the cloth got further and further to the back of my throat, I heaved with so much force it came flying out of my mouth along with vomit and saliva. With a scorched throat, I forced out a scream.

"Gaetano, I'm in here!"

I tossed and turned in the bed to try and free myself. I lowered my torso and with all the strength I had left to muster, yanked my wrists so hard I heard a pop.

I'd separated my shoulder.

I wailed.

"José, take his gun and go find her."

José burst into my room. He gaped at me with wide eyes.

"*Ay, Dios mio,*" he said as he untied me from the bed. José wrapped my body in the sheets around me and picked me up in his arms. "*Pobrecita ¿Qué te hizo ese monstruo?*"

The most unbearable pain radiated from my shoulder and ribs. It snaked its way through my body, assaulting me to my core.

"My arm," I cried as it dangled at my side.

José carried me down the hall. I looked over his shoulder to see Gaetano on top of Frank. Gaetano's fists came down hard and fast on Frank's face in a series of vicious blows. Left, right, then left again. Gaetano pressed his hands around Frank's throat.

"I'm not just gonna beat you, I'm gonna kill you, you fucking bastard. You deserve to die after what you did," Gaetano yelled into Frank's face. Gaetano pressed down on Frank's throat. Frank's face turned three shades of red, then white. His eyes looked like marbles about to pop out of his face.

Paulie barged in through the back door and pressed a gun to Gaetano's head.

"No, Paulie. Don't!" I cried out as José carried me toward the front door.

José turned around and placed me on the floor. He reached into his jacket pocket and pulled out his pistol. Gun in hand, he charged toward Paulie, ready to put a bullet in my brother's head.

Inches away from ending Paulie's life, José yelled, "Drop da fuckin' gun, or I kill you."

"Stop this, please," I screamed out with my last energy. "He's my brother."

José looked confused. He looked at me, then back at Paulie. Gaetano released Frank's neck. In one final, brutal blow, Gaetano punched Frank's face and made his body go limp.

José held Paulie in the gun's sight, ready to fire.

Gaetano ran to me and scooped me up in his arms. "I'm right here. You're okay," he whispered as he assessed my face and body.

I looked back down the hall at José and Paulie.

"Paulie, stop. I'm your sister, for God's sake—your flesh and blood," I pleaded, gasping for breath.

Paulie looked at me, then back to Frank who lay lifeless on the floor.

Paulie dropped his gun. "Go. Never return here, Vi. You know I'll have to come for you now. Do yourself a favor and be hard to find." Paulie knelt and patted Frank's face. "Frank? Frank, get up."

Gaetano carried me to his truck and lifted me into the passenger's side. José followed behind, walking backwards out the door to the truck while covering all their movement with his weapon. Gaetano started the truck, and José jumped in. With his gun in one hand, José rolled down his window, ready to fire at anyone until we were safely away.

"Hold onto her," Gaetano commanded.

José looked down at my face. "She's hurt bad, boss."

"I know," Gaetano said, then shifted his sad eyes at me. His bottom lip quivered as he looked down at my ravaged body. "You're gonna be okay. I'll take care of you. I'm getting you out of here for good."

Gaetano's foot slammed down onto the gas. The engine roared as we made our way down the dirt road and away from the ranch. I pressed my head against José's shoulder and let go of any conscious thought.

Chapter 24

Tending to Wounds, Old and New

VOICES SPOKE AROUND ME. I TRIED TO OPEN MY EYES TO WAKE from my nightmare, but they wouldn't budge. Occasionally, I caught flickers of light and faint movements.

"Whya you bring her here?" a familiar woman's voice asked as she tended to my wounds.

"Mama, stop it. I love her. Look at what that bastard did to her," Gaetano said.

"Dey willa coma now," *Signora* Sanna said.

"I know. We'll be ready. Right, José?" Gaetano asked.

"*Si señor*. De men will be here in two days. I tell *mi primo*. He know one of da border patrol agents. He gonna pay him off. If dat no work, I have udder ways to get dem here. No worry. Dey coming. Until den, I tell da men who work here. Dey gonna fight for you, boss."

"As soon as she's strong enough to travel, I'll take her somewhere far away from here. I'm sorry to put you through this. You can leave at any time, José. I don't want any of you to get hurt."

"No, boss. Dis is our home now too. We stand wit you."

"Thank you," Gaetano said. "Violetta, my love, I need you to open your eyes and look at me."

Gaetano's hands cupped my face. I pushed my eyes open. My eyelids fluttered as I tried to gauge where I was. The pain made me realize I wasn't dreaming.

Faces stared at me. I was partially blind in one eye. From the little I saw, I was in a room I'd been in before but couldn't place. I forced my lids higher. Trying to focus hurt my eyes. My head throbbed, and my body felt weak.

"Violetta, stay with me." Gaetano placed his hand on my arm.

I opened my eyes again and looked around the room. White lace sheers draped over the bed's canopy. I looked out the window. Rows of green were in the distance. My fuzzy brain made the connection. I was in the guest house of the Sanna Winery. The place where I'd given my body and soul to my lover—my grape grower—Gaetano. It was my home away from home. Thoughts of the ranch flooded my eyes.

The rope.

The sock.

The bed.

Frank's eyes and Paulie's face as he put a gun to the back of Gaetano's head.

Paulie.

My stomach shriveled with disgust. How could he betray me like this? The answer sprouted tears and stung my eyes. Gaetano stood over me next to the bed. His mother taped my fingers together.

"Ouch," I yelped as she manipulated them.

"We need to set them," Gaetano said. "We gave you some medicine for the pain."

"No, I can't take medicine," I said frantically, worried that it would reignite my addiction.

"Violetta, listen to me. You've suffered enough. You need the pills to rest. You've been beaten head to toe. It's the only way you can heal. Just for another day, my love, so you can get stronger," Gaetano assured.

I tried to move but the pain was too great. I nodded without protest.

"Here, drink some water, *sole mio*." Gaetano placed a glass under my lip. There was a thick wrinkle between his brows. I'd never seen him so worried.

I craned my neck and took a sip. My throat still ached from when Frank shoved the sock down it, but the water felt good. It was cool and moist, but a bitter taste in my mouth remained. I reached for my stomach.

"I'm going to throw up," I said.

"Mama, Espi, hurry. Hand me that towel," Gaetano yelled, then looked at the young woman who stood in the back of the room. She had long black hair that jetted down her back. She handed Gaetano a towel.

My body contracted and spasmed as I hurled bile onto the towel. The medicine came back up onto my tongue. It tasted like it always had: poison. I tried to roll over onto my side, but my body shook in pain and the tape over my ribs pulled at my skin. Gaetano wiped my face and mouth with a cool cloth.

On my side, I focused on the young woman. This wasn't the girl I'd met years ago. No, she was a woman now, beautiful and exotic. Long legs, flowing hair, and a body to match. We caught each other's eyes. She stared at me with an uncomfortable intensity. Her lip curled up on one side. She sneered then looked away from me. She'd had a crush on Gaetano since she was young. It was obvious she didn't want me here.

Gaetano looked back at her. "We need to get her some food. Maybe some broth? Please tell the chef to prepare something at once."

Espi's nostrils flared. She shook her head at Gaetano, then marched from the room.

"We're going to get you some broth. It should help." He grazed his hand against my cheek.

I winced.

"I'm sorry." Gaetano pulled back his hand.

"It's okay." I grabbed for his hand. "I'm just sore."

Gaetano's eyes moistened. "I hate to see you like this. It's breaking me."

I held his hand. "You saved my life. Thank you."

"I love you," Gaetano said as tears streamed down his cheeks.

"How can you still love me after this? Look at me." I tried to cover my face with my bandaged-up hands. "I'm hideous. He raped me." I turned my head away.

Gaetano's body stiffened. He grunted, then cleared his throat. He bent down over my face. "I will always love you, no matter what. I'm sick just thinking about what happened, but I'm glad I got there when I did."

I turned back to him. "How did you know it was him?"

"The scar on his face. Then I heard you scream," Gaetano said in a shaky voice. He swallowed hard. "I had to get to you." Gaetano swept his thumb over my cheek gently.

"You hand isa mended. I coma back to giva you da *medicina* later. You should take a hot bath to clean you self," *Signora* Sanna said. "He soiled you." She grabbed the wet towel and bandages, placed them in a bag and stood. "Imma go see you *papà* now." *Signora* Sanna placed her hand on Gaetano's shoulder.

"*Grazie*, Mama."

Gaetano walked his mother and José out.

After everyone left, Gaetano sat beside me in bed. "I'll start the bath." Gaetano leaned over and kissed my forehead.

"I'm ashamed. I hate for you to see me like this." Tears welled.

"You have nothing to be ashamed of. Frank did this. I should've killed him, but when you called out for your brother, I didn't want to do anything you'd hate me for later. I know that deep inside you love your brother."

"I do, but how could he do this to me? My mother and father would be so ashamed of who he's become."

"He's no longer the brother you thought you had. You can't trust him."

"A part of him is dead to me."

"If he harms you again, I'll make sure he's dead." Gaetano got up and peered out the window with a cold, blank stare.

"Of all the times Frank beat me, it was never this bad. If you hadn't come, he might've killed me."

Gaetano walked back over to the bed and sat next to me. "You're safe now." He reached for my hand and held it in his. "I thought he was in jail?" Gaetano asked, perplexed.

"So did I. When I opened the door to see him standing there, I was in shock. Before I could shut it, he'd already pushed his way through. I don't know if he's flipped, or if he's back out here doing Molanano business. He said he got something called parole? He's always wanted his revenge." I examined my taped fingers. "This is my fault. When I came home, I told my family about us and our plans. Sadly, it was Paulie who told him I was back home."

"I'm sorry." Gaetano pressed a gentle kiss on my swollen lips. "You know how they work. Frank's either working for Molanano or the cops. Either way, what he did to you is immoral, and he'll be punished in hell for his actions."

I grabbed for Gaetano's arm with my one good hand. The movement caused thunderbolts of pain to surge through me. "Ouch. My shoulder hurts."

"You dislocated it. José and I had to push it back in." Gaetano cringed. "We waited until you were asleep from the medicine, but it was one of the hardest things I've ever had to do. To know that I hurt you like that . . ." He grimaced and turned away.

"Hey, look at me. You didn't hurt me, you saved me. I'm sorry things had to come to this, but Frank won't stop. He'll find us."

"Don't worry about that. It's over now. You're safe here with me. Let's get you up so I can help you bathe."

Gaetano picked me up and carried me to the bathroom where I'd wash away years of servitude and sacrifice to a worthless cause of betrayal.

Chapter 25
Embers of My Heart

LYING IN THE BED THAT ONCE PROVIDED ME SANCTUARY WAS bittersweet. The place where I'd shared my body with Gaetano now functioned more as a medical infirmary.

The drugs forced me to sleep deeply, only waking to use the bathroom. Gaetano was attentive and watched my every move. I don't think he slept much the entire night. Every noise, from a hoot owl to the crackling branches of wind in the trees, forced Gaetano to get up and look through the windows. I wasn't sure what to expect, but something was on its way—ready to come for us.

I slowly moved around in the bed and looked down at my body. Deep splotches of bruising had set in along my arms and legs. I grazed my fingers over my swollen bottom lip—another obvious sign of Frank's handiwork. With my arm in a makeshift sling, I leaned over to the side of the bed to get up when Gaetano appeared with a food tray.

"Here, let me help you. Do you need to use the bathroom again?" Gaetano placed the tray at the end of the bed.

"No, I want to see what I look like."

"No, my love, it's too soon. Let your injuries heal first." His eyes were sullen.

"I need to see. Please. I need to see what that monster did to me."

Gaetano pressed his lips together, then walked to the bathroom and handed me a small hand mirror. "I love you, body and soul. This isn't permanent, but my love for you is. Time heals all things, as we have learned."

My hand shook as I held the mirror before me. New tears spilled down on what was left of my face. Both cheeks were black and blue. Embarrassed, I tried to blink away my sadness. My eyelids looked like balloons and one of my eyes was blood red. My lip was split straight through and was hot to the touch. I was used to seeing my face like this, but not for Gaetano to see me this way— that was too much to bear. I threw the mirror on the bed and looked out the window.

"Please go away," I whimpered. "I'm monstrous."

"No, you aren't." He crawled into bed next to me.

I turned my face away from him.

"Please look at me."

I turned back around.

"I love you. What happened doesn't change the way I feel about you. In fact, it only makes my love stronger. You will get through this. *We* will get through this. You need to eat, my love. Build up your strength so you can heal." Gaetano grabbed the metal fork on the edge of the tray and stabbed a mouthful of eggs. "Here, open your mouth."

I looked down at my hand, then back up to him. A lump formed in my throat. I couldn't even feed myself.

He gently tilted my chin back toward him. "Let me help you, *tesoro mio*."

Defeated and humbled, I opened my mouth while he fed me like a child.

In between Gaetano helping me to the bathroom and dozing off, I adjusted to my physical confinement. My only real fear was what I would do when I had to do more than pee, but I figured when I had to do *that,* Gaetano would get his mother or maybe Espi to help me. Those options didn't look promising either. Either one of them would probably leave me in my own shit.

Espi. Esperanza. If we made it out of this situation alive, one day I'd ask Gaetano about his relationship with her.

A groan escaped my throat.

Beside me, Gaetano shifted. "What's wrong? Are you in pain? Do you need more pills?"

"Not now."

"How do you feel? Any better?"

"A little better. I can move my fingers again. It hurts, but I can feel them."

"That's good." A slow smile spread across his face. "You'll get better every day, I promise. I would've called a doctor, but I didn't know who to trust. My mother tended to enough of my father's wounds over the years that I knew she'd help."

"I understand. I know your mother doesn't like me being here. Let's leave before anything happens." My stomach flipped against my bruised ribs.

"It's too late for that. If your brother told him who I am, he knows where we are. Let him come. I don't care." Gaetano's eyes squinted and the muscles along his jaw bones pressed together tightly. "Rest, *bella mia.*" He pressed a soft kiss on my forehead. "I know it's only been three weeks since I said goodbye to you in Italy, but after everything that's happened, it feels like a lifetime ago. I've missed you so much." He cupped my cheek and smiled.

"We're together now, and that's all that matters." I put my hand over his.

"I should've taken you with me that day, and none of this would have happened. I'm never leaving your side again."

"You've been through so much. First your father's stroke, and now me." Guilt enveloped me. "I'm so sorry. You look so tired. Did you get any sleep last night?"

"A little." My favorite crooked smile emerged and comforted me. "I'm fine."

"I'm worried about you."

"Don't be. With you here, everything is okay. Mama will be by later to check your wounds. Sleep, *tesoro mio.*" He placed the covers over me.

The feeling of something cold on my forehead jostled me awake.

Startled, I recoiled and yanked it off.

"You have *febbre,*" *Signora* Sanna said.

"Oh, I'm sorry. It was cold. It scared me," I whispered and shook from chills.

Signora Sanna grabbed the towel and put it back on my forehead. "Do you wan *aspirina*?"

"*Si, per favore,*" I said.

She handed me a pill and some water. I swallowed it quickly.

"I tink da cut on you lip isa infected. I gonna clean it." She dipped a clean cloth in a bowl of something and rubbed at my lip.

I winced and pulled away from her touch. I licked my lip. It was pure rubbing alcohol, and it burned like fire.

"I needa clean," she said with a stern face.

I carefully pressed my swollen lips together while she dabbed the pungent liquid on my cut. The pain made my face sizzle. I bit the sides of my cheek while she worked. When she was done, she gathered her things and the rest of the medical supplies.

I reached for her arm. "*Signora, aspetta.* Please, wait."

"*Che c'è?* Wassa wrong? You wanna me get my son?"

"No, it's not that. Thank you for helping me. After everything that's happened, I know you have negative feelings about me and my family. But I want you to know that I love your son. We don't get to choose our families. I want to be with Gaetano now. We love each other. I'm sorry that I've brought harm to you and your family."

She stared at me. "My son, he love you. He hurt bad when you leave. I cry for him. I helpa you not only becausa he ask, but becausa what happen when da Cosa Nostra attack me in my house in *Sardegna*." She paused. "And for you mudder. She helpa me dat day at you house. I neva forget."

"Yes, Mama was a strong woman." I blinked back tears. I thought back to the day she spoke about. Mama told her they were *paesani* now, and our family wouldn't let anything happen to them as long as they earned. And if they couldn't, she'd teach her how to protect herself, and had pointed at her gun.

"I see *Cosa Nostra* all my life. Dey only do bad. I no wan *la mia famiglia* wit dem. Der are too many mudders who lose der sons to dis life. I neva wan Gaetano to suffer like dat. I hate dat we giva dem money. But my husband, he decide. I pray every night we find a way to be free of dem. No pay dem anymore. And dey no coma here no more."

"You can never stop paying them. If you did, that would be an act of war. Even my father has thought about ways to become legitimate, but there is no way out for him either. I'm sorry."

She shifted her gaze from me to the floor, then got up slowly and straightened her skirt.

"Gaetano isa man now. I canno tell him what to do, but he hava responsibility to his *famiglia*," she explained. "If you love him, you willa do what isa right. I no wan him hurt again."

"Yes, I will. I understand."

She paused at the door. "Like you mudder, I no let anyone hurt *la mia famiglia* again. I kill anyone who try," she threatened.

She cast a warning stare, then left the room. The door slammed shut.

She was right. I never wanted my daughter, Adelina, to suffer the consequences of this life. I would've protected her from it at all costs.

I thought about the sacrifices that Mafia mothers had to make. Mama would be so upset with Paulie for betraying his blood. More than anything, she'd be scared for his life.

I slumped back into bed and pulled the covers over my face to hide my tears.

Exhausted, Gaetano slept deeply beside me. I needed to use the bathroom, but I didn't want to wake him. I rolled over to my side and walked toward the bathroom, when I smelled smoke . . .

I hobbled to the kitchen and looked out the window.

A flood of panic gripped me.

The vineyards were on fire.

Huge, bright orange and yellow flames blazed through the hundreds of acres before me. Thick smoke billowed up to the night sky and covered the stars. A shiver crawled its way up my swollen body. I limped as fast as I could back to the bedroom.

"Gaetano, get up!" I screamed. "The winery's on fire! Everything is burning."

Gaetano leapt from the bed and threw on his pants and shoes. He looked out the window then back at me with terror.

"It's Frank. He's here. He did this," I yelled when something pounded against the door.

Gaetano grabbed his shotgun, aimed, and threw open the door, ready to shoot.

"No, boss," José's voice bellowed. "Is me. Der isa fire everywhere. Fields to da north have burned to da ground. I try to turn on da water, but it no work."

"Did you get everyone out? Where are they?"

"The men, dey try to fix da water. I tell dem to get the women and children off da property. Espi, she go to check on you family and call da fire department."

"Good." Gaetano's body stiffened. He looked outside, then back at me. "Don't leave this room. The fire is still a few acres out. I'll come back to get you. I need to go to the main house and check on my family. José, stay with her. If anyone comes here that you don't know, shoot, and shoot to kill. You understand me?" Gaetano seethed.

"*Si Señor*. We will kill dem all." José reached for his gun.

"And if the fire gets too close, drive her off the property. Take her to GiaDomella. They're good friends. They'll help us."

"*Si*," José said with a strained face.

Gaetano came to me and kissed my forehead. "I love you." His eyes were hard and fierce.

"I love you too. Please, be careful." I wrapped my sore arms around his waist.

I didn't want him to go. He gently slipped from my grasp. "You'll be safe here with José. I'll be right back, and I'm getting you out of here. We are *all* getting out of here—somewhere we can stay until things die down." Gaetano wrapped his jacket around his face and pushed past me through the door.

I coughed as clouds of smoke gathered around us. José closed the door.

"*Señora* Violetta, please go lie down. Is no good for you to cough," José implored as fear crossed his face.

I went to the bedroom, sat on the bed, and looked out the window. It felt like my blood had drained out of me. Years of Gaetano's hard work, ruined. It would take his family decades to recover from this.

My stomach knotted, and I felt sick again. I looked down. My St. Anthony's medal still hung from my neck. Even with the countless blows from Frank, it was still intact. I held it between my fingers until I heard another knock. I walked back to the door to see if it was Gaetano.

"Stay back," José said.

I shivered, and my mouth went dry.

José went to the door.

"*Papá, ¿estás aquí?* It's me. Espi. Please, let me in. I'm scared. I can't see where I'm going with all the smoke," I heard her say, followed by some heavy coughing.

José opened the door. "*Ay, Dios mio,*" he said.

"Please, let me go," Esperanza shouted.

I peeked out from the bedroom door. Frank stood behind Esperanza with a gun held to her side. Paulie stood next to Frank, pointing a shotgun at José's face.

"Not so fucking tough now, are ya?" Frank said as he edged his way through the guest house. He smelled of gasoline.

My legs felt watery, like I'd melt into a deep puddle on the floor. I held onto the wall for fear of falling.

"You said that if I showed you where she was, you wouldn't hurt me or my father," Esperanza yelled. She clawed at Frank's forearm, which was wrapped around her neck.

The depths of betrayal were countless. First Paulie, now Esperanza. It all made sense. She'd always loved Gaetano, and I was in the way. I'd known it from the moment I'd met her. I shook my head at her, but she avoided my stare.

"Leave her alone, *pinche cabrón.*" José cocked the hammer of his gun, which he pointed right at Frank's head.

"Paulie boy, take care of this guy. Will ya?"

Paulie's face went blank. He took a deep breath, adjusted his neck to focus. "*Viva la famiglia* Molanano," he said.

Then fired.

"No, Paulie!" I screamed and dropped to my knees.

Time slowed as José's body fell to the ground. Red splattered everywhere. He lay surrounded in pools of blood as the fluid gushed from his head and onto the floor.

"Oh my God, no," I choked out.

"Nooooo! *Papá,*" Esperanza screamed, trying to break free from Frank's hold.

Frank laughed as he watched.

"Stop it, Frank," I yelled. "Let her go. I'm the one you want. Take me instead. You win." I stood with my arms out to Frank.

"For being a good little girl, I'll let you live this time," he said to Esperanza. "But you say one word, and I'll come back and put a bullet in ya like your daddy."

He tossed Esperanza aside. She ran screaming toward her father and wept over his dead body at my feet.

Paulie grabbed José's gun while Esperanza hovered over her father.

"It's true. He'll do it, Espi," I warned as Frank came toward me. "I know you'll want your revenge, but if you say one word, he'll kill everyone on this winery. Your mother, your sisters. Even Gaetano. It's not worth it."

"Enough talkin'. Let's go." Frank grabbed me by my hair and shoved his gun to my side.

"We gotta get outta here. Fast. The fire's surrounding us on every side," Paulie warned.

"Get out of here while you can," I screamed back at Esperanza. "Save yourself. The family will need you now more than ever."

Frank forced me out the front door of the guest house and through the burning fields. I was barefoot and dressed in nothing more than my silk shift. With a gun at my back and a fistful of my hair in his other hand, Frank pushed me through the vineyard. Sparks of orange, yellow, and red flickered around us as we moved through the blazing fields. Sweat trickled down my back and dripped off my chin. The smoke was so thick, we coughed uncontrollably. Frank stopped and hacked so fiercely he threw up on the dirt.

"Come on. We gotta get outta here!" Paulie yelled.

"Yeah, yeah, give me a God damn minute. I can't breathe ova here," Frank said, winded.

As Frank retched, he released his grip on me. Adrenaline kicked in. I broke free of his hold and bolted through the smoky blackness. Through the maze of burning embers, my raw feet gained traction against the rough earth beneath me. The inferno's light guided my way.

With every stride forward, the wind picked up around me. Strong and hot, it swirled around the tiny trees with vengeance. Flames jumped from vine to vine, causing more destruction. For the first time in my life, the wind frightened me.

The heat of the fire burned my cheeks and stung my eyes. Panting now, I drew in a deep breath. Blackened air burned my throat and chest, making me croak and wheeze. The smoke was so dense that I couldn't see two feet in front of me. With clouded sight and swollen eyes, I struggled to get my bearings. I had no idea where I was going.

Something yanked at the back of my hair and forced me backward.

"Get over here, you stupid bitch." Frank slapped my face so hard I fell to the ground. "Get up, you lousy whore."

He dragged me through the vineyard. The ache in my shoulder returned. I tried to fight against his grip, but my shoulder screamed in pain. My hand and swollen fingers crippled in agony as I clawed at Frank's forearm.

"Let me go!" I yelled. My legs hung like limp spaghetti and caused me to slump to the ground.

"Get up," Frank roared, trying to hoist my body back up. "I want you to see this."

"See what? You crazy, sick bastard!"

Grunting, Frank pulled me through the barren fields while my feet trudged through the dirt and ash to a clearing. A massive light flamed in the distance. It was so bright I thought the sun had risen before us. It got brighter and brighter with every step forward. Between the howls of the wind and the crackling of fire, screams lifted in the distance.

Frank stopped and looked to the left.

"Noooo!" a woman's voice shrieked.

"This is what happens when you fuck with Frank Di Natale."

Frank held me up. My eyelids fluttered in the heat as I tried to focus. We were at the winery's entrance, a few feet from the main building. The mammoth structure was lit with flames that must have reached fifty feet high. Hotel guests screamed and ran to the main road for safety.

Gaetano's mother wailed into the darkness as she bent over *Signor* Sanna's lifeless body. To their right was another body on the ground—a smaller body—a girl's body.

Gaetano rushed from the main building carrying another small bundle.

Oh no. Gaetano's sisters.

My heart jumped into my throat.

Gaetano's face was covered with black soot. He placed the lifeless body down. His shirt was on fire and most of his hair had been singed off.

Signora Sanna screamed over their corpses. There lay her family, dead and burned. All except Gaetano, who cried over his sisters' bodies. In clouds of black smoke, Gaetano fell to his knees next to his mother and held her while she shook with grief.

Frank laughed.

Gaetano's head snapped to attention.

Frank pressed his gun to my side.

Gaetano stood, reached for his rifle, pressed it to his shoulder, and charged into the smoky darkness toward us. "Let her gooooo!"

Frank looked to the right. Paulie's car was parked up the hill about fifty feet away from the main building. Frank dragged me toward the car.

Gaetano fired at the car.

The side mirror broke clean off. Shards of glass flew into the air.

Paulie squared his shoulders.

"No, Paulie, don't do it," I pleaded, sobbing and clawing at Frank's forearm to break free of his grip.

Paulie looked at me and back at Frank. He hesitated as a shadow of fear crossed his face.

"If you eva wanna be a boss, now's your chance. Kill that son of a bitch," Frank ordered.

Paulie glanced at me again, then straight ahead at Gaetano.

"He's lying to you, Paulie. He's using you to do his dirty work."

"Shut up." Frank slapped me again.

Another shot came from Gaetano's gun and grazed Frank's arm.

"Ahh, fuck," Frank yelled. He loosened his grip on me as blood streamed down his arm. I stepped forward and wriggled out of his arms.

He yanked me back by my hair. "Get back here," Frank scolded, then dragged us a few feet closer to the car. "Do it," Frank roared at Paulie between coughs. "Do it now. Your *capo* gave you an order."

"No, Paulie. Don't," I screamed, trying to escape Frank's grasp. "Please don't. I beg you, brother. Don't do this. It's not worth it." I reached for Paulie's arm as he pushed past me.

"Get off me, Vi," Paulie shouted.

Frank pushed me through billows of dense smoke and ash toward the car. I could barely see Gaetano.

"No. I don't want to go with you." I kicked and screamed.

Frank backhanded me.

My legs buckled, and I fell to the ground.

I pressed my swollen eyes together and squinted through the dark haze to search for Paulie and Gaetano. Gaetano stalked us until he caught sight of Paulie. He stood firm then fired a shot at Paulie's feet, missing my brother by inches.

"That's it, you son of a bitch." Paulie planted his feet, rolled his neck, and pulled the trigger.

Gaetano clutched his chest, fell to the ground, and curled into a ball.

Time stood still.

My heart stopped.

"*Nooooooo!*" I wailed as Frank lifted me over his shoulder and shoved me into the car's back seat.

I looked out the window to see if Gaetano was moving.

He wasn't.

Fire engines barreled down the road.

"Come on. Let's get outta here," Frank yelled.

Frank tied my hands and feet. Paulie slammed the door, ran to the front seat to start the car, and then slammed on the gas. We peeled out past the firetrucks with nothing but blankets of smoke behind us.

"Paulie," I choked out through snot and tears. "How could you do this? Kill me. Kill me now. Please. Put me out of my misery. I'd rather die than be with Frank."

"Shut up," Paulie said in a commanding voice.

"You should be ashamed of yourself. You fucking murdering bastard," I roared. "I hope you rot in hell."

"Frank, shut her up. Swear to God, man, shut her up, or I'll pull over and do it myself," Paulie roared as he sped through the dark roads of the sleepy wine country.

"Shut up, the both of yous," Frank fired back. "My head hurts from the screamin' and the damn smoke." Frank held me down with one hand, the other was on his gun.

"Oh shit." Paulie's voice shook. "What if someone saw us? What if they saw the car? I ain't getting pinched. I just killed two guys."

"No one saw us. There was too much smoke. Even if they did, you'll be fine," Frank said as he held me down. "I take care of my men. You're gonna drop me and your sister off at the ranch and then go to the Bay Club Casino like I told you. Ask for a guy named Tommy the T-bone. Tell 'em I sent you. He'll know what to do. Do not contact me or call anyone. I'll reach out to you when it's safe."

Sweat poured from Paulie's face. "Okay." He gripped the steering wheel tight.

"Don't worry about it, kid. Was this your first hit?"

"Yeah," Paulie admitted.

"You earned your ceremony. When we get back, it's *La Omerta* for you, kid. You earned it tonight. We'll have a party and everything," Frank said, then coughed again.

Paulie stared at me through the rearview mirror.

"How could you?" I mouthed as my body drowned in grief and disgust. Blackened tears trailed down my cheeks and dripped off my chin.

Paulie looked back at the road.

I closed my eyes. I prayed to my mother, my daughter, and God. *Please God, take care of Gaetano. Let him live and take me instead. If I'm too late, then you've got yourself another angel. Lord, hear my prayer.*

I peered down at the St. Anthony's charm he'd given me. This would be all I had left of him.

My Gaetano. My Guy. My grape grower.

The love of my life . . . gone.

Chapter 26
Body of Evidence

Frank carried me into the house and threw me on the bed. It was late, and the lights were off in Pop's clinic.

"I hate you. You killed innocent people. When you die, you'll burn in hell. Your father raised a lousy bum of a son," I hissed. "Murderer!"

"*Basta*," Frank yelled. "Shut that big hole in your face, or you'll get it again." Frank raised his arm to strike.

"Do it. Fuckin' kill me. If you don't, I'm gonna tell everyone what happened. Now I'll be the rat that you thought I was. I have nothing to lose anymore."

"I said shut up," Frank slapped me again.

I was numb. The pain didn't hurt anymore. I wanted more. I wanted him to kill me. It was the same feeling I'd had the night the cops came to our door in Brooklyn. This time, I would end it all. This time, there was no going back. I knew the one thing that would push him over the edge and end my misery.

"Is that the best you got, you rotten piece of shit? I never told you this before, but I killed our daughter."

Frank looked like he'd seen a ghost.

"Yeah, it was me, Frank. Remember all those pills you used to give me? Well, I took them, and more. That's what killed our little girl. I did it. I never wanted to bring a child up in this life, anyway," I said, trying to get him to snap and end all the misery.

Frank's face went from white to bright red. He jumped on top of me and clenched his hands around my throat. He pressed down so hard ligaments in my neck popped.

"I should have done this a long time ago," Frank screamed at my face. "Now you die, you worthless bitch." Frank frothed over me like a rabid dog.

I didn't fight back. I let go. This was what I wanted—to be free. I welcomed my eventual passing. I put my hands to my sides and counted down from one hundred. In seconds, I'd be reunited in heaven with all the people I loved.

There was no sound. My sight changed, as if I was looking through water.

I must be close now.

I quieted my mind and stopped fighting for air. My body was as weightless as a floating cloud in a vast sky.

Please, God, take me now. I'm ready. Gaetano, I'm coming.

Suddenly, there was a thunderous boom, then something wet spattered all over my body. Frank's full weight crushed me.

I tried to open my eyes, but the warm substance covered my face. It dripped down my cheeks and into my mouth. It tasted of rust and salt. I tried to wipe it away, but I was covered in it.

It was blood. Lots of blood.

I wiped the red liquid from my eyes. A huge part of Frank's head had been completely blown off. Pieces of his skull and brain were missing.

Tony stood at the foot of the bed with Mama's shotgun pointed right at us. Wisps of smoke came off the barrel and rose to the ceiling. "Burn in hell, you son of a bitch," Tony fumed.

My father rushed in and stood next to Tony. His eyes were as wide as saucers. "*Minchia*." Pop shook his head. "We needa get rid of da body."

I shut my eyes. White light crept under my hooded vision. It must have been my guardian angel protecting me from all the events I'd endured. My body lifted, and I was carried away to the nothing.

My nose tickled. I opened my swollen eyes.

The harsh scent of bleach stung my nostrils. It was strong and burned my throat. I was in a hospital bed in my father's clinic, dressed in a fresh nightgown and wrapped in clean linens.

It must have been a dream.

A deep yawn developed in my diaphragm, making me stretch my body. I yelped in pain.

This was no dream.

Like a puzzle, I tried to put the hazy pieces together in my mind—a product of all the pills. Truth left me breathless.

"Oh my God, Gaetano," I whimpered. I hobbled my broken body to the phone in my father's office and dialed the operator. While I waited for a voice, the cuckoo clock chimed. It was four a.m. Seconds passed like hours. Visions of high flames and bodies on the ground made my heart pound against my chest. "Oh God, please no. He has to be alive," I spoke into the phone. My voice shook.

The operator answered.

"Can you connect me to the Sanna Winery in the Napa Valley, please?"

"Connecting now." After a brief pause, the woman said, "Ma'am, there's no answer. Should I try a different connection?"

"They had a fire there last night. It must have warped all the telephone lines out there," I said frantically. "Can you connect me with the Napa Valley Fire Department, then?" I asked desperately.

"Hold, please."

The phone slipped down my sweaty palm as I waited.

"Napa Valley Fire, Captain Eli Willis speaking. Are you reporting a fire?"

"No. Well, yes. There was a fire at the Sanna Winery last night."

"Yes. A terrible one. Almost took down their whole operation. We were able to salvage some of it. Are you from the press?"

"No, I'm a friend of the family. Do you know if Mr. Sanna is alive? I tried to call but the telephone lines are down."

The officer cleared his throat. "Ma'am, unfortunately, Mr. Sanna suffered life-threatening wounds and died last night at the scene. May I ask your name? Would you like me to deliver a message to someone out there?"

I took in a big gulp of air.

I screamed and threw the phone across the room, ripping the cord from the wall. My rage was back in full force. It flowed through my veins like hot poison, consuming me once again.

I pushed everything off my father's desk. Various papers, pens, and medical equipment dumped onto the floor. I tossed over the file cabinet, breaking a lamp on its way down.

The light bulb sparked, and glass shattered around my bare feet.

"I hate this life," I bellowed and fell to the floor. "I hate the Mafia. Why, God, why didn't you take me last night, why?" I cried, trying to push over my father's chair.

A big, warm hand grabbed my arm in midair.

"Stop it," Tony's voice roared. "Stop it right now," he commanded, then confined my body into a tight ball.

"No, Tone," I fired back. "Let go of me." I tried to push my brother's arms away. "They're all dead. He's dead. Gaetano's gone. Paulie did it," I yelled through tears.

"Hey, you shut your mouth, you hear me?" Tony's voice was stern and threatening.

A flux of anguish flooded my eyes.

He hugged my shaking body tightly. "You're okay, Vi. I have you."

"Tony, oh God. What am I gonna do now?" My words trailed off as my legs gave way. I slumped to the ground.

Tony gently laid me on the floor and sat beside me. "It's okay." Tony patted my back. "You're okay, Vi," he said while I whimpered on his shoulder "It's all over now. *Shhh,*" Tony hushed as he rocked me back and forth.

I pulled away and stared at my brother's face through wet eyes. "Wait. I remember now. You shot Frank. You . . . you . . ." I pointed my finger at my older brother, recalling the bits and pieces of Frank's skull scattered around me.

"I don't know what you're talking about." Tony quickly looked away.

"Yes, it was you. I remember. Frank's head . . . the blood . . . Oh God," I muttered, then threw up. Yellow bile fluid flew from my mouth along with streams of saliva onto the floor next to Tony's feet.

He ran to the bathroom and returned with a towel.

"Here. Clean yourself up." Tony carried me back to the bed and pulled the covers over my bruised body. "You shouldn't be movin' much. Look at you. You're all busted up."

"Paulie's to blame for this. He's the one who told Frank where I was."

"I'll deal with Paulie." A vein in Tony's forehead pulsed.

I grabbed for his hand. "Don't play games with me. I know what happened. I'm not a child. If you won't tell me the truth, Pop will." I slung my leg over the side of the bed and ran out the door.

"Get over here," Tony yelled from the house.

"Papa, where are you?" I screamed and ran past the chicken coops. With only small hints of light in the distance, I scanned the ranch. Pop was talking to Sal Sunseri by the barn. I walked through the tall grass toward my father.

"Donna worry about notin'. We take care of everyting," Sal said while my father wiped his blood-stained hands with a towel.

"Papa," I choked out.

The two men shot me a bone-chilling stare. Angelo came out of the barn carrying a body wrapped in a sheet over his shoulder.

Angelo stopped, looked at his father, then back at me. Breathless, I fell to the ground.

Two heavy hands grabbed onto my shoulders and yanked me back up.

"Get back in the house," Tony demanded.

"No. Let go of me. Papa," I screamed, trying to break free of Tony's grip.

"Violetta, go back to da house," my father commanded, then shot me a grave stare. "Tony, get her back in da house and keep her der."

Tony picked me up. I kicked and screamed against my brother's body. "Papa, Paulie killed Gaetano," I roared.

"Shut up, Vi. I mean it, or I'll make you shut up," Tony yelled.

Tony held me down on the bed while my father came in behind him.

"Papa, Paulie killed Gaetano!" I screamed with a hoarse voice. "Please take this pain away from me. I want the pills. I don't want to live anymore. I'm going crazy," I shrieked. Then I looked at Tony. "You killed Frank. You shot him while he was on top of me. This is all too much. Please. Help me," I begged.

My father held me in his arms.

The Mafia had taken so much from me and stolen any shred of sanity I had left. I struck my father repeatedly as years of anger poured from me because of his association with the Mafia. "You did this! If you hadn't made me marry that bastard none of this would have happened," I yelled and pounded on his chest.

Tony pushed Pop aside and held me down.

"She's hysterical, Pop. You have to do something. She's threatening to go to the cops."

Pop went to the medicine cabinet and pulled out a syringe. "Hold her down," my father ordered.

"Make it strong enough to kill me," I seethed. "You owe me that."

Tears fell from my father's eyes, and he shoved the syringe into my arm.

I hoped that I'd be listening to angels sing. I was dismayed to find that I was still in the clinic. The door to the room was open. I heard Pop and Tony talking in the hallway.

"Pop, she knows too much. We need to talk to her."

"No. Not yet. We mussa keep her sleep for a little while so she no say nutting."

"Fuckin' Paulie. Where could he be? He's definitely runnin' scared. Vi told me what happened. He shot the Sanna boy. I'm sure Frank made him do it. I hope for his sake no one got the plates, or that could get the feds over here, snoopin' around."

"*Maronn.*"

"But look what Frank did to her," Tony said. "Paulie's my brother and I love him, but I want to beat his stupid face in. Brother or not, he betrayed us. Blood is blood."

"For you brudder, Molanano blood courses tru his veins more dan mine. He made hisa choice. He knew what it mean to get hisa hands dirty. He willa needa be a man and face up to his consequences, to Di Natale or da cops. I willa do all I can to protect him, but if someone did see, how long you tink da mayor willa help us?"

"We have to hope no one can identify him, or we'll have to grease their pockets to keep them quiet. Or kill 'em."

"Lika everyone else we deal wit, itsa always da same. Da mayor isa slippery man. I no trust him, but we needa him on our side. To him, glory is wort more dan gold. We canno win. We needa help you brudder and da mayor. How you tink biziniss been runnin' so smoothly all deez years? Tony, we needa be smart."

"Yeah, Pop. You're right. What do we do?"

"I willa do what I canna for you brudder, but I make no guarantees. I neva wan dis for any of you, but what choice did I have? Der were times I had to do tings dat I no proud of to help us survive. Now look at my beautiful daughter." Pop's voice cracked. "Looka wassa happened to her."

"Don't cry, Pop. Violetta's strong. She'll pull through this. I won't let anyone hurt this family again. I should've put a bullet in Frank a long time ago."

"I glad we took care of da body when we did. Da feds willa be here any day now askin' questions."

"I'll take care of everything," Tony said.

"I more worry about Di Natale. When he canno find his son and word gets around he was here, he'll blame me. Di Natale gonna be here sooner or later. We needa be ready."

"We'll deal with that when the time comes. I heard Frank was on parole. I think the son of a bitch flipped. I bet the cops knew he was here," Tony said.

"Word is, he on da run. Don Molanano always wan him in da casinos. I tink das why he wassa here. But if he did work for da cops, I wonder how much dey know. Da mayor, he play both sides. He never tell me everyting. I trust no one."

"Sounds like we got two big problems now. The feds and Don Molanano. God help us. I'll get a couple guys together. You know, people we can trust—Sal's guys."

"I no wan a war, Tony. Itsa bad for biziniss. Wars cost lotsa money."

"We'll figure it out, Pop. It'll be all right. But one thing's for sure—I ain't never gonna eat Sal's sausage and peppers again."

Wait, what? I'd heard of guys drowning with bricks tied to their legs, but this was far worse than I could've ever imagined. Frank deserved this ending. I suppressed a slow grin. Afraid my father would sedate me again, I stayed quiet with my eyes closed. I'd heard all I needed.

Chapter 27
Cover-Up

My father stood in front of me with dark circles under his eyes.

"You should've killed me." I turned my face away from him.

"No speaka like dat. Please, donna be mad. You were hysterical. Tings are dangerous right now. I sorry for everyting."

I ignored his apology. "How long have I been out?"

"You needa rest. You body needa heal."

"How long?" I demanded.

"Two days."

"Two days? I need to find out about the funeral arrangements." I tried to get up to use the phone but my head was still woozy. I quickly lay back down. "Whoa." I put my hands over my face.

"Da *medicina* willa get outta you blood soon."

I closed my eyes, then reopened them to focus. "Pop, Paulie is dead to me. I never want to see or speak about him again."

Pop shot me a careful glance. "You needa be verra careful what you say. Itsa only a matter of time before da cops gonna coma here. We canno find you brudder."

"I know where he is. He's in Tahoe. Frank told him to go there."

Frank.

"I'm glad Tony killed him. I'm finally free of that monster. Free, but for what?" The emptiness in my chest would surely crush me.

Pop rubbed his chin and then looked down at me. "I sorry, Violetta."

"If and when the cops come here, I'm gonna tell them everything. Paulie deserves to rot in prison for what he did."

"You canno do dat. You put us in danger if you tell," he cautioned.

"I've followed Mafia rules before and never said a word, but this goes too far. Let them come and kill me. I don't care."

"You breaka my heart when you speak like dat. You my daughter. I canno let dat happen," Pop pleaded.

"And you think my heart isn't broken? The love of my life is dead," I snapped. "I'll never be the same now."

"I know you angry, but Paulie is still my son." He looked at me with a pained expression. "If da cops coma here, I needa you stay quiet. We not only dealin' wit da *polizia*, but we deal wit Don Molanano and Di Natale too."

"I'm not afraid of any of them. I was so happy when Gaetano came back into my life. I had a second chance at happiness, and now this." My voice shook and tears followed. "It's always been about you and your place in this sick, twisted, disgusting world," I sobbed into his face. "I hate you."

Whack.

My father slapped my face.

I gasped.

"Now you listena me. I love you and neva mean to hit you, but you no disrespect me in my house. Everyting I do is for you—for *la mia famigila*." His voice shook. "I no let you put our *famiglia* in danger." He grabbed his handkerchief from his pocket and handed it to me. "Dis isa no game. Itsa matter of life and death, and you not da only child I have left to protect. Tink about Antonio. Tink about Carmela and Vincenzo too."

A huge lump formed in my throat as I rubbed my cheek. Pop's slap wasn't as painful as Frank's, but it hurt more. I didn't care what they'd do to me, but not to Tony, Carm, and Vinny. Vinny was innocent, with a bright future ahead of him. No, I had to protect Vinny. "What do you want me to say? What lies do you want me to spin this time?"

Pop grimaced, then went on. "You tell dem dat you husband..."

"He was never my husband . . . not by *my* choice anyway. He beat me and raped me."

Pop hung his head. "He neva hurt you again. Itsa over."

"I know what happened. I'm not stupid. I'm glad Tony did it, and I hope Frank rots in hell."

"If you want you brudder to live, you neva speaka dis again," he warned. "You hear me?"

The thought of my anger causing Tony's death stopped me short.

"Yes, I hear you."

"Remember, anger and sadness make you vulnerable, and dat isa what dey looking for."

His words were few but wise.

"You a smart girl. You know what I ask of you."

"*Maronn*," I fired back and rubbed at my temples.

"Tell dem you no see Frank, and you tought he wasa in jail. And you brudder, you no see him since Saturday night."

"That's it? And you think the mayor and the cops will believe that, and leave me alone? What if someone saw me, or got Paulie's plates? Come on, Pop."

"You letta me worry 'bout dat. I willa take care of da cops and da mayor. He owe me a favor."

"Fine, but first I need to make a phone call. Don't worry, I won't say anything you don't want me to."

"Who you call?"

"The Sanna Winery."

"Dis willa be your last call. I donna know if da feds gonna tap da phones," Pop whispered, then looked over his shoulder.

"It wouldn't be the first time I've had to watch what I say on the phone," I huffed, thinking back to my days in Brooklyn. "I need to find out where Gaetano's services are so I can say my goodbyes."

My God. The services? What was I even saying? This felt unreal.

"He's gone. The love of my life, dead," I whimpered and clutched at my chest. "Papa. I want to rip out my heart."

"I'm here, *bella mia.*" He touched the hot handprint on my cheek. "Forgiva me." He leaned over and hugged me tightly. "I remember how it was after you mudder die. I feel lika you. I wan to die and go wit her but den I see Carmela get marry. I see you go to war and coma back alive and how proud I feel. My daughter. She save men. She serve our country. And now wit Vinny goin' to college, I know why I still here. Der is more life to be lived, Violetta. More memories to be had. You willa get tru dis. We willa helpa you, *bella mia.*" He held me tightly.

After a few minutes of sobbing into his arms, I blew my nose into my father's handkerchief. I walked past him toward his office. In the two days I was out, Pop and Tony had put the office back together. A new lamp sat on the desk, and the phone had been connected again. I mustered the courage to reach for the receiver.

There was a feeling of numbness and despair now that I'd never be able to shake. The world was a different place without Gaetano in it. Flashes of that dreadful night appeared in my eyes. Paralyzed in guilt, I remembered how Gaetano's face looked as he watched his mother grieve over his father and sisters. And the way his body lay limp on the ground while he gasped for air. He lost everything in one night, all because of me and my family's connection to the Mafia.

Anguish wrapped around my heart, making it hard to breathe. I cleared my throat and dialed, knowing my call wouldn't be well received. I had to try.

After a short time, the operator connected me.

"Sanna Winery," a woman answered.

"Oh, thank God. I wasn't sure I'd get through. Last time I called the lines were down."

"Um, yes, ma'am. The telephone company was able to restore the line this morning."

"May I please speak to Mrs. Conchetta Sanna, please?"

"Sorry, ma'am. The family has requested no more inquiries. Are you a reporter?"

"No, I'm a friend of the family. Do you know when she might return? I need to speak to her."

"I can leave her a message if you'd like. But she's leaving for the hospital and won't be back until after visiting hours."

"The hospital?"

"Yes. To see her son."

"Wait, Gaetano's alive?" I asked, confused. "The fire chief told me he died."

"No, ma'am. His father, Efrem Sanna, died in the hospital. His son suffered a bullet wound to the chest. He and his mother were the only survivors in the family."

My heart stopped, then started again. My grape grower was *alive*. I closed my eyes as tears of joy cascaded over my cheeks. It was as if God had restored my faith and given me a third chance.

"Which hospital is he at?" I asked impatiently.

"Sorry, ma'am. I can't give out that kind of information."

"Please, I must know."

"Who is that?" I heard another woman's voice in the background.

"Oh, sorry, Mrs. Sanna. I thought you'd left already," she muffled. "Can I get your name, ma'am?" she asked, returning to the call.

"Violetta Giordano."

"She says her name is Violetta Giordano, and that she needs to speak to you," the woman explained.

"Give me da phone," an angry voice said. "You no calla here no more," *Signora* Sanna snapped. "I lose my husband and my two beautiful daughters. Dey burn everyting. My son isa fighting for hisa life. You stay away from us, or I kill you," she screamed through the receiver.

"I'm sorry. I'm so sorry." My voice shook. "Please *Signora*, I never wanted this. I love your son. Please..."

"Gaetano isa all I have left. If you coma here again, you willa be sorry." She hung up.

My hand shook as I put down the receiver. Gaetano was alive, but how would I get to him? How could she keep me away? After everything that had happened between us, I couldn't let that happen. I'd wait a few days and then go to him. Waves of emotions enveloped me. My stomach knotted and lurched. I ran to the bathroom and threw up.

In the days that followed, I thought of nothing but being with Gaetano. I wanted to run to my lover's side as he recovered alone in his hospital bed. I wanted to hold his hand and tell him that everything would be fine and that we didn't have to hide any longer.

From the little I'd gathered from Tony, no eyewitnesses came forward. It didn't surprise me. The smoke provided the perfect veil for our escape, but there was always a chance someone would come forward.

The test would be how the Molanano family covered it up.

Two things had happened at once: the fire, and Frank's disappearance. This meant involvement from the cops and, eventually, the Molananos. Pop was right. It would only be a matter of time before someone asked about Frank.

A week later, the first string of officers showed up with the mayor. They came with a warrant and probed around. They didn't mention one word about the fire; they only asked about Frank's whereabouts. They wanted to know where their informant was.

After what Frank said to Paulie in the car, it was safe to assume that Frank had been sent out here to feed information to the feds about the Molanano involvement in the casino business. Their incessant need to find my deceased ex-husband caused them to lurk around the ranch almost daily. Thankfully, Pop got rid of the body.

Because Frank worked with the cops, it made things sticky. If this were just Molanano business, things would be dealt with in the old way—the Mafia way. It put us on edge, especially Pop, because it always slowed business when the feds got involved.

But every time I was asked, I lied so the cops would back off and make the Molanano family happy at the same time. My answers to their slew of questions were simple but ambiguous. This frustrated them, and they probed for more answers.

The police chief took pictures of my injuries. According to Tony, the officer told the mayor that he'd reviewed the notes from the medical examiner of what happened back in Brooklyn and that this case screamed of a possible domestic dispute that may have resulted in Frank's mysterious disappearance. He went as far as to say that I was the key suspect in Frank's case.

When asked about my injuries, I told them it was a horse-riding accident. They nodded but came back with even more questions to see if I'd break, always trying to find motive and any possible leads of Frank's whereabouts.

The minute Pop found out they might arrest me, he had a sit-down with the mayor and the chief of the police. Immediately after their meeting, which I'm sure involved some greasing and leveraging, the mayor and the cops backed off. The mayor even apologized to me and said he was sorry for the disruption. He shook Pop's hand, and the police chief tipped his hat. They left. The only question that remained was the investigation in Napa. What did they know about the fire?

I didn't know how the investigation would go, but with José

dead and Gaetano shot, I was pretty sure a manhunt was underway. I prayed that no one identified me that night, but every day someone knocked at the door, I was sure they'd take me away. With Gaetano alive, I didn't want anything else to jeopardize our possible future.

I put faith in one thing: the Mafia mentality. Gaetano knew, as I did, that if he said it was Frank, the Molanano family would breathe down his neck. Knowing him, he'd want justice, but he knew who bankrolled the winery. On death's door, he'd have to lie, as I had.

Molanano lawyers would be engaged. They'd feed the Sannas a story of what to say and instruct them not to press charges or they'd be dealt with. In Mafia fashion, it would be another huge cover-up. Tony kept me in the loop, but there were things he couldn't share. I'd have to learn more as the days passed. Without communication with Gaetano, my only answers would be in the newspapers.

Sun poured through my window and forced me to rise early. I'd forgotten how much I despised the summer heat at the ranch. I went to the kitchen to get something to drink. Tony stood at the stove, cracking two eggs in a frying pan alongside some bacon. The smell was heavy and made my stomach feel off.

"You want some?" Tony asked.

"No thank you." I clutched at my gut. Oddly it felt firm and swollen. "I think I'll just have some coffee. Too much pasta fagioli from last night." I poured myself a cup. "Did you bring it?"

"It's on the table. You sure you don't want to eat?"

"After everything that's happened, my stomach isn't doing so good. Must be nerves." I sat and rubbed my belly.

"Well, ain't you gonna read it? You been pumping me for information every day. It's all in there."

My heart fluttered as I opened the newspaper.

I flipped to the third page. There, in black and white, was an article about the mysterious fire, José's murder, and the attempted murder of Gaetano.

SEVERAL CASUALTIES AND 50 ACRE FIRE LEAVE FAMILY AND STAFF IN PERIL.

Authorities continue to investigate what led to a five-alarm fire at the famous Sanna Winery. Three individuals succumbed to smoke inhalation, and one died from a gunshot wound. One other remains hospitalized.

Police chief Eric Bradford states there were reports of fireworks and loud noises coming from the estate, possibly a late July Fourth celebration.

Fire captain Eli Willis said, "There were several possible causes of the fire. Traces of gasoline were found at the scene. There may have been a spark from a firework. A winery representative confirmed that gasoline was used that day to power various equipment. This appears to be an accident rather than arson, but we are looking into every detail due to the homicide and attempted homicide."

Fire crews discovered owner, Efrem Sanna, and his two daughters had died at the scene from smoke inhalation.

The investigation took a strange turn when Chief Operational Manager Gaetano Sanna, son of the late owner, was found unconscious from a gunshot wound to the chest. He was taken to a local hospital for emergency surgery. Sanna also sustained third degree burns but is expected to fully recover.

Family lawyers stated that when Mr. Sanna woke from surgery, the famous vintner said he didn't know who shot him, stating "with everything that was happening around me, I couldn't get a good look through all the smoke."

Head groundskeeper José Cortez was also shot at close range and died at the scene. When questioned, Cortez's daughter, Esperanza Cortez, stated she found his body lying in a pool of blood in the winery's guest house. The grieving daughter and hotel manager said, "I'm devastated. I loved my father. He didn't deserve this. There are crazy people in this world who only mean to do harm."

The investigation remains open. Anyone who may have seen something that night is asked to contact the Napa Police Department.

"It's a sad day for our community. Please keep the Sanna family in your prayers. Let's help them rebuild." —Justin M. Fitzpatrick, Editor in Chief

I placed my hand over my chin. "Well, I'll be a son of a bitch. They did it again. They're gonna get off, scot-free. Smoke provided the perfect alibi for a hidden escape."

"Not all of them." Tony laughed under his breath, as if I didn't catch his meaning. "The lawyers will take care of everything."

"Gaetano's not stupid, he knows they'd come back for his mother. She's the only family he has left." I put my head down. "But the girl, Esperanza, she hates me. She's in love with Gaetano. I thought she'd be the one to say something, but I guess she listened to my warning. She's the one who brought Frank and Paulie to us."

"Bet she wishes she hadn't," Tony said with a smirk on his face.

"It's not funny, Tone. José was a good man, and Paulie shot him like a dog in the street."

"That's business. Not personal."

"Not personal? Paulie shot Gaetano and he's fighting for his life in some hospital bed," I clipped.

"I know you're pissed at him, but he didn't have a choice. I'm sure Paulie feels bad, but it's kill or be killed. You know that." Tony shook his head. "Besides, you didn't think Don Molanano was gonna take the rap for any of it, did you? No way was he gonna let one of his capos go down. That would lead to a full-on investigation. The bookkeeping, the shell companies that put up money fronts, the lost profits. I bet the old man is pissed about that all right." Tony slid his eggs and bacon onto his plate. "But that's where the insurance comes in. What happened is just a nuisance to him."

"I don't think the Don liked Frank much. He'd become a huge liability. I wonder if he questions Frank's father's loyalty at this point. Frank made them look like fools."

"Frank *was* a real character." Tony said under his breath, completely unaffected, while shoving mouthfuls of eggs down his throat.

I folded the newspaper in half and fanned the greasy bacon

odor from my nose. "Jesus, Tone. Don't you even chew? Watching you eat is making me sick." I rubbed my stomach.

"I'm hungry, damn it," he snapped. "Don't look, then."

I turned away and cast my eyes back to the words in print. "And *Signora*. I wonder if she'll ever say anything. She threatened to kill me if I came around. She hates everything about the Mafia. I can't say I blame her."

"The old broad knew well enough what would be waiting for her if she talked. She doesn't want a dead son." Tony wiped his mouth with his napkin. "If she'd told the cops it was Mafia related, the whole operation would've been investigated and seized. Even now all parties are gonna lose money, and that's what's gonna piss off the Don. So, if anything, that's how Frank fucked the family."

"Paulie better hope that the family hasn't found out that he helped Frank burn down the winery. I'm sure that wouldn't sit well."

"Paulie can always say his *capo* gave the order and get out of it."

"It's that easy, huh? Paulie can get away with shooting two guys, killing Gaetano's family, and burning his dreams to the ground?" I huffed.

"Yeah, it's that easy."

I shook my head in disgust.

"Even if someone did see somethin' and they squealed to the cops, the Molanano family would find out who they are and kill them."

I threw the paper down on the kitchen table.

"Look, I know you're upset, but I'm gonna give it to you straight. This is what we were trying to warn you about when you came home."

"Are you saying this was *my* fault?"

"No." Tony slammed his fork down on his plate. "After what Frank did to you, the son of a bitch had it coming." Anger clouded Tony's face.

Tony knew as I did that Frank had broken the cardinal rule. His anger exposed his truth. I didn't say anything, just nodded. There was an unspoken understanding between the two of us.

"Look, I'm sorry for raisin' my voice," Tony apologized. "I don't want to upset you. You've been through a lot, sis. We all have."

I let out a deep breath. "Have you heard from Paulie yet?"

"No. He's probably staying put somewhere."

"Frank told him to find some guy named Tommy something. Frank said he'd contact him when he thought it was safe. But with Frank gone, I don't know."

"You mean Tommy the T-bone?"

"Yes. That's it."

"If that's true, Di Natale already knows who Frank was with that night. It's only a matter of time before he comes around asking questions, and that's not good. If he can't find Frank, he'll seek justice the old way." Tony rubbed at his chin.

"If Gaetano hadn't survived . . . you don't know how close I came to telling the cops everything. But then I thought of you, and Carm, and Vin. But Tone, this . . . all of this . . . it's gotta stop."

"In this family it'll never stop, and you know it. And if you would've done that, you'd have been killed too. If you don't care about Pop, think about how tore up I'd be if I lost you, huh? Huh, Vi?" Tony rose from his chair and stood before me with his palms on my shoulders. "Please don't make me suffer like that. You're my sister, and I love you," Tony pleaded, then pulled me up into his frame and hugged me tightly. "I wish things were different, but they aren't. I don't make the rules, I just live by them. I can't lose you, Vi."

I sniffed and looked at my big brother. "I love you too. You won't lose me. Not yet, anyway."

"Good." He pressed a kiss on my forehead.

Tony put his plate in the wash basin and walked outside.

As sad as it was to admit, Tony was right. Human life was never high on the Mafia agenda. It was always about business and power. Nothing else. Anyone who got in the way of that died, plain and simple.

Once again, they'd gotten away with murder. From what I'd read, their control also helped get me off the hook. But I'd never thank them for my freedom. I'd earned my freedom long before this. I'd paid my dues and more.

It had been over a week since I'd heard anything. Antsy, I thought about ways to steal my father's keys, but Pop and Tony were smart to me now. They probably hid them somewhere I'd never find.

I sorted through the mail as my mind wandered for ways to escape to see Gaetano. There was one letter addressed in a hand that I recognized immediately. It was from Gaetano. I ran to my room and locked the door.

July 19th, 1947

"Sole mio, I am writing you from my hospital bed. It's the first day I feel strong enough to write. I hope this letter finds you alive and well. I hope you were able to get away and that you are safe back at the ranch. I would've called, but there is no phone in my room.

I've developed an infection and may have to stay in the hospital another week or so. They say I can't leave until I stop spitting blood. I'm weak and sleep most of the day.

I feel sad for my mother and Espi. We've lost so much.

Being confined to this hospital bed makes me feel powerless. I can't be there for my mother as I wish. When I'm feeling better and return home, I need to speak with you in private. There's much to discuss. Please know that I love you and am thinking about you.

I pray you get this.

I'll reach out again when it's safe.

-G

Ps. If what I think has happened, happened, I'll do everything in my power to make it right and see you well again.

His letter was cryptic—never using my real name, never mentioning anyone by name, and even referring to Esperanza as Espi. Gaetano was smart. He didn't know who would intercept the mail. With no return address, I was left with only his words—that he loved me, and that he'd call me when he got home from the hospital. As much as I wanted to see him, I'd wait for him to contact me. He'd know when the time was safe. I'd need to avoid any possible further interrogation from any pain-in-the-ass cops and any possible run-ins with his mother and Espi.

I hid the letter at the bottom of my hope chest.

I heard Carmela's voice from the other room. I hadn't seen her since she left for LA with Louie.

"Hey, Vi, you in here?" She knocked.

"One second," I said and opened the door.

"Hey, what happened to your lip?" She looked concerned.

"Sit. I need to tell you what happened."

I told Carm everything that day. I needed to speak to another woman—someone who understood this life. Like me, she was a Mafia wife. She knew the rules. She'd never tell a soul—not even her husband—or Tony would be locked away forever. She thanked me for taking over the duties of the ranch and for giving her time with Louie, but after hearing what I divulged, she said she felt guilty for leaving me. I told her if she had been here, Frank would have hurt her too. I told her what Paulie had done and that I never wanted to see him again. She cried and wondered if he'd ever return.

Her time in LA was eye-opening. Because Louie had lots of business down there, he talked to her about moving that way. She didn't want to leave us but wanted to start a family. I tried to be happy for her, but with what I witnessed, I couldn't imagine raising a baby in this environment.

While in LA, Louie heard from one of his guys that Frank's dad made a lot of noise about Frank's whereabouts. Even went as far as to say there were rumors that Don Molanano himself wanted to visit Pop. We were both worried about that news. She said she'd tell Pop so he'd be ready for anything.

Di Natale was bound and determined to find his son. Little did he know he'd be looking forever.

Chapter 28

The Sit-Down

The summer sun stung my back as I picked tomatoes from the garden. It had been a month since the fire. I wanted to go up to Napa and see Gaetano, but it wasn't safe yet. I didn't know how many cops might be lingering around, asking questions, not to mention *Signora* Sanna's threat to kill me if I stepped on her property. And then there was Esperanza. She'd hate me even more for getting her father killed. There'd be no limit to the wrath that waited for me at the winery.

Not only did I worry about Gaetano's family, I worried about Pop and the rumors swirling around about Frank's father coming to the ranch and demanding justice for his missing son. I didn't know what Di Natale had planned, but I didn't trust him. Not one bit.

I had many enemies now.

The whole thing made me sick. Nerves twisted up in my gut, leaving me nauseous. To settle my stomach, I took a sip from the water hose and placed my basket of tomatoes on the porch. Hoping to get another letter from Gaetano, I went to the front to retrieve the mail. Sadly, there were only a few envelopes from the Franchise Tax Commissioner and medical board for Pop's business.

With letters in hand, I walked back to the house when a black limousine crept down the road. Dust billowed in its wake. I opened the screen door and stood behind it to see who it was.

The limo parked in front by the old oak. The driver opened the back door. Three men with black hats sat in the back. Pop and Tony came out to greet them. *Consigliere* Rapino was first to step out, then Frank's father, followed by the man himself, Don Molanano. The men were dressed in black suits with pocket squares. Pop and Tony shook their hands and kissed Don Molanano's ring.

"Don Molanano, *è così bello vederti*," Pop said. "I wasn't expecting you. You come to visit da horses?"

"No, no, Giuseppe. Dis isa about a different matter, my friend. We needa talk *privately*."

"Coma wit me. We go to da back." Pop motioned Tony to walk the men to the big house for a surprise sit-down.

I peered out of the clinic window and watched the men march to the big house. The door slammed shut. My stomach knotted. That meant private conversations and no entry to anyone.

As much as I wanted to sneak around and hear what they said, I couldn't take the chance of my father-in-law seeing me. After what happened in Brooklyn, he didn't like me much. I didn't want to be caught in the crossfire.

I stood in front of the window and waited for the men to leave so I could ask Tony what happened.

After almost an hour, I spotted Frank's father storm out of the sit-down, cussing and hollering. *Consigliere* Rapino ran after him to the front. Shortly after, Pop and Don Molanano walked out with Tony behind them. Pop shook his head while Don Molanano pointed to the barn. He probably wanted to see the horses—they were his money makers, and the only reason he and my father remained close after all these years. Pop was a good earner for the family and in this life that was his only life insurance policy.

I waited for the men to leave so I could get Tony alone. Another twenty minutes passed. Pop and Don Molanano walked to the front. Tony wasn't far behind.

"*Pssst*," I hissed as Tony walked by. He stepped into the house and I shut the door behind him. "What happened? And don't tell me 'Nothin', Tone."

Tony huffed at my words.

"Don Molanano wouldn't come way out here if he wasn't fishing for something," I said.

"Di Natale wants to know where his son is. He says Pop was responsible for his son and blames him for his disappearance," Tony explained. "Says if Pop doesn't produce his son soon, he's gonna start a war."

A shiver ran down my spine.

"From what it sounded like, Don Molanano respects Pop. They were telling stories about the first time they met in the old country. They go way back. I don't think the Don will make any orders against Pop, but Di Natale is a different story. He's pissed. He started makin' threats and insulting our family and . . . you. That's when I called him a son of a bitch."

"Jesus, Tony." My voice jumped an octave. "You have to be careful. That man is a lunatic. He's looking for an excuse. What did he say about me?"

"Nothing. I took care of it. I won't let anyone talk bad about our family."

"Tell me."

His face grew pained. "He thinks you were the one that turned in his son back in Brooklyn. Says you're an animal for biting Frank's cheek."

"He deserved it," I fired back. "Is that all?"

"No." Tony paused. "He called you a *puttana*. That's when I lunged at him."

"Have you lost your mind?"

"Pop and the *consigliere* got between us. That's when he accused me of killing Frank. He said Frank told him of our fight the night before your wedding, and that I wanted to take my revenge."

"Did the Don believe him?"

"No. That's when Pop spoke up. He told the Don that he thought it was Frank's smart mouth and stupid behavior that caused Di Natale's son to vanish into thin air, and that he probably deserved it. Di Natale spit at Pop's feet, but that's when Pop asked him where Paulie was. Pop said he thought Di Natale knew more than he was saying about Paulie's whereabouts. Even went as far as calling Frank a rat and that, with his sources, he could prove it."

"The mayor," I said, putting Pop's plan together.

"Yeah. Di Natale tried to plead his case, but the Don asked for the proof. He said he needed to know who he could trust, and that he could ensure Pop's safety if he provided facts. That's when Di Natale came unglued. He said he felt betrayed, then flicked his cigar at Pop and stormed out, but not before threatening that if he found out anyone had anything to do with his son's disappearance, we'd all suffer. It pissed him off that the Don sided with Pop over him."

"Don Molanano is smart. He knows Frank was a liability and that his father covers for him any chance he gets. After what happened in Brooklyn with the Sambino murder, the family took a ton of heat for years."

"I gotta get back to Pop. After everything that was said, he's gonna wanna get some guys over here. We need to be ready in case Frank's old man makes good on his threats. As much as we tried to avoid it, a war may be coming." Tony walked out of the clinic.

My brother was right. Pop would do anything to protect us. I also knew Frank's father was ruthless, like his son. Pop had never given Don Molanano a reason not to trust him, but in this life, loyalty was fickle. Paulie was an example of that. I hoped Frank's father would believe what my father told him, and leave us alone. But what Pop said about Frank being a rat—that wouldn't sit well with Mr. Di Natale. I didn't want another war. I'd seen and experienced enough violence and bloodshed to last a lifetime. I wanted to get to Gaetano and run away with him so we'd be safe.

This situation was far from over.

Chapter 29
The Morning the Sun Didn't Shine

After the sit-down, things were tense. My father beefed up security. I wasn't allowed to leave the ranch—not even for a loaf of bread. Carm and Louie moved back in to help. Things felt different at the ranch. I missed Gaetano, but as much as I wanted to drive up to Napa, my father wouldn't let me leave.

After Don Molanano's visit, Pop assembled an arsenal in the event Di Natale made good on his threats. Different wise guys at different times showed up every day at the ranch. Pop took them straight to the big house and into the basement. Lots of sit-downs meant lots of food and drinks. Cases of beer and whiskey were dropped off weekly. Sal and Angelo brought trays of meats and cheeses while Carm and I made pounds of pasta and gravy. Gangsters never worked well on empty stomachs.

Pop invited many of his closest friends and confidants to the house—San Jose's finest. He'd say he was having "meetings" and not to disturb him. Things were so hush-hush that Vinny stood guard, so even I couldn't snoop anymore. From the looks of it, things were brewing.

I'd seen Mafia wars in my past, and this had the signs of a full-on battle. I was certain that lines had been drawn after everything that was said between Pop and Di Natale. Pop knew it and prepared for the worst.

Pop had a lot of friends who would protect him to the death. Over the many years, he'd served Don Molanano's men faithfully. He helped wise guys on the run. He tended to their wounds, gave them a place to live, and protected them from the cops. He even gave them money. They remembered his generosity and came to my father's call. Although they loved my father, sadly, cash was the only way to ensure loyalty. So we paid, and we paid big.

In between the cooking and cleaning, I decided to ask Tony to take me to the winery. I wanted my brother there in case things got out of hand. I needed to see Gaetano and hoped he wanted to see me.

Water flowed over my hands. My fingers were caked with dough from the five pounds of pasta Carm and I had made for our *new visitors*. I wiped my wet hands on my apron. Vinny whizzed by with a box of whiskey in his arms.

"Hey Vin, you know where Tony is?"

"He's in the stables."

"I'll go find him." I followed him out. "How's everything going out there? You think it will come to a war?"

"I hope not. But you never know."

"Thankfully, you'll be starting school soon—away from this crap—to live a good life—a legitimate life. I'm proud of you, squirt." I ruffled up his hair. "You'll be the first in the family to graduate from college."

"Hopefully." He shot me a quick smile, then looked down at the whiskey box. "Do you think Paulie's alive?" Vin looked back up with desperation and hurt in his eyes. "Think he'll ever come home?"

I placed my hand on his shoulder. Vin stopped to face me.

"I know you love Paulie, but he's changed now. This life promises money, prestige, and power, but it also serves up its share of consequences. At some point, Paulie will have to face his."

Vinny nodded.

"I love you, and I don't want this for you. After college, move away and never return, or the next time, *you* might be the one who's running. Everything's gonna be fine, brother." I patted Vin's face.

"Yeah." Vin smiled back at me.

"I'm gonna go find Tone. Remember what I said."

With hands full, Vinny nodded and continued for the big house. I walked into the barn. Tony placed hay around the stalls.

"Hey Tony, I need to talk to you," I said as he dug into the bale.

"What is it? I'm pretty busy today."

"I know things have been crazy lately, but I need a favor."

"What is it now? Can't you see I'm busy?"

"If you get some time this week, could you drive me to Napa?"

"*Maronn*, here we go." Sweat dripped from his chin. "I don't know, Vi. It's not a good time for me to be leavin' the ranch, and with the cops and Di Natale . . ."

"Then can I at least borrow your truck? I was going to ask Pop, but I know what he'd say."

"Things aren't safe right now."

"I know, but if I don't see him soon, I feel like I'll go crazy. Please. Don't you remember how it feels to be in love—real love? It's a miracle he survived after what Paulie did to him."

Tony placed his pitchfork against the stall and wiped sweat from his forehead with his shirt. "Yes, I know what it feels like to be in love. I haven't told anyone this yet, but I was planning to ask Christina to marry me. I'm going over there later to ask for her father's permission."

"Oh Tony, I'm so happy for you." I hugged him. "I was wondering when you were going to tie the knot." Tears leaked down my cheeks.

"Why you cryin'?"

"I don't know. After everything that's happened, I'm a ball of emotions lately."

"Don't tell anyone. Not even Carm. I want to tell them when I'm ready."

"I promise." I paused and looked around the stall. It was the same stall where Gaetano and I had our first sexual encounter. Thoughts of his naked body on top of mine made my breasts feel heavy in my bra and my nipples ache against the fabric.

"What are you thinking about? You look like you're miles away."

"Sorry, so, um . . ." I swallowed deep. "Do you think you can take me?"

"I'm not promising anything. It would kill me to see your name on a headstone. I can't let anything happen to you."

"Please, I beg you. I need to see him. After everything I've been through, I need to speak with him. There are things I need to say," I said with a tight throat. "What if this was Christina?" More tears poured.

"*Minchia*," Tony said, defeated. "All right, all right. I'll take you. Just don't cry. I hate it when girls cry."

"I'm sorry. I don't know what's got into me lately."

"Jesus Christ. If Pop finds out, he's gonna be pissed."

"He won't find out."

"I'm not promising anything. Things can change at a moment's notice. Pop wants me to pick up some supplies in San Francisco at the end of the week. I ain't gonna wait there all damn day either. In and out, Violetta."

"I promise. You and Vinny are the best brothers a girl could ever have." I kissed him on the cheek.

Tony's gaze shifted downward.

"What is it?"

"I don't know if Paulie's runnin' or dead. I'm worried about him."

"Not sure if I'm the best person to have this conversation

with. I don't want him to suffer. I know Frank pressured him, but he deserves to pay the consequences. He tried to kill Gaetano, Tony. I'll never forgive him for that—ever." I stepped back.

"I'm worried for the kid. The same way I was worried for you when you left for Brooklyn. The same way I worry for you now."

"You have a huge heart, and soon you'll be a husband and maybe a father..."

"A father? Jesus, Vi, slow down."

"Yeah, and maybe you'll have all girls," I giggled.

"*All* girls?" Tony's voice rose. "I don't know about that, but if they turn out half as good as you, I'll be happy." Tony planted a kiss on the top of my head and grabbed the pitchfork.

"Wait, I need to say something to you."

His face became serious. "What?"

I looked over my shoulder to make sure we were alone. "Thank you."

One of his brows shot up "For what?"

"For saving my life that night." I wrapped my arms around my big brother. "When it was happening, I wanted it to be over, but with Gaetano alive, I have another chance now." After the last words were out, Tony didn't confirm or deny, but he hugged me a little tighter.

"Now go. Get outta here, I gotta get back to work." He adjusted his gloves and dug back into the hay.

Roosters crowed and the sound of my father crying loudly came from right outside my window. I grabbed my robe and ran outside. The mayor was there with his arm over Pop's shoulder. With bare feet, I ran to them.

"What happened?" I yelled and joined Pop's side. "Pop, what is it? *Cosa c'è che non va? Cos'è successo, Papà?* What's wrong?"

Pop wept in my arms. "No... Nooooo," he wailed, his hands over his face.

The mayor looked at me as I tried to keep Pop from falling.

"I'm sorry, but we just fished Tony's truck from the bottom of Calero Reservoir," the mayor said. "It was reported early this morning."

Tony? *Dead?*

I felt like I'd gone deaf. Breathless, the life had been sucked out of me once again. When I looked up, early morning stars spun above us. A violent tremor of fear traveled down my arms and legs, leaving me with watery feet. Like feathers in the wind, our bodies swayed as shock consumed me.

For fear of falling, I had one arm around my father and the other I placed on the mayor to steady myself. "How? It can't be his truck. This can't be true. He said he was going to his girlfriend's house?" I stuttered.

"If I didn't know your family like I do, I wouldn't be sure. But it's him. When they recovered the body, I knew right away."

"How'd this happen? Did he lose control of the truck or something?" I asked with blurry eyes.

"I'm afraid not. Your brother was shot. From the looks of it, he suffered two rounds to the chest. I'm so sorry, Giuseppe." The mayor put his hand on Pop's arm. With a sullen face, he looked back at me. "I'd like to take your father to the morgue to start the paperwork."

"No paperwork. I know who do dis . . ." Pop mumbled through snot and spit. "If he wanna war, he gonna get a war," Pop whimpered and fell to his knees.

Carmela and Vinny came outside to see what all the noise was about.

"Cosa c'è, Papà?" Carm searched my father's eyes as tears fell down her face.

"Carm," I mumbled. "Tony's dead. He was shot and they found his body in the Calero reservoir." It felt like I'd swallowed a beehive. The words stung as I tried to get them out. The look on my sister's face was indescribable.

Carmela screamed. Vinny fell next to us and placed his arms around us.

We wept together. For the first time, I saw my father's powerlessness. I recognized that look, because I'd worn it for so long after Adelina's death. It was the look of agony and despair. With one son to bury, he felt the full weight of his choice to serve in this life. Like me, my father had now paid the ultimate sacrifice.

My big brother was dead.

Unfathomable sadness and grief filled the days leading up to Tony's funeral. With his passing, we were lost. Moping about and crying, we tried to comfort each other, but sometimes it was too much. We were a family of hollowed-out souls that needed to heal. For fear of losing another child, my father put up a bounty for Paulie. He offered any wise guy who found my brother five grand—no questions asked.

That's the day we got a phone call from Paulie.

My father broke the news to him. Paulie cried on the other end. He didn't say where he was—just that he was safe and couldn't contact us again for a long time. Pop hung up. He looked lost and defeated. With war imminent, who would help us now?

Tony had been my father's right-hand man—our rock—the one we turned to when Pop wasn't around. We couldn't trust Paulie, and we knew he wouldn't be around. Vinny was still too young for all of this. My father never wanted him in the business. He wanted to shield him from this life. Because of that, Vinny didn't know how to lead this family now. He was still too green. He was the accountant. The student. The civilian. And everyone knew it.

Pop barely functioned as he grieved and tried to heal his heartbreak for his firstborn son. He closed the clinic and left the businesses to stall. We were vulnerable, and Di Natale knew it. Without true leadership, the men would falter, and their loyalty would be shaken and tested. We were sitting ducks in a world that looked for any sign of weakness.

I was afraid for my father and worried he wouldn't recover from this. With Mama, he had been sad, but it was her time. She was sick and dying. He wanted her free of the pain. But Tony had a wonderful life ahead of him, full of hope and possibilities—the two things Pop always told me to hold onto when I was low. Now there was no possibility and no hope—only darkness.

Tony said it would kill him to see my name on a headstone, and now I'd see his.

There is a silence in death where no words can truly depict the grief felt by everyone. For some, the sound can be peaceful—a natural transition between this world and the next. For me, who loved to hear the sound of my brother's laughter, the silence deafened.

The morning of my brother's funeral arrived. I didn't want to get up. I didn't want to see them put him in the ground. The whole thing made me sick. My stomach ached something awful. From all the grief, food wasn't agreeing with me. I couldn't keep anything down.

To block out the world, I pulled my blanket over my face. As my arms grazed my breasts, a strangely familiar sensation rippled inward. I sat up quickly and rubbed at my flesh. It was sore to the touch, and my breasts felt enlarged. I ran to the bathroom, locked the door, and stripped off my nightgown.

I examined myself in the mirror. My breasts and pelvis were larger. I rubbed at the bulge under my belly button, then turned to the side. My gut stuck out about two inches.

Oh no. I pressed against my bloated belly. *This can't be happening. Not now. Pop said it was impossible. How? This can't be real.*

My throat caved in as I counted the days since my last period, which had been wildly irregular since Adelina. It had been nearly two months since I'd returned from Italy. I'd had some light spotting a few days after I returned home. That must have been a light cycle.

How did I miss this? Frank's child?

Chills rippled across my spine followed by a flood of thoughts.

The throwing up. The aversions to smells. My emotions were all over the place—crying, anger, exhaustion.

Once again, I'd been so preoccupied with everything, I didn't see the signs. The bulge in my gut was proof enough. I was pregnant again.

With Frank's baby.

Impossible.

Fear crept over me. Could something be wrong with the baby already? Gaetano loaded me up with pills for my injuries and to keep me quiet; Pop shot me up with something that put me out for two days. This wasn't good at all. Would I lose this baby too? Only time would tell.

How could this happen?

My mind spun from my discovery. I slid onto the cold tile floor of the bathroom, wrapped my arms around my legs, and rocked myself back and forth. What would I do now? There'd be no way Gaetano would raise Frank's child, not after what happened. My future with Gaetano was uncertain again.

I remained in the bathroom in a state of hopelessness. Thought and reason evaded me. With nothing more to give, I pretended my arms were my mother's. I held myself tight and dreamed of the days she rocked me back and forth in her chair. My eyes blurred. For a moment, I was safe.

After the funeral, I put my father to bed and pried the whiskey bottle from his hands. He'd been drinking all day, saying that Tony was now with his mother. I already missed seeing Tony around the ranch. Since childhood, he'd been my hero. He was the one who sat with me when I had the pox and the one who taught me how to ride horses.

I looked out onto our land and thought about the life he would have lived. I would've loved to see his children chase after the chickens in the fields. He'd had a wonderful life ahead of him, yet he was taken away too soon.

Anger bubbled up in my throat.

My distaste for this world and its ugliness prompted me to search for my father's keys. I wanted to drive away and never return. I'd go to Gaetano and beg for his forgiveness. But as much as I wanted to see him, how could I face him like this? This would not be the reunification I'd dreamed about. This was a dilemma I never expected to have. For so long I'd grieved over my daughter and wanted another child in her absence, but not with Frank.

The conversation would have to be handled delicately. I wasn't sure of the right words. Even in death, Frank had power over me. His actions had the strength to close doors to my dreams forever. How would Gaetano react to such news? Would it be too soon after what had happened?

I hadn't seen Gaetano in weeks. Our love felt like it was slipping away. Time can be a strange thing when confronted by turmoil. Adrenaline made my mind rush, causing some days to go by fast; the rest of the time, minutes felt like hours. Moments of reflection reaffirmed the life that grew inside me.

My thoughts betrayed me, and my selfish yearning for my lover stopped me cold. What about my family? I couldn't leave them now.

No, I couldn't do any of it.

Chilled with confusion and powerlessness over my reality, I questioned my future. How could I subject my child to this world when they could end up like Paulie—or worse—dead, like Tony?

I crumpled up my brother's prayer card in my hand. The phone rang. I didn't know if it was another reporter, but a small voice inside secretly hoped it was Gaetano calling to pay his respects. I rushed to the phone. "Hello?"

"If you don't want the rest of your children to die, return my son," Frank's father said and hung up.

I ran to my father and shook him awake from his drunken stupor.

"Pop, wake up. It's Di Natale. He called and said that if we don't produce Frank soon, he's gonna kill us."

My father blinked and blinked again.

"What do we do?" Ripples of dread crawled up my back.

"I needa call Don Molanano. Pack your tings."

"Where am I going?"

"I needa get all of you outta here. I canno lose any more of you." He rubbed his face to wake himself up.

I ran to my room and threw clothes in a bag. I reached for a pen and paper and wrote.

Dear Gaetano,

I received your note. I'm alive. I don't know if or when you will get this letter. Your mother has made it clear that I'm not welcome anymore, but if by some miracle you do get this, please know how much I love you.

I'm sorry for what happened and for your family and the lives that were lost that day.

For some unforeseeable change of events, I must leave for a while. My brother Tony was killed. Something's happened, and there are things I need to say to you. Things that can only be discussed in person.

I don't know how long I'll be gone, but when things settle, I will try and reach you when I can. Please know that I will be thinking of you every day and praying for the time when I can be in your arms again. Until then, be well.

I love you, Vi.
P.S. The devil can no longer invade my dreams.

Like him, I didn't know who would retrieve the mail, so I left out details purposely. Apologizing incriminated me, and I couldn't tell him I was next on Di Natale's list. I hoped he would read between the lines and understand what happened since he, too, had to flee his hometown in Sardinia because of the Mafia.

At the bottom, I drew a heart with the letters *Vi* in the middle. Then I ran outside and put the note in the mailbox.

When I returned, my father was on the phone. He spoke so low, I barely made out the words.

"Don Molanano, da informant tell me dat Franco wassa workin' wit da feds to take down da Molanano operations in da casino biziniss. He has agree to speaka to you for more details, but he willa wan a piece in tings. He has photographs and udder tings proving dat Franco was involved. All for a price, of course. Da cops might have been hidin' him because dey know hesa dead man," Pop lied smoothly. "Yes. Yes, I see. I coma to you, or I canna arrange a meeting."

Pop listened in silence.

"After Antonio's death, I needa make arrangements for *la mia famiglia*. I canno help wit da horses until I feel safe. I needa guarantee for my safety."

There was more silence.

Then my father said, "*Grazie,*" and hung up the phone. He walked over to me and said, "We leave at midnight."

Chapter 30
Among the Hidden

IT WAS AFTER MIDNIGHT WHEN WE PULLED UP TO THE BACK OF Zavlaris's thrift shop. Pop and I exchanged glances.

"What are we doing here?" I grabbed my coat and purse. "Where are Carm and Vin gonna go?"

"Louie agree to drive Carmela to hisa *Zia* house in LA tonight. Vinny, Ima send him to Italy to stay wit you *Zia* Angelina. Dey canna protect him der. He willa be under da protection of Don Guerra."

"Why am I not going back to Italy with Vinny?"

"I hava split you up. Itsa safest way. I no wan to take any chances. Da men almost find you da last time . . . and becausa you wit baby." He stared at my midsection.

Reflexively, I threw my hand over my stomach. My mouth dried. "How long have you known?"

"For a while now." His eyes were tender and a faint smile spread across his face. "I too old to run now. If dey coma for me, dey coma. But I no run. Dis isa my home, and I stay so dat I helpa deliver you child. I only pray dat itsa boy. A strong boy like Tony was." He wiped away a straggling tear from his cheek.

"I . . . I . . ." My tongue was locked in my mouth. I didn't know how to feel about my father's admission.

"Coma, we mussa get you out of sight before someone see." He reached for my bag.

"But Pop . . . Mr. Zavlaris?" I whispered in the cold night air. "Are you sure?"

"Yes. He a civilian. No one willa suspect you be here. Itsa safest place I know. I wanna take you to Antonelli. He'sa *paesano*, but itsa too dangerous. Dey gonna look der first. Now be quiet."

As we walked closer to the building, a small light shone behind the store. I followed Pop to the back door. Pop knocked and glanced around.

Mr. Zavlaris opened the door to greet us. The two men shook hands, then Pop looked back at me.

"Come, get inside." Mr. Zavlaris motioned us in.

We walked down a hall into what appeared to be an old storage room. Pop laid my things across a mattress on the floor. Fresh blankets and linens were folded at the edge of the tiny bed. Hundreds of boxes sat on shelves, and there were racks of secondhand clothing. The smell of mothballs tugged at my nausea.

"As we agreed, she willa do you books and she can sew as good as my wife used to."

"Ah yes, Adelina. God rest her soul. So many times, she'd come here to buy and sell various things on consignment." Mr. Zavlaris turned and looked at me. "I remember the day she bought the material to make your communion dress. It seems like only yesterday." He smiled. He turned back to Pop. His face got serious. "And for the other part of the arrangement we spoke of . . ."

Pop looked at the man, then back at me. "A truck willa coma here once a week to deliver various tings for you to sell or keep."

"What kind of things?"

"Lots of tings. I suggest you keep soma da *nicer* tings for yourself. We no wanna tip off any nosey cops. But der might be a new radio for you house or even a new fur for you wife." Pop enticed the stout Greek man with the details of the arrangement.

Mr. Zavlaris's eyes widened. "Yes, that would be nice."

"I pay you tree honna dolla a month to watch over and protect my daughter from da men we spoke of. Here da first payment." Pop handed him the money.

Mr. Zavlaris fanned out the cash, then he eyed me cautiously.

"If you suspect anyting, or if anyone ask you questions about me or *la mia famiglia,* calla me at once so dat I canna move her somewhere else."

"Agreed. She will get three small meals a day and there is a bathroom she can use down the hall. But let me be clear, Giuseppe, I don't like the kind of business you run or the company you keep. I'll do this for you because I've known your family a long time, and you have been good customers to the shop. I don't want trouble. If things get messy, you'll have to make other arrangements."

My father's eyes narrowed. "Nicolas, I have known you a long time, and I tank you for what you doin', but neva forget, I canna be a ruthless man. Now more dan ever, I willa protect wassa mine. I woulda hate to end our relationship da hard way, my friend."

"What are you implying, Giordano?" Mr. Zavlaris pointed his finger in my father's face.

With his hands in fists, Pop stood toe to toe with the shopkeeper. "Donna put you finger in my face," Pop warned. "Dat's unwise. I can hava twenty guys over here in an hour. Dey can make it so you neva seen or heard from again." Pop's eyes burned with rage. He took a deep breath and stepped back from Mr. Zavlaris, trying to compose himself.

"Hey, what kind of deal are you trying to pull? I never say nothin' about how *you* people work. For so many years, I know what goes on in this town. I've always treated your family well, but think of the kind of position I'm in by doing this."

"*You* people? Now you wanna disrespect me? You act lika we below you, when last mont you ask for money to grow you biziniss.

Don Molanano bankrolled you. Donna forget dat. I canna put you out of biziniss, and you and your *famiglia* canna starve," Pop said through clenched teeth. "It seems to me dat you have been well paid for you services. We canna make another deal if you like, but dat would mean I kill you, den you wife and son. I know where you live, where your son go to school, and where your wife buy her groceries."

"How dare you threaten me. You, you . . ." Mr. Zavlaris's face turned three shades of red.

"Be careful, old friend. You willa guard my daughter wit you life, or I'll be back." Pop moved his jacket away from his vest to display the gun at his side. With his hand on the gun he said, "When we coma, you'll neva know. Neva forget dat. Now go be a good neighbor and do what we agree. One day when you needa someting, you canna come to me, and I willa owe you a favor. I make you a rich man, Nicolas. All you havta do isa keep your mouth shut, and besides," Pop said and drew in a breath, "you owe me. How many times did I helpa you when you son was sick wit his heart? If it wasn't for me, you son would be dead. Hava you forgotten?"

In humbled silence, Mr. Zavlaris's gaze fell to the floor. "No, I haven't forgotten." The shopkeeper's shoulders slumped. "I must apologize for my rudeness. Thank you for all that you've done, Giuseppe." He paused for a few seconds. "She'll be safe with me," he reassured.

"Glad to hear you came to you senses. For you sake." Pop shot him a warning glance.

This was Mafia power at its finest.

Pop kissed my forehead. "You'll be fine here, *bella mia*. I coma check on you when itsa safe."

My throat tightened. "But Papa . . ."

"*Shhh*. Rest now. If tings work lika I tink, you should be out of here sooner dan later. But I no let Di Natale take another one of my children from me. Now or ever," he said in a steely tone.

"Okay, Pop."

He held me tightly, kissed my cheek, then made his way to the door. Pop glanced back at Zavlaris. "If anyting happen to her . . ." Pop reminded.

"You have my word," Zavlaris said.

Pop shot him a stern look, turned, and went out the back door.

Mr. Zavlaris's eyes shifted back to me. "There's water on the dresser over there, and my wife made some food. Make sure to keep the door locked. We can't take the chance that someone might see you."

I looked at my new quarters, and a feeling of bleakness took over. "I'm sorry, Mr. Zavlaris. I've never seen my father act like that. He's having a rough time with my brother's death and all."

"Those things tend to happen when you work for the Mafia," he replied in an icy tone.

"My brother didn't deserve to die. He was protecting me," I said, afraid I'd given away too much.

"If it wasn't for needing your father's money, I wouldn't have taken the deal. The damn war took a toll on my business." He shoved the handful of hundreds deeper into his pocket.

"Please excuse me when I say this, and I mean no disrespect, but when someone from the family comes forth to offer you a deal, you take it or you're dead. There are no options."

"You're just like your father. You're trying to frighten me," he huffed.

"No, quite the opposite. I'm telling you the truth about how this works to save your life, because I like you and my mother liked you. I don't want anything bad to happen to you or your family."

"You'd better get to bed, missy. You'll start early tomorrow."

"Um . . . where's the light?"

"Get used to the dark at night. There's no light in this room except for the crack under the door.

I looked around the cramped, walled-in space. "Oh," I sighed. "Do you have a candle then? Or something I can use to see my way around, so I don't fall?"

"No, and I'm not gonna install a light either. In case you've forgotten, no one can know where you are. So, at night, this is as good as it gets. Goodnight," he said and stormed from the room.

I sat on my new bed in the dark. With no windows, there was no light and no air. I was trapped again, and I hated this feeling. It reminded me of the time I wandered off to eat strawberries in the fields as a kid and was lured into a strange home, drugged, and kept from my family for days. Only difference was, this time I couldn't scream and cry. This time, I'd have to be silent for my child's sake. I couldn't take any chances.

I lay on the bed and pulled the tiny blanket over me. Afraid to open my eyes to the void, I thought about Gaetano. Ribbons of shame, grief, and loneliness wrapped around me and bound me to my new solitude. I placed my hands over the bulge in my stomach and prayed for a miracle.

Chapter 31
Dear Diary

THE NEXT MORNING, A BELL CLANKED AGAINST THE FRONT door of the store, followed by some heavy steps. "It's me," Mr. Zavlaris said and knocked at my door. "You can open up now. It's safe."

I jumped up and opened the door.

He handed me a bag. "Some food."

"Thank you," I said, squinting my eyes as I tried to adjust to the light.

"Is it safe to use the restroom now? I didn't want anyone to see me."

"Yeah, but make it quick. Remember, Violetta, no one can see you through the store windows. You must remain back here at all times."

"I understand. I was too afraid to go last night. It was so dark I thought I might trip on something."

"It's down the hall to the left," he said softly.

I grabbed a few items of fresh clothing from my bag and a washcloth. I tiptoed to the bathroom and stripped off my clothes. With nothing more than a small wash basin, I gave myself a sponge bath and wrapped up my hair in a bun.

Newly dressed, I returned to my room with my dirty clothes and sat on the bed. I opened the bag of food and peeled a banana. I needed something to soothe my morning sickness. Mr. Zavlaris came in with a black book and two large sacks.

"Here, you'd better get started. Receipts are in the book, along with the deposit slips. Here's the cash from yesterday."

"And the sacks?" I asked.

"This one is some clothing that people need stitched and fixed. I pinned a note of what should be mended. Those need to be ready by tonight. I'll need you to press them." He pointed to an ironing board hanging on the wall.

"Okay."

"The other bag is some yarn and crochet needles. Your father said you can crochet and sew as good as your mother."

"Yes, I do fine."

"I'd like you to make a few blankets that I can sell. I'll put them up in the window."

"How fast do you need them by?"

"End of the week."

"Um . . . okay. I think I can get them done at night, but without any light, I can't work well. Isn't there something I can use?"

Mr. Zavlaris folded his arms. "Well, I suppose I can bring a small room lantern. I have one to sell out there," he said. "But I don't know, Violetta . . ."

"Don't worry. I don't think anyone will see. The door seals shut. I promise to turn it off after ten."

"Well, okay. I'll need that deposit by this afternoon."

"Yes, I'll have it ready by then." I held the black book between my fingers. "Um, Mr. Zavlaris, my stomach doesn't feel so good. I need to throw up." I got up quickly.

"What's the matter? You sick?"

"Yes."

"Well, you better find a way to throw up quietly or someone will hear you. Use the bathroom this time, but once I open the store, you'll have to be absolutely silent. Understood?"

"Yes, sir." I ran to the bathroom to throw up my half-eaten banana.

After I was finished, I got up slow and wiped my mouth. When was this ever going to stop? I hated early pregnancy. It was awful—the throwing up, tender breasts, not to mention the heightened emotions. I rubbed at my stomach and walked back to my private room. I decided if someone were to come, I would throw up into a towel to muffle the sound. I kept the towel close, then grabbed the pen and started counting.

The day passed smoothly. Every time the bell rang, I stayed quiet. I finished my deposit by noon and was able to keep half a sandwich down. After the books, I started with the shirts. A few blouses had armpit holes. A few others needed new buttons, so I set them. Once the shirts were done, I started on the pants. One pair needed to be hemmed. Another had a large hole in the crotch. Poor guy must have eaten too much, bent over, and there it went.

Sometime during the day, Mr. Zavlaris brought me two glasses of water. One for me to drink and one for me to make starch with. I unfolded the ironing board and heated the iron. I pressed the shirts and formed a crease down the middle of the slacks. Once I was done, I hung them up on a coat rack in the back of the room.

I opened the second sack to find six rolls of yarn and three crochet needles. I pulled out soft spools of colored yarn. I decided to start with white as the base. By the end of the day, I had half of it done.

Mr. Zavlaris handed me the cash and receipts from the day along with a small bed lamp. "Here," he said. "Remember to turn it off, and only use it when you're in your room with the door shut. That way no one can see it on if they were to walk by at night." He sounded paranoid.

"I will. Look, I'm halfway done." I showed him the work on the first blanket. "I was thinking of making red flowers to weave into it. It will be beautiful on someone's bed." I looked proudly at my handiwork.

"That's nice. Did you eat?"

"Yes, sir. I finished the other half of the ham sandwich you brought. Please tell Mrs. Zavlaris I said thank you."

"She doesn't know you're here. She can never know. I can't tell her I'm involved with this. She thinks I was extra hungry because I told her to make me two sandwiches."

"Oh, I understand."

"I'll bring you more food tomorrow. Get some rest."

I locked the door behind him, but I was instantly lonely. He was the only one I'd talked to all day. With no interaction, I was left to my thoughts, and more alone than I'd ever felt. I turned on the light and sat on the edge of the bed. I grabbed the blanket and laid it over my stomach as my baby fluttered inside me. Tears pooled in my eyes and spilled down my face. It had only been one day, and yet I was already miserable. How would I last here until the baby came? I would go crazy in here with no conversation or interaction. I looked down at my belly and talked to my stomach.

"Well, little one, it's just me and you. I'm sorry I got you into this mess, but I didn't have a choice in the matter," I whispered and wiped my tears. I reached for a crochet needle to continue my work and found an old journal on one of the wooden shelves behind my bed.

After I blew off the dust, I unfastened the small wooden bead latch to see what was inside. In a hand that might have been Mr. Zavlaris's, there were a few notes that read:

September 1921

Today was the grand opening of the store. I've met many new friends in this community. I am excited yet nervous. I hope we do well here.

November 1921

It's been cold, but sales are picking up with Christmas around the corner. We live in a predominantly Italian community, and it makes me feel like an outsider. I'm the only Greek in this area. Most have been friendly, but a few Mafia men came into the store a few days ago. I think one of the younger guys stole some shoe polish. I considered calling the police, but then I remembered what happens to people who do that. I hope they don't come back. I don't like their kind in here. I don't want problems. Maybe I should bring my gun to the shop to be safe. Mary found out she's carrying our child. A man in town by the name of Giordano has a small medical practice. He seems nice and said he does house calls. I met his wife for the first time. She doesn't speak good English, but she is nice enough and appears to be a good customer. Yesterday, she even brought me some needlepoint doilies and offered to let me sell them here for a small commission. I agreed because of how good her husband has been with Mary. She likes him and trusts him. I pray our child is born healthy.

January 1930

It has been so long since I've written. I thought I'd lost my journal, but found it in the back of the shop. Times are hard. We are desperate. I'm not sure I can stay open for much longer. Baby boy Pete is 9 years old. I want to teach him how to tend to the store, but a part of me wants more for him. I'd like him to be a lawyer. That's a respectable job and high paying. That way he won't have to suffer like the rest of us bums.

June 1935

I'm not sure why I write in this stupid thing anymore. Times have been tough. We're making it through—but barely. Mary had to get a second job. Poor Petie, Mr. Giordano says his heart sounds abnormal, and that he will keep a close eye on him. I hope it isn't anything serious. I'm not sure I can afford the medical bills right now. Thank God for Mr. Giordano. He hasn't charged me a dime for the last three visits. He also gave me a name of another doctor who is a friend of his in San Francisco. I owe him one.

I closed the journal. Now it made sense. Pop helped his son, and that was why Mr. Zavlaris felt indebted to him. I remembered his boy. Good-looking kid. I remembered the day at the dinner table when Pop said he heard the problem in his heart. Mrs. Zavlaris was so worried, but Pop said he was glad he caught it early so they could monitor it. Tomorrow I'd ask about his son, but tonight I'd write in the journal and chronicle my time in this little room. I didn't know how long I'd be here, but it might help pass time.

August 1947

I'm not sure what day it is. I think it's Wednesday, but I might be wrong. I haven't been paying that much attention since I don't read the newspaper every day. I stopped looking through the newspaper after reading Tony's obituary. I cut out the picture of his truck and put it in my hope chest. Not sure why.

I lie here on the tiny bed as my child grows in my belly. I'm sad and alone. It's only been a few days, but I miss my family and hope they're okay. I also miss Gaetano. I pray he got my letter and is healing from his grief. I want so much to be in his arms, but I don't know how things will go. We were so close to a real life together and now with this—

I've lost so much. I don't even know what is real anymore. All I can do is keep busy and healthy for my child's sake.

Not sure how much I will write in this journal, but I'll try when I can. Every time the front door opens and the bell rings, I get scared. God, when will this end?

October 1947

Pop came and visited me today. He comes when he can, but not when he thinks he's being followed. He brought me home-cooked food. I'd forgotten how good homemade pasta tastes. He told me that a few Di Natale men have been lurking around Goosetown, asking questions. He has a few guys staying with him at the ranch if Di Natale tries something. He says he's ready for whatever they have planned. He's kept the clinic closed, claiming a medical sabbatical after Tony's death. Some of the townspeople are upset because they only go to him for their medical needs. He said it's too dangerous. He doesn't know who he can trust.

Paulie's still running but is said to be safe somewhere deep in the woods of Tahoe. My brother—gangster turned mountain man? I'm sure it's only a matter of time until Paulie tries to get his beak wet in the casinos out there. Who knows, maybe he'll go to Vegas? I remember Rose said that the heads of the five families are trying to make their stake out there.

Gaetano came to the ranch, looking for me. Pop told him he didn't know where I was because he doesn't know who he can trust. I'm sad. I miss him. Pop says there is a lot of tension between the East and the West and that he sees a great divide in leadership. He's not sure what will happen, but he's ready to die to defend his family and land if need be. Things have gotten out of hand.

December 15th, 1947

    I'm huge and uncomfortable. This is a big baby; I can feel it. I'm glad I'm further along than I was with Adelina, but I think he's coming sooner than later. My back aches from lying on that lumpy mattress. I'm not sure what will happen, but I feel like I'm gonna burst. I stay under the blankets I make at night. It's freezing in here. I have a cold and a slight fever. I haven't seen sunlight or been outside in months. Pop came to check in on me. He says I'm measuring bigger than I should be, considering the dates I gave him. I may deliver early.

    The baby is resting on my bladder. I spend half of the night in the bathroom. I make sure not to flush until Mr. Zavlaris arrives in the morning. I don't want anyone to hear me. I've thought of ways to escape. I need to see Gaetano, but what would he say if I showed up to the winery like this? Would he tell me to leave? Would his mother hurt me if I showed up? I can't let anyone hurt my baby. I have to get another note to him somehow. But how? Then I can tell him the truth. Maybe he'll understand. Then again, maybe he won't. I'll ask Pop when it's safe to go.

December 25th, 1947

    Merry Christmas, but I don't feel merry. I don't have anyone to celebrate with. Pop didn't visit me, but Mr. Zavlaris brought me some treats—pastries made with spinach, and some made of nuts and honey. I've gotten used to Greek food. It's pretty good, but what I wouldn't give for some ravioli. This baby is always hungry! I want to go to sleep early tonight and forget this day ever happened. I want to get out of here. I've been here so long.

    Last night, I dreamt that Gaetano and I decorated a Christmas tree at the winery. He strung the garland, and

I hung the ornaments. We listened to Christmas music. We were happy and laughing. Oh God, I wish it was real.

Goodnight, heavenly Father. Happy Birthday.

January 2nd, 1948

New Year's came and went. It was uneventful. Men have been shooting their guns outside. I don't know if it's for the New Year celebration, or wise guys ready to kill each other. The sound of guns scares me now. I've heard too many of them with the war, then what happened at the winery. By now, I'm sure Gaetano is frantic about where I am. It's been so long. Gaetano needs the truth. With so much time and no explanation, I asked Pop if he would deliver a letter. He refused and said it was still too dangerous. Apparently Di Natale has gone rogue and no man is safe. I hope they shoot the son of a bitch so I can go.

Would Gaetano love my baby as if it were his, even if it's Frank's? It's my child. My responsibility. Gaetano will have to understand if he wants me. But this is bigger than even me. I must do what's best for my baby.

On a happier note, Pop said Carmela's pregnant and doing well in LA.

January 15th, 1948

Something happened today that frightened me. I heard some guys yelling at Mr. Zavlaris. I couldn't make out what they said because I hid under a pile of clothes. Once they left, he came into my room. His face was busted up. He said a few men were asking questions about me. He lied and said he hadn't seen me. I felt so bad seeing him like that. I hated another person getting hurt on my account. I wonder if Pop will want to move me now?

I've been having strange thoughts and dreams. How can I bring my child up in this crazy world?

January 21st, 1948

Just got word from Pop that the cops picked up Paulie for a slew of crimes. He was picked up in Carson City and is looking at up to ten years in prison. Pop's sad that Paulie's going in, but at least we know he'll be out of the game for a while. I hope he doesn't flip like Frank. If he starts squealing, the cops might reopen the investigation.

I wonder how long it will be before my child gets stuck in this world. I feel sorry for Pop. He has one kid going to prison, another dead, and the rest of us ... well ... we're all in hiding, not to mention Di Natale's threats to kill us all if he can't find Frank. It's only a matter of time before someone gives us up. Money talks. This is no way to live. I'm truly scared now. I don't want them to hurt me or my baby. If word got out that I was with Gaetano, Frank's father would take my baby as leverage, in exchange for Frank. And when I can't produce Frank's body, he'd kill us both, claiming I was a whore and the baby was a bastard. He'd do it to make an example out of us. I can't take that chance. After what happened to Adelina, I must protect this child. My child deserves better. Much better.

February 12th, 1948

The pains have come. Mr. Zavlaris told me Pop is coming to get me. I need to move locations. He says it's no longer safe. He's worried about me delivering in the shop. I can't say I blame him. I don't think I can be quiet during labor, and a new baby's cries would surely cause a stir. I don't want to put Mr. Zavlaris in any more danger. I never loved it here, but it's become part of my routine. I don't know where I'm going next. I have tough decisions ahead, but deep down I know what I have to do. There's no denying it.

And I'm taking the journal with me. Not sure when I'll write in it again. The baby is coming soon. I feel it.

February 13th, 1948

The contractions are strong, and everything hurts. Pop drove me to Antonelli's in the middle of the night. I lay in the back of the truck with a burlap sack over me so no one would see me. My water broke on the way over.

They put me up in their back room. Pop and Signora Antonelli come in and out to check on me while ole man Antonelli keeps watch. Signora gave me a leather belt to bite down on and sometimes I scream into my pillow. I bit down so hard that I chipped a tooth. I'm frightened. I wish my mother was here. I feel alone. This hurts so much I can barely write. Please God, let this child live so I can do what I need to do and give me the strength for what's to come...

February 14th, 1948

Baby boy delivered at 8 p.m. Born on Valentines' Day. He was big, despite coming more than a month early. Nearly 8 pounds. Big eyes and a small tuft of curls on the top of his head. He was born with a small defect. One of his feet curled up slightly. Maybe it was from the less-than-ideal conditions I lived in for the last few months. I can't be sure. Pop called it piede valgo — club foot.

Pop wrapped him up tight in a blanket to soothe his cries. When I heard my son's first screams, Rose's voice echoed in my head. She said it's hard to have children in this life, and that it's always a personal choice. I thought about everything that led up to this moment. I'd been hidden from the world. I would probably be in hiding for the rest of my life. With Tony dead and Paulie in prison, I knew what I had to do for my son—I remembered *ruota degli esposti*—the church in Italy with the bell and the little door.

Pop would never understand. I will wait for him to leave, then ask *Signora* to drive me to the church. The next few hours will be the hardest. I'll make sure to leave a note so that one day he'll know why I'm doing what I'm doing. I won't let him grow up in this life. I have to let it begin with me. This all has to stop.

As dawn approached, I swaddled my son in the afghan I'd made for him, then ran as fast as my legs would allow to the truck parked in front of the Antonelli farms. While ole man Antonelli slept, *Signora* Antonelli sat in the driver's seat, dressed all in black. She wore a scarf around her face and neck.

I opened the truck door and got in.

"Get down," she commanded. "And put dis blankets ova you so no one see."

I pressed my son to my chest, crouched down to the floorboards, then threw the blankets over us.

Blood dripped down my legs from the birth.

The clutch popped as she put the truck in neutral and we coasted down the hill. After a few seconds, the truck's engine came alive, and we were on our way. A few minutes later, the truck stopped.

"You mussa hurry. I tink someone follow us," she whispered cautiously.

I threw the blankets off, opened the door and climbed out. I turned back to *Signora* Antonelli. "Thank you for doing this and for helping me. I'll never forget what you did for us tonight." I looked down at my son while he suckled my breast.

"Dey took my son, but dey willa not take yours." She looked through the windshield and over her shoulder. "Now go," she demanded.

With the cold night air on my face, I trudged forward to do the unthinkable. No one could know I was here and what I was about to do.

I gathered any remaining strength I had left and walked up the steps to the church door. I bent down and laid him onto the cold, concrete floor and tucked a note inside with him.

I peered down at his little face and tiny lashes that flickered in the night's wind, then pressed a kiss to his cheek. "You deserve better than me. Better than this life." My words came out no stronger than broken whispers. Tears clouded my vision, turning his precious face into swirls of regret and a lifetime of immeasurable sadness.

"Goodbye, little one. I will love you forever and now you'll be safe." I banged on the tall doors and hurried back to *Signora* Antonelli. He screamed for me. I clawed at my chest, hoping to dig out my own heart with my nails. I put my hands over my ears and got in the truck. We drove away. I looked back only once to see the church door open.

February 15th, 1948

We made it back with no one seeing us. Thankfully, Signora Antonelli agreed to drive me. She understood why I made the decision, and I'm glad she was there with me. I don't know if I could have gone through with it without her.

Of all the people in this world, it wasn't surprising that it was another Mafia queen who stood in solidarity with me in my darkest hour. We were a silent sisterhood of lost souls who'd sacrificed to a cause that never cared about our well-being. We were the baby makers of future gangsters. Enablers. Arm candy. Partners in crime. And when those jobs were done, we were punching bags and rape victims. We were the forgotten pieces of this secret society, and we all spoke the same language.

We didn't speak on the way back. There were no more words, just tears felt by two mothers who'd suffered their share of grief in this life. For those brief hours in the night, her allegiance was only to me, my son, and his future.

Leaving him all alone on the steps of the church is a memory I hope to bury forever. Any shred of happiness that I've held onto these past few years has been sucked out of me.

All I can hope for now is that the nuns will find him a home filled with love and happiness. I pray he's placed with good people who will protect him from the harms of this world. I saved him from Di Natale, the mob, my father, and even myself.

Today was the hardest day of my life. I've spared him from a life of misery. He'll never have to choose, as I did, or be exposed to the corruption. He'll never have to get his hands dirty to provide for his family. He has the opportunity to live a good life. Now his children and their children will have the same.

I've done all I can to free my future legacy from this insanity. I can only hope one day my father will forgive me for what I've done. Hopefully, one day I can forgive myself for giving a piece of myself away. My child. Piccolino mio.

Tonight, I was brave. I won the battle. The next hours will be long. I need you, Father in heaven, now more than ever.

I named him Anthony, after my brother.

February 15th, 1948 — evening

    I feel lost. All I have left now is this journal and an empty heart. This is my second entry today. My father will be here any minute to check on me. He'll find me alone. I don't know what he'll do, but I don't care anymore.

    I know I did the right thing, but I want to hold my son in my arms again. I want to smell his skin and feel his eyelashes flicker against my cheek. I want to hold his tiny hand. Oh God, what did I do? I feel as if I have to mourn him, but he isn't dead — I am — inside. The only thing that will help me heal is time and prayer. Not even seeing Gaetano can take this pain away. I need time, so much time, to collect my thoughts and feelings. I hope that one day I will see him again. I'll tell him why I had to say goodbye, and ask for his forgiveness. I hope, my son, you have a good life, filled with happiness and laughter. I will think of you always. I love you. One day you'll understand just how much.

Part Three

Il Passagio Della Corona

Chapter 32

Saving the Best for Last: The Queen's Wish

Giordano Estate
San Jose, California
July 2003
Barbara

"I GAVE HIM UP. I LET MY SON GO, ALL BECAUSE OF THIS DISGUSTING life . . ." Ms. G. screamed and cried. Her words were tainted with unimaginable fury and despair. She climbed out of her bed and threw pillows around the room. She tossed old picture frames to the ground, shattering glass everywhere.

"Calm down." I approached slowly. "Don't move or you'll cut your feet."

Alessandro stood behind me, ready to restrain her.

"Easy, *Zia*. Easy. It'll be okay," Alessandro said as worry clouded his eyes.

She picked up a picture of Tony and peered down at it. "Look at how handsome my brother was, and they killed him. Those bastards killed him," she roared. Her hands shook as she held the wooden frame, then she peered down at the newspaper clipping. "This was Tony's truck the day they pulled it from the water."

My heart froze. I lowered my gaze, then looked back up at her.

"Please, hand me the picture." I reached out my hand.

Her eyes were empty. Not a single flicker of light remained in them. Every word and every secret were out in the open. Raw from her admissions, she looked at me.

I pulled her close. "It's okay, sweet girl. I'm right here and will always be here, no matter what. I love you," I whispered in her ear, took the photo out of her hands, and rocked her back and forth while she cried.

"Alessandro, get the broom from outside so we can sweep this up."

Alessandro hurried to the kitchen.

Ms. G. looked up at me. "I'm a sinner. I was a horrible mother. I'm gonna go to hell with Frank."

"No, you're not."

"What kind of mother gives up their son? How could I do that?"

"The kind of mother who knew what would happen to her child if he grew up in this life, and one who loved selflessly. You did what you thought was best to protect your son."

"I wanted to save him, but now it feels like regret. That's why I'm here alone. This is God's punishment for me," she whimpered. "I'm the last to go."

Alessandro returned with the broom and swept around us as I held her in my arms like a helpless child.

"In truth, my son was a product of rape. A beautiful child of God, but nonetheless not planned, and a result of Frank's revenge. A small part of me was scared he'd grow up with a mind like his father. I'd seen how Frank tried to emulate his dad, and I worried it was in his blood. But my biggest fear, bigger than Gaetano and even my feelings, was that he would suffer. I didn't want my son to spin around on the wheel of generational destruction. No matter what I did, he would be exposed to this craziness at some point. It's who we were, and still are." She looked at Alessandro standing behind me. "The family I was born into."

Alessandro put his head down. "Some of us are still trying to get out."

I reached for his hand and gave him a reassuring smile.

"Do you hate me, Barbara?" Ms. G. asked with tear-stained cheeks.

"I could never hate you. I love you, and you know how much. You saved my life."

She sniffled, then wiped her nose.

"Please help me find my son before I die. I need to see him and tell him that I love him. It's my dying wish." She put her hands over her face.

Alessandro and I exchanged glances and nodded.

"Yes, Ms. G. We'll find your son."

After a few minutes of hugs and tears, we walked to the living room, where I sat her down in her tattered brown recliner. Alessandro brought her a glass of water.

"So, you'll help me?" She stared up at me.

"Every time I think you're the strongest woman I've ever met, you go and tell me something like this. Then I realize I've only scratched the surface." I moved straggling pieces of her hair from her eyes. I looked at Alessandro.

A thick crease had formed between his eyes.

"I didn't think I was able to get pregnant after Adelina. With all the scar tissue that followed, I had painful cycles. Some months, I never got my period. Nor did I ever think I'd ever be trapped again like I was when I was a kid. The only friend I had was that damn journal. And here I am, still trapped, this time in the confines of my withering brain with only memories of the past." She stood.

"Where are you going?"

"To get the journal."

Alessandro and I followed her to her room.

Deep in her closet was another old shoe box. "Here. It's all in there." She handed me the box.

I blew off the dust. Inside, red tissue paper wrapped the small leather journal. I opened the book and scanned her entries.

"Those were some of the saddest months of my life. I had almost no communication with the outside world. From then on, I got used to being alone."

My fingertips glided over the words on the yellowed pages.

"For a long time Pop never told anyone where I was—not even the mayor," Ms. G. said. "Well, Mr. Zavlaris knew, but he wasn't going to say anything—not after what Pop told him. It wasn't until about three months in that the mayor asked him why he didn't see me around anymore. Since I was never part of any formal investigation, my father said I'd gone to visit my aunt in Italy until the Di Natale business was taken care of."

"Yeah, what happened with that? How did your dad get Di Natale off your back?"

"Shortly before my son was born, the mayor relayed the message and photos of Frank with the feds to Don Molanano—for a small price. Moving forward, he agreed to turn a blind eye on Molanano operations as long as he got a bigger cut. Don Molanano tried to slow play his request, the two had a few words, but the mayor had another card up his sleeve. He threatened to blow the whistle on all operations, including shutting down my father's medical practice, stating he shouldn't be practicing medicine and that his license was falsified. He even went as far as having the Board of Medical Examiners try to revoke my father's license."

"Could he do that?"

"Yes. Well, he tried anyway."

"Did they ever shut down your father's clinic?"

"No. My father worked until he died in 1953. Everyone has a price—including the medical examiner."

"Yes, you've told me how it works, once or twice." A slight smile escaped my lips.

"The mayor knew how to bring down and cripple our underground economy. Don Molanano knew he had to comply and grease him. He couldn't afford to let them close my father's businesses. The shells were working perfectly, and he made a killing at the track, so he complied. They came to an understanding. After that, no local official bothered us again. But Don Molanano was always smarter. The worst was when I found out about Vinny. About a year after the fire, Vinny went to work for Don Molanano. He was Don Molanano's insurance policy that my father would stay loyal to him."

"That's why you said what you said to that man at the funeral."

"Yes. My brother was a pawn. He was sent to New York to be Don Molanano's righthand man and personal bookmaker."

"But I thought he wanted a legitimate life?"

"He did, until he heard how much money he'd make in the business."

"Oh, the allure."

"Yes." She shook her head. "I realized no matter how much I tried, I'd never get out, and neither would my son. I knew he'd be lured or forced, and I couldn't take that chance."

"At least now I know why you crochet all those blue baby blankets." I reached for her hand.

She nodded, then her gaze dropped to the floor. "I used to think about how he was doing in some orphanage. For so long I prayed that he'd grow up strong and healthy with a loving family. I hoped he'd become a doctor like his grandfather, free to make his own choices and free from the crime and death. I knew I'd never be the same, but I tried to cling to the phrase about hope that my father told me years ago. He said that life is about hope and possibility. And that is what keeps us going. I had hope for my son's future. More hope than I'd had in a long, long time. I sacrificed my happiness one more time and let him go. I let my son go so he could live."

Tears fell down my cheeks. I turned to Alessandro. His eyes were wet and vacant from her admission. It was as if her words were meant for him.

"Sacrifice. What a powerful word, and one that has been felt over and over by us old mob wives. Hell, that's all we did back then." She grabbed for her pendant and rubbed it between her fingers. "When I came out of hiding after Frank's father was killed—"

"Frank's father was killed?" I interrupted.

"Yes. After Don Molanano received the pictures of Frank consorting with the cops, he made his move. Some time after the birth, Frank Di Natale Senior was gunned down on a rainy night in Brooklyn. They never pinned down who did it, but I knew what my father had told Don Molanano. I knew what the plan would be once they found out that the son of the underboss was a traitor."

I looked at Alessandro. His eyes were wide from his aunt's revelations of the past. I shifted my glance back to Ms. G. while she continued.

"There were rumors that Frank's father had grown tired of Don Molanano's ways and wanted to assassinate him so he could be the boss. I realized his plan when I first met him. He called Brooklyn 'his little town.' Don Molanano knew it, too, so he did what he had to do."

"I'll be a son of a bitch," Alessandro spit out. "The old bastard gave the order? I heard it was the Sambinos. I still can't believe my dad was the one who got rid of Frank's body."

"Go on," I said.

"Pop came for me when it was safe to come out of hiding. We didn't speak much after. He was angry with me for giving up my son. Even up to his death, a few years later, he never approved of what I'd done. But I think deep in his heart he understood why. We never talked about it again. Carmela never even knew I'd been pregnant, and it was better that way. I didn't want her to say anything to the wrong person. The only people who knew were me, my father, Zavlaris, and the Antonellis. Zavlaris wasn't gonna say anything. He was too afraid of what would happen. We trusted ole man Antonelli. Antonelli was my father's oldest friend and confidant. He wasn't the kind of man who was motivated by money. What they had was a true friendship. Kinda like ours, honey," Ms. G. said, then patted my cheek.

I smiled at my patient. It all made sense now. Years of pain had created a poisoned heart from countless sacrifices. Everything fit into place except one thing—Gaetano.

"But what happened to Gaetano? Why didn't you seek him out? Why didn't you go back to him?"

"He never received my letter."

"Wait, let me guess. *Signora* Sanna threw it out, right? All so you'd leave him alone."

"Yes. Worse. They lied to him." Her expression hardened. "As soon as it was safe for me to return home, my father handed me letters from Gaetano."

My heart pounded in my chest for answers. "What did the letters say? Where are they?" I asked, looking around the room.

"I threw them out."

My chest felt like it would cave in. "Why would you do that? You kept everything else."

"I was hurt. It had been almost a year when I returned home. I sifted through a stack of letters, all with a Napa address. Gaetano wrote that he'd come looking for me numerous times after he left the hospital. Most times, no one even answered the door. I think my father had too much on his plate to play Cupid. The one time he did talk to Gaetano, Pop told him not to look for me anymore and that I'd left. In one of his letters, Gaetano wrote that he hired a private investigator, and there was a lead that I'd stayed with my aunt in Italy. He promised to search all over Italy until he found me, wrote that he needed me in his life, and asked me to call him immediately if his letters reached me."

I gripped at my chest as Ms. G. continued.

"He wrote dozens of letters from Italy. Postmarks from all over, including my father's hometown of Tricarico. He even paid a visit to Calabria, where he found my aunt. She told him she hadn't seen me in months, but that didn't stop him. His mother cautioned him to give up the search and move on with his life. It wasn't until I received this that I realized what happened."

She pulled another letter from the shoebox and handed it to me. I opened it.

"Read it out loud. I gotta hear this," Alessandro chimed in.

March 1948
Dear Violetta,

It's with a heavy heart that I write this letter. I've written many letters, hired a private investigator, placed missing persons ads in several of the local newspapers, made dozens of phone calls and trips to the ranch. I've searched most of California and Italy for you. I even thought to go to Brooklyn to see if you could be there, but upon my return from Rome, my mother informed me of your note. I'd be lying to say I wasn't heartbroken. She told me of your latest plans to rejoin Frank, and that you had been running from the law.

I don't know where you are, but I hope you're safe. I didn't believe her at first, but when Espi confirmed that she was the one to retrieve the letter and that you'd even signed it with a heart and your initials, I knew it had to be true. That's the way you'd always signed your letters to me in the past.

I may never know why you've decided to return to Frank, but I have my suspicions. You're probably trying to protect me, thinking of everyone else besides yourself. Or maybe I'm wrong— maybe some part of you does love him after all. You both share the passing of your daughter. Maybe in some way you're trying to heal the pain that's been haunting you for so long. Maybe this life of violence and death is all you know. But I wanted to show you a life free of all that.

From the little that I've heard, Frank's gone missing. I can only guess that the two of you are together somewhere, hiding. I pray he doesn't hurt you anymore, and if he does, you find the strength to leave him, once and for all. You deserve so much better.

I've decided to give up my search, and will remain here at the winery with my mother and Esperanza. It's time for some healing.

Although Italy will always be my home, Rome feels different without you. I went back to the pensione we shared just to feel close to you. I've walked the streets several times, hoping I might magically run into you again. But after all that's happened, I don't believe in magic anymore. I don't know if you'll ever get this, but this is the only address I have.

I need you to know how much you've meant to me. You were my first true love and will always have a special place in my heart. As much as I'll never understand your reasons for returning to him after everything he's done, I won't fight you anymore. My mother is the only family I have left, and that's who I need to focus on now. She and Espi need me.

I must let you go, Violetta. Seems that no matter how many times we tried, forces kept us apart. If you ever need anything, you know where I am, and I will be there for you, always.

When I'm out in the fields and I feel the sun press against my face, I'll know it's you, sole mio. And when the wind tickles your lips, let it be me you think of. I can't keep writing. I feel as though I'll surely lose my mind.

I pray you're still alive.

All my love eternally,

~G

My lips quivered as I stared at Ms. G.

"I can't believe this," I choked out.

Ms. G. added, "After I read this, I was about to drive up to see him. Then I opened the newspaper to this . . ." She dragged out another newspaper clipping and handed it to me.

NAPA'S FAMOUS WINE TYCOON MARRIES IN PRIVATE CEREMONY SURROUNDED BY FRIENDS AND FAMILY. GAETANO SANNA MARRIES ESPERANZA M. CORTEZ IN THE SUNRIPENED NAPA VALLEY.

There he was. Ms. G.'s grape grower. Gaetano stood beside a woman with long black hair in a wedding dress amongst the vineyards. Everyone smiled but Gaetano. He looked sad and lost—not the look of a groom in love.

I threw the clipping on the bed. "How could he do this? There has to be more to the story. He loved you so much. I don't understand."

"After almost a year of not hearing from me, and no letter to tell him that I was dead or alive or even with Frank, I'm pretty sure his mother and that girl had quite an effect. I hated them for a long time after that."

"Do you mean to tell me this is all a big misunderstanding?" I put down the letter and cried, "You should have fought for him, Ms. G. You should have gone to the winery and told him the whole truth."

"You must understand, I wanted to. But when I got home I was in a deep depression, and I was sick, very sick—from the loss of blood in the delivery, and from the lack of nutrition and sunlight during my time away. I was anemic. I slept most of the day. I slept for lots of reasons, I suppose. My dreams were the only way for me to see my son. Being awake made me miserable. I relapsed a few times, and after I read that he had married, I overdosed. I almost died. For weeks, Pop tried to wean me off the pills, but I kept going back. It wasn't until my father died that I quit drugs all together."

"That must have been so difficult."

"It was. After everything I'd been through, I didn't have the strength or the words to tell Gaetano what had happened. I didn't have the words to admit it to myself. Hell, I didn't want to speak to anyone about what had happened. After some time, when I was clean enough to think straight, I mustered the courage to drive up to the winery. I was ready to tell him everything. I didn't want to change his life, and I was no homewrecker, but after all we'd been through, he needed to know I was alive. He deserved that much. But something stopped me."

"What?"

"The look on his face." She swallowed deep. "When I walked back onto the Sanna Winery grounds, reconstruction was happening everywhere. It was loud and people walked around, fixing this and that. The damage reminded me of what my relationship with Frank had done to his poor family. Still, I tried to compose myself and gain the strength to say what I needed to say. He was married, and I didn't want to flip his world upside down, but he deserved the truth—my truth. I came upon a large field full of new growth where two silhouettes made shadows across the ground. Gaetano stood in front of Espi, smiling, his hands pressed to her mid-section."

"She was pregnant?" I clutched at my chest.

"Yes. Just a few months, it seemed. It was the picture I dreamed about for as long as I could remember. Only difference was it was supposed to be me. He looked joyful and at peace."

Her voice crumbled, so I reached for her hand.

"I couldn't disturb his new life. I'd done enough. So, I drove away and never looked back. He was happy, and that's all I ever wanted for him."

My heart broke into tiny pieces. The fairytale romance she'd told me for months was over.

"Not long after I left the winery that summer day, I received a letter from Esperanza. She said she wasn't sure I'd ever get the note because no one knew where I was, but she apologized for what she'd done the day of the fire. She wanted me to understand what Gaetano meant to her and said that if anyone understood why she did what she did, it would be me. She said they'd lost their baby from a car accident and that she'd been struggling with medical problems ever since. The doctor told her she wouldn't be able to have children after what happened. She thought the miscarriage was some sort of punishment from God for all that she'd done. In the letter, she begged for my forgiveness. I never replied. I knew how it felt to have a miscarriage, and I figured that was enough punishment for anyone. She closed the letter by telling me that Gaetano was at peace with things, and they'd discussed adoption. She wished me well, and that was it."

"I can't believe this." I reached for Alessandro's hand. He wrapped his arms around me. "It's all over and this is how it ended? It can't be. So that's it? After all these years, you never contacted him?"

"No. I would've been a disruption. He had a happy life in front of him, and I didn't want to get in the way. I loved him too much to ever hurt him again."

"Yeah, but what about you? What about your happiness?" I asked.

"I was content knowing that the people I loved most were living the lives they were meant to live, even if that meant without me," she said. "Gaetano came to the ranch some years ago. I saw him through the door's peephole, but I didn't open it." Her eyes drifted off.

"What? Why?"

"I'd changed since he'd last seen me. And not just physically. I stood there quietly, listening to how he breathed and spoke my name. I couldn't watch him walk away again. Like a coward, I ran to the bathroom and locked myself in. Staring at myself in the mirror, I realized that I wasn't just old, I was different. I was afraid. Afraid of what he'd say after all these years. I didn't know if he was still married. I didn't want him to see me alone and feel pity for me. Time alone and away from the world changes a person."

"He came here and you never even thought to talk to him?"

"I didn't want to get hurt again. The last time almost killed me."

"You had so much more life to live, and yet you decided to stay here alone for the rest of your life?"

She let out a small laugh. "Well, I did date, once. Carm tried to set me up with your father, but that ended quickly." Ms. G. shot a smile toward Alessandro.

"Pop?" he choked out. Alessandro's eyes were wide. "He never said a word."

"Yeah, Angelo was a big flirt. A regular Romeo, but he was too young and only my friend. I'm the one who set him up with your mother. It's a good thing I did, or you wouldn't exist, kid."

We laughed.

"Marie was good for Angelo. She understood what it meant to be a wife in this world and all that came with it."

Alessandro put his head down. I patted his back to comfort him.

"Besides, it would've never worked out with anyone. My heart was, and always will be, Gaetano's. No matter how much we fought it, this was our fate. We were both tired of messing with God's plan. But just because our relationship didn't work didn't mean that the time we spent together was any less amazing. Moments are all we ever have."

She raised the diamond-studded St. Anthony's medal to her mouth and pressed a kiss, then laid it back down on her chest.

"Since then, I've gotten used to hiding feelings, and, well, everything. But now that I know I'm dying, I have to fight this time. I have to find my son. I can't let another relationship slip away. I can't hide anymore. I need to face the choices I've made so that I can die in peace."

"You don't know that you're dying."

"Yes, I do. I can feel it in my bones. When you get to be my age, you know."

I grabbed for her hand.

"I know I'm a pain in the ass, but I can't do this alone. I may have lost Gaetano, but I hope I haven't lost my son. I want to see him with my eyes before they close forever."

"We'll do whatever you need. Right, Alessandro?"

"*Zia*, for you, I will scour the ends of this earth. Where do we start?"

"Well, the first place would be the church."

I folded the articles and letters, placed them on her side table, and gave her a long hug.

"I love you, kid. And now you know everything."

A year ago, her stories of her life as a Mafia queen almost made me run away, but now I saw her in a different light. I understood why she'd become so bitter. Why she didn't trust. Why she wanted to talk about her love story—because those moments were all the joy she had left. All the love she'd given my children and me was because she couldn't give it to her own children, and she didn't want to be alone anymore.

Her story, memories, and plight had become part of me. I'd been placed here for a bigger reason than just to care for her. I was sent here to help her find her son and give her her last wish. As Ms. G. had done her duty to her family, it was my duty to reunite them. Every moment, conversation, and story had led to this moment. This was my destiny.

I placed my arms around her frail body. "Thank you for trusting me with this. I love you. We're gonna find your son. And when we do, we're all gonna live happily ever after."

Alessandro came over and wrapped his arms around both of us. "I love you, *Zia*."

"I love you too. Take good care of this lady right here. She deserves goodness." Ms. G. sniffed. "Don't let what happened to me happen to you. Hold on, and don't ever let go."

"I love her, and she knows how much. Now it's up to her." Alessandro looked at me tenderly.

I swallowed down hard, knowing that my answer was right here all along. If Ms. G.'s story proved anything, I needed to seize the moment. Tomorrow wasn't promised. It may have been the emotion in the moment, but the answer was clear.

I winked at Alessandro and whispered, "Yes, I will marry you."

Chapter 33

A Mother's Love

THE NEXT MORNING, ALESSANDRO AND I GOT TO WORK. We made a large pot of coffee, sat with Ms. G. at the kitchen table, and wrote down all the pertinent information. Luckily, she remembered most of what she'd told us the day before—only leaving out bits and pieces of Tony's involvement in Frank's demise. Even in death, she tried to protect her brother.

I started a folder of the letters, dates, timelines, newspaper clippings, and addresses of past and present family members and friends. Darnell agreed to watch Ms. G. while we went to inquire at the church. I'd called Sofia and told her we might need to retain one of her private investigators. She agreed, pending our investigation at the church.

As we marched up the steps of the old church, I thought about the cold night when Ms. G. dropped off the baby. I wondered what it must have felt like when she left that little boy alone with nothing more than the blanket his mother had made for him. Emotion bubbled up in my eyes with every step forward.

"You okay?" Alessandro asked.

"I'll be fine. It's these steps. I can't even imagine . . . That poor little boy . . ."

"Come on, baby. Let's find him."

The church was small, with rows of wooden pews and a few stained glass windows. I looked at the altar and thought about how Ms. G. stood at that same spot to marry Frank. That was the day she was coronated as a Mafia queen. On the right was the confessional where she and many others had asked for forgiveness for their sins. This religious temple had many stories to tell.

A nun approached us. "Hello," she said in a small voice. "Can I help you? Are you here for the marriage classes?"

"Um, no. Not yet, anyway." Alessandro shot me a glance, then looked back at her. "We're here to speak to someone who keeps the church's records."

"What kind of records are you looking for?" she asked.

"We have a friend who gave up her son to this church to be placed into an orphanage, and we'd like to know which orphanage."

She looked at me skeptically.

"It happened in 1948."

"I'm not sure we keep those kinds of records anymore. That was a long time ago."

"It's of the upmost importance that we track down the child taken in on the night of February fifteenth, 1948. His mother is critically ill, and time is of the essence. She wants to be reconnected with him in her last days."

The nun stood silent for a moment, then nodded her head. "Come with me. I'll introduce you to Father Michael. Maybe he can help. He's been with this church for a long time. This way."

Alessandro and I followed her through a corridor. She knocked on a tall wooden door.

"Father, may I come in?"

"Come in, Sister Annie."

She went in and shut the door behind her.

After a few minutes the door creaked open. "Father Michael will see you now."

Alessandro grabbed my hand, and we walked in together.

"Come in, come in," the priest said. "Please, have a seat." He motioned us to the chairs in front of his desk. "Sister Annie informs me that you're inquiring about some records regarding a child taken in by the church in 1948. Is that right?"

"Yes, sir. That's correct," I said.

"I'm sorry to say I don't think we have records going back that far. Even if we did, we're not allowed to provide that kind of information. It's confidential to protect the mother and child."

"We're trying to find out what orphanages he may have gone to after arriving here and who adopted him. We're hoping to get the child to meet his mother. She's fallen ill with Alzheimer's. I'm her caregiver, and this is her godson, Alessandro."

"I've seen you at Sunday mass a few times, but we've never met." Alessandro extended his hand. "Alessandro Sunseri, Father. Pleased to meet you."

The two shook hands.

"Sunseri. Where have I heard that name before?" the priest asked, looking Alessandro over.

"I'm sure you've met my father, Angelo, from time to time. I bet you've heard of Angelo's Deli in Goosetown. My family has supported this church for years. The woman we speak of had her first communion here and was married in this very building."

"Oh? Who's that?"

"Violetta Di Natale. She goes by her maiden name, Violetta Giordano."

"Giordano. Giordano." The priest rubbed at his chin. "Any relation to the notorious mob family that used to live up the hill?"

Alessandro's eyes pressed together into fine lines. "Yes. The very same."

Father Michael's eyes widened. "Yes, well, I'll do my best to get you any documents you need." His voice trembled slightly, and beads of sweat glistened on his forehead. "Please, come this way. Do you need any water, tea or coffee? One of the nuns can bring you something to eat if you'd like."

"You hungry, Barbara?"

"No. Thank you," I said, surprised at how quickly he became attentive.

"We're fine. Just the files, please," Alessandro said.

We followed Father Michael down a dark hallway to a room. He flicked on the light. An old desk occupied a corner. Wall-to-wall shelves held mismatched boxes. The space smelled of aged wood and dust.

"Take all the time you need. And if you require anything else, please don't hesitate to ask. We're at your service." He disappeared quickly.

"Thanks, Padre. And peace be with you," Alessandro yelled after him, then made the sign of the cross over his face and chest.

"Wow. He was really nice. And so accommodating."

"Yeah, well, with a name like Giordano, people tend to go the extra mile. Did you see the look on his face once I told him who *Zia* was?" He pulled me up to his chest.

"Now that you mention it, I did. No wonder. Your aunt really does have power."

"Yes, she does. Our family has given this church loads of money over the years and he knows it." He leaned in and kissed me.

I pulled away with a smile. "Quit distracting me with those lips. We have work to do, mister."

"All right. All right. Where do we start?"

"We need to find anything that says February 1948."

"Okay. But when we get home? *Maronn*. You'd better start praying now," he teased.

"The faster we search, the faster we can get home. Grab those boxes over there."

I looked down at my watch. It was already eight p.m. We'd searched through almost every folder but come up with nothing.

"It's late. Why don't we stop for the night and start back in the morning? If we don't find anything by tomorrow, we'll call Sofia's private investigator. Those guys know what to look for. We don't." I stacked the hundreds of files back together.

"I swear we looked through every one of these things. No babies or kids recorded before 1955." Alessandro looked around the room. "Hey, wait a minute. We never looked in here." He opened a closet door and pulled the chain of the single bulb that hung from the ceiling.

"Jackpot," he said.

I sprang up and hovered behind him in the closet where more boxes of paperwork were stacked. Years were written on the outside.

"1944, '45, '46, '47 is over here, and '48. Here it is, 1948." He pulled down the box.

My heart smacked against my chest as he placed the box on the desk. I opened it. Inside were hundreds of manila folders with handwritten dates on the front. The folders contained more of the same: marriage licenses, communions, and confirmation certificates.

A date on one file snagged my attention.

"Here it is. February 1948." I removed the contents.

The first document read:

```
Baby boy found alive.
Location: Arc Angels Church
San Jose, CA
Height 20 inches long
Weight 8 pounds 2 ounces
Mother: unknown
Father: unknown
Child was found on the steps of the church at 5
a.m. with a note. See attached.
Follow up instructions per the archdiocese
of California. Will reach out to a few of the
orphanages in the local area to have the child
placed.
```

I inhaled sharply. "Praise God. The church saved his life." Alessandro peered over my shoulder as I turned to the next page.

```
Child was placed in a temporary home for the night.
Notes for Diocese records-
Case assigned medical notes upon evaluation:
Febuary 20th 1948—Dr. Smith
Extrinsic Talies Equinovarus Mild Club foot (left)
Severely Jaundiced. Lab work required.
March 15th 1948—Dr. Leonard
Medical notes: Child experiencing severe case
Pertussis. Will follow course action with
medications.
June 30th 1948
Treatment of left foot. Child shows signs of severe
Asthma. Possibly type two mild Polio—blood work
and medication to follow.
Child will be admitted to hospital facility, then
placed into a foster home until a prospective
candidate comes forward and can be determined.
Signed, *Samantha Santoro*, Case worker # 3710 of Santa
Clara County
```

I lifted the page to view the one under it. There was a small note attached to a form.

These were sent from the orphanage.

They belong with the documents for recovery and archive for the county.

Please keep with our records,

Sister Julie.

Date: September 24, 1948
Prospective Parent 1. Mr. Gaetano Sanna

    I jumped up and down. "Oh my God. Oh my God," I screamed. My hands shook like leaves holding the document.
    "What is it?" Alessandro peered at the papers.
    "Look at this," I said, and we continued to read.

DOB: April 20th, 1921
Race/Ethnicity: Italian American
Gender: Male
Occupation: Vintner
Employer: Sanna Winery
Address: 1600 Silver Way, Napa, California.
Relationship Status: Married
Signature: *Gaetano Sanna*

Prospective Parent 2. Mrs. Esperanza Sanna.
DOB: July 11th 1926
Race/ Ethnicity: Mexican
Gender: Female
Occupation: Assistant to the President of Sanna Winery
Address: 1600 Silver Way, Napa, California
Relationship Status: Married
Signature: *Esperanza Sanna*

    "Holy shit!" Alessandro looked at me. "Wait. This can't be." He pulled the application aside and looked at the back page. His eyes widened. "It's *Zia's* baby all right. Look," he said, then handed me the pages.
    I skimmed the last page.
    The journal.
    My heart jumped. "Give me my bag."
    Alessandro ran to get my medical bag, which was filled with papers, newspaper clippings, and Ms. G.'s leather journal.
    I opened the journal and fanned the pages until I found one

page that had been ripped out. "It's been ripped right from here. Look," I said, and put the note to the old diary. It was the same paper, same typeset, same everything.

I read it out loud.

February 14th, 1948

Please take my child and provide him a home full of love and understanding. A safe place where he can be free and play in green pastures. One day when he is old enough, please show him this letter so that he knows how much I will always love him and that I did this to protect him and save him from a life that would only harm him. I pray that God may let me atone for my sins on this day. Today, I have committed the ultimate sacrifice—one that any mother would do to save her baby from imminent danger and death. I give him to you to love and protect for the rest of his life.

My little son, Tony. I will love you and think about you every day for the rest of my life. May God watch over you. I hope that one day you'll forgive me for this. I know it's for the best.

All my love, your mother.

There it was—her special signature mark that she'd written on almost every note, and sewn into the blanket she'd made for me at Christmas and the Afghan she'd given to Gaetano at Alum Rock Park, so many years ago.

"How?" Tears welled in my eyes. I stared at the crucifix hanging over the door frame. "It's a miracle."

"We have to tell her. We have to take her to Gaetano."

"We need to talk to him first to see if he wants to be part of her life. I don't want to bring her there for either one of them to reject her. She's been through enough. That would kill her."

"I agree. Let's take these papers and go up to the winery tomorrow."

"We may need to make an appointment to speak with Gaetano. We should speak to him first so he can talk with his son."

"I'll make the appointment," Alessandro said. "I'll tell them I need wine for the shop. That ought to get them moving quickly."

We drove back to the ranch with the adoption papers in my bag. With shaky legs from the adrenaline, I struggled to walk to the house. I yanked open the gate. Darnell ran over.

"What's wrong?" My heart ticked up.

"I don't know. She isn't talking. She's just lying there. I tried to ask her what's wrong, but she doesn't answer."

I ran to the house, threw open the slider, and dashed to her room. Ms. G. lay still. She had no words for me, no signs of recognition.

"Ms. G.? It's Barbara. What's wrong?"

I checked for obvious signs of a stroke. Her face wasn't drooping, and she followed my finger. She didn't speak or move any part of her body except to blink her eyes.

"What happened? Should I call 911?" Alessandro asked.

"I'm not sure yet. Ms. G? Do you know who I am?" I scanned her expression. "Do you know your name?"

No response.

I turned to Alessandro. "Call 911. I think she's had another stroke."

"You got here just in time," the doctor said as he shined a light in Ms. G.'s eyes. "According to the tests, she suffered another small stroke.

I've given her some different medication that should help. I'd like to monitor her overnight."

"Can she speak? Does she know where she is? Please doctor, I'm her caretaker. I need to be in there with her."

"Give us a few minutes. They're getting her comfortable and adjusting her IV."

"Thank you." I turned to Alessandro. "Yesterday might have been too much for her. Too much stress. Too many emotions caused this to happen."

Alessandro hugged me tightly. "*Zia's* tough. We need to tell her before it's too late."

"You're right."

"You can come in now," the nurse said.

I rushed to her side and kissed her forehead.

She looked at me.

"Hello, beautiful," I said. "Remember me?"

"Oh, yes, Barbara. But where's my baby? Where did they take him?" She looked down at her medical gown.

A huge lump formed in the back of my throat. "Don't worry. I think I know where he is. I'm going to find him for you, okay?"

"Yes. I'd like that." She stared at the walls.

"*Zia*, you all right?"

"Yeah, but I wanna get outta here. If I'm gonna die, I wanna do it back at the ranch."

"If that's what you want, *Zia*, that's what we're gonna do. Get the nurse. We're getting her outta here."

"Agreed." I went to find the nurse and call Sofia from the lounge.

We arrived home after midnight. After settling Ms. G. in her bed, I sat next to her and placed my hand in hers.

"Can you open my window so I can hear the windchimes?"

"You got it."

"I've been alone too long. I don't want to be here anymore. I want to be with Mama and Adelina. I'm no good to anyone here."

"Don't talk like that. I'd miss you too much. We need to get you better because I hope to have a surprise for you soon." I prayed the words wouldn't blow up in my face, or I'd never forgive myself. If she had something to look forward to, maybe she wouldn't give up.

Her eyes got wide like a child's on Christmas morning. "Oh yeah, what surprise?"

"What if I told you I have a lead on where your son is?"

She cocked her head to the side. "How do you know about my son?"

"You told me yesterday."

"I did?" she asked with wide eyes.

"Yes, you did. It's all right, honey. You don't have to worry. Your secret is safe with me." I patted her hand. "But I need a favor. I need you to hang on a little while longer so I can find him. Can you do that for me?"

"Well, you'd better find him quick because I saw Pop and Carm in my dreams and they want me to come home to them. I even saw Tony. I miss them."

"I know you do. Have hope, like your father told you. More hope than you've ever had before that something wonderful will happen." I grabbed her St. Anthony's pendant. "Hold this tight and pray to Saint Anthony that he finds what you've lost."

"You think?" She looked up at me with child-like eyes.

"I know," I affirmed. "I have one too." I pulled my St. Christopher medal up and kissed it. "This was given to me when I needed protection. It worked. I was protected, and I am still protected."

I looked over at Alessandro, who stood in the doorway. We exchanged smiles.

"I'm starting to think miracles are real, and you're overdue for one."

The corners of her mouth edged up as a bright smile gleamed across her face.

"We have an appointment at ten o'clock," Alessandro explained. "We'll need to leave early."

"I'll be ready. Darnell doesn't work tomorrow. He can stay with her while we go, and I'll alert Leticia to be on stand-by."

"I'll tell Pop to check in on her tomorrow too," Alessandro said.

"I hope I dream about my son tonight."

"You won't have to dream for much longer, honey," I whispered as waves of excitement and emotion engulfed me.

Tomorrow meant everything. Time was the enemy now.

Chapter 34
Found

ALESSANDRO PRESSED A TENDER AND SOOTHING KISS AGAINST my hand. "We're almost there."

We drove down the long drive to the Sanna Estate. Acres of green vineyards surrounded us on both sides. A massive building stood in the distance. Alessandro pulled into the circular driveway. A bellman opened my door.

"Are you hotel guests?" The man offered his hand to help me out of the Ferrari's bucket seat.

"No. We have an appointment with Mr. Gaetano Sanna."

Alessandro tipped the bellman, then came around to me and reached for my hand. His deep blue eyes held me in place. He pulled my hand up to his chest and kissed my forehead. "I'm right here with you. We'll do this together."

"Do you think she's all right? Maybe we should call and check on her."

"She's with Leticia and Pop. If anything happens, they'll know what to do. This is our last chance. After what happened yesterday, we can't wait much longer."

The main building's lobby was bright and open with windows on every wall. Huge chandeliers hung from tall cathedral ceilings. Leather sofas and chairs were arranged across the tiled floor and a gigantic fireplace stood dead center. Near the reception desk were framed photos and newspaper articles of the fire. Alessandro and I stopped to look at the devastation. Much renovation had been done to restore the building's charm.

A receptionist stood with her glasses halfway down her nose and her hair in a tight bun. "May I help you?"

"My name is Alessandro Sunseri. We have a ten o'clock appointment with Gaetano Sanna."

"I'll have Tomas take you up to his office immediately."

"Thank you." Alessandro squeezed my fingers.

A few minutes later a tall man in a suit came up to us. "Please, follow me." He escorted us to the elevator. The third floor opened to a large hallway with offices that lined the walls.

"First time at the winery?" Tomas asked.

"Yes," I said as we exited the elevator.

"Mr. Sanna's assistant will be right with you."

"Thank you," Alessandro said, then Tomas returned to the elevator.

I looked up at the huge double doors of his office where a gold nameplate read:

GAETANO E. SANNA
PRESIDENT

I drew in a sharp breath. In seconds, I'd meet the man I'd only heard stories about—the love of Ms. G.'s life.

A tall woman came out from the office doors to greet us. "Hello, Mr. Sunseri. Mr. Sanna will see you now."

"Thank you. This is my fiancée. She'll be accompanying me today."

With Alessandro's hand on my lower back, we followed her to another set of doors.

"Everything will be fine. I promise," he whispered.

I nodded and licked my lips.

The heavy door swung open, revealing a man in a blue three-piece suit.

He greeted us with a warm smile. "Hello. Gaetano Sanna. Nice to meet you." He reached out to shake our hands. His dreamy eyes blinked. Small, curly whisps of grey hair were brushed back behind his ears. "Come in, come in. Take a seat."

Gaetano motioned us over to the two chairs in front of his desk. He moved behind his desk and sat in a high-back leather chair. He grinned. I recognized that *crooked smile* Ms. G. loved so much. He looked comfortable in a suit. "And you are?"

My eyes scanned his face as I marveled over his hands, hair, and eyes. He was everything Ms. G. had described. Time had been good to him. For eighty years old, he was in good shape. If it weren't for the faintest wrinkles by his eyes and the strands of silver that weaved through his hair, he could pass for someone in his sixties.

I took a deep breath to ground myself in the moment. His office smelled of citrus, and many pictures of children were on the windowsills behind his desk. Beyond his broad shoulders was one of the prettiest views of the Sanna Vineyards.

"*Ahem*." Alessandro cleared his throat, interrupting my blank stare.

"Oh yes, I'm sorry. My name is Barbara Jackson."

He smiled, then looked at Alessandro. "And you must be Alessandro?"

"Yes, pleased to meet you, sir. Thanks for taking this meeting."

"So what can I do for you today?"

I nodded, rising to the moment. "Mr. Sanna, the reason for our visit today is personal. You see, sir, I needed to meet with you as soon as possible, so I had my fiancé make the appointment under false pretenses. I'm sorry, I didn't think you'd agree to see me any other way."

A crease formed between his brows. "You aren't a reporter, are you?"

"No, sir. I'm a nurse and private caretaker."

His face looked perplexed, then softened into a smile. "Well, I'm not sure I'm ready for a nursing home yet, but I could be wrong." He laughed. "Who put you up to this? My son?"

"No. It was my patient—"

A knock at the door interrupted us.

A proud grin spread over his face. "Speak of the devil. Come in, son."

A tall man wearing a grey suit and tie entered. He had curly brown hair, and the same dreamy eyes as the man sitting in front of me.

Alessandro gasped. "Holy shit. No way," Alessandro whispered.

I kicked his leg under the desk.

"I'm sorry? Did I miss something?" the young man teased, then cocked his head to the side, looking confused.

"Oh, nothing. You look familiar, is all," Alessandro lied smoothly.

"Have we met?" the younger man asked.

"Not officially," Alessandro said.

"Sorry to disturb your meeting, Dad, but can you sign these invoices? They were supposed to be in yesterday." He handed the papers across the table.

The young man had the same face, hair, and eyes. He even had the same build. *It couldn't be, could it?* The resemblance was remarkable. Then I thought about all the events that led me here. My heart beat like a hummingbird's wings against my ribs.

Alessandro leaned over and whispered, "Are you thinking what I'm thinking?"

"Yes, it has to be," I whispered back. While the two men talked, my medical training went into overdrive and my early days working in an obstetrics office kicked in. I couldn't believe I'd missed it, but I had. Implantation. My pulse pounded in my ears with my discovery.

"Oh, I'm sorry, where are my manners?" Gaetano said, snapping me out of my thoughts. "Let me introduce you to my son, Valentino."

He reached his hand out. "Pleased to meet you. Sorry for the intrusion." With only a few strands of grey at the sides of his head, both men seemed to defy the effects of time.

"Yes, nice to meet you," I said, floored at the resemblance.

"We call him Val for short. My wife and I named him Valentino because he was born on Valentine's day," Gaetano explained. "At least that is what the papers said the day my wife and I adopted him." Gaetano smiled at his son. "God rest her soul," he said wistfully.

Valentino moved behind the desk and placed his hand on his father's shoulder. "Please excuse my father. He can be sentimental at times. Mom's looking down and she's proud, Pop."

Gaetano nodded with a twinkle in his eye.

"Are you two here for a tour or are you from the paper? I know we were expecting someone from the Chronicle to do a piece on the winery," the younger version of Gaetano asked.

"No. We're here to speak to Mr. Sanna on a personal matter," I explained.

"Okay. I'm sorry. Thanks for the signatures. I'll get out of your way and let you folks talk. It was a pleasure to meet you both." He reached out his hand again for a farewell shake. "I didn't catch your name?"

"Barbara Jackson."

"It's a pleasure to meet you." He smiled.

"You don't know what a pleasure it is to meet you," I said.

The man looked at me skeptically.

On his way out the door, I glanced at his feet. He wore a pair of orthopedic shoes. One of the soles was higher and thicker than the other. It was him.

Chills ran up and down my spine. I'd just met Ms. G.'s son.

"You have a beautiful family." I pointed to the pictures by the window. "Is he your only son?"

"Yes. My wife and I talked about adopting another child, but then she got sick. My son took her death hard." Gaetano's face went sullen. He appeared to be miles away.

"I'm so sorry."

After a few seconds, he shook his head and forced a smile. "So, Ms. Jackson, you said you wanted to discuss a personal matter with me?"

"A long time ago you knew a woman named Violetta Giordano."

Gaetano straightened in his chair. "Have you found her? Is she alive?" His voice rose an octave.

"She's alive, but she's battling Alzheimer's. In the last few months, she's become very ill and suffered a few strokes."

"Oh, no." He put his hand over his mouth. "I searched for her for months, but no one knew anything. I was told she went back to her husband." His voice trembled.

"You were misinformed, sir."

"Misinformed. How?"

"About a year and a half ago, I became Violetta's caretaker. During our time together, I've become acquainted with your story. She asked me to help her find her son, claiming that she'd surrendered him on the stairs of the Arc Angels church in February, 1948—February fifteenth, to be exact."

Gaetano's eyebrows shot straight up.

"After much research, we discovered that you and your wife adopted Violetta's son. From the looks of it, he appears to be the son you and Violetta had together."

Gaetano jerked back. "What are you saying?" His eyes were wide.

"Well sir, after seeing him with my own eyes, haven't you noticed the resemblance? It's rather incredible." I stared at Gaetano's face.

Gaetano threw up his hand and rubbed at his forehead. "He's always been my son in my heart, but *my biological* son? My blood?"

"Yes. You both have the same dreamy eyes that Violetta described, same stature, same wavy hair, same facial features. He looks exactly the way you appear in old photographs."

"You can say that again. He looks like your twin," Alessandro piped in.

"This can't be true. I . . . I . . . Violetta . . . pregnant? With my baby? That's impossible."

"Please excuse me, sir, but I'm Violetta's godson and my aunt wouldn't lie about something like this," Alessandro explained, protective of his aunt.

"She said she couldn't have children. She never said a word."

"She was in hiding. She couldn't tell anyone. Her family was at war. She was afraid someone would try and hurt her or her unborn child because of her involvement with the Molanano family."

"That's a name we don't take kindly to around here anymore. I had to buy my way out years ago." He walked over to his liquor cabinet and poured himself a tall drink. "All this time I thought she was dead. I thought he'd killed her. Oh my God . . ."

"I didn't put it all together until I saw your son. Then I remembered what Ms. G. . . . *er* . . .Violetta told me. I don't mean to go into too much detail, but now it all makes sense. Forgive me for what I'm about to say, but I come from a medical background, so please bear with me."

Gaetano sat down. "Go on." His eyes widened.

"Ms. G. explained that after the miscarriage with her daughter, she had strange cycles, even stating that a few days after she returned from Italy she had light bleeding. She was likely spotting because of something called embryo implantation—that's when a baby embeds itself in the womb. Oftentimes, women mistake this for menstruation. That's why, all along, she thought it was Frank's baby and not yours."

Gaetano remained pensive, digesting my explanation.

"I didn't think it was a possibility until now, but when Violetta returned from Italy, she wasn't having her time of the month. She was already pregnant—with your child. And from what I understand, she came into contact with Frank weeks after seeing you in Rome. In those days, it was difficult to determine the exact time of conception. She said she'd counted the days after what happened with Frank, but she was surprised by how big your son was for coming so early. The reason he came early was because the pregnancy was further along than she'd thought.

"After seeing your son today, I believe the child you adopted that day at the church was the one you share with Violetta. She told me her son was born with a club foot, and it appears that your son has the same condition. The only way to be sure is a DNA test, and your son would have to agree. But after seeing both of you today, the physical resemblance is uncanny."

Gaetano ran his fingers through his hair, and took another swig of his drink.

"I understand that this is a lot to take in. I have paperwork and a note so you can see for yourself." I unzipped my medical bag and pulled out the papers.

"What note? The church never gave us a note."

I handed the note across the table. "It's time you knew the truth."

Gaetano reached for the paper and his reading glasses.

"They probably kept it for the mother's and child's privacy."

Gaetano thumbed through the paperwork then read the letter. His eyes were misty. He pulled out his handkerchief from his inside pocket and wiped his nose. Then he set the note back down on the desk. "I didn't believe you at first, but it's Violetta's handwriting, all right. Even this little heart at the bottom. That's how she always signed her letters to me. There's no denying it now."

"I'm sorry. I know it's overwhelming. Violetta has shared some things with me, personal things about the two of you. I've seen the letter you mailed her, and it appears that you were led to believe, by your mother and your wife, that Violetta wrote you a note stating that she was leaving you for Frank. That wasn't the case."

"It wasn't?" Gaetano rubbed at his chin.

"No, sir. Quite the opposite. In her letter, she stated that she was being forced into hiding because the Mafia killed her brother Tony and that she didn't know when it would be safe to contact you again."

Gaetano's brows shot up. "Tony was murdered?"

"Yes."

"Violetta was so close to Tony. She must have been devastated."

"She was."

"So Violetta never went back to Frank? She was here all along?"

"Yes. I believe your mother and your wife read the letter and knew if they told you how she signed it, you'd believe them and leave Violetta for good." Gaetano went silent as his eyes measured my words. "Not many people draw their signature with a heart and their initials."

"True. She even put it on a blanket she made me years ago. I still have it," he said.

"Violetta tried to contact you when you were in the hospital, after you were shot, but your mother threatened to kill her if she ever came to look for you. And it was your wife who led Frank to the guest house. She said she didn't know they were going to kill her father. She wanted to punish Violetta, and have her leave with Frank, once and for all. The reason I know this is because she wrote to Violetta, asking for her forgiveness."

Gaetano's face paled. "Dear God, no. She did?"

"Yes, it was sometime after your wife's miscarriage. Something about a car accident? How else would Violetta know about that if it wasn't true?"

Gaetano's lips pressed into a thin line, then he leaned back in his chair. "As much as I want to say this isn't true, I know in my heart it is." He rubbed his forehead. "How was I so stupid? I should've known. I guess I believed it because she'd left me once before for Frank."

"You weren't stupid. After everything that happened, your mother was the only family you had left. Of course you believed her. And Espi, she helped your family for so long that you trusted her."

"Yes, I did. She was family to us. We'd gone through a lot together." He looked down at his glass. "The accident. I haven't thought about that in years. It was painful. My wife was in a car accident right after we were married. Some drunk maniac ran her off the road, and she landed in a ditch. The steering column broke off and lodged itself into her diaphragm, killing our child and any chance we had at having another baby. When the police pulled her from the car, she was barely alive." He grimaced. "The doctor had to perform an emergency hysterectomy. That was the same night they told us we'd never have children of our own." He cast his gaze downward, then back up at me.

My heart went heavy in my chest. "I'm so sorry. That must have been devastating."

"It was."

"Sir, I don't mean to pry, and it's probably not my place, but I feel like I'm missing a piece of the puzzle."

"Call me Gaetano. And what is it that you want to know, exactly?"

"From the sound of it, you and Violetta were crazy about each other—like soulmates. How could you . . . ?"

"Marry someone else?"

I nodded.

"Truth is, I never thought I'd marry anyone but Violetta. Then something happened that I didn't expect . . ."

I grabbed for Alessandro's hand and listened intently for what he was about to share.

Gaetano stood and walked to the window behind his desk. With his back turned, he spoke. "I'd been hurt by Violetta in the past. So, when I was told she went back to Frank, the pain was familiar. A small part of me hoped it was a lie, but I'd been disillusioned before. I didn't trust myself or my feelings when it came to her."

My heart broke for Gaetano. His face was pained.

"When I returned from Italy after months of searching for her, I fell into a deep depression. My hopes for our future were gone. My mother told me Espi was taking her father's death hard and to go check in on her. She was the one person in that moment who understood what I was going through. Deep conversation mixed with a bottle of tequila. We comforted each other. It was the drunkest I'd ever been, and in that moment I didn't care. I'd lost everything and everyone I'd ever loved. I guess I felt sorry for myself. I didn't know where to turn. In our drunken stupor and misery, one thing led to another, and, well . . . I think you know the rest." His words dropped off and guilt covered his face. He looked down at the glass and swirled his ice.

I squeezed Alessandro's hand.

"I won't lie and say that I didn't have any feelings for Espi. When Violetta left me the first time, I created a real friendship with Espi, and I know she cared about me. But the incident made me feel dirty and full of guilt. I tried to avoid her. I even told her that what we did was a mistake. She said I was crazy for still caring about a woman who'd left me twice. A month later, I found out that Espi was pregnant with my child."

I put my hand over my mouth.

"In that moment everything I thought my life would be, changed. I still loved Violetta with all my heart, but after the note and Esperanza's condition, I couldn't leave her in that state. I respected her father too much to disrespect her like that. So, with a broken heart, I did the honorable thing for the mother of my child—I asked her to marry me. Over time, I grew to love her. Still, I think Espi always knew Violetta had my heart. I hated myself for that for years. I was married to one woman but in love with another. I'm not proud of it."

"You've been through a lot and made a mistake. Then you tried to make it right and do the honorable thing by marrying José's daughter. You were respectful. It makes sense now, and it explains a lot."

This is who he always was and why Ms. G. loved him. Despite his mistake, he was a man of honor. Like Alessandro, I couldn't judge him for it.

He wiped his cheek and sat back down at his desk. "After the accident and miscarriage, my mother told me to call an old friend of ours, *Signora* Antonelli. She and her husband were the ones who took us in when we fled Sardinia."

"I'm familiar with the Antonellis."

"They told us of a child who'd been left at the steps of a church and who needed a home. I wasted no time and filled out the papers immediately. I wanted to heal my wife's heart."

Oh my God. Signora *Antonelli was looking out for the child! That's why she told him. She knew. Like Ms. G. said, it was one Mafia wife looking out for another. The sisterhood. The bond.*

"When I went to see him, he was already six months old. He was sick and quarantined in the hospital for whooping cough. I was surprised no one had adopted him yet. Babies usually get adopted quickly. Then I learned that he was born with a deformity—his foot. I knew that was the reason no one had adopted him. A lame leg meant no help in the fields and high medical costs. My grandmother had club foot. It was a slight case. My wife and I never cared about that. We just wanted a baby, so we made the decision to love him as our own. I had enough money to take care of any medical care that he'd require."

"Ms. G. never mentioned anything about your grandmother having a club foot."

"My grandmother died years before I met Violetta. She wouldn't have known."

"Studies show it's hereditary."

"Apparently."

We shared a smile.

"Sadly, as much as I wanted to scoop my son up in my arms and take him away from there, he couldn't come home with us right away. He'd been in and out of the hospital. Whooping cough, jaundice, you name it. Poor kid suffered. Not to mention all the paperwork and bureaucracy.

"I'd been shot, and there was an open investigation into José's murder. I can't tell you how many times we met with different people from social services. We were interviewed almost daily about the safety and wellbeing of the child. They don't give babies to just anyone. You have to pass several tests before they relinquish a child to you. It was months before we were able to bring him home." He choked up. "I'm sorry. I haven't felt these feelings in a long time."

"Thank you for trusting me with this and for filling in the details. We came here today to help Violetta reconnect with her son before she dies. It's her dying wish. She's done so much for me. It's the least I can do to reconnect all of you. She's suffered for too long."

He rubbed the tears from his eyes, then sat upright in his chair. "When can I see her?" he asked with renewed hope.

"The sooner the better. I don't know how much time she has left."

"Is tomorrow okay?"

"Yes. That way you'll have some time to speak with your son so he can process all of this too."

"Yes, I need to tell him. I still can't believe it." Tears brimmed in his eyes. "After all this time, it was Violetta who gave me the biggest gift a man could ever have—a beautiful son." A huge smile swept across his face. "You know, I've always seen the resemblance, but I thought it was just some strange, heavenly coincidence." He appeared deep in thought.

"Your story is the kind that makes people believe in miracles. I know the two of you have had your share of grief, but you have a son together now. Because of him, your love will go on forever."

His smile ebbed, then a small line formed between his brows. "I'll still never understand why she didn't pick up the phone to tell me she was alive, and what happened to her. I looked for her for so long."

"When she found out she was pregnant, she was afraid to tell you. She thought it was Frank's child and that you would treat her and the baby differently. She thought you'd reject her."

"I would've never done that. That's not the kind of man I am."

"She was trying to protect herself and her baby—your baby. Once her father discovered that Frank's father was coming for the rest of his family, he hid them all to keep them safe. While in hiding, your child was delivered in the Antonelli home, and that is how you came to know about his existence. It was *Signora* Antonelli who drove Violetta to the church on that cold February night in 1948."

With blood shot eyes, his jaw hung down. "Do you mean to tell me *Signora* knew all along?"

"Yes. It wasn't until you told me that it was *Signora* Antonelli who informed you about the baby that I made the connection. She'd also lost a son to the Mafia, so she kept the secret. Violetta is one of the strongest women I know. She made the ultimate sacrifice for your son. She didn't want him to suffer at the hands of the Mafia. Once he was born, she took him to the one place she knew he'd be safe—with the nuns at the church."

His eyebrows shot up. "*Ruota degli esposti.*"

"Yes."

"When we were in Rome I told her about the foundling wheel. My grandmother was a foundling wheel baby, so I was open to the idea of adoption."

"That's how she knew what to do."

He ran his hand over his tear-stained face.

"Poor Violetta. I hate those Mafia bastards. They're nothing but lying murderers. What happened to Frank? How did Violetta get away from him? For so many years I thought he had her on the run with him, or he'd killed her."

Alessandro shifted in his seat.

"Violetta claims he brought her back to the ranch that night and left to do a job. He was never found again," I said, keeping the family secret.

Gaetano shot me a telling stare. He wasn't stupid. He had his suspicions, but I wouldn't clarify one of the biggest unexplained disappearances in San Jose history.

"Let's not dwell on the past. Let's focus on the future and getting you all back together before she passes."

"I'll speak to my son tonight. What time should I arrive tomorrow?"

"Let's say ten a.m?"

"Where should we go?"

"The ranch."

"Wait, Violetta's still living at her family's ranch?"

"She never left."

"Years back, after my wife passed, I went to the ranch to see if she was there. I knocked on the door. But nobody answered, so I left."

"She was there but was too afraid to speak to you, after everything."

"Afraid? Of me?" he asked in disbelief.

"She hasn't had an easy life. For years, she's battled drug addiction, domestic abuse, the loss of two children, and now Alzheimer's. With the only strength she had left, she walked away from everything she loved so you all could have better lives. She never remarried and has been living the life of a recluse, afraid of the world. Her biggest fear was to watch you walk away and feel alone all over again."

His gaze lowered then returned slowly. "I feel so bad. I wish I'd known. Maybe I could've done something to help her. It breaks my heart to hear that." His face looked empty. "What if she doesn't forgive me?" A mist of worry clouded his eyes.

"She already has, a long time ago."

He smiled with renewed hope.

"You can't change the past. Only the future. You'll always be the love of her life." I smiled.

"And she has always been mine," he said with a soft grin. "We'll be there at ten a.m."

Gaetano came around and shook Alessandro's hand, then opened his office door.

"Gretchen, hold my calls and cancel my appointments for the week. I'll be out of town for the next few days."

"Is everything all right, sir?" Gretchen asked.

Gaetano looked back at me and smiled. His eyes were soft and dreamy again. "Everything is great," he said with a twinkle in his eye. Gaetano hugged me. "Thank you, Barbara, for everything. And for having the courage to come here and tell me the truth. For the first time in a long time, I don't think I'll be able to sleep tonight. I can't wait to see her beautiful face again. *Sole mio.*" A warm smile bloomed across his face.

To hear him say the words out loud made me warm and fuzzy inside. I squeezed him tight. "No, Gaetano, thank you. You don't know how much today has meant for me. I was so nervous to come here and meet you, but I feel like I've known you all my life." I pulled away slowly. "I don't know about second chances, but maybe the third time's a charm?"

"*Hmm*, you never know. After today, I've learned that anything is possible." He smiled again. "I'll see you tomorrow."

I stood in the Napa sun and let it warm my face. It felt as if I'd lost one hundred pounds.

I was light.

I was strong.

The valet handed the keys to Alessandro, and Alessandro hugged me.

"We did it," I yelped and pressed my cheek against his face.

"No, baby, you did it. You handled yourself in there like a champ." He smiled proudly at me.

"In less than twenty-four hours, Ms. G. will meet her son. A son she has no idea was Gaetano's. Oh my God, she's going to see Gaetano again tomorrow too." My heart leapt. "Do you think it'll be too much for her?" I bit my lip.

"No. It'll give her more of a reason to live." His hands cupped my face. "When you love someone, you live for them and because of them." He pressed a soft kiss to my lips, then gently pulled away. "This is why I fell in love with you. You take care of people, and you fight for them. Here." He handed me the keys as he pressed my body against the passenger side door of his Ferrari.

"Me? Drive?" I turned to look at the long hood of the Ferrari "This?" I asked. "I'm not sure . . ."

"You afraid?" he challenged. "Chicken?"

I pulled his body close to mine and pressed a strong kiss to his lips. I grabbed the keys and pulled out of his grip. "Get in, Mr. Sunseri. I'm gonna give you the ride of your life."

Alessandro opened the driver's side door. I threw my bag in the back and kissed his cheek. "No back seat driving."

"I have a feeling I'm going to regret this. Remember the time you flew out of the mortuary parking lot? You have a heavy foot."

I sat behind the wheel of the sports car, turned the key, and revved the engine.

"*Maronn,* my ears," he yelled over the noise, then climbed into the passenger seat and slammed his door shut.

"Put on your seat belt," I ordered.

He eyed me dubiously. "Go easy on her."

I rolled down the window and turned the radio up loud. With my left foot on the clutch, I put it in gear.

"Hold on tight." I looked at the side mirror to see guests staring. I let the clutch out slowly and pressed the gas. The engine roared while the tires screeched forward. The race car peeled out of the driveway.

With my hair blowing in the wind and nothing but the open road in front of me, I sped toward home. I wanted to get back to the ranch to tell Ms. G. everything. Tomorrow, she would be reunited with her son, and I would witness one of the greatest love stories in history come to life—again.

One hundred miles an hour didn't feel fast enough.

Chapter 35

Queen in Training

I DOWNSHIFTED AS I TURNED THE LAST CORNER ONTO THE ONE-lane road to the ranch. I was excited to get into the house and tell Ms. G. everything. I wanted to see her smile light up when she heard the miraculous news.

Once I passed the old oak tree in front, I noticed a strange black car with tinted windows and low-profile tires parked in front of the main house.

"Whose Camaro is that, and where are my men?" Alessandro's eyes blazed.

"I don't know. I've never seen that car before. Leticia started work an hour ago. She said Darnell would take over when she left. I hope this isn't one of Darnell's new *friends*. If they make any noise, Ms. G. said she'd kill them. Did you hide her gun, like I asked?"

I edged closer to get a better look. A man stood over Darnell, kicking and punching him in the face.

A pit formed in the bottom of my stomach. "Oh no, Darnell's in trouble," I shrieked and rolled down the window.

"Where's my money, motherfucker? Huh? Today's payday, bitch," he roared and continued to punch Darnell in the face.

"Stop. I was gonna get it to you today," Darnell yelled between blows.

"We have to do something. He's going to kill him," I said to Alessandro and pressed the brakes. "He must be the prank caller." I honked the horn to startle Darnell's attacker.

The man looked up.

Alessandro dialed his phone. "Joey, where is everyone? Get over to the ranch right now. We got trouble," Alessandro yelled into the phone.

"What are you going to do?" My heart pounded in my ears.

"Stay in the car. Don't get out, no matter what. I don't know if he's alone. I don't want you to get hurt. I'll handle this. Do as I say." Alessandro opened the glove compartment and pulled out his gun.

"No. Stop. You need to call 911."

"They won't be here in time." Alessandro flung open the door with his gun in hand and charged at the man standing over Darnell's bloodied body. "Get the fuck off my son, or I'll blow your fucking head off," Alessandro roared, pointing the gun at the attacker.

The man released Darnell, then stood up slowly.

"Darnell, get back in the house and lock the door," Alessandro ordered.

Darnell got up and hobbled back to the house.

The man stood tall. He was a giant with the physique of a bodybuilder.

"We can do this the easy way or the hard way. Your choice. Get off my property. Drive away or you're a dead man," Alessandro warned.

"That punk owes me five grand, and if I don't collect today, I'm a dead man anyway, so I'll take my chances with you. I ain't leaving here until I get my money."

"Wrong choice. Looks like we're gonna have a problem then," Alessandro threatened, ready to fire.

"No," I screamed from the car.

"Stay in the car," Alessandro yelled back at me.

The man charged toward Alessandro. Alessandro let off one shot, hitting him in the shoulder, but the attacker didn't even flinch. He continued his pursuit. Alessandro fired again. The shot grazed his thigh. The attacker lunged at him and knocked the gun from his hands. The gun slid across the gravel and under the Camaro. The two men fell to the ground. The attacker held Alessandro down, then hit him in the face and ribs. Splotches of blood bloomed from the man's shoulder and thigh. Two shots and he still didn't go down.

Like a wrestler, Alessandro swung his legs up and around the man's neck and squeezed.

The attacker's face turned blue and his eyes bulged in their sockets. Alessandro held him there until the man let go and he could escape from under him. The man coughed and rubbed his neck.

Alessandro got up and reached his hand under the car to get his gun when the attacker pulled him out by his legs and dragged him across the dirt. In one swift move, Alessandro twisted his body around and kicked the man in the gut and again on his thigh. The attacker grabbed at his leg, releasing Alessandro from his grip.

Alessandro jumped to his feet and threw the man's body up against the Camaro and punched his ribs. Left, right, and left again. After a finishing punch to the gut, the man fell to his knees, gasping for air.

Alessandro spun around and planted a round-house kick onto the attacker's face. Blood splattered everywhere. The man collapsed to the ground. Alessandro jumped on top of him and landed several more punches to the face until the man's body became lifeless under him.

Panting, Alessandro looked up at me and put his arms down by his sides. He peered back down at the man under him, shook his head and climbed off the intruder.

After only a few seconds, the attacker got back up and tackled Alessandro to the ground.

The two men started hitting each other again. Their bodies rolled around in the dirt until the man grabbed a large rock and hit Alessandro in the face.

Alessandro's body lay motionless.

My heart stopped.

The giant man pulled Alessandro's wallet from his pocket and removed its contents, then walked back to the Camaro and pulled out a gun. It must've been the same gun he'd fired the night he called. Recalling the sound sent chills down my spine. The man cocked his gun, then turned back toward Alessandro.

I had to do something.

He'd kill Alessandro.

"Your turn, asshole. No one fucks with the people I love." I shifted the car into gear, slammed on the gas, and struck him, dead-on, pinning him between his Camaro and the Ferrari.

He screamed and dropped the gun as I crushed his legs between both cars.

Four white Angelo's Deli catering vans came out of nowhere. Loads of men poured out and pointed their shotguns at the attacker.

"Put your fucking hands up, man, or we'll blow your fucking head off." Joey came up on the guy. "Oh fuck, I know this piece of shit."

Alessandro stirred, then hauled himself to his feet. He limped over to Joey. Blood rushed from his head. He looked at the attacker, then back at me with wide eyes.

"Alex, give us the order," one of the guys yelled, pointing his gun at the man's head.

"She's broken my fucking legs," the man pleaded. "Tell her to back up." He hit his hand against the car's hood. "Please, man, I beg you."

"Back up, Barbara. He ain't going anywhere," Alessandro said as he reclaimed his gun from the ground.

I put the car in reverse. The man fell to the ground. Alessandro's crew surrounded the attacker with their guns as Alessandro grabbed the man by his hair and lifted his face to the sky.

"You low-life, drug-dealing piece of shit. Dealing dope to young kids, you worthless fuck." Alessandro pressed the pistol to the guy's forehead, ready to fire. Rage filled his eyes as he steadied his hand.

"Come on, man," he pleaded. "I didn't know you work with these guys. Joey, you gotta vouch for me. Tell him. The kid owed me money. I was here to collect."

"If I knew yous was dealing to kids, I woulda killed you myself," Joey threatened.

"I didn't know the kid was your kid. I don't want any problem with you guys," he said in pain.

"You made a big mistake coming here," Alessandro warned. "You fucked with the wrong family, and now you know who I am and what I'm capable of. Consider Darnell's debt clear. You got off easy today, motherfucker, but if I ever see you around my family again, I'll kill you and I won't think twice about it."

"Okay. Hey man, I gotta get to a hospital."

"You'll live. I didn't hit any vital organs. As for your legs, get yourself a fuckin' cane!"

"What do you want us to do with him, boss?" another Molanano man said.

Alessandro walked over and whispered something to Joey.

"Sure, boss, we'll take care of it." Joey grabbed the man by the arms, tied his hands with zip ties, and threw him into the van.

"Where you taking me?" the attacker yelled.

"You're going on a little vacation," Joey said and slammed the van door shut.

Loud screams came from the back of the van.

"You shut up in there, or I'll make you shut up. You worthless fuck," Joey banged his hands against the van doors.

"The piece of shit emptied my wallet. Frisk him and clean him up. Pop doesn't want blood all over the seats. And get his car outta here," Alessandro ordered.

"You got it, boss," Joey said.

I threw open the car door and ran to Alessandro.

He put his arm around my shoulders and scanned my face. "I'm sorry. I tried to let him go . . . It was self-defense."

"I know. It's okay."

He put his hand behind my head and drew my face to his. "Are you all right?"

"Am I all right? I'm fine, but look at you. You're bleeding. You need stitches."

"Well then, I'm glad I have a nurse as a fiancée."

"You're crazy, you know that?"

"I'm crazy? You're the one who ran the guy over." He spit out blood from his mouth. "The son of a bitch dented my hood. Luckily I have insurance. But the whole car thing? That was amazing."

"Take off your shirt. We need to stop the bleeding."

Alessandro ripped off his shirt.

I crumpled it up and applied it to his cheek. "Apply pressure. I'll disinfect it when we get inside."

I put Alessandro's arm over my shoulder, and we tottered toward the gate.

Darnell staggered toward us. "I saw everything in the cameras."

We stopped. The three of us stared at one another.

"You okay, kid?" Alessandro put his hand on Darnell's shoulder.

"Yeah, but it hurts to breathe," Darnell said.

"That happens when you have a few cracked ribs. Trust me, I know," Alessandro said.

"That's nothing after I get through with you. Darnell, what in the hell were you thinking? You lied to me."

"I'm sorry, Ma. I tried to sell enough to get him the money, but then I started smoking it and giving some to friends, and then I didn't have enough to pay it back."

"You're grounded . . . for the rest of your life," I scolded.

"Your mom and I care about you. We don't want you into that

shit. It's bad for you. You have a good future ahead of you. Don't blow it on that crap."

I turned and looked deep into Darnell's beautiful brown eyes. Tears trickled down my cheeks. "I love you, son. More than my own life. I've proven that more than once now. Don't make me prove it again. I know what happened with your dad has messed with your head, but I'm going to do everything I can to make things right. Drugs and alcohol are never the answer."

"I love you too, Ma. I'm sorry." Darnell hugged me gently. "And Alex, thank you for all you've done for my mom and me."

"You're welcome, kid. I want you guys in my life for a long time. I want us to be a family." He looked at me, then back at Darnell.

His words warmed me as a huge smile swept across my face. Alessandro and I exchanged glances.

"We have some things to talk about with you and your sister, right, Barbara?"

"We do, but not before I clean you guys up. And not before we talk to Ms. G. Oh God, Ms. G. She's been all alone." My heart fell to my feet.

"She's fine, Mom. She's watching a rerun of *Judge Judy* and cussin' at the TV. I already know what you guys wanna talk to me about, and you don't have to worry. I'm fine with it. I want you to be happy, Mom."

"Thank you, Darnell," I said.

"Yes, thank you. Your blessing matters a lot to us," Alessandro said. "Now, let's get inside so your mom can check us both out."

"What are you going to do with that guy?" I asked nervously.

"He'll live. Far away from here, but he'll live. If he's smart, we'll never see that piece of shit again. I promised you that I've changed."

I smiled. "Come on, you two. Let's get inside." We hobbled to the big house.

Alessandro winced and slowed. "Hey, Joey," he yelled, "before you take off, I could use some help over here."

The surge of adrenaline must have worn off. I hated seeing him in pain. I touched his side with my free hand.

"I'll be fine. It just needs to be taped. I'm getting old," he mumbled as he hobbled past the gate with his arm around Joey.

The screen door snapped shut.

"What in the hell is going on here?" Ms. G. yelled from her front porch. She stood in her nightgown with her mother's rifle at her side. "What's with all the God damn racket? I was gonna take a nap. Joey, is that you?"

"Yeah, it's me, Ms. Giordano."

"What in the hell are you guys doing? Can'tcha walk? Darnell, what happened to you?" Ms. G. asked with her rifle at her side like a walking stick.

"It's a long story," I said. "I'll tell you about it later. Alessandro, her gun?"

"What do you expect me to do? She practically sleeps with the damn thing," Alessandro clipped, grimacing from pain.

"It's too dangerous. She might hurt someone or herself. With how she talked the other day, I don't want her getting ideas. She's been so depressed."

"After tomorrow, she won't be depressed anymore."

"Why? What happens tomorrow?" Darnell asked as he held his side.

"Did you make her wear her hearing aid today?" I asked Darnell.

"Yeah, she's wearing it."

"Then I'll tell you everything when we get inside."

"Tell me what?" Ms. G. snapped.

"See?" I said as we trudged slowly to the back. "Don't worry, Ms. G. Some guy was giving Darnell a hard time. He's gone now."

"You want my gun, honey?" she asked and pulled it up from her side.

"No. Now put down your gun. We took care of it."

"Barbara took care of it all right," Alessandro yelled to his aunt.

"She ran into the son of a bitch with the car. Broke both of his legs." He beamed.

My cheeks flamed. "Don't tell her that," I whispered.

Ms. G.'s brows shot up. "She did?" she said loudly. "Atta girl. Give 'em hell, honey. Don't let no man mess with your family. Now get over here. I'm starvin'. Where you been all day?" she said, with one hand on her rifle.

"I'll be over shortly. Please go back inside," I said.

Alessandro lowered his voice. "Joey, when we get inside, get my *Zia's* gun and hide it."

"I heard that," Ms. G. said. "The hell he will. You try and take this here gun, Joey, and I'll shoot you right between the eyes, you hear me? Why you here, anyway?"

"Easy, Ms. Giordano. I heard you. We're here to help. Alessandro called us," Joey explained.

"Help with what?" asked Ms. G.

"Well, she must be feeling better." Alessandro laughed.

"Yeah, much better," I said.

"Answer me, damn it," Ms. G. hissed as she followed us to the back. "Joey, what in the hell are you doing here?"

"Neighborhood watch."

"Neighborhood watch, he says. *Minchia*. Get outta here. You guys make too much noise. Go on and let an old lady rest."

"Hey Alessandro, maybe you should hide her gun. Your aunt scares me," Joey said.

"Tell me about it," I said, and we all walked into the big house.

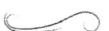

I sat beside Darnell's bed and watched him sleep. I'd given him some pain medicine and told him I'd make an appointment to see a family therapist. After everything that had happened, he didn't argue. Now and again, he'd grimace from pain. I'd come so close to losing him again. I kissed his forehead and went to my room.

Alessandro lay half-naked in bed. His eyes were closed.

I lay next to him and placed my hand on his chest.

"Darnell okay?"

"A little banged up and in pain. I'll check on him again later. How are you? You want something for the pain?"

"How about another shot of that whiskey? I'm getting too old for this shit." He winced and grabbed his glass off the side table.

"You're not old. Here, let me help you." I grabbed the bottle and poured him a shot. He took a sip, nestled back into the pillow, and closed his eyes. Gently, I rested my head in the crook of his neck. In silence, I held him.

I replayed the day's events in my head. So much had happened in twenty-four hours it was hard to comprehend. Gaetano. Valentino. Ms. G. Alessandro. Darnell. The fight. It was the first time I'd witnessed Alessandro act as a boss for a family that, for so long, I had feared. A family who once again came to my rescue.

Alessandro had put his life on the line for my son and me. I was powerless against my love for him. He was a semi-retired, true-to-life Mafia man. An antihero of sorts, and I loved every inch of him. A man who wanted nothing more than to love me for the rest of my life, and I believed him. He wasn't an abuser like Marcus or Frank. He was a man who just wanted to be loved.

Loved by me.

My whole life, I thought men left their families when times got tough, like my father did, or controlled women by fear, but Alessandro disproved all of that. He stepped in as a father figure to my children and promised to be a partner to me forever. Time and time again, he'd shown me that he'd fight anyone and anything that tried to keep us apart. He never let our skin color define our relationship. He wanted me for me.

Strange as it was, this life that I'd been warned about many times felt dangerously familiar. It wasn't the allure. It was the unyielding power and unwavering loyalty that this family had that made me want to be a part of it. I was forever in their debt. The words *a favor for a favor* took on a new meaning.

This was my life now. My family. With that came great responsibility. Every story I'd heard had prepared me for this.

Today, I was brave.

Today, I saved the people I loved. Ms. G. would be so proud of me for not falling victim. I wouldn't be afraid anymore, and I accepted my new role as a soon-to-be Mafia queen. I loved this feeling, and I loved Alessandro.

"Hey, Alessandro?" I whispered in his ear.

"Yes, beautiful?" His eyes were shut, but he grabbed my hand and pulled it to his chest.

"I'm gonna need that ring."

He opened his eyes. A huge grin played across his lips. He reached into the side table drawer, pulled out the black box, and placed the ring on my finger.

"The ring's been here all this time?"

"Yes. I put it here the day you said yes. I planned to give it to you on a night when I could hold you in my arms as we watch the sunset take our breath away, but we've been pretty busy these last few days." He laughed and a warm smile remained. "You're my queen. I promise to love you forever." He pulled my hand up to his mouth and kissed the diamond on my finger.

I looked down at the ring, a symbol of my future service to this family. "When I saw how close I came to losing you today, I knew I couldn't live without you. I love you, Alessandro. Thank you for making me feel beautiful and cherished. I'd be honored to have you as my husband. We're a good team, you and I."

I kissed him.

He tangled his fingers into my hair and pulled me into a loving embrace.

Chapter 36
Reunited

"Ouch. God damn it," Alessandro shouted as he pulled the shirt over his chest. "For this much pain, I should've had him killed."

"No, you shouldn't." I gently placed my arms over his shoulders and leaned in for a kiss. "I know it's hard, but you did the right thing." I inspected his cheek. "The stitches look good. You'll heal up nicely," I said and put a bandage over the wound.

"Thank you for taking care of me." He smiled.

"You're welcome. We need to head over soon. Gaetano should be here in the next hour and I have to prepare Ms. G." The thought made butterflies swarm my stomach. Ms. G. would soon see the love of her life, and the son she gave away more than fifty years ago. The kind of day that people write stories about. I wasn't sure how she'd handle it all. I hoped and prayed that her debilitating Alzheimer's would subside, if only for a moment, to remember him.

"Yeah, but first I need some industrial-strength coffee and another aspirin."

He winced again and clutched at his side.

"Let me get them out of the medicine cabinet," I said and turned toward the bathroom.

"I'll get them. Go check in on Darnell and then we'll go over. Okay?"

"Yes, okay."

I peeked into Darnell's room. He snored lightly and remnants of a half-eaten sandwich led me to believe he was on the mend. I pulled the covers over his body, kissed his forehead, then shut his door.

"How's he doing?" Alessandro asked, handing me my coffee and my medical bag.

"He'll be fine. If it still hurts by tomorrow I'll take him in. Maybe I'll reach out to that family doctor who came to check on Ms. G. I don't think he'll ask too many questions, and he does housecalls."

"That's a good idea, my little nurse." Alessandro pulled my waist into his frame and pressed a kiss to my cheek.

"We better go. Today's a big day."

"Don't worry. I'll tell our guests I was kicked by a mule."

We laughed.

"You ready?" he asked.

"Yes."

"Let's go, then. Time to watch a miracle."

Ms. G. was in bed. Her eyes were soulless again and bereft of any shine. She stared off into space. Alessandro sat next to her and held her hand. She was unresponsive to his touch. Her chest rose and fell with each breath.

Oh God, not today. Please let her hang on for a few more hours. I grabbed her pills.

"I don't like seeing her like this," Alessandro said. "I'll go out front to greet our guests when they arrive,"

"Sounds good." I winked at Alessandro. "Time to get dressed and take your pills, Ms. G."

She turned to look at me. "What for? I'm dying. Those pills can't help me anymore. Pills were never the answer for me."

"I need you to take your pills because you'll have a visitor." I handed her two tablets and a glass of water.

With eyebrows raised, she sat up in bed. "A visitor?" She swallowed the pills.

"Yes." I grabbed the cup from her hands and set it on the nightstand. "And you'll want to hear what they have to say." I placed her hearing aid into her ear and searched her dresser for one of her finer nightgowns. "Let's put this on. Here, lift your arms." I helped her out of her slept-in bed clothes and slid the rose print satin garment over her frail body. I fixed her bedding and brushed her hair. "You look beautiful." I smiled at her.

"Who'd want to visit an old dying lady like me?" she asked while gliding her fingers over the satin gown.

"I do," a familiar voice came from the doorway.

Gaetano stood in the entry of Ms. G.'s bedroom. He was dressed in a grey three-piece suit with a hat in his hand. He walked toward her and stopped at her bedside. Valentino stood behind him. Tears welled in his eyes as he witnessed his mother for the first time.

Ms. G.'s eyes lit up when she saw Valentino. She reached for him. "Gaetano. It's you," she said to her son. "You came back for me," she whispered.

Gaetano glanced at me then tilted his head. I walked over to Gaetano, put my arm around his shoulder, and then looked at Valentino.

"She thinks you are your father. You look the same as she remembers you."

"Ms. G., this is your Gaetano." I placed one of her hands with Gaetano and the other with her son. "And this, Ms. G., is your son, Valentino. I promised we'd find him, and we did," I choked out as a knot formed in my throat. Feeble against my emotions, my tears spilled over the tops of my cheeks.

Her eyes searched both men's faces.

There were no words in the moment, only investigative silence.

Her eyes widened. "My son? How?" she asked while studying Valentino's face.

"I adopted our son. A son we share together. I didn't know he was our son until your friend here made the connection," Gaetano said, weeping.

"How?" she asked.

"*Signora* Antonelli knew that my wife and I couldn't have children. She called to tell me that a child had been left at the steps of the church close to her home and that I should seek out the details. Yesterday, Barbara told me that the child I adopted was ours." His thumb grazed over the top of her hand. "What I'm trying to tell you, *sole mio*, is that God brought us back together by placing our son into my life."

An incredulous expression flitted across her face, followed by slow smile. "I can't believe it." She marveled at her son. "It can't be, but somehow it is . . ."

"You were off on your dates, Ms. G., that's all."

"You look just like your father," she whispered in awe. She smiled at her son, then back at her grape grower. "After all this time, I thought . . . but I was wrong . . . so very wrong. God had a better plan, after all."

"He always does. This is evidence of that," I said.

Valentino knelt at his mother's bedside. Tears streamed down his face.

"Mama," he said, "for the longest time I've wanted to know what you look like. You're more beautiful than I ever imagined." Valentino bent forward and laid his head on his mother's chest.

"Let me look at you." Ms. G. put her hands through her son's curly hair. "Same curls, same honey-brown, dreamy eyes and lashes. Look at these lashes, Barbara."

"He's beautiful, Ms. G. You have a handsome son there." I put my hand on top of Valentino's shoulder.

"Mama, I love you," Valentino cried and fell into his mother's arms again.

Gaetano kissed Ms. G's forehead. "We don't need tests done, Barbara. He's our son. I know it. He looks like me, but he also has her loving heart and courageous spirit. Both of them being brave and overcoming so much through adversity." Gaetano smiled on them fondly. "Him, as an orphan with all his medical problems and her, with everything she's been through. The more I think of it, the more I see how alike they've always been," Gaetano said, witnessing his beloved and their son together for the first time. Tears slid down his cheeks.

With her son's head on her chest, Ms. G. reached for Gaetano's face and patted it. He held her hand. "*Sole mio*," Gaetano stammered out between sniffles. "Oh, how I've missed you, my love." He kissed the back of her hand. Gaetano leaned over her body, placed his face down to hers, and whispered something in her ear. With Ms. G.'s arms around the two men, they all wept.

Ms. G. had reconnected with her son and the love of her life and on my watch. This time, it would be forever. I took a few steps away to let this little family have their moment.

I ran to Alessandro's side. "We did it," I said with a sniffly nose.

"You did it and I'm so proud of you," Alessandro said as we looked at the trio before us.

"Are those tears I see, Mister Tough Wise Guy?" I teased.

"Don't tell anyone." He laughed. "Guys get whacked for less, and the boys will tease me."

"I promise. You can cry in front of me anytime you want." I kissed him and enjoyed the miracle before us. "This is better than any medicine. This right here will make her want to live. I'm sure of it."

"Yes, it will." He brushed away my tears. "World's best nurse and caretaker, Ms. Barbara Jackson, reporting for duty," he teased. "Your love for her is remarkable—all the time and effort you've put into making her healthy and happy. Look at what you've done," Alessandro said and nodded in their direction.

"No. All along it's been her helping me. I just didn't know it until now. Through her stories, she's the one who taught me about resilience, the importance of family, and the power of selflessness, and above all, she taught me about love." I rubbed his shoulders. "Look at them. It seems that no amount of time and distance has changed them. Their love story is the kind that makes people believe in love in the first place. It just happened in God's time, is all."

"When we're that age, do you think we'll have that kind of love?" he whispered in my ear.

"I know we will." I smiled at the incredible phenomenon unfolding in front of us. "Let's give them some time alone. They have much to catch up on."

After a call to the deli, the house was filled with warm and delicious food. Smells of garlic, onion, and basil tickled my nose as trays of food lined Ms. G.'s table. Between smiles and tears, Ms. G. seemed to come alive again. She walked her son around the house and showed him pictures of his new family, including every detail of every family member. He took much interest in hearing about his grandfather and his medical practice, admitting that a part of him always wanted to go down the medical path and he never knew why. But because of his upbringing, he decided to work alongside his father to run the Sanna empire one day.

Valentino told Ms. G. of his wife, Liz, and their three sons. The oldest, Gaetano, was named after his grandfather. Their second son, José, was named after his adoptive mother's father, and then there was baby Efrem, named after Gaetano's father—the man who started their family's legacy. One of her grandsons was newly married with twins on the way—a boy and a girl.

My heart swelled as my Mafia matriarch beamed with pride

for her expanding family. Every now and again, I'd catch a glimpse of Gaetano—how he looked at her with complete reverence and an indescribable adoration and affection.

After the food, pictures, and stories of her family's lineage, Ms. G. looked weary and returned to her bed to rest. Alessandro took Valentino outside to show him the ranch. Gaetano followed me into Ms. G.'s bedroom and sat by her side while I fluffed her pillows and gave her pills.

"Violetta, you're still so beautiful. Just to touch you again. I never stopped loving you." He reached for her hand and pressed it to his lips. "When I reconnected with you again in Rome, it was a miracle. I thought, *This is it—I found her*. And then you were stripped away from me again. There I was, roaming the Earth, searching for the other part of my soul again, only to hear you'd returned to Frank. All I could do was pray you were alive and happy. To find some peace within myself, I thought I needed to let you go, once and for all. But I screwed up. I let my emotions get the best of me. Esperanza filled the void created by your absence. I had to live a life with half a heart—so I did. The only time I smiled is when I held my son. If I'd known what I know today, things would have been so much different. I should have never stopped looking for you. Forgive me."

"That's all water under the bridge now. I'm glad you told me everything. I don't want to waste any more time. We've both made mistakes. You couldn't have known where I was. I'm the one who created mistrust when I left you the first time. It seems my entire life I've tried to protect everyone I love from the Mafia's clutches, but it came at a great cost." She shook her head. "I couldn't lose another child to this life, so I had to make tough decisions. It's because of those decisions that our son's alive. Up until today, I felt shame for giving him up. After seeing him, I know that I did the right thing. If I hadn't done what I did, he would've ended up dead or in jail somewhere."

Gaetano leaned forward and held her hand to his chest. "Thank you, Violetta. You're the bravest woman I know. You love selflessly. Val's the best gift you could have ever given me."

"Everything happens for a reason. If you had never married Espi, then you wouldn't have adopted Valentino and I might have never found him. You and Espi have done a fantastic job raising our son in love and happiness. That's all I ever wanted for him. As much as I disliked her for stripping me of a life with you, a part of me owes her for what she's done. It wouldn't be the first time I've had to bury the hatchet. I forgive you."

"You're the love of my life. You always have been and always will be. *Mia bella ragazza, sole mio. Ti amo. Sei la forza che mi dona la vita e la luce che mi toglie l'oscurità.*"

"Still the poet," she teased.

"You're the only woman I've ever written poetry for—ever. Now that I've found you, I'm never letting go. We have Valentino now, and because of him we are bound together forever. I can never lose you again, because everytime I look at our son a piece of you will always be with me." He bent down and kissed her forehead.

"So much time has passed." Her lips quivered, and she cupped his cheek in her hand.

He smiled fondly at her. "No amount of time can change how I feel about you. I want you to come back with me to the winery. Let me take care of you now. Please, let's be in each other's lives until our last days," Gaetano pleaded.

"I don't know. Who will take care of the ranch? My life is here," she said.

I politely cleared my throat. "Your life belongs where you're the happiest. We can arrange for you to go to the winery. Sofia and I will understand."

"But, Barbara, I only trust you." She reached out her hand for mine. "You're like a daughter to me now. I can't lose you."

"You'll never lose me. Like Gaetano, I'll always be here for you. I want you to be happy. Besides, you won't lose me because we're going to be family now. Alessandro proposed, and I accepted. So you're stuck with me."

"Finally. That kid is thinking with his brain and not his . . ." Violetta stopped herself. A small smile crept up. "Well, good for you. Alessandro will be a good man to you."

"He already is." I smiled.

"I heard my name. What did I miss?" Alessandro asked as he and Valentino entered Ms. G.'s room.

"Ms. G. is moving to the winery."

"Wait, what? *Zia,* are you sure? Is that a good idea? Can she do that in her condition?"

"She's a grown woman, and she can do whatever she wants. She won't be trapped here. She'll never be trapped again—not on my watch. There's no time to waste, and if anyone can take good care of her, it's you, Gaetano."

Gaetano looked at her intensely. "Violetta, if you wish to stay here, I'll move here with you," he said. "I'll have to go back and forth to oversee things, but I just want to be with you."

"Yeah, Pop, don't worry. I can run the winery. Do what's best for both of you."

Ms. G. cradled Gaetano's face in her palm. "I want to go to the winery. As much as I love this place, I want to see my grandchildren and great-grandchildren run through the vineyards. I've dreamed of that all my life. My place is with you, Gaetano. Where you live, I live."

As Valentino nudged forward to sit with his mother, Gaetano pulled me aside. "May I have a word in private?" A mist of worry floated across his face.

"Sure." I walked with him down the hallway.

"How much time do you think she has?" His eyes were pained.

"No one knows for sure, but I'd say after watching her, it could be anywhere from three weeks to three months. Now that you and your son are back in her life, she has a reason to live. If we can get a handle on the medication and she doesn't have another stroke, it could be longer. I can't say. It's up to God now."

"I don't want to endanger her life. I can make other arrangements if you think it's best that she stays here. I want her to be safe. That's all I've ever wanted," he said, then looked to the ground. "Come with us. I have a large estate. I'd be happy to give you live-in quarters—whatever you need."

"I don't think I can move in permanently. My children live here in San Jose. My daughter is attending her medical program in town, and my son has just finished high school and has a job in town. Things have been rocky lately with my son, and I don't think I can leave him right now."

"I can watch the ranch and keep an eye on things here with the kids," Alessandro interrupted. "You go. We'll be fine."

"Thank you." I smiled at Alessandro, then turned back to Gaetano. "I can come up three or four times a week to check in on her—even some weekends to make sure she's okay with her meds and to visit her."

"That would be wonderful. In the meantime, I'll make it my mission to give her the best medical care she can receive. I will spare no expense to make the rest of her days pleasant ones. I'll take full responsibility for her now."

"Ms. G. is like a mother to me. As you know, with what's she's confided in me, we have a very close relationship, one I never dreamed of. She's taught me many things—saved my life—even given me a safe place to live. I'll be there wherever and whenever you need—even to help her transition, but I believe she'll thrive now. I've never seen her as happy as she's been today." I looked over his shoulder. Ms. G. beamed as she looked at Valentino. "You'll have to stay on top of her medication, and she'll need a low-salt diet."

"When can I take her with me?"

"If the past has taught us anything, there's no time like the present. I can pack most of her things, and the rest can be delivered. I'll need to speak to her niece Sofia first. She holds her medical power of attorney, so the decision isn't all mine. I don't think Sofia will protest. She wants her to be happy too."

"Do whatever needs to be done, but I won't leave her side again."

After a long, private conversation in which I revealed Ms. G.'s past, Sofia agreed to the move. She said she'd visit in the next few days to talk with Ms. G. about what to do with the ranch. Alessandro said we could move in with him if Ms. G. decided to sell the place.

Alessandro and I packed up the Sanna truck with her clothes, medications, and crochet supplies. I even made sure to pack her yellow dress if she wanted to look pretty for Gaetano. I hoped it would serve for great memories of their time together.

While Valentino helped his mother get in the truck, I ran back to get something she'd want. I grabbed the step ladder from the kitchen and went outside to her bedroom window. I yanked down the two wind chimes that had hung there for years. They were weathered and rusty but they'd brought her so much joy over the years and had helped her fall asleep to the sound of the wind.

I ran back to the truck. "She'll want these." I handed the chimes to Gaetano.

"Windchimes?"

"Yes. You were her wind and she was your sun, remember? That is how she coped for so long. When she'd hear the windchimes, she thought of you. The sound makes her feel like you were talking to her."

He grinned and peered down at the chimes.

"She listens to them at night, so please hang them by an open window so she can feel safe. It helps her sleep." I felt the full weight of her departure.

He smiled. "I will."

"I'll have the boys come by tomorrow, pack up the other stuff, and deliver it by the end of the week," Alessandro said.

"Thank you," Gaetano said.

"I wrote a medication list and the times to give her the different pills. They're in her overnight bag along with extra hearing aids. I'll be up on Mondays, Wednesdays, and Fridays. Alessandro and I agreed that I'd live at the winery temporarily if things progress. He'll look after my kids while I'm away. So it won't be a problem."

"Thank you, Barbara, for everything." Gaetano hugged me, then turned back toward the truck to help Ms. G. put her seatbelt on.

"I can do it. Give me a minute," she yelled from the passenger seat. "It's the damn arthritis." She looked for me for help.

I walked to the truck and opened the door. With everyone watching I grabbed the belt and plugged it in. "Okay, you're in. You all right, Ms. G.?"

"Yeah, yeah. Now let's get goin'. I'm getting older by the minute."

We all laughed.

I shook my head at her. "I love you, you know that?"

"Yeah, I know that." She patted my cheek. "I love you too, kid."

I fought hard to hold back the tears flooding my vision.

"I'll visit you in a few days to see how you're doing. If you need me before that, call me."

"Okay," she said with softer eyes.

"Oh, a word to the wise," I said to Valentino and Gaetano. "Whatever you do, don't make her turkey sandwiches. She hates them." The thought brought a smile to my face. "Please make sure her crochet bag is within arm's reach and, last but not least, she loves to watch *Judge Judy*. Don't you, Ms. G?"

"I'll be fine. I got the man I love right here with me and my son, see?" She smiled fondly at the men in the truck.

"Yeah, you're right. You're gonna be fine. I'm so happy for you," I mumbled through tears.

"No goodbyes, kid."

"Yep, no goodbyes. How about, I'll see you soon?"

"I love you, my beautiful daughter Barbara. I'll see you soon. You're in my heart forever."

"As are you." I leaned in for a hug and closed my eyes. "Okay, okay, I know. It's time to go." I moved away from the door.

"Love you, *Zia*. See you soon." Alessandro kissed her on the cheek.

Valentino turned the key and the truck's engine roared. I looked down at the side of the door at a picture of the sun rising over the hills—the Sanna Winery emblem. She was in good hands.

Alessandro and I waved goodbye as the truck's tires kicked up the dirt on the one-lane road.

"You did a wonderful thing today. I can't wait to marry you." He kissed my forehead.

"Thanks for putting me back together again and showing me what real love looks like."

"You deserve nothing less." He leaned in and kissed my tear-soaked lips. Alessandro held me close as a feeling of warmth flooded my soul.

Chapter 37
Arrivederci

September 2003

"BARBARA, YOU AND ALESSANDRO SHOULD COME. SHE ISN'T doing well." Valentino's voice shook through the receiver. "She doesn't want to eat, or she forgot how. Yesterday, the doctor said she's in the later stages of the disease. I don't think it will be long."

"I'm packing up now. We should arrive by noon."

"It's unfair. I just got her back in my life. It was only a few weeks ago when she and dad said their vows. Now, she barely recognizes us."

"I'm so sorry, Val. This disease is an ugly one. Just know that this isn't her. It's the Alzheimer's talking. She loves you and your father very much."

He sniffled. "It's like she's withering away right before our eyes."

I drew in a deep breath. "Sadly, she is." The words cut like razors in my throat. "I'll reach out to Sofia and tell her to gather as many family members as possible. If anyone wants to see her, now's the time."

My final goodbye would come soon. The thought of that made my heart shrivel up. I grabbed my medical bag to distract me from the painful thoughts.

"We should get going or we'll hit traffic," Alessandro called from the kitchen.

"I'll see you soon. Stay strong. I'm on my way."

No matter how many times I'd driven to Napa, seeing the Sanna Winery sign still gave me chills. It meant I'd see Ms. G. For the past two months, things had gone smoothly. She and Gaetano had a private wedding ceremony on the hills of the estate, surrounded by her closest family and friends. They looked happy, and she glowed in her yellow dress. It was one of the best days of my life to watch her marry the man she loved.

I'd gotten used to my new routine. I came up to the winery three times a week. Sometimes, I'd stay an extra night or two on the weekend. Once she was asleep, I'd walk the grounds with Gaetano, and he'd tell me how she was *really* feeling. He said there were days she'd stare off into space and no matter what he said or did, she wouldn't return to him.

It was those days that I'd come to appreciate our time together and my love for the winery. So much so that Alessandro and I decided to have our wedding there in June. Of course Gaetano agreed, and told us he wanted to pick up the expenses in exchange for everything we'd done for her. I asked him to walk me down the aisle, since my father was absent from my life. He was gracious like that. A true gentleman. The more I'd gotten to know him, the more I understood why Ms. G. loved him so much.

My stomach twisted in knots as the dozens of tiny trees flew by. Alessandro raced time. I was nervous to see Ms. G. I suspected she might have had another small stroke. She was adamant that she didn't want forced medical intervention—just me to check in on her, and a local doctor close by to give her pain meds as needed.

Alessandro zipped through the gates and parked the Ferrari in the circular driveway. A valet opened my door. "Hello, Ms. Jackson. They've been expecting you. She's not in the main house. We have a golf cart ready to take you to our guest quarters."

The guesthouse. I should've known she'd want her final days to be there. "Yes, of course." I grabbed my medical bag.

After handing his keys to the valet, Alessandro came around to my side and rubbed my back. "It's gonna be okay."

"I hope so," I said when a small green golf cart drove up.

Alessandro and I got in, and the cart whizzed past the main building and through the acres of vineyards. After about a mile, we pulled up to a small building. I got out and walked up to the door as chimes sang in the wind.

"She's here, all right," I said.

I knocked. Gaetano opened the door. Despondent and withdrawn, his face told a sad story. His once-dreamy eyes were puffy and red, and his gaunt cheek bones looked like he hadn't been eating.

"Come in," he whispered.

I hugged him tightly.

"I'm glad you're here. Things look grim." He spoke in my ear. "In the last few days things have changed drastically. I can't explain. She asked me to move her here, and that's when I knew she knew something was coming."

Alessandro shook Gaetano's hand as I surveyed my surroundings. In my mind, I'd been here before: floor-to-ceiling windows that looked out onto vast and deep orchards. A small living area with bookshelves filled with pictures of Ms. G. and Gaetano at their wedding, along with other photos of her, Valentino, and her grandchildren standing in fields of green vineyards. There were smiles on everyone's faces. Ms. G. beamed with pride and joy. It was a new look on her—one I hadn't seen when she lived at the ranch. Just as I hoped, she'd come alive here.

I stared at the floorboards under my feet and thought about the man they called José. My heart hurt. I'd seen old pictures of him and Gaetano as they started this empire in the main house, but I'd never been here—at the place where he lost his life.

"She's resting, but come. She's in here." Gaetano motioned me down the hallway.

Alessandro and I stepped into the bedroom. A king-sized bed sat in the middle of the room. Long, white sheers hung from the bed canopy. Ms. G. lay with her hands folded over her chest, covered with a white sheet and a fluffy goosedown comforter. Valentino stared at his mother as she slept.

"Look how beautiful she is," Gaetano said, smiling at his beloved.

Valentino stood, shook Alessandro's hand, then wrapped his heavy arms around me. "Thank you for coming. I'm sure she'll be happy to see you. She stopped eating, but maybe you can talk some sense into her."

Powerless, there was nothing I could say or do to prevent the inevitable from happening. I shook my head at Val and walked closer to where she lay. I'd seen this look before. She was in transition.

"She asked for you yesterday. She said she had some things she wanted to say to you," Gaetano said as he rubbed her tiny hand.

I put my medical bag down and reached for her other hand. It was cold. Even with my touch, she didn't open her eyes. There were shadows across her cheekbones—a sign of malnourishment—and her skin had lost its glow. I'd seen this look many times before. Death was near.

I pulled my stethoscope from my bag and listened to her heart. The beats were slow and weak.

"Ms. G.? It's me, Barbara. Take a deep breath for me. Can you do that?" I gently jostled her frail body to get a response. A crease formed between her eyes as I continued to probe her. "Ms. G., I'm not going to stop until you look at me. I want to see your pretty eyes." I put my fingers on her wrist to check for a pulse. "Please don't do this to me. I need you. I'm not ready for you to go. Please." I blinked back tears.

"Get your damn hands off me," she shouted and finally opened her eyes.

Alessandro laughed. "There she is. Love you, *Zia*."

Confused, Ms. G. reached out her hand for Alessandro. "Alessandro," she muttered. "Tell your father how much he's meant to me all these years. I'll never forget what he did that day," she said, then closed her eyes.

"I will, *Zia*." Alessandro's smiling lips quivered. "He wanted to come today but he's catering a wedding."

"I love you. You've a been a good boy, and I know things have been hard, but you came through the other side." She panted, then slowly opened her eyes. "I'm proud of the man you've become. My wish for you is that you never have to answer to them again, that you're free to live the way you want. And that one day you get reunited with your son, like I was."

"That's what I want too." Alessandro wiped his eyes. "I'm trying . . ." Alessandro's gaze fell.

"I pray you find a way," she whispered against shallow breath. "I'd like some time with Barbara alone, please."

"Yes, of course." Gaetano pulled her hand up to his lips and pressed a kiss. "I'll be right outside the door if you need me, *sole mio*."

Alessandro bent over Ms. G.'s frail body and hugged her. She held onto him tight and patted his back.

When he came up there were tears in his eyes. "Give 'em hell up there, okay?"

"You better believe it, kid." She tried to smile.

Alessandro squeezed my shoulder and made his way toward the door.

My throat tightened.

As the three men left, I turned back to my little patient and held her hand. The room got quiet between us and the moment closed in. Sunlight crept in from the windows, and tiny dust motes floated through the air as I thought about what to say. I listened to her shallow breathing as a gentle breeze blew in from the window, making the windchimes sing and the white lace sheers on the canopy move like angel wings.

I'd been in this moment many times in the past, but this felt different. This was Ms. G. She was family, and that made it hard. I couldn't just say my condolences to the family and move on to the next person who needed my help. No, not this time.

"I'm glad you came," she said, breaking the strange silence between us. "There are some things I need to say to you before I go."

I swallowed past the giant lump in my throat. I rested my head on her chest. My head rose and fell with her breath.

She patted my hair. "How you doing, kid?"

"I'm sorry I haven't been here in a few days. My mother was down to meet Alessandro for the first time," I said, regretting my short absence. "I missed you."

"I missed you too. How's Alessandro treating ya?"

"He's great. I finally found the one man who loves me the way I always wanted."

"Good. That makes me happy. You and I, we've had our share of *stronzos* in our past."

"Yes, we have. That's all over with. We're with the good guys now."

"Help him get out of the business, if you can. Otherwise, he'll be made to do things that you may not like."

My neck stiffened. "We've talked about that."

"He won't want to do them, but you know how it works. It's a life-or-death oath," she warned. "You must understand this, know what's expected, and accept this role wholeheartedly, or your relationship will fail."

"I know, and I know the risk I'm taking by marrying him, but I love him. Unconditionally."

"I know you do," she smiled. "From the little I've heard, things are changing. Hopefully the Molanano name will be a thing of the past."

I nodded.

"And those babies of yours?" she asked.

"They're good. Family therapy is going well. The kids had much to say about the things they saw and how it made them feel. I learned that it was my abandonment issues with my father that led me to Marcus. I was seeking love from someone who couldn't give it to me." I looked down at the stitching in the goosedown. "We promised to go back if more feelings came up, but I'd say it was a success. Leticia is at the top of her class, and Darnell's decided he wants to learn the restaurant business. Must be from all the time he spends with Alessandro at the deli. He stepped in as a father figure, and I'm grateful."

"Darnell's gonna do fine. They both will. You're blessed."

"I am."

"Did you know I have grandchildren, and two great grandchildren on the way? Can you believe it?"

"Yes, I heard something about that," I said vaguely, so as not to remind her about her declining memory.

"They're going to name the litte girl Violetta Adelina, after me and my daughter, and the boy Antonio, after my brother."

"That's wonderful news." I swept the hair from her eyes.

"Hey, let's play some cards for old time's sake."

"I didn't bring any with me." I looked around the room. "You sure you're up for it? I'd be happy to sit here and talk with you. Or maybe you'd like to nap."

"I'll sleep plenty when I'm dead. Right now, I want to play some cards. I have some in the drawer. Sometimes I play with my grandchildren when they visit."

I searched the side table drawer and found a pack of cards.

"So what'll it be?" I said, fanning the deck out. "Best out of ten?"

"Sure, kid. Sure." She reached for her glasses at the bedside table.

"Cut the deck, please."

With our cards in our hands, we smiled at each other—like old times.

"Barbara, I need to tell you something," she said with a cracky voice.

I took a deep, reluctant breath for what she was about to say, knowing it would bring me to my knees.

She placed her cards face down and reached for my hands. "I've been having those dreams again. This time it was Mama. She came to me. She was sitting in the old rocking chair on the porch. You know, the one she used to rock me on? The one she held me on after they found me when I was a kid?"

"I remember the story. The day you wandered off and ate the strawberries."

"Mama sat on that old rocking chair, and she had her hands out for me like she wanted to hug me. I was about to go to her when a small voice called to me, 'Mama, Mama.' It was my daughter Adelina, but she was older somehow. Like an angel, she flew over to me and whispered the words I so longed to hear. She'd forgiven me, and kissed me on the cheek. I wanted to stay, but that's when I heard your voice."

I drew in a deep breath, knowing she had seen the angels and that her time was near.

"The thing is, I wanted to stay with her. I know I'm gonna die soon. I'm not afraid of it anymore. It's my time. But before I go meet my family and daughter up in heaven, I wanted to tell my daughter on Earth how much she's meant to me." Emotion flooded both of our eyes.

Reflexively, I turned my face away. I wasn't ready to hear her words.

"Look at me, *bella mia*." She reached under my chin and gently tugged my face toward her. "You brought me back to life at a time when I thought I'd die alone. You cared for me, made me laugh, and pissed me off sometimes with your pointy needles, but through it all, you loved me."

"Yeah, I know you hated the needles."

We both laughed.

"There are no coincidences in life. Because of you, I lie here in this bed that I share with the man I loved from the moment I saw him. And now, here you are with me, holding my hand at the end of it all. I'm grateful for you and everything you've done for me."

I placed my hands over my weeping eyes. *Why can't I do this?* I'd said goodbye to so many patients in the past. It was all part of the job—something I'd been trained to do my entire career. With her, I couldn't. "Please, Ms. G. This is too hard. I . . ."

"No more tears, my brave girl." She placed her hand on my cheek. "You've endured much harder things in your life, and I'm proud of who you've become. I'll be watching over you. But most importantly, I ask one thing."

"Anything, Ms. G. What is it?" I held her hands again.

"Don't forget what I've told you. Don't forget the stories and the lessons. You're the only one who knows the whole truth." She gently touched my fading scar. "Remember that no scar, physical or emotional, can ever define you. You are beautiful inside and out, my dear Barbara. Stay strong and lead by example. Never let anyone harm you or your family again. And don't take shit from anyone— even my godson." We both laughed. "You have a wonderful life in front of you—filled with hope and possibilities. And remember, God's time is always the right time. Please don't forget that."

"I will never forget you or anything you've told me—ever. Promise."

"Teach your kids the importance of family, and pass on the traditions. Show them the pictures and tell them the stories so that they may tell their children, as you're all part of my family now. Let our family's legacy live on through you. One day, take my grandchildren and great-grandchildren to the ranch and show them where I grew up. Tell them everything, and let them know how much their grandfather and I were in love. Tell them our love story."

I drew in a big gulp of air. "I will."

"I love you, my dear Barbara."

"I love you too." I bent down and hugged her tight in my arms. We cried into each other's shoulders.

After a few games of poker, Ms. G. grew tired again. "You win," I said.

"I did?" she asked, confused.

"Yes, you won." I fibbed to let her have the last win, but knowing that in life she'd already won.

"How about some *Judge Judy*?" I searched for the remote.

"Not now. I'm tired." She stared off into space.

I kissed her forehead. "It's time to rest." With everything I had I rose from the chair. "I will never forget you, Violetta. Never."

"Love you too, kid. Now go and leave an old lady to die in peace," she said, then shut her eyes. Eyes that might never open again.

Unafraid, she laid there, peaceful, ready for whatever came next.

We'd come through a lot, she and I. Different backgrounds, different families—even different skin colors. But in the end, none of that mattered. We were two souls brought together by unimaginable circumstances. We shared a common bond—a sisterhood of sorts—but Ms. G. was always more like a mother. The mother I needed when things were hard. We helped each other, and she taught me that family wasn't always blood. She was my best friend, and soon she'd be gone.

Immeasurable sadness engulfed me.

I wiped my tears and bent down to whisper in her ear. "Ms. G., if you can hear me, the next time Adelina comes to you, you can go to her. We'll be okay down here. Be with your family now. In heaven, no one can hurt you. There, you will never feel trapped or alone, and your memory will never fade. Your sacrifices will never be forgotten and you'll live on through the souls of the people you leave behind. God bless you, Violetta. Fly with the angels. I'll miss you, my sweet girl." I kissed her cheek, grabbed my medical bag, then turned to walk out the door.

My hands shook as I fumbled with the door knob. My legs felt like they were about to give way when I managed to open the door and see Alessandro standing in front of me. My body let go and I fell into his arms. He carried me to a wooden bench outside that looked out over the hills, where I cried in his arms the rest of the afternoon.

Chapter 38

All Queens Wear Crowns

June 21st, 2004
Sanna Winery Guest House

While Leticia pinned my hair, I fumbled with the lace on my gown.

"Time for the crown." Leticia grabbed the diamond-studded headpiece from the box. "I love the veil on this. It's so soft and elegant. Here, turn toward me." She placed it on my head.

My eyes scanned the hills through the windows of the guesthouse as she applied the final touches. Leticia fixed up my makeup.

"Here, let me do it." I reached for my compact, then stared at myself in the mirror.

"Be careful. You don't want to get anything on that dress."

"You'd be surprised how good I am at doing my own makeup." I patted on more makeup to hide the faint line of my scar. "You know, it's strange. As many times as it's reminded me of my painful past, today it feels like a distant memory. Scars, emotional and physical, never completely go away but dissolve over time." I placed the compact back on the vanity, then patted my hair.

"Stop fidgeting." She batted my hands away. "You'll ruin my masterpiece."

"Sorry." I moved my hand to my lap. "Nervous habit, I guess."

"You look beautiful." She smiled.

"Thanks, baby." I reached for her hand.

"When Alessandro sees you today, his jaw's going to drop to the floor. He loves you."

"I know he does." I smiled. "And I love him. He makes me feel beautiful every day."

I looked at my reflection and touched the shiny crown on my head. A small chuckle escaped my lips.

"What is it? What's so funny? You don't like it?"

"Oh no, I love it, and it's quite appropriate for the occasion, considering who I'm marrying." I tried to hold back more laughter as I realized I was the one wearing the crown now, like a true Mafia queen.

She cocked her head. "I don't get it."

I smiled. "Just a private joke. Here, I want to give you something." I took off my St. Christopher's necklace. "It's for protection." I placed the pendant in Leticia's palm.

"For protection?"

"Yes, that necklace has saved my life many times, and now I want you to have it. Think of it like someone's watching over you. With Alessandro in my life now, I don't need it anymore."

"Okay." She put it on.

"It looks great on you. Take good care of it. It was given to me as gift from one of my past clients, Mrs. Passerelli."

"I will." She studied the pendant.

There was a knock at the door.

"Can we come in?" Darnell asked, slowly opening the front door to the guest house.

"Yes, come in."

Darnell and Val walked in, wearing black tuxedos.

"Well, don't you two look amazing?" I adjusted Darnell's bowtie.

"Uncle Val said we had to come get you. We gotta get going. The ceremony starts in ten minutes."

"Yes it does," Valentino said, "but not before we give your mom a few things. Here are your bouquets." He pulled out a small white and pink rose bouquet and handed it to Leticia. "For the maid of honor. You look beautiful, Leticia." He gave her a big hug.

Leticia raised them to her nose. "*Hmm*."

"And this, my dear sister, is for you." He pulled out a much larger bouquet filled with dozens of white, pink and red roses. There were even a few Stargazer lilies tucked inside.

I pulled it up to my nose. "They're so beautiful. Thank you."

"Not as beautiful as you." Val beamed. "Okay that's your 'new'. Here's your 'borrowed' and your 'old'." He handed me Ms. G.'s St. Anthony's medal. "Let me help you put it on." He placed the necklace around my neck.

"But I thought . . ."

"She made me promise to give this to you. She said she wanted you to wear it on your wedding day and that you'd know why."

I placed my hand over the diamond-studded pendant. I shook my head as I held it between my fingers. "Kind of appropriate, considering."

"What is it, Mom? What does that one symbolize?" Leticia asked, touching her new necklace while I touched the borrowed heirloom.

"This is Saint Anthony. You're supposed to pray to him to help you find lost things." I fought back the tears. "This necklace has a lot of history."

A feeling of warmth came over me when I thought about how powerful these two necklaces were, and what they'd meant to Ms. G. and me.

"And this is your 'blue'," Val said, handing me a small black box containing a pair of blue topaz earrings. "These are from Pop."

I gasped. "Oh my God. They're gorgeous. Thank you." I admired the tiny turquoise stones. "They remind me of Alessandro's eyes."

"Then they're perfect." Val's eyes were misty.

I squeezed his hand. "We better get going, then."

"Yes. There's a man out there who really wants to see you." Val smiled.

"Time to go marry the man I love." I grabbed my flowers as Leticia held my train.

I walked from the guest house. We piled into a Sanna Winery golf cart and drove to the man of my dreams.

My protector. My lover and my future husband—Alessandro.

The sun shone on the flowered vines of the arbor as the priest held his bible. Alessandro, stood next to him, looking as dashing as ever. He wore a finely tailored suit that hugged his frame perfectly. *The man always looked good in a suit.* To Alessandro's right was his son, Dominic, who, after several months of getting to know him again, had agreed to be his best man.

With every step forward, I searched for his eyes—they were my home now. His black suit matched his hair and eyebrows, making the blue of his eyes shine that much more. His warm, comforting smile pulled me forward.

I dug my nails into Val's arm as we moved toward the altar. Hundreds of people stood at their seats as the wedding march began. I looked around at all the guests, old and new. Everyone was smiling, winking, and blowing me kisses in the crowd. My mother and sister smiled at me as we passed them in the aisle. She mouthed, "I love you" as we walked toward the altar.

I was happy that they'd made the trip and that, after meeting Alessandro last summer, she'd come to fall in love with him and accept our union. To the right, Angelo sat with a few men dressed in three-piece suits and pocket squares. They smiled and nodded at me. Angelo had given us his blessing after he heard what had happened at the ranch with Darnell's attacker. He said, "Only people who love each other put their lives on the line to save one another." I smiled back at my soon-to-be father-in-law as I made my way to the grassy knoll.

Val placed my hands into Alessandro's. Like a live wire, his energy zinged through me as my skin touched his. I was spellbound, the warmth of his magic stirring my soul as it always did, making the whole world fall away.

"Take good care of her," Val said to Alessandro.

"You bet I will." Alessandro smiled at me with his perfect grin. We stood in front of the priest as Leticia fanned out my train.

"There are no words for how incredibly beautiful you are today. I'm so lucky to have you," Alessandro whispered and kissed the back of my hand. I handed my flowers to my daughter and smiled adoringly at the man who promised to love me forever.

As the priest spoke, I listened and repeated our vows. We both promised to love and honor each other for the rest of our days. The priest's voice faded as I dove into the pools of Alessandro's eyes. I wanted to drown in them and remain there—safe, protected, and loved. Forever.

The priest cleared his throat, jostling me back into the moment. "It's time for the rings."

We placed our rings on each other's fingers and held hands as the priest continued.

"Do you, Alessandro, take this women to be your wife, to have and to hold until death do you part?"

Alessandro smiled at me adoringly. "Hell yes, I do," he said.

We all laughed.

"And do you, Barbara, take this man to be your husband, to have and to hold, until death do you part?"

"I do."

"Then with the powers vested in me, I pronounce you husband and wife. You may kiss your bride."

With tears in his eyes, Alessandro wrapped his arms around me, and we kissed. The kiss was a declaration of our commitment and love for one another.

Thunderous applause filled the air.

With my husband at my side, we walked down the aisle. Dozens of guests smiled back at us. Everyone came around to wish us well.

Everyone except for two.

"I need to go see someone," I said as Alessandro stood amongst our family and friends.

"I'll go with you." He pulled me close and studied my face.

"No, I'll be fine."

I walked up the dirt road, flowers in hand. The sun had just begun to set. I stopped at the top of the hill and placed my flowers next to the headstone.

Violetta Sanna
Loving Wife and Soulmate
Your light will always brighten our days

"Hey, Ms. G. It was a great ceremony. I wish you could've seen it. Well, I guess you were there in spirit." I wiped my tears away. "You like the crown? Don't laugh." I felt the stones on my head. "I wanted to say how lucky I am to have known you, and for all the things you taught me about myself, and how you treated me like a daughter—your daughter," I choked out. "I will miss you every day for the rest of my life, but I know you two are together now."

I glanced to the right, where Gaetano's headstone stood next to hers.

On the other side of Gaetano's headstone was Esperanza's headstone. Gaetano made sure that he'd be remembered always as a gentleman and a respected father to his son until the end. He passed away six months after Ms. G., with no known ailments. The doctor said Gaetano must have died from a broken heart.

He loved Ms. G. with every bone in his body until his last breath. He was a man I'd come to love like a father, with a big heart and a vision for greatness. This glorious, fruitful land was evidence of that. The Sanna Winery was now one of the biggest wine producers in the world. Through it all, their dreams became reality and their enduring love for each other was proof of hope and possibility—just as Ms. G.'s father had reminded her, years ago—important words that I would live by for the rest of my life.

With blurry eyes, I looked toward the horizon. The last of the day's sunlight touched my face, and in the same moment the wind blew through my hair.

"Ya, you two are here all right. I love you both. See you on the other side." I pressed a kiss to my hand and touched their headstones, then walked down the path, where Sofia greeted me.

"Thanks for letting me borrow this." I unclasped Ms. G.'s St. Anthony's charm.

"You're welcome. I know *Zia* would've wanted you to wear it today."

"I'm happy you have it now. I know why she wanted you to have it." I handed it back to Sofia.

"Oh yeah, why?" she asked, putting the pendant back on.

"Because it's known that Saint Anthony is about more than lost things. He is supposed to be a symbol of love. Some say that symbol is better at finding love than even Cupid or Saint Valentine."

"Really?" she asked.

"Yes. Besides, I've already found my love." I looked in Alessandro's direction. "Now it's your turn." I smiled.

"*Zia*," she laughed. "Always trying to be a matchmaker. How are you adjusting to life on the ranch? You look gorgeous, by the way." She touched the lace of my gown. "And the crown? Nice touch. It's beautiful."

"Thanks. We're doing great. Alessandro is talking about getting some chickens and pigs."

"I'm glad you decided to stay at the ranch. *Zia* was adamant when she had me change the will. She wanted you to have that land. She said you'd know why and that you were the only one who knew how important the ranch was to her, and that you'd take good care of it." Sofia smiled. "It's good to know that it went to someone in the family. Someone who understands. Someone we can always trust."

"Thanks for trusting me and giving me the job. Best job I ever had."

"Oh yeah? Surprising, considering what you now know."

"Best perk of the job is that it came with a wonderful family, full of rich history and incredible memories. I'm blessed to be a part of it." We smiled and hugged. She let go and I was whisked away in someone else's arms.

My husband's arms. Alessandro pulled me into his muscular frame and kissed behind my ear.

"Stop monopolizing the bride," Sofia yelled.

"Today, she's all mine," Alessandro beamed.

"Okay, you two, I'm going to get another glass of that fabulous Sanna wine. See you both on the dance floor," Sofia said, then walked back to the party.

Alessandro stared into my eyes. "Thank you for making me a better man."

"You're welcome, and thank you for making me feel loved."

He flashed a flirtatious smile, then kissed me long and deep. We broke away to catch our breath. "I have big plans for us tonight, Barbara," he teased.

"Oh, you do, do you?" I asked, still winded.

"Yes, I do."

"I can't wait. How long is the reception, anyway? Think we can sneak out?"

"Maybe." He gripped at my hips. "So how's my feisty aunt today? Did you tell her how much I love you?" He smiled tenderly.

I looked toward the hilltop where she lay in her eternal resting place next to her beloved. Waves of memories filled me with love. "She knows. She's always known everything. She's perfectly happy in heaven with her family, her daughter, and the man she loves—forever. She's like one of those homing pigeons her father used to have." I pointed up to the sky where dozens of birds soared beyond the hills. "She returned to the one place where her soul would be redeemed—a place where her memory and love story will live on forever."

Blissful, I smiled as Alessandro held me in his arms. Cheek to cheek, we watched the sun disappear behind the mountains of the famous winery.

Word of mouth and honest reviews are critical to an author's success. If you enjoyed this book, please consider leaving a review at your favorite online retailer.

Thanks for reading *Crown of Confessions*!

About the Author

E.J. Tanda lives in Northern California with her husband and three sons. Growing up, she was surrounded by a large Italian family. With a rich, cultural background guiding her writing, she weaves her heritage throughout her stories. She graduated from Southern New Hampshire University with a degree in English and creative writing. When she isn't writing, she travels the globe to gain experiences for her next book.

Acknowledgments

A huge thank you to all my readers who have supported The Mafia Matriarch Series through to its end. It has been an absolute honor and privilege to meet and speak with some of you at the various signings and events this past year. And to all my supporters and fans on social media, thank you for your unwavering enthusiasm for this book. I am forever grateful to you all. I hope this story of family, hope, and love endures long after you read the final page.

To my husband, Eric: Once again, my lovey, you sat with me day after day, being a second pair of eyes to guide me in my edits. How many times did we go through that editing checklist? A hundred, maybe two hundred times? Thank you for supporting me so I could fulfill one of my biggest dreams. Love you, B.

To my son Michael: Thank you for listening to me tell you about all the trials and tribulations of writing and publishing on your drive home from work, and for telling me how proud you are of me. Your words kept me going in times when I wanted to give up. I love you.

To my son Patrick: Thank you for helping with promo graphics and for coming to my book signings to support me. I love you.

To my son Justin, aka 'Puddin': Thank you for the endless hours you helped me with social media. Thanks for being patient with me and teaching me. I owe you one, kid. I love you.

I am so grateful to my parents, Michael and Annie Tanda. Thanks for your enduring love throughout this process, and for supporting me at every event. Dad, thanks for showing me what hard work looks like. If I hadn't had you as a role model, I might have given up. Mom, thanks for all the phone calls and for being my cheering section when I doubted myself.

To my editor, L.A. Mitchell: I type this in tears. I couldn't have written this book without you. And I don't just mean the writing-coach stuff. I mean, like on the day when you told me, "E.J., we can edit later. Go say goodbye to your grandmother before it's too late."

She died the very same day.

Your words became a part of this story's themes. And thank God I listened because it was in that moment that I could bring my real-life experience to the page in a genuine, heartfelt way.

And thank you for encouraging me to continue to write after my grandmother was gone. You knew me well enough in our three years together to know that writing was always my way of escaping pain, and you reminded me. Thank you for coming on this incredible journey with me and for holding my hand when things got hard and saying, "We got this." That meant the world when the vision for this book was unclear. I will be forever grateful to you, Laura. You are a dream maker. Love you. You are my friend and the best coach and editor in the world.

To my sister Samantha: You helped lighten my mood after problem writing days at the computer. Thanks for all your support and for steering me back on the path. Love you, sissy.

Big thanks to my beta readers who took time out of their busy lives to read and review Crown of Confessions and for providing excellent feedback: Michael and Annie Tanda, Vicki Langone, Kevin Gildea, Mathew Morrone, Marco Di Ianni, Mavis Burford, Kari Schoch, Bob and Linda Langone, Lorre Jimenez, Jasmine Youngs, Donna Morrissey, and Monet Ortega Kerr.

Many thanks to my sensitivity readers, Nikki Langone Traore' and Malon Ruffin: Your input was invaluable. I've learned so much from both of you. Let this story's message bring us together.

To my street team, Samantha Alarcon, Karin Barbaria, Christina Melo, Monica Alarcon, Joanne Zavlaris, Monet Ortega-Kerr, Vicki Langone, Natalie Morrone, Brigitte Wiegand, Donna Bowron Morrissey, Julie Boydstun and Kelly Clark-Nelson, who rallied behind me and helped spread the word: Thanks for all the times you shared a promo graphic, and for every time you told a friend about the series. I treasure you. You are my people—my friends, the ones I trust on this journey. Big hugs, ladies.

To Kelly A. Way: Thanks for reading the manuscript and providing your superior, expert legal counsel.

To Kate Willette, who agreed to be my research assistant: Thanks for all your countless hours providing me the much-needed and thorough research of post-war Europe. I appreciate the level of detail you provided in your reports. The data helped me forge my way through the story with a historical lens.

To my proofreader, Sabine Sloley, who worked tirelessly at proofreading and editing Crown of Confessions: I appreciate all your help in ensuring this story's overall readability. You did a commendable job, and it was a pleasure to work with you.

To my phenomenal cover artist, Tatiana Vila: You knocked it out of the park again! Your artistic talents are in a league of their own. I came to you with a vision for each book, and you nailed it—exceeding all expectations.

To my formatter, Stacey Blake: You are a formatting ninja! I always feel safe with my manuscript in your hands. You've done a fantastic job with both books. I look forward to our future work together!

To my cousin Lena Caruso-Commisso: Thanks for telling me about the foundling wheel and of our family's history. I remember getting chills because it was exactly how I thought the story might go anyway. I learned so much about its history and its importance. Love you, cousin!

To the Langone, Tanda, Guerra, and Zavlaris families: Thank you for everything. For all the stories I heard, growing up, and for supporting me through this writing adventure. I'm so blessed to know you. You've all made such an impression on my life that I needed to tell the world about our shared history. Please keep talking about the stories with your children and grandchildren. Nani would be so happy if you did. Let us never forget where we came from.

And last but not least, to my cousin Dougie Sousa: I remember the night we watched the news together and learned of the COVID lockdown. You said that this was my chance to do what I loved and to write the book I've always wanted to write. It was that very same night that I opened my laptop, and a story I didn't know existed poured out onto the page. Thank you for encouraging me to live my dream, because here I am, three years later, a published author with two books under my belt. You were the spark to my writing fire. I love you—you are my Tony.

To anyone suffering from domestic abuse, drug addiction, or thoughts of suicide, I hope this book serves as a beacon of hope and possibility. We share a common bond. Please know that you are never alone.

Made in the USA
Columbia, SC
21 August 2023